❀❀❀

BURNING DOWN THE DARK

❀❀❀

BRENDA POPPY

First published by Glass Fish Publishing 2021

Copyright © 2021 by Brenda Poppy

This novel is entirely a work of fiction. The names,
characters and incidents portrayed in it are the work of the
author's imagination. Any resemblance to actual persons,
living or dead, events or localities is entirely coincidental.

First edition
ISBN: 978-1-7356181-6-6

www.glassfishpublishing.com

To all those who have been with me from the beginning. Thank you for joining me on this amazing adventure.

Prologue

The man on the table was naked, although the group gathered around him didn't seem to care – or even notice. They were more focused on the tube snaking into his arm, feeding a sluggish purple liquid into the crease of his pale white elbow. Any state of undress didn't matter. In fact, not even the man mattered. He was merely there for show.

It was an intimate assembly, a small collection of men and women gathered together in the cold, shivering as one. Some wore lab coats, others uniforms, others suits, but all of them felt the bite of frost. The two standing by the door wore layers of armor, covered head to toe in black, yet even their lips were beginning to bear a tinge of blue.

They weren't used to the cold. Under the dome of Kasis, the temperature barely wavered, barely dipped below warm and into the realm of cool. Yet this was different. This wasn't a natural chill, but rather one piped in through the walls, keeping the room at a constant.

They didn't ask why – or what or how. Merely when. They told themselves that the less they knew, the more easily they could sleep at night. The truth was that most didn't care. The process was immaterial. All that mattered were the results.

The white wardrobes that lined the walls, the surgical tools, the vials of blood, the shapes lurking beneath sheets stained with rust. They were all necessary evils, insignificant parts of a larger plan.

These players were part of something bigger than themselves. What they were doing would transcend time. It would bring peace to a warring world. It would usher in an era of equality. A few dozen people could save thousands. That was a small price to pay.

"Thank you for joining us today," said one of the doctors, imbuing his voice with enough gravitas to suit the situation. The group turned, focusing their attention on him. "You all know why we're here – and it isn't to listen to me talk." Chuckles greeted him from around the room, indulging his attempt at levity. Yet beneath the mirth, an impatience lingered like an obscuring fog, urging him on.

"I don't need to tell you how important this work is to the cause," he continued, placing himself behind the motionless man on the table. "This project has consumed our time and our resources for years, with a multitude of dead-ends and roadblocks along the way. But now we stand at the cusp of a breakthrough. Your dreams will soon become a reality. Ladies and gentleman, behold the future of Kasis."

Turning his attention to the specimen before him, he flicked his finger over the tube, slowing the flow of inky liquid into the man's arm. For a moment, nothing happened, and the group remained frozen on the edge, their eyes wide and their breathing shallow. Then, in an instant, the man's eyes snapped open and he screamed.

Chapter 1

Auburn stood, staring into the mirror at a reflection that wasn't hers. The woman that peered back was achingly beautiful, like some precious porcelain doll. Delicate, breakable. Untouchable.

Where Auburn's hair was a straight and muddy brown, cropped short for ease of maintenance, this girl boasted soft golden waves, which fell down past her shoulders and shimmered in the light. The eyes that stared back were even stranger. Instead of dark and piercing, these were bright and tender, and they sparkled with an innocence that she had long since lost.

Auburn's face was sculpted of sharp lines and hard expressions, relics of a life spent fighting against fate, but neither appeared in the mirror before her. Instead, round cheeks and a full mouth set off the small nose, and the soft lips were upturned in a permanent smile.

This was a face that hadn't known hardship, hadn't

known what it was like to want. It was the face of a woman who still believed in the world – and the people in it. That definitely wasn't Auburn.

She was…skeptical. Cynical, even. She'd learned at a young age that the world was not on her side and nor were the people who ruled it. If she wanted to succeed – or even survive – trust and faith weren't luxuries she could afford.

Yet today she had given that trust, blithely placing herself in the hands of another.

That's why as she moved her hand up to her face, resting it gently on her cheek, the woman in the mirror did the same. And as she tilted her head to the side, her eyebrows knitting together in concern, so did the girl in the glass. Because that woman – that poised and perfect doll – that was Auburn.

Now, finding herself in someone else's body wasn't a common occurrence for Burn, as she was often called. In fact, this was a first for her – one that was truly messing with her head. And her sense of balance.

While Burn was more or less a normal height (emphasis on the less), this girl was tall, with arms and legs that felt both too long and too light to truly be hers. These were arms that had never labored, never fought, never carried a family's future in their grasp. This was a girl who had been carefully shaped and molded to be placed on a pedestal, to be envied and wanted, to be desired and withheld.

That was not Burn – but it was exactly the girl she needed to be. She was fighting a war, and she intended to win, whatever that required.

It was a strange path that had led her here, so of course it would be a strange road ahead. Burn couldn't think of another word to describe it. Taking possession of someone else's body certainly wasn't normal – or comfortable or natural or easy. Although, to be fair, the real Ellis was alive and well and still encompassing her own form. Burn was merely her double.

Even for a planet as peculiar as Kasis, though, this was unusual. It was a harsh world, an unforgivable landscape where radiation ruled and the atmosphere was unsuited for human habitation. It wasn't somewhere that people should have settled. Yet they had. They'd created a domed city of the same name, a vertical maze that broke the metropolis into tiers and separated its citizens by classes.

The repercussions of building on a wasteland were not subtle. After hundreds of years, mutations had sprung up amongst the populace, warping the people from human to subhuman – or superhuman, depending on your outlook. Either way, people had started to develop gifts and abilities, things that set them apart from the norm. And in Kasis, being anything other than normal meant being in danger.

Burn herself was one of the gifted. Hers was not an ostentatious gift; it didn't demand attention or command respect, and it wasn't physically apparent to passersby. Yet it was part of her, part of how she understood the world and the people in it.

Burn could hear the city – the people, their movements, their words. By sending her thoughts out across Kasis, she could hear through walls and over bridges, across alleys and between tiers, casting her net wide to reel in the darkest secrets and sweetest lies.

Sometimes she could even hear what wasn't said – the

thoughts left unwhispered and the dreams unspoken. That facet was new, a byproduct of her weeks spent in the wildlands outside the confines of the dome. For some reason, the harsh environment had allowed her to crack the barrier between word and thought, giving her access to others' ideas and secrets, to their desires and fears.

With Burn safely back inside the dome, however, she was no longer exposed to the planet's unforgiving atmosphere – and nor were the dozens of people who had returned with her. That meant that their gifts were starting to wane, receding back to their pre-exile levels. For her and Hale, who had only been exposed for a matter of weeks, their gifts were fading the fastest. For the others, whose banishment spanned years or even decades, the decay was slower.

But the fact that they were weakening at all was a problem – especially when it came to Eyana. Eyana could change a person's face. Well, more than their face. She could transform someone completely, removing their identity and replacing it with another. That's what she'd done with Burn. And with Hale, the strongman who'd given himself up to step into a traitor's shoes.

They'd both done it because they had hope – hope that they could bring down the city's tyrannical government, free the people of Kasis, and return to their lives. Return to each other. Yet if Eyana's powers faded, if her ability weakened and blinked out, it was possible they'd never return to normal. Burn and Hale would be stuck this way, cursed to live out other people's lives in other people's forms.

It was a terrifying thought, but Burn had to risk it. After all, if she was unwilling to change, how could she possibly change the world around her? And theirs was a world that desperately needed changing.

The Peace Force ruled Kasis with an iron grip. Sure, they feigned fairness and play-acted justice, but it was all for show. Behind the curtain, they were judge, jury, and executioner. They decided people's fates on a whim, saving and condemning based on what suited them best.

It was worse for the *freaks* like Burn. They were seen as mistakes, evolutionary missteps in need of eradication. Of course, it wasn't something that was spoken aloud. There were no laws against them, no rules barring their existence, but they were not accepted. They were not wanted. The Peace Force made that perfectly clear.

Their safety was never a certainty. Their lives were dangerous. They could never lower their guards, never walk through the city with confidence, never fully trust that they'd make it through another day. They deserved a better life – and Burn had the power to make that happen.

Burn steeled herself, raising her head to stare into the unfamiliar eyes in the mirror before her. This was her chance to make a difference, to finally craft a future free of the Peace Force. Sure, it was an unconventional plan – and it was dangerous as hell – but it was something she had to do.

With a grim smile, Burn turned away from the mirror and strode to the door. Taking a deep breath, she turned the handle and stepped into her new life.

Chapter 2

Scarlett looked up from her work and blinked at Burn. Or, rather, at Ellis. Because there was nothing left of Burn now, no trace of the woman she had been. From head to toe, everything had changed, morphing and shifting until she was indistinguishable from the original. Even her voice had been altered, rising half an octave until it tinkled like fine china.

Which was why it sounded so strange when Burn smiled at her sister and casually said, "Hey, Scar. It's me."

Burn didn't know what she expected her sister to say, but it certainly wasn't what came out of her mouth next.

"You look ridiculous," Scar said flatly, promptly returning her attention to the complicated contraption in her hands.

Burn stood there for a moment, collecting herself. Scar lived in a different world than the rest of them, a world of machines, algorithms, and electronics, a world where circuits and code made far more sense than people. Her gift was to understand these machines, but her curse was to be like them. Patches of her skin shone like the metal of a bot, while her bright red curls were threaded with wires that tended to spark at any hint of emotion.

Sometimes people – and their conversational customs – confounded her, and the subtle art of tact often eluded her. She wasn't mean, merely honest to a fault. Although, in this case, Burn found it refreshing.

"I feel ridiculous," Burn said, taking a seat on the floor next to her sister. "This girl is too tall, too blond, too…pretty to ever be taken seriously."

"You don't need to be taken seriously," Scar shot back, raising an eyebrow in her patented sardonic style. "In fact, the less seriously people take you, the more chance you have of getting out alive."

Scar had a point. The Lunaria had targeted Ellis because she was well-connected. An accident of birth had landed her with a family on the top tiers, a family endowed with power and money and the knowledge necessary to wield them. As their precious only child, Ellis had access to all the best circles, to the Peace Force *and* their superiors.

Not much was known about the council of officers and influential citizens that made up the city's highest rank. Their identities were a secret even to most of the force, ensuring absolute impartiality – or at least that's what they claimed. In reality, their secrecy was a mask to hide behind, a mask which allowed them to rule without consequences.

The Lunaria had taken to calling them the Shadow Assembly. It was a fittingly ominous name. Together, the assembly sat on top of the world and dispensed their own crooked brand of justice, slowly suffocating those cursed to live below them. It was on their orders that the Peace Force targeted the mutants, the poor, the vulnerable. If the Peace Officers were their lords, then the Shadow Assembly were their kings, ruling with impunity. Now it was Burn's job to bring their reign to an end.

Well, technically her job was to discover their identities, but Burn knew that was merely the beginning. She intended to unearth not only their names, but their weaknesses, their vices, their faults and flaws and failings. She was going to reveal their true colors and watch with glee as the citizens tore them from their perches. Because this wasn't merely a mission; it was a revolution. This was the beginning of the end. And it was only slightly nerve-wracking.

"Do you think it will work?" Burn asked, looking up at her big sister with hopes of reassurance. She should have known better.

"Maybe. Maybe not," Scar said with a shrug. "There are a thousand ways it can go wrong. One misstep, one wrong word, and your cover's blown."

As if Burn needed reminding. She knew all too well that if she said the wrong thing, was found in the wrong place, or pushed the wrong buttons, she faced a fate worse than jail.

The Peace Force wasn't kind on a normal day; this was something else entirely. If they learned about her plot, if she fell into their clutches, they wouldn't rest until they'd bled her dry. They would squeeze out every morsel of intel and enjoy every moment.

"But you're prepared, right?" Scar continued, bringing Burn back to herself. "I mean, you've gotten everything you need out of the real Ellis?"

"I think so," Burn sighed, running her hand through her hair – the length of which still seemed strange between her fingers.

While her powers of telepathy were fading, it was still possible to see inside someone's mind under the right circumstances. Some emotions, for instance, intensified thoughts, acting as an amplifier. Emotions like anger and jealousy – and terror. When it came to a spoiled girl like Ellis, it was surprisingly simple to stoke the flames of fear. They hadn't even needed to threaten her…much.

Burn had spent hours poring through Ellis' brain, searching for every crumb about her life, her family, her personality – or her utter lack thereof. After vision upon vision of balls and parties and afternoon socials, she'd come to understand that the rich had no need to develop defining characteristics; they could simply buy them. Money was, after all, the most powerful attribute. Why bother making yourself unique when you could pay to fit in?

"She's so dull," Burn continued, untangling her fingers from her mess of blond hair. "I don't understand how someone can live like that, with no job, no mission, no purpose. I don't know if I can fake that level of emptiness." Burn couldn't imagine anyone more different than herself.

"Oh, poor baby," Scar cut back, drenching her words in sarcasm. "You get to live in the lap of luxury while the rest of us toil away in hiding, waiting with bated breath for your next update. Don't act like you're not going to enjoy it. You'll be living the life most of us can only dream about."

"Except for the whole 'being in mortal danger' part. It won't exactly be a walk in the park, Scar."

Scar scoffed. "Oh, come off it. You look like Ellis. You sound like Ellis. As long as you don't scream 'Down with the Peace Force!' at dinner, no one's going to notice the difference. People are far stupider than you give them credit for."

Burn couldn't help but laugh, despite the fact that her sister was completely serious. Something about Scar's rant made her realize the true insanity of her situation, and the realization loosened something inside her. Scar was right yet again. No one was going to see through her disguise because no one would think to question it. The whole concept was absurd – and that absurdity would protect her.

"Thanks," Burn said, letting out a loud sigh of relief – and releasing some of her tightly coiled tension along with it. "I needed to hear that. I think I'm just scared to leave all of this. You, the Lunaria, this place," she said, gesturing to the safe house they currently occupied. "It's not easy to let go."

"It's not like you're dying," Scar said, once again acting as the blunt voice of reason. "Besides, you'll still have us. Well, you'll still have me, at least," she said, waggling her eyebrows.

From the pocket of her cloak, Scar produced a black wrist cuff, which she offered to Burn with a smile. Taking it, Burn spent a long moment looking it over before clasping it around her arm.

"Let me guess – a comms device?" Burn ventured. She knew her sister well, and Scar was always coming up with new ways to reinvent the wheel.

Scar smirked. "You didn't think you were going in alone, did you?" She leaned over and pressed a hidden button on the bracelet's side, which immediately started blinking with a soft red light.

"Push that button to connect with us. There should always be someone on the other end. If there's not, your message will automatically be relayed to my tab."

"And if you want to talk to me?" Burn asked, intrigued.

"The cuff will vibrate. If you're alone and can talk, press here," she said, pointing out another hidden button along the edge. "If you can't talk, we'll leave a message, and the button will flash blue."

"Oh, how I've missed your contraptions," Burn said wistfully. Her time in the wildlands had been painfully devoid of Scar's clever creations, although it was more than that. She hadn't just missed Scar's harebrained inventions; she'd missed Scar.

Her weeks in the desert had been difficult in their own right, packed with ferocious creatures and bloodthirsty foes, yet being separated from her sister had made them excruciating. The two had never been parted for so long, and it had been a sweet relief when they'd finally found each other again. The thought of leaving her behind was eating at Burn. More than once she'd considered backing out. She'd considered handing the reins to someone else, but she knew that no one else in the Lunaria could do what she could. No one else could hear the truth.

"Well, that's not the only one of my gadgets you'll be taking," Scar said, her smile widening. "Don't worry, little sis. I've got your back."

Burn wanted to thank her sister, to express her gratitude for more than just the gadgets, but the sudden appearance of several more Lunaria members put an end to their conversation. Burn stood abruptly, preparing herself for the inevitable stares.

Eyana herself was one of the first to enter, and she gave another self-satisfied smirk at her work, checking Burn up and down like a jeweler appraising a stone. Burn's mentor, Meera, came next, closely followed by the fire-wielder Ansel. Scar's onetime ally Cali trekked behind them, accompanied by Coal, whose appreciation of Eyana's gift verged on jealousy. The man, who was able to change his own face at will, stared at Burn with a mixture of envy and awe. Several more Lunaria piled in after them, filling out the ranks. Bringing up the rear of their small troop was Hale. Or, rather, Raqa.

Unlike Hale, whose burly form commanded respect, Raqa's body was small and scrawny. His ears seemed too big for his face, and his scraggly hair stuck out in every direction. Compared to Hale, he looked plain and mousy, a twitchy hare next to a thoroughbred stallion.

The sight of him still made something in Burn tighten, and she glanced away hastily to hide her expression. It was the same look that the others gave him: pity mingled with revulsion and sadness. Raqa's face – the face of a traitor who had brought death to their ranks and turned the Lunaria into fugitives – still carried so much pain, even though it was now attached to Hale's soul.

Raqa had sold them out, bartering away their secrets for coin, betraying their plans for his own gain. He had thrown the Lunaria to the wolves, revealing their schemes to break through the dome and turning Burn's homecoming into a bloodbath. It wasn't something she could easily forget – or forgive.

Burn finally mustered the courage to raise her gaze and

train it on Hale. Looking into the eyes of the man who used to hold her, whose mere presence used to calm her racing heart, she was shocked to see the same look in his eyes that she held in hers.

She wanted to say something, to explain, but Meera called the room to attention, demanding silence. Turning to face her friend, Burn was surprised to find an old woman in her place. The shocks of gray in her long brown hair had taken over, coating her mane in white, and the new lines around her eyes made her kind face appear tired.

These past few months had taken a toll on all of them, so Burn supposed it shouldn't come as a shock. Yet it did. Meera was the closest thing to family that she and Scar had, and she'd long thought of the woman as invincible, a pillar of stability in a rapidly changing world. But even she couldn't make it through this war unscathed. It was one more reminder of the price they had to pay for progress, of the true cost of revolution.

"It is with heavy hearts that we meet here today to say goodbye to one of our own," Meera started, her voice grave. "While she is not leaving us forever, it will be a long time before we see her face again." Meera shot a look in Burn's direction, reinforcing her double meaning.

"We've worked hard to get where we are, and we've lost many good souls along the way," she continued, bowing her head to acknowledge their sacrifice. "But this journey isn't over yet. In fact, the most difficult times are still to come. We have a lot of work ahead of us, and I would be lying if I said that I knew how all of this would end."

The people around her nodded grimly, as if silently

confessing their own fears. They all knew that victory wasn't a given, that their years spent fighting might all come to nothing in the end. Yet here they were. They were willing to take the chance, to risk everything for even the slightest possibility of success. That fact in itself was heartening.

"As most of you know," Meera went on, getting down to business, "Auburn Alendra will be stepping into the life of Ellis Hyde, effective today. The Hydes have been one of the most powerful families in Kasis for decades. Based on our intel from the top tiers, we have come to believe that they have formed important connections inside the Shadow Assembly. Their patriarch, Baylor, may even have a seat on the assembly himself."

Murmurs of conversation danced across the room, with surprise and delight evident on the Lunaria's faces. So little was known about the Shadow Assembly that any hint of information − even just a rumor − was cause for excitement. Meera waited for the whispers to fade before continuing.

"It is our goal to uncover all of their identities, to unmask them, and to bring them down once and for all." She said it with such conviction that a shiver of excitement ran down Burn's spine.

"While Auburn's away, the rest of us have our own parts to play. This city deserves to know the truth about its leaders, and it's our job to give it to them. We intend to share the news of the Peace Force's corruption with the masses, to uncover their lies and expose them to the world. With the public on our side, the Peace Force won't stand a chance. And when it comes time to fight, we'll have all of Kasis on our side."

A cheer of support rang out around the room, bolstering her rousing words. Even Burn, whose stomach was twisted into tight knots, managed a shout of approval and a stiff smile. No one seemed to notice her reserve, however, as the excitement rose to a peak and crested, carrying with it the contagion of hope.

The meeting came to an end shortly thereafter, and the members took their time dispersing, enjoying the comfort of each other's company. Burn, on the other hand, just wanted to leave. She was rapidly tiring of the blatant stares, as well as the blunt questions that accompanied them. Quietly, she untangled herself from the clusters of people and slipped away. She needed a moment to herself, a moment to think and assess and prepare, but fate had never been her friend.

"Hi," came a squeaky male voice from the doorway. Burn didn't turn. She knew who it was. She had heard him coming, but she didn't want to look.

"Hi," she said softly, her back to the man and her eyes cast to the floor.

Hale wasn't deterred. He ventured farther into the room, placing his hand on Burn's shoulder in a gentle plea for her to turn. Yet she didn't.

She didn't want to see him like this – or have him see her. If she didn't turn, didn't look, maybe they could both pretend that everything was as it had been. With her back to him, Hale was still *her* Hale, the same man that had walked by her side through a desert and lain by her side under the stars. And he could pretend she was the same woman, too – the woman who had shared his thoughts and his pain and his bed.

But no amount of belief could make it true. So Burn turned, looking into the eyes of a stranger. The stranger stared back, looking into a face that was equally unrecognizable.

"You look perfect," Hale said after a beat, gesturing to her new form. A flash of pain tore through Burn, and he hastily amended his statement. "I mean, you look like her. Although personally I prefer the old Burn."

Burn tried to smile, although she wasn't sure she quite managed it. She wanted to say so much, to reach out and grab Hale and draw him close, but a chasm had formed between them. It was a rift of their own making, yet she didn't think she had the strength to cross it.

The worst part was that he'd done it all for her. He'd been happy in the wildlands. They both had. But he'd returned because she'd asked him to. He'd stepped back into the fight because he'd wanted to be by her side. He'd given up his identity because she'd given him something to fight for. And now she couldn't even look him in the eye.

"It feels strange," was all she managed to say, her voice once again sounding foreign to her own ears.

"I know what you mean," Hale responded simply.

"Does it get better?" Burn asked, needing to know.

Hale shrugged, a move which looked bizarre on Raqa's small body. "You get used to it, I guess. But no. It's never better."

"I miss you," she whispered after a beat, putting all of her pain and sadness behind the words.

"I know," was all he said. Reaching out, he gave her hand a light squeeze before turning and walking out of the room.

Chapter 3

Burn saved Scar's goodbye for last. It wasn't an emotional affair. There was no hugging or crying or heartfelt last words. That wasn't Scar's style. Instead, there were gadgets and weapons and everyday items with hidden electronics sewn into the seams. That was her sister's language. That was how she showed love.

Burn walked out the front door, her small purse laden with an arsenal of technology and her heart heavy with the recent farewells. Sighing, she rubbed at her eyes, trying to drive the doubts and misgivings from her mind.

Without warning, a hand appeared on her shoulder and she shrieked, spinning around and crouching into a defensive pose. Yet instead of an enemy, she was met with the smiling face of Kaz Petala. Peace Officer Kaz Petala, to be precise.

"You scared me," Burn said once her heartbeat had mellowed back into a steady rhythm. "You're getting pretty good at the whole sneaking around thing, aren't you?"

Kaz chuckled, apparently pleased with himself for his stealth.

"Well, are you just going to stand there, or are you going to accompany me home, Officer Petala?" Burn asked, a playfulness coloring her tone.

"Why of course, Miss Hyde," he said in his best gentlemanly style. "It would be my pleasure."

Together, the pair turned their backs on the safe house and began their trek through the city.

It was strange, being alone with Kaz again. They'd barely laid eyes on each other since the ManniK Battles, a brutal series of skirmishes choreographed by his employers on the force. Led by the loathsome general, Illex Cross, the officers had released a drugged gas that turned citizens into monsters, creating chaos in the streets.

Although Kaz had taken no part in the proceedings, their goodbyes after the battles had been less than cordial. He had said some things – and she had returned them in kind.

It was Burn's fault that he had gotten wrapped up in all of it to begin with. If she hadn't stumbled into his house – broken, bleeding, and on the run from the Peace Force – his life would have been so much simpler. He never would have become a pawn in her plot to bring down the force. He never would have been arrested and beaten and suspected of treason. He never would have learned her real motives, called her a traitor, and looked at her with such disappointment that it had broken her heart.

He had taken the discovery of her real allegiance as a betrayal, a personal insult that had hurt him to his very core.

21

In return, he had hurt her.

Still, in her absence Kaz had apparently made amends, not only helping Scar find the truth about the wildlands but also aiding the Lunaria as a double agent. He'd even helped the Lunaria bring Burn and her friends back into the city. When their plan had dissolved into chaos, pitting Kaz's comrades on the force against the rebels, he'd chosen to stand by the Lunaria. He'd chosen mutiny over complacency, the wild unknown over the comfort of the familiar. He'd chosen her.

It was a stroke of luck that the Peace Force hadn't seen Kaz helping them – and that Raqa hadn't reported on his true loyalty – although luck wasn't entirely to thank. Kaz's supernatural gift of stealth had also played a part. That and the fact that Raqa hadn't actually known his name.

Kaz had only recently learned he was one of them – a *freak*, a mutant, an abomination. After his initial shock, he'd soon come to realize that being gifted had its advantages, especially for a spy. Since Burn had returned, Kaz had been instrumental in the Lunaria's plans, particularly those involving Ellis.

After they'd formed their plot to infiltrate the highest tiers, they'd devised a short list of candidates for Burn to impersonate. These were minor players in the games taking place atop Kasis, people who were prominent yet invisible, respected yet insignificant. She needed to step into a life without notice, to assume responsibilities without blunder. The higher she aimed, the more likely she was to fall.

Once the Lunaria's list of targets had been crafted, they'd handed it over to Kaz, placing their trust and their future in his hands. With his access to Peace Force files, he'd been able to delve into the darkest corners of the candidates' lives, poking and prodding to determine their worth. Through his efforts, the list had steadily dwindled, ebbing until only one name had remained: Ellis Hyde.

Ellis was a blank canvas that craved color, a timid blossom begging for life to begin. Her world was small, with her parents at the center pulling the strings. A few years younger than Burn, she was new to the realm of "polite" society, with few friends – and fewer expectations set upon her graceful shoulders. She was unencumbered, unhindered by a complicated past or an arduous present. In other words, she was the perfect mark.

Yet finding their target was only one part of the problem. They also needed a way to get to her. As a daughter of the elite, Ellis was well-guarded, secured in her tower at the top of the city like some fantasy princess of yore.

They knew that infiltration would get them nowhere. A stealth mission to wrench the princess from her castle would only end in failure. So they did the unthinkable; they told the truth. They were going to kidnap Ellis, and they told her family everything. Well, maybe not everything, but enough to make them scared. Because a family that's scared is a family in need of protection, and a family like the Hydes could afford the best protection money could buy: their own personal Peace Force guard.

What they didn't realize was that the man they hired to protect Ellis was the very man hired to kidnap her. Once Kaz had slipped his name to the top of the bodyguard pile, it was only a matter of time before he took his place at the girl's side. Then, with a trusted officer in tow, Ellis had walked directly into the Lunaria's hands, descending through the city like a lamb to slaughter.

Of course, that had been the easy part. Now it was time for the actual work.

Burn walked beside Kaz in the fading evening light. The soft rays of sunset that broke through the tiers caught on the particles of dust and haze, creating an otherworldly glow. It made Kasis look almost magical, at least for the moment. Soon, though, darkness would fall, consuming the streets and the houses and the people within them, and stealing the magic from their grasp.

Silence had set in between them, and Burn struggled to find the words to fill it.

"Kaz, I wanted to say I'm sorry," she began, but Kaz raised a hand to cut her off.

"Don't," he said gently, lowering his gaze to the ground. "You don't need to apologize. I didn't understand then. I didn't realize why you needed to fight. I do now. I'm only sorry it took me so long to see it."

Burn nodded, a wave of relief coursing through her. She hadn't realized how much she'd been dreading this, how much she'd feared seeing him again and facing her past. His words eased something in her, and a new lightness took hold in her chest.

"Thanks," she said sincerely. "I'm glad you're here."

And she meant it. This whole plan was ludicrous. Taking over someone else's body – someone else's life – was absurd, and if she wasn't careful, she knew she could end up losing herself in the process. With Kaz at her side, at least she had something familiar to hold onto. She hoped it would be enough.

"I'm glad you're here, too," Kaz stated, refocusing his gaze on the street. "The city wasn't the same without you." He risked a glance at Burn, and she thought she spotted the familiar twinkle in his green eyes before he looked away.

Another silence descended between them, but this one was easy, comfortable. Side by side, they climbed toward Kasis' peak, leaving the dirt and despair of the lower levels in their wake.

As they rose, the city brightened around them, coming to life before their eyes. Up here, people walked instead of shuffling, smiled instead of coughing, stood out instead of blending in. The streets were more detailed, sharper, and more alive. It was as if this was the real world, and the one below was merely an echo, a figment, a dream.

Burn marveled at the architecture, how one tier fed seamlessly into the next, with stairs and walkways and bridges branching off like tributaries of a stream. It was elegant, meticulous, precise, a work of art soaring atop a broken city.

While it wasn't Burn's first time amongst the elite, the experience never failed to shock her. The colors, the cleanliness, and the brilliance of it all made her blink, and she took her time to absorb the excess.

She had no idea how to survive in this world, how to act like she belonged in a community that thrived on exclusion. As if to emphasize her fears, a roadblock rose up in their path, barring their entry to the next tier. Two armed Peace Officers stood rigid against the barricade with their arms crossed, glaring at the street as if daring passersby to test them.

This was a new feature in the city, and it was a direct result of the Lunaria's recent endeavors. Bombing the air intake points and, later, placing decoy explosives along the upper tiers had rattled the rich and powerful, and the Peace Force had since taken extra steps to ensure their safety. It meant that the Lunaria were getting somewhere. Their actions were making waves, and soon the storm would be unstoppable. In the meantime, though, it did make travel a tad more difficult.

Thankfully for Burn, a Peace Force escort made bypassing the roadblock a breeze – as did her new identity. Instinctively, she shrank back from the officers, shying away from their gazes. Yet at her appearance, they stepped aside, instantly recognizing her and granting her access.

Burn hastily strode through, secretly afraid that a word or a gesture would give her away. As she passed, though, the guards merely nodded, quickly refocusing on the crowd. She breathed a soft sigh of relief as Kaz joined her, and together they continued on.

It was quieter up here, a fact which Burn's sensitive ears seized on. The painful discord of the busy city streets was fading to a hum, and the factories' constant clatter was muted to near silence. In their place were the light tinkling of porcelain, the laughter of children, the chimes of distant shop bells. It all combined to form one unending song, a tune of such overwhelming sweetness that it practically begged for dissonance.

With the darkness falling in earnest, Burn and Kaz quickened their pace, cognizant of the coming curfew. While the rich were likely unrestricted by such rules, Ellis' family was no doubt wondering where she was. By this point, the girl had been gone for some hours, and the last thing she needed was for her parents to raise the alarm. So the two hurried through the still streets, winding their way toward the top.

By the time they reached the Hydes' street, Burn was beginning to feel lightheaded. Everything seemed like too much – too big, too bright, too quiet – and the eerie feeling clung to her like cobwebs.

"The house is right over here," Kaz said from beside her, startling Burn out of her thoughts and making her jump.

She looked in the direction he was pointing, and her mouth fell open beneath her mask. A palatial mansion lay before her, composed of steel and glass, standing tall against a backdrop of stars. The light cascading from the windows and the brilliance of the streetlamps combined to create a ball of brightness that almost rivaled the planet's twin suns.

Burn had seen this house in Ellis' mind, traced its shape in her thoughts, but it couldn't compare to the reality. In theory, Burn knew every room, every hall, every statue and painting, but that didn't mean she'd been prepared.

Standing in the building's looming shadow, she suddenly felt hopelessly small. The house, with its three towering stories, was solid and strong and menacing in its rigidity. She felt no sense of home, no comfort or life emanating from its walls.

Even from outside, she could glimpse the lush furnishings and glittering accents that dotted the interior. The house itself was a gallery and the gaping windows its frames, giving passersby a carefully curated picture of the lives unfolding inside. Looking down the street, Burn noticed that the other houses were much the same, inviting glances into their sumptuous rooms and their sumptuous lives.

For some reason, the sight made a small ball of anger ignite inside Burn's chest. It wasn't just that these people had so much when others had nothing; it was that they chose to flaunt it with such reckless abandon. Their lives were on display, put on a pedestal and shown to the world in a vain attempt to garner envy and praise. For all that they had, Burn thought, their lives were still so empty.

It made Burn want to turn around and run. She wanted to flee back to her real life, back to her family and friends, back to a world that made sense, where things had value beyond just their worth.

Sighing, she ignored her instincts and pressed on, inching closer to the home's glowing front door. Unlike the grand glass windows, the door was opaque, and it radiated a soft orange light. Bracing herself, Burn stuck out her hand and scanned it on the pad. It took an agonizing second to verify her identity before softly beeping in acceptance.

Burn strode inside, and Kaz followed silently behind. Outwardly, Burn ignored him, adopting Ellis' veneer of lofty superiority. But underneath, she was glad to have him there, and his presence helped calm the anxiety that flitted like sparks through her mind.

Burn wasn't even 10 steps into the house when a cool voice greeted her, sending an uneasy chill down her spine.

"Ellis, darling. Where have you been? We've been worried sick," the woman said with cool indifference.

Burn turned to her right, finding the woman seated in a low onyx chair in what appeared to be a living room. The sunken space gleamed with glass, set off by stylish upholstery, and the woman seemed right at home amidst the grandeur. She held a crystal tumbler and made no move toward Burn. Instead, she merely raised her eyebrows, feigning concern.

The expression looked strange on her. The woman was beautiful, of course. She had bright blond hair that verged on white, with a dramatic purple streak coloring one side. Her bob was cut short in the latest fashion, curling under her chin and framing the sharp lines of her face. Her clothes boasted the same stark elegance. The tailored green ensemble hugged her tall, thin frame and accentuated the length of her legs as she sat staring at Burn.

Yet something was off about her. Burn couldn't put her finger on it, but something about the woman made her skin tingle as if in warning. Maybe it was a memory – something she had seen in Ellis' mind. Or maybe it was simply a normal reaction, an ingrained response to the innate dangers of the elite.

Burn flashed through her mental images, sorting through names and faces until landing on a match. This was Una Hyde. This was her mother.

Before Burn had a chance to reply, another figure appeared, rising from a high-backed couch and turning to face her. This man was softer, more padded, and Burn realized with a start that he looked like her. Well, technically he looked like Ellis, but they were one and the same now. Round cheeks, full mouth, small nose. Except unlike her, his lips were turned into a cruel scowl, which stripped his face of any hint of kindness.

"Take off that god damn mask this instant," he snarled

in a low, threatening tone. "I warned you not to set foot in the lower tiers, but clearly you haven't listened. What do you have to say for yourself?"

Burn's mind reeled, trying to latch onto something – anything – she could use. She knew instantly that this was Ellis' father, Baylor. And she knew from Ellis' memories that he was not a man to be crossed.

"I'm sorry, father," she replied breathlessly in Ellis' high, girlish voice. "I just wanted to go down a few levels to shop. It's not too dangerous there. Besides, I had Officer Petala to protect me."

A noise between a sigh and a growl escaped from Baylor's throat. "I'll deal with Officer Petala later," he said between clenched teeth. "Right now, *you* are my priority, and you have disobeyed me."

Baylor stalked closer to Burn, his eyes boring into hers. "There is nothing down there for you. Do you understand me? Those people are worthless – just like the trinkets they peddle. You have no business fraternizing with them. It's best for everyone if you stick with your own kind."

Burn kept her face blank, fighting her scorching desire to lash out, to defend the lower tiers and the people in them. She bit her lip, focusing on the pain instead of the rage. Ellis would never lash out. Ellis would stay silent. So Burn stayed silent too.

"These rules are for your own safety," Baylor continued, crossing his arms across his portly chest. "You know the threats *those people* have sent to us. They want you dead. They want all of us dead, and they want anarchy to reign in our place. If I find out you've gone down there again, I'll have no other option than to tag you. At least then I'll always know where you are. Do you understand?" he asked again, as if she were a simpleton who couldn't comprehend his basic reprimands.

"Yes, father," she forced herself to say, keeping tight hold of her fury – and her shaking fists. She glanced over at Una, hoping to find sympathy painted on her sharp face, but all she found was icy disinterest.

"Good," her father continued, drawing her attention back. "Now go to bed. I'll see you in the morning." Without warning, he grasped her shoulders and kissed her lightly on the cheek.

Burn walked away in silence, too stunned to protest. She wove through the house without thinking, relying on memories to guide her while her mind whirled. Was that how those people always acted? Was that how they treated their daughter?

That man had threatened to implant a traceable chip into his own child, to effectively steal her autonomy and relegate her to the realm of property. She steamed at the thought, bitterly resenting their attempts at control.

Then something Meera said drifted into her thoughts and she froze. *Their patriarch, Baylor, may even have a seat on the assembly himself.* Was that horrid man part of the Shadow Assembly? Was he one of the masked faces behind the atrocities plaguing the city – the persecution, the murder, the escalating disappearances of *freaks*?

She had known it was a possibility, that she might be walking straight into the lion's den, but until that moment she hadn't fully understood. Now that she did, the thought made her sick.

Without realizing it, Burn had reached her room. Channeling her fury into movement, she yanked the door open and stormed inside. Slamming it shut behind her, she slumped against its cool surface, lowering her head into her hands. She was surprised to find that they were shaking. And soon, so was she.

Chapter 4

Scar didn't feel lonely, at least not in the way other people did. She felt an absence, a lack of something that should have been there but wasn't. It made her uncomfortable, like an itch she couldn't scratch.

It had felt like that a lot over the last several months. First Symphandra had gone, claimed by the ManniK Battles which had taken so many. Then Burn had disappeared into the wildlands, leaving Scar alone in a city that despised her.

It was better now that Burn was back inside the dome, safe and relatively unscathed, but this new distance had its effects, making her feel restless and unsettled.

Scar didn't sleep much to begin with. It felt unproductive and, frankly, unnecessary, just one more component of her peculiar nature. Typically she didn't mind it. The nights, with their glorious stillness, were the perfect time to work without disruption, without the threat of idle chitchat.

Yet that night, despite the silence, she couldn't

concentrate. Something was off – or, rather, something was coming. Scar felt it looming on the horizon, a monumental event that held all of their fates in its grasp. It was simultaneously thrilling and terrifying, and Scar was impatient for it to begin. Waiting wasn't one of her strong suits.

She tried to work, to meld her mind with that of the machine in her grasp, but it was futile. Her mind didn't want to toil away in the darkness. It wanted action.

Tossing aside the wrist cuffs she'd been tinkering with, Scar rose from her seat and poked her head into the hall. Since she'd been declared a fugitive – along with most of the other Lunaria members – she'd been spending the majority of her time trapped with them inside a safe house. It was crowded and chaotic, and Scar craved the solitude of her own home.

Yet going outside was more dangerous than ever. Disappearances were on the rise, and the Peace Force had upped their patrols, scanning everyone they could in search of rebels. Typically, Scar would have used her pet PeaceBot to explore, to tiptoe around the lines and gather intel on her behalf, but the force had sidelined that, as well. Once they'd realized that their own creations could be used against them, they'd decommissioned the droids and left them to rot.

Her sole remaining PeaceBot, which she'd previously used as a scout and now lurked like a relic in her room, would no doubt be spotted in an instant and taken down in the next. Even if they couldn't trace it back to her, it would still be a waste of a perfectly good bot – and it wouldn't get her any closer to the info she needed. That left Scar only one option: She was going outside.

Invigorated by her decision, Scar suited up, donning dark clothes that concealed the metal across her skin and a black scarf that extinguished the brilliance of her fiery red curls. Pulling on her mask and goggles, she risked a glance into one of the mirrors dotting the hallway and paused.

It didn't have to be like this, she reminded herself. Eyana had given her the chance to change, to relinquish this problematic exterior in favor of a new one. Someone who wasn't a fugitive. Someone who wasn't a freak.

Each of the Lunaria members whose identities had been compromised had been given the choice. Some of them had snapped at the chance, eagerly seizing the opportunity to shed their skin in favor of something better, but most had not. It was hard enough to hold onto yourself in the midst of a war, they reasoned. Why make it even harder?

Scar was in the latter camp. Sure, it would have been easier to be normal, to look like everyone else. She'd entertained the notion for a few minutes, letting a vision of her metal-less body float in her mind's eye like a dream. But that's all it was: a dream. Because this was who she was – and this was who she intended to remain.

Turning her head back and forth, Scar watched herself in the mirror, checking to make sure her identity and her *defects* were sufficiently concealed. By this point, the move was second nature to her. She longed for the day when she no longer had to hide herself, when the world came to realize that standing out was better than fitting in.

It was something Symphandra had known – and something she'd made sure that Scar knew, as well. She had loved Scar not in spite of her differences, but because of them. Now that Symphandra was gone, the idea of changing, of giving up what made her unique, seemed unfathomable. Even if it meant she no longer had to hide away, trapped behind the face of a fugitive, she couldn't do it.

Scar lowered her goggles over her eyes and turned away from the mirror, quietly stepping out the door and into the night. The air outside was cool and thick, with a cloudy gray haze obscuring the lane. Overhead, a streetlamp flickered in uncertainty, casting Scar's body in and out of shadow as a cloud of moths battled for the light. Wrapping her cloak tightly around her torso, she stepped fully into the darkness, fading into its familiar embrace.

The route was clear in her mind, with the destination lit like a beacon in her thoughts. She was headed for the news hub. As the headquarters of the Peace Force-controlled media, it was where pro-government propaganda was wrung from the realm of fiction and disseminated to the masses. The Lunaria had realized early on that in order to win a coup, they needed those masses on their side. To do that they had to show them the truth. Seizing the news hub was the obvious solution.

Naturally, Scar was the first one they'd turned to. She'd taught herself how to hack into news feeds over a decade ago, and she'd utilized her skills for years to help further her sister's career. Blackmailing, it turned out, was far easier when one could threaten to expose the target on city-wide channels – and follow through in the rare instances where threats were not enough. But splicing in one or two salacious stories was different than manipulating the entire feed. For that, Scar needed control of the hub itself.

Of course, she wasn't reckless enough to believe that she could bring the hub to its knees on her own. As a government building, it was heavily fortified, with several teams of Peace Officers on round-the-clock guard. Taking them on alone would have been suicide. Instead, Scar's objective that night was observation. The infiltration would have to wait.

Scar needed to find a weak spot, a flaw in their defenses. Such a staid and steadfast company had to have at least one, and once she found it, she could slip by unnoticed – along with a crew of likeminded Lunaria. Yet even with all her gadgets, discovering such a handicap wouldn't be easy, especially for a fugitive like her.

If she had wanted, she could have sent someone in her stead, someone whose mere presence wouldn't raise alarm bells and calls for backup, but she didn't trust anyone else. Not with this. Missions like these were safer when undertaken alone. If you had to put your life in someone else's hands, there was always the chance that they'd drop it.

Of course, she could have turned to Cali, her onetime partner and ally, with whom she'd explored the tunnels beneath the city and crafted a plan to break through the dome. They'd grown close during their days together – or at least closer than Scar got to most. Yet Cali was a fugitive just like Scar, and she had no desire to put the woman's safety at risk yet again. The last time she had, Cali had nearly died, shot through the shoulder during their bid to bring Burn back into the city, and in the wake of it neither had fully recovered.

That's why Scar stalked through the city's darkest streets alone, clinging to the shadows for safety. Her goggles relayed a sharp picture of the grime-encrusted walls and trash-strewn alleys, and she tiptoed around a minefield of bottles and cans so as not to break the eerie silence of the scene.

With the curfew in effect and the Peace Force on high alert, the nights in Kasis had become bleak and desolate, a wasteland of fear and reckoning. Gone were the ManniK peddlers, the petty thieves, the junkies. Now the only thing that prowled in the dark was the true enemy.

There were a handful of tiers standing between Scar and the hub, each patrolled by officers who roved in random formations. There was no way to plan around their positions, nor anticipate their moves. Theirs was an ever-changing puzzle, irregular, erratic, too much for your average citizen to solve. But Scar was not your average citizen.

Tucking herself into the grip of a disused alley, Scar grabbed her pack and withdrew a clunky contraption, dominated by a wide screen, a mess of colored wires, and a delicate protruding scope. It was a prototype, an amalgam of bits and bobs, a thing of function over beauty.

Pressing her hands to its sides, she heard the gentle purr as it rumbled to life. The screen flickered for an instant, then resolved, settling into a map of colors and darkness, of shapes and straight lines. In the middle, Scar could see herself, radiating red and orange and cool blue like some colorful ghost haunting a monochromatic city. Jutting out from her in every direction were the roads and alleys, the buildings and tiers, the valves and ventricles of Kasis.

She'd overlaid the thermal data onto a map of the city, giving her a godlike view of its inhabitants – or at least the ones left lurking outside. With it, she could see everyone who wandered the streets, everyone who ventured out, everyone who posed a threat. She could see the force and their minions, and she could skillfully evade them. Slinging her bag across her shoulders, Scar took off at a light run.

Loping through the city alone in the dim light, Scar felt unstoppable. Her wild hair had come loose from its prison and now flowed freely behind her like a cape, gracefully rising and falling in the cool evening air. She smiled beneath her mask, relishing the emptiness of the city and the stillness that came with it.

Only once during her travels was the glorious stillness broken by the presence of others. As soon as Scar spotted their glowing forms, she stowed herself away in the shadow of a stall, unable to find a path around them. Then she waited, listening to the sound of their footsteps against the pavement and the echo of their lighthearted laughter.

As they drew nearer, Scar peered around the cart, her curiosity winning out against her unease. With a few quick taps on the side of her goggles, she zoomed in on the far end of the street. Soon enough, two Peace Officers appeared from around the corner, armored and armed and strutting like they owned the world. Scar cringed, shrinking back behind the cart and making herself one with the night.

She held her breath as they passed, an unconscious reaction to the presence of a predator. The men, however, were far too distracted by their own high spirits to ever notice a lone woman perched in the darkness, tracking their every move.

Scar waited, listening with all her might as their footsteps receded. Then she waited some more. Finally satisfied that the patrol was gone, she pushed herself up and stretched, her limbs having grown stiff from the stasis. Moving slower, she embarked on the final stretch to her destination.

It wasn't far now. The hub was located on a central tier in the center of the city, just within reach of the Peace Station. Or, rather, just below it. While the morgue and state rooms lay resplendently above it, crowned by the station like a jewel, the hub was hidden away and often overlooked. It was like an offshoot of the Peace Sector, a forgotten cousin forever languishing beneath.

Yet that didn't mean it wasn't protected.

Scar's map lit up red at the presence of patrols, and she cursed beneath her breath. Officers scoured the perimeter, covering every inch. No matter her stealth, she'd never be able to slip by unnoticed. As she watched, they traveled in predetermined paths around and around, protecting the building from every angle. Well, almost every angle.

Glancing up, she spotted the rooftops several stories above her, their peaks muted by the haze, and an idea formed in her mind. Sprinting into a nearby alley, she scoured the bricks for a way up, a way to scale the surface and reach the summit. Her eyes landed on a rickety set of metal stairs and she ran to them, beginning her climb.

The rusted iron groaned beneath her, the sound reverberating like a cry through the hushed night, and she flinched. Her breath caught in her chest as she listened for patrols, but none came running. Refocusing her attention on her steps, Scar made quick, careful movements up the remaining stairs and onto the roof.

Lying flat on her back, she paused to catch her breath before leveraging herself up and absorbing her surroundings. Through the dimness and haze, she could just make out the fuzzy edges of buildings, which stretched on into the darkness. The ceiling of the tier, the walkways, and stairs were consumed by the night, drenched in fog and blurred into mere ghosts of shapes. In front of her, though, the rooftop was open and empty, as if inviting her for a stroll.

Now, traveling by rooftops was not a common way to get around the city. The uneven buildings and sporadic chasms made rooftop ramblings a perilous endeavor. She prayed that no soldiers would look up – and that no citizens would glance out their windows – as she ambled over their heads, hopping over crevices and leaping gaps until the news hub rose within view.

The hub wasn't a grand building. Where the Peace Station stood tall and majestic, with polished stone walls that glittered in the light of a hundred bulbs, the news hub was dull and flat, with a squat countenance that nearly blended into the shops around it. It didn't seem like the centerpiece of a news empire, the post from which all of Kasis received their reports. Only the guards posted outside hinted at the building's importance.

Several pairs of soldiers flanked the front and sides with a small armory at their backs. All told, she counted eight officers stationed around the scene – with each man looking more bored than the last. Some smoked, some paced, some sat playing cards by the meager light of lanterns. Others rested on the ground, their backs to the hub, arms crossed, and eyes closed in peaceful slumber.

It was a quiet sight, a serene slice of life, and Scar sat for a minute studying them. Then she got to work, snapping pictures of the guards and their positions for later dissection.

These would be their blueprints for battle, the Lunaria's life-line to the hub. This was precisely what she'd come for.

She spent a quarter of an hour in study – looking, listening, capturing – until nothing in her sights was left unexplored. Eventually, it was time to go. Yet for some reason she couldn't move, couldn't bring herself to leave.

Scar should have been content with her findings. She should have taken her pictures and left. Yet she remained perched, craving more. Contentment was, after all, an overrated emotion. All it meant was that you didn't have the gumption to strive for more. And Scar had never been one to leave good enough alone.

Moving slowly so as not to draw attention, Scar crawled toward the rear of the building and peered over the edge. Unfortunately, no staircases – rickety or otherwise – were conveniently placed along the side, providing an easy route to the ground. There was, however, a sturdy-looking pipe that led down to an overflowing trash bin. It wasn't ideal, Scar thought, but it could work.

Stowing her spy gadgets in her pack, Scar readied herself for descent. In one nimble move, she hopped over the side, keeping hold of the ledge while wrapping her legs around the duct. Once secured, she moved her hands to the tube and began to slide, inching toward the ground.

She'd only made it a few feet when an uncomfortable sensation registered, first in her hands and then her legs. It began as a tingle, then a warmth, then an all-out burning. Scar was clutching a heat vent. It was just her luck. Her instincts took over and she let go, dropping like a stone.

The fall was over in an instant, yet the shock remained,

coursing through Scar's system. She expected pain to blossom in her body, but it didn't. Instead, a mild discomfort and general breathlessness were all that took hold. Well, that and the smell.

She realized belatedly that the towering pile of garbage and refuse had broken her fall, saving her from serious injury while muffling her impact. She listened briefly for any approaching footsteps, any indication that someone had heard her, but the street remained silent save for the sound of her own heavy breathing.

Momentarily reassessing her plan, Scar weighed her general idiocy against her luck, trying to determine if she should press on. On the one hand, she wasn't dead or injured. That was good. On the other, she had nearly brought a squadron of Peace Officers down on herself simply because she couldn't tell that something was hot. It was a rookie mistake.

Still, she'd come all this way. She wasn't about to leave without getting a full picture of the hub's security.

Taking a deep breath – a move which she instantly regretted – Scar sat up and grabbed hold of the sticky steel rim, slipping farther into the squalor before clambering over the edge. Lowering herself onto the pavement, she did her best to brush away the filth, wincing at the mysterious liquids that had seeped into her gear. She shook her head, watching as bits of moldy food and metal detritus fell from her hair, before securing the scarf around her curls.

Setting off, Scar crept softly around the corner, her eyes peeled for any sign of movement. Sensing none, she plastered herself against the wall, grating her body against its rough surface as she inched toward the hub. Once the building was in sight, she stopped, sinking down to make herself as small as possible.

From her vantage point, she could see only the right side of the building, where two guards stood facing each other in lazy conversation. Manipulating her goggles – and wiping away a smudge of grime that had made its way onto the lenses – she zoomed in on the scene. She also activated her lip-reading program, which she'd been perfecting on and off for the past several months.

"Nah, that would be a waste," a robotic voice whispered in her ear, catching the men mid-conversation.

"Then what would you choose if you had to be one of *them*?" the man on the left asked, crossing his arms over his chest.

"Definitely something powerful. Like being able to control people. Or being able to shoot bullets from my hands. That would be awesome."

"You can already shoot bullets from your hand, you idiot," replied the second man. "It's called a gun. Maybe if you'd ever used one, you'd know."

"Shut up," said the first man, going on the defensive. "It's way better than invisibility. How could you want that? It's so weak!"

Scar was rapidly bored by the conversation. These men clearly weren't the brains behind the operation – if there were any brains amongst these guards at all. Scar seriously doubted they had a brain cell between them. Maybe if she got into range of the men out front, though, she might be able to pick up something a tad more useful.

Scar crept forward, intending to get a better view of the building, but a large hand suddenly clamped onto her shoulder.

"Don't move," came a deep male voice from behind her, freezing her in place.

Chapter 5

"Keep your hands where we can see them and prepare to be scanned," said a second man, coming to stand in front of Scar. He was a broad man, clean-shaven and bald, and his gear clearly marked him as a Peace Officer.

Scar cursed herself for getting caught, for being so swept up in the investigation that she couldn't even watch her own back. Her skin prickled in dread as her mechanical mind stuttered, struggling to change gears from predator to prey, from reconnaissance to resistance.

She couldn't let them scan her. That much was clear. Once they figured out who she was – and who she worked for – she'd disappear for sure, carted off to some Peace Force holding cell to be tested or tortured or killed.

Making a split-second decision, Scar disobeyed her direct orders and reached into her pocket, pulling out a pen. Blue sparks sprang to life as she pushed the button, aiming the weapon at the hand still clasped on her shoulder.

She just managed to connect with the man's arm before he wrenched it away in a panicked flurry of movement. In the next instant, a kick sailed her way, striking her hard in the stomach and sending her flying. As she hit the wall with a thud, the pen dropped from her grasp and clattered to the ground, jumping away in jagged bounds.

She prepared to lunge for the weapon, but the first officer grabbed her by the arms, shoving her roughly into the wall. From this vantage point, she could see him clearly – see his greasy brown hair, his sallow skin, his snarl. Moving one of his bony hands to her chest, he readied a punch with the other. Letting loose, he struck her once, then twice, missing the metal of her body and finding only tender flesh.

Scar's head spun as pain and dizziness took hold. She couldn't see. She could barely even hear. Yet she felt it as someone shoved her to the ground, tearing away her pack and casting it aside. It landed with a muted thump somewhere down the alley, taking with it Scar's only hope of escape.

A kick collided with her midsection, and Scar winced, curling into herself. Another kick struck her, but this one met metal, sending a jarring reverberation through her body. The man who'd hit her howled in pain and surprise, hopping uncouthly to soothe his injured foot.

Scar's reprieve was short-lived. She barely had time to sit up before the bald man took over, using the butt of his gun to inflict yet more damage. Every time the gun hit metal, he laughed and hit her harder, fueled by her freakish state.

Scar tried to crawl, to get away, but the barrage was too constant, too fierce. Dropping to her stomach, her strength rapidly dissipated amidst the onslaught of pain. Shaking, she brought her arms up over her face and wished for it to end.

Now, wishes are a curious thing. In Scar's experience, they'd never done much good, what with being a last resort in times of crisis. She had no faith in fate, no belief that things would work out in the end. Life was merely a game of chance, and luck and destiny had no part to play.

Yet somehow, on this night, against all the odds – and all her doubts – her wish came true.

Through the gaps in her arms, Scar watched as something small and dark whizzed through the air, sinking into the bald man's back. His eyes went wide as the arrow bit into flesh, and he sank to his knees, clearly struggling. Meanwhile, the sallow officer swiveled, pointing his gun into the night but finding no monsters at which to aim.

The monster, however, knew exactly where to strike.

Out of the darkness and haze, a fury appeared, bent on vengeance. Twirling a steel spear between her hands, she approached slowly, methodically, as if savoring her opponent's unease. She had no business being as confident as she was. She had, after all, brought a stick to a gun fight. Yet that didn't seem to bother her.

When the sallow man trained his weapon on the woman and moved his finger to the trigger, Scar tried to warn her, to tell her to run, to save herself – but the woman didn't need a warning. In fact, she didn't appear to need anything at all. By the looks of things, she could handle herself just fine.

Leaping to his side, she brought the spear down on the gun, knocking it from his grip. With another swing, she sent the weapon skittering down the alley and into the night.

Yet the greasy officer didn't concede. He reached around, pulling another weapon from its holster, but the woman was faster. Her spear whooshed through the air in a blur of movement, striking his arm with a resounding crunch. As bones broke and his useless weapon dropped, the man let out a pitiful howl and crumpled to the ground.

With two men on their knees before her, Scar's savior circled them, weighing her options. She had yet to speak, to explain her presence, so Scar remained where she was, curled into a ball in the dirt. Her mind told her to run, to seize this distraction and slip into the night, but her body wouldn't obey. She cursed its weakness – her weakness – and watched.

The next events happened so rapidly that Scar wasn't sure which came first. Maybe it was the ashen man pulling himself up and turning to run. Maybe it was the knife, dislodged from the woman's belt, flipping through the air toward him. Maybe it was the appearance of three more officers, armed and angry, at the mouth of the alley.

Whatever it was, it finally spurred Scar into motion. Pushing down the pain, she uncurled and straightened, crawling sluggishly through the alley toward her pack. Clutching the bag, she rose, gripping the wall for support.

While Scar steadied herself, her newfound ally sent two more knives sailing toward the trio of newcomers, with each one finding its target. Yet she wasn't quick enough for the third man, who raised his gun and began to spray the street with bullets. Diving to the ground, she released her final knife, which flipped end over end before embedding itself into his hand.

The officer wailed, letting go of the gun but remaining

upright. Pulling out the knife with a cry of pure fury, he advanced on the woman, blood streaming from his injured hand. He swiped at her wildly with the dagger, a crazed rage overtaking his senses. The woman parried with her spear, and the clash of steel against steel echoed off the walls in ragged clangs.

Scar was so mesmerized by the blur of hands and weapons that she barely registered the bald man rising to his feet beside her. Despite the arrow still sticking from his back, he seemed to move with minimal discomfort. With a burst of speed, he ran at Scar, pinning her to the wall with surprising force.

Fear and adrenaline coursed through Scar's body as the man reached up to tear away her mask and cover her mouth with his hand. Instinctively, she jerked her head forward and bit down, feeling his fingers crunch between her teeth. The sharp, metallic taste of blood filled her mouth as he jerked his hand away with a growl.

Scar savored the momentary freedom before his other hand shot out and closed around her neck, slowly squeezing her windpipe until all she could do was croak. She clawed at his hand with feral abandon, but his grip didn't loosen. As greedy shadows began to claim the corners of her mind, she did the only thing she could think of. Reaching around the man, she raked her nails against his back, searching for the arrow still lodged in his skin.

A short eternity passed as she groped helplessly for the shaft, her tired fingers finding only cloth and armor. With her last ounce of strength, she pulled the man in tighter, combing her hand down his body until it finally met its target. Grabbing hold, she twisted, driving it deeper.

The man writhed in anguish, yanking his hand from her neck. The relief was instantaneous. Cool air flowed into her ravaged throat, burning as it traveled to her lungs. The world blinked back into focus, clear and sharp, and a new anger roared to life within her. With her hand still clasped around the arrow, she pulled the shaft with all her might, tearing it from the man's flesh.

Agony, hot and fierce, took hold of him as he tumbled to the ground, a bloody hole in his back. Scar waited for him to move, to come at her for revenge, but he stayed limp on the pavement, cast into painless oblivion.

Scar looked down at the arrow in her hand and nearly choked at the sight. Muscles and tendons and skin still clung to it, impaled upon its head and dripping onto the street. With a shiver of disgust, she tossed it aside and looked away.

Farther down the alley, the woman and her adversary were still locked in combat, trading blows with less force but the same manic ferocity. Both had suffered injuries in her absence, and she cringed at the sight of the woman's skin, torn and bleeding.

Scar knew she had to do something. More officers had to be on their way, called in as backup or alerted by the flurry of shots and screams, and neither woman had the strength left to fight them. Retreat was their only option – but that required a diversion. Digging into her bag in search of a solution, Scar's fingers closed around the cool metal of a coin.

She waited for the perfect moment to act. The officer missed a strike, and the woman dealt a blow that sent him to his knees, and Scar whistled, grabbing her attention. With a few quick hand signals – and a painful jerk of the head – Scar communicated her plan. The woman nodded, already running toward her with a sprightly gait.

Scar chucked the coin, and a small explosion rocked the alley, sending a cloud of smoke and debris billowing around them. The women didn't hesitate. Together, they took off down the road, twisting and turning through the tangled maze of streets to lose themselves in the city.

Scar's throat burned as she ran, and the grime of the city seeped freely into her lungs, but she didn't stop. She knew they needed to get clear of the scene, to disappear into the darkness without a trace. So they kept going, kept running until they were certain they were free.

What felt like miles later, they finally slowed and stopped, ducking into a service tunnel for shelter. Scar's breathing was labored and ragged, and it felt like her throat was bleeding. She swallowed once, then again, trying to rid herself of the feeling, but it persisted.

It was only then that she glanced up at the woman by her side.

"Who are you?" she asked bluntly, her throat chaffing painfully at the words.

Sighing, the woman lifted her goggles and lowered her mask, revealing a familiar face. Scar squinted at Nara through the gloom, attempting to piece together the mystery of her sudden appearance.

Nara had been a member of Burn's crew in the wildlands. Her gift of enhanced vision had apparently come in handy during their journey across the desert – and their subsequent re-entry into Kasis. In fact, she and Scar had fought alongside one another in the ensuing battle, but they'd had few interactions since. They weren't friends. They were barely even allies, since Nara was only a tentative member of the Lunaria. Yet here she was. Why?

Sensing Scar's curiosity – no doubt aided by her clearly bewildered expression – Nara began to explain.

"I don't sleep much," she said, wiping the blood and dirt off her hands as she spoke. "I'm used to being a guard, to watching the city's gate at all hours. I guess old habits die hard." She sighed, not making eye contact.

"I saw you leave and I followed. None of us should be going out alone, especially at night. I tracked you through the city, and when you got into trouble, which was inevitable, I intervened."

"Inevitable?" Scar scoffed, her hackles rising. "Why were you so sure that I couldn't handle myself?"

Nara finally looked up, meeting Scar's eyes with fire in her own. "You're not invincible. You're not a superhero, no matter how much you may believe otherwise. You can be killed – and you would have been, too, if I hadn't stepped in."

Annoyance, shame, and a good dose of wounded pride mingled in Scar's chest, tightening it uncomfortably. Yet she kept her face blank, unreadable. She didn't want to give Nara the satisfaction of knowing that her words had hit home.

"Thank you for your help," Scar replied coolly, staring straight into Nara's deep black eyes. "Next time I won't need it."

Nara let out a dubious snort. "Next time? Don't you understand? There won't be a next time. There can't be. You're too important to the Lunaria. And to Burn."

"What's important is getting control of the news hub," Scar replied, inching her face closer to Nara's. "If we want a chance of winning this war, we need access to their communications. And in order to get it, we need to know what we're up against."

Nara's eyebrow rose in a look of amusement. "There are eight guards patrolling the outer flank," she said, ticking off the items as she went. "Six are on a roving patrol of the tier. There are three more inside, one with a full surveillance feed of the building's interior. The broadcast room is in the rear, accessed through fingerprint and retinal scans. Would you like me to draw you a map?" she asked with a sardonic smile.

Normally, Nara's cocky attitude would have grated on Scar's nerves. She didn't do well when others celebrated their own genius. But this time it was different. This time, Nara had surprised her, and that wasn't an easy feat.

Scar didn't think. Closing the gap between them, she kissed Nara firmly, feeling the woman's soft lips give way under her own. It only lasted a second, which was the amount of time it took for Scar's brain to catch up with her body, but that second was glorious.

Scar withdrew as quickly as she had advanced, retreating back into the wall – and back into her shell – but she couldn't take back her actions. Instead, she pressed on, pretending as if nothing had happened.

"I was wrong," she said, adopting a smug tone that rivaled Nara's. "Next time I might need you after all."

Scar risked a glance up, finding a small smile on Nara's lips. She didn't know if it was from what she'd said – or what she'd done – but the expression warmed her, sending a pleasant tingle through her chest. If she were capable of blushing, she would have done so. Instead, she returned the smile with a tentative one of her own.

"Good," Nara said firmly, her smile widening. "Now that we have that settled, may I suggest that we make our way back to the safe house? Morning is coming, and we don't want the others to worry."

Scar reached around to her bag, intending to grab her thermal tracker, but Nara stopped her.

"Oh no," she said, shaking her head. "You don't need gadgets when you've got me." She winked at Scar in an expression of pure self-assurance before lowering her goggles back over her eyes.

Scar did the same, positioning her goggles securely before rising. As she did so, a stab of pain shot through her ribcage, and she cringed. Without a word, Nara wrapped her arm around Scar's waist, propping her up. Her touch was fortifying, and Scar welcomed the assistance, draping her arm over Nara's shoulder and trusting her to lead the way home.

Chapter 6

Burn awoke early, confusion clouding her senses. The light streaming through the veiled windows was glaring, and even with her eyes closed it still managed to seep in. She felt disoriented, out of place, and she couldn't quite remember where she was.

The sounds around her didn't help. The noises and voices that trickled in were unfamiliar, and they lacked the harshness that she was used to. There were fewer footsteps outside, fewer shouts, fewer rumbling machines with their comforting rhythms. She missed them, missed the chaos and the congestion. This place seemed too quiet, too calm, as if it were hiding some sinister secret.

A sudden knock on the door made her jump. Before Burn could even process the noise, a small brunette woman entered, dressed from head to toe in black.

"Morning, miss," she said with quiet deference, bowing her head in greeting.

Without waiting for a reply, she strode farther into the room, making a beeline for the windows. In one fluid movement, she drew back a pair of velvety curtains, bathing the room in brilliant light before moving on to the next. Soon, the light streamed in from every angle, alighting on every surface, every object, and bringing them to life. Burn blinked at the brightness, unaccustomed to such intensity.

The room was beautiful in its opulence, and Burn had to consciously pull her attention away so she could focus on the woman. She scanned her mind for a name, sifting through her stolen thoughts, but all she landed on was *servant*, *maid*, *other*.

As Burn deliberated, the servant approached, drawing back the soft blankets and silky sheets and folding them neatly at the foot of the bed. Burn watched her work with genuine curiosity, making note of her graceful movements and quiet steps.

"Breakfast will be ready in half an hour," she remarked once she'd finished, folding her hands in front of her in a practiced stance. "Would you like me to draw you a bath?"

Burn was startled at the offer – and delighted at the idea.

"Yes, thank you," she said, surprised at the sound of her own voice.

The maid seemed surprised, as well – not by her voice, but by her expression of thanks. Burn realized with a start that Ellis wouldn't say such things. Ellis would command servants, not thank them. She'd show them indifference, not gratitude. Burn made a note to amend her interactions in the future.

Overcoming her shock, the maid nodded and fetched

Burn a robe before departing into the adjacent chamber. Burn rose and donned the flowing garment over her night clothes, listening with interest as the woman turned on the taps and began filling the tub with water.

Taking a deep breath, she considered her surroundings. Last night, with the shock of the Hydes' behavior fresh in her mind, she hadn't processed the glamor of it all. Now, with the interaction fading to a hazy memory, she took the time to truly appreciate the space.

It was stunning. Everywhere she looked, something vied for her attention and competed for her awe. The room itself was towering and open, with space enough for an entire family to dwell. The windows that spanned two of its sides were nearly as tall, forming walls of glass that overlooked the magnificence of the tier beyond.

From her perch, Burn felt like she could see forever, with no clouds of dirt or debris to obscure her vision. Streets fanned out around her, dotted with gardens and people and sprawling homes that glinted in the light of the suns. Above her, the dome towered, acting as both her guard and her jailer, her protector and her prison.

It was all so clean, so bright, so colorful that it didn't even seem real. It felt like a toy world, a fantasy in which to play, a momentary distraction from the hardships of life beyond.

Inside, the room was no different. A rainbow of colors greeted her from across the space, beckoning her to reach out and touch. The walls were dressed in ivory, with golden flowers dancing elegantly across their breadth. Deep red curtains dripped from the ceiling like blood, hugging the windows and framing the world beyond.

In its center, the room cradled a towering bed, complete with four grand posters and a canopy of the deepest blue. It called to Burn even now, inviting her into its embrace like a lover with promises of blissful oblivion. She yearned to fall back into its soft caress, to lose herself in the silence of sleep, but she resisted, knowing she couldn't succumb to its temptations.

Elsewhere in the room, elegant furniture rose from the floor in graceful curves, more art than equipment. To her, furnishings were mere objects, useful articles that did their job with sturdy resilience. These, however, were sculptures, beautiful bits of engineered wood and metal that sang through the space, giving it life.

If she could, Burn would have spent the day exploring the room and its secrets, marveling at this world and the treasures it held. Except she had a job to do, and she knew she'd never achieve anything if she remained at the mercy of her awe. Turning her back on the room, she strode into the bathroom beyond.

Her first reaction was to marvel at that space as well, but she resisted its pull. Stripping out of her garments, she lowered herself into the tub, relishing the warmth as it loosened her muscles and seeped into her bones. The bubbles in the bath tickled her skin and a scent like flowers rose in smoky tendrils to her nose, eating away at her tension. Without knowing it, she sighed, slipping deeper into the heated bliss.

Back home, warm water wasn't a luxury they'd been allowed. Theirs was a world of icy jets, of freezing showers and tepid baths. There were no warm pools, no long showers. This ecstasy was reserved only for the rich, and it made Burn realize the true chasm between the classes, the yawning crater that lurked between their life and hers.

She allowed herself a few more minutes of euphoria before pulling herself from its depths. Throwing on the robe once more, she crept into her room and dressed, choosing a simple blue ensemble from a closet that held hundreds. Twisting up her hair, she pinned it in place in a simple style before turning to the mirror to check her work.

The sight was still a shock. She wanted to see her own eyes, her own hard face and dark hair. She tried to find them beneath Ellis' soft curves, but they were gone, devoured by the perfection of this girl, hidden behind her soft skin and long lashes, her rosy cheeks and pouting smile.

Burn took a moment to focus, to remind herself of where she was and who she was supposed to be. She flicked through Ellis' memories, centering herself in the girl's world and immersing herself in her thoughts. With a fortifying breath, she stepped into the hall and away from the safety of her room.

It wasn't difficult to find the dining room. If Ellis' thoughts hadn't led her there, she still would have been able to hear it plainly, to decipher the tinkling of glasses and the clatter of silverware. Despite the lack of discussion, she could tell that Ellis' parents were already present, tainting the room with their censure.

She paused at the door, the conversation from the night before still clear in her mind. She didn't want to face them, to relive that scrutiny, but she knew she had no choice. These people were her connection to the underworld, her key to finding the hell hidden amidst the heavens, as the top tiers were often called. She needed them to trust her.

Plastering on a small smile, she turned the corner and floated into the room. Burn kept her face placid as she greeted her parents and took a seat at the long wooden table. Outwardly, she was the model of decorum. Inwardly, she was mesmerized.

Just like the rest of the house, this room was breathtaking. Its walls were coated in a blood-red paper that shimmered in the light. Each surface dripped with gold-framed art and beveled mirrors that cut the room into pieces and reflected it upon itself. Overhead, a monstrous light fixture of solid glass cascaded from the ceiling, swirling down in subtle curves. Throughout the space, sculptures and statues and silhouettes looked on like some frozen audience, their attention forever cast on the lonely stretch of wood.

Yet the room itself couldn't hold Burn's attention for long. Her gaze was drawn toward the table, pulled toward the food that was piled on its plane. Burn feasted with her eyes, consuming the sight with a painful mixture of envy and glee.

She'd never seen so many dishes. They called to her with their scents, ranging from sweet to savory to sour. On one end, towers of fruit and pastries put the room itself to shame. At the other, bowls of salty meats and fluffy eggs and steaming bread made Burn's head spin and her stomach growl.

Burn wanted everything. She couldn't even name half the items, but she craved them, her body welling up with desire. Back home, plain porridge or runny eggs or tinned soup filled her stomach most mornings, leaving her full yet unsatisfied. A pastry was a luxury, one she couldn't often afford.

These people had pastries to spare. They had pastries for half the Lunaria – and bacon and eggs and sausage for the rest. It was a stark contrast, one which Burn was acutely aware of. She felt guilty for their excess – and infuriated that they didn't even seem to notice. Still, a girl has to eat.

Trying to quell her eagerness, Burn carefully scooped food onto her clean white plate, obscuring its perfection with an equally perfect pile of buttery baked goods and steaming eggs laced with cheese.

Only after she'd demolished a delectably flaky croissant and two strips of bacon did she finally look up, considering the others at the table. Baylor sat at one end, focused on his food. Una sat at the other, her plate empty and her lips drawn into a tight line. She was considering her tab with knitted brows, shaking her head and sighing. Her hand rested lightly on a delicate porcelain mug, and every few seconds she brought it to her lips, savoring the inky liquid.

In the middle, Burn felt invisible. Neither noticed her presence, and she realized belatedly that she needn't have feared their fury. These people wouldn't admonish her; they barely acknowledged her. Somehow, that fact made her feel safer in her ruse, more confident in her con.

They'd never think to question a girl they barely knew, even if she shared their blood. If she kept her head down and stayed out of trouble, they'd have no reason to doubt her. Although that last part could prove challenging; Burn had never been able to resist the lure of trouble for long.

As if to prove her own point, she spoke up, drawing her

parents' attention.

"Do we have any plans today?" she asked innocently, pushing the remaining eggs across her plate with idle ease. "I was thinking of stopping by the shops, but I wanted to make sure I wasn't needed here."

Her mother, who had barely lowered her tab to look at her daughter, merely shook her head and refocused on the screen. Baylor, however, took a keen interest in Ellis' words, squinting his beady eyes in a look of quiet reproach.

"What, you didn't get enough shopping time in the *ghetto* yesterday?" he asked with a punch of malice.

Burn bit her tongue to stop herself from spitting out the first reply that came to mind. Instead, she took a breath and shook her head, putting on a look of surrender.

"You were right," she said quietly, as if resigning herself to the inevitable. "They didn't have what I was looking for. Everything I need is right here."

She was no longer talking about material goods, although Baylor was none the wiser. What she was searching for couldn't be purchased in shops – and it was all right here in the heavens. All she needed was time to find it.

Baylor grunted in response, but she could tell he was pleased with her pandering.

"Fine," he barked gruffly, scooping up another bite of sausage and bringing it to his mouth. "Take that Peace Officer with you. I don't trust those *freaks* to stay on their own levels. And if I hear one word about you going down there, you're getting that chip." With that, he thrust his fork into his mouth and tore apart the meat, staring at her as its juices ran down his chin.

Across the table, Una lowered her empty cup and rose, flicking her eyes between her husband and her daughter before stalking out of the room. Burn listened as the woman's shoes clicked on the cold floors, retreating down the hall before disappearing beyond a distant door.

"She seems busy," Burn ventured, curious. She wondered what Una did to fill her days. She hadn't seen a job in Ellis' mind, yet the woman seemed to have plenty of work.

Baylor didn't look up from his plate, which was nearly empty. With a spoonful of eggs in his mouth, he mumbled a reply. "You know your mother's social engagements keep her occupied. She should resurface in a day or two." Swallowing, he looked up at Burn, squinting in mild confusion. "What's wrong? You're usually so happy to see less of her."

His suspicious glare made Burn realize she'd slipped up, and she scanned her mind for a way to cover her faux pas.

"You know me so well," she tried, accompanied by a girlish laugh.

The statement seemed to pacify him, and he nodded, pushing his plate away. Swiping his beefy hand across the table, he revealed a hidden screen inlaid in the wood. He tapped a button with fervor and the table before them began to move, springing into action.

Like a sentient jigsaw, its pieces rearranged, some dropping from view and others taking their place. Within a minute, the surface was clean and shining. Not even a crumb was left on the gleaming wood, and Burn had to consciously control her features to hide her surprise.

"I'm heading to the factory," Baylor declared, more to himself than to Burn. Still, she turned her attention to him, eager for any morsel of information. "The workers have been acting up," he continued. "It's all that talk of the Lunaria. It's not good for them. Gives them ideas. But we have ways to make sure they stay in line."

Then, as if realizing who he was talking to, he frowned and turned to leave. Stopping in the doorway, he spun back, his eyes focused on his daughter.

"Remember what I said. You will not disobey me again." He turned once more and ambled away, leaving Burn to her thoughts.

Everything about this world was a shock to the system, and its residents dealt in opposites like currency. These people and their homes were beautiful to the extreme, yet they were filled with such ugliness that it hurt to behold. They were rich beyond measure but lacking any true worth. Their families were whole, yet they knew nothing of love. This wasn't a life. It was a game, and all that mattered was to win.

And that's exactly what Burn planned to do. She was going to beat them at their own game.

Rising from the table, she strolled back to her room, taking the time to mentally map the house and its halls. She tracked the servants as they moved, floating like ghosts through its dead rooms. She listened to the walls and the floors and the windows, searching for secrets. She heard Baylor leave and Una stay and felt her own relief at their absence.

Closing her bedroom door behind her, she took a second to bathe in the solitude. Then she got down to business. Within a few minutes, she'd armed herself with a small arsenal of gadgets, each hidden under the illusion of the ordinary. Necklace, earrings, bracelets, purse. She looked the part of the pampered princess, but underneath she was ready for action. All she needed now was her escort.

"Call Kaz," she commanded the mirror beside her door, watching as it transformed from a clear picture of Ellis' face to a foggy opalescence, searching the house for its target. Within a moment, it changed again, resolving into an image of Kaz.

The man was seated at a small table in a dim room, flanked by two more of the hired help. Burn hadn't seen these men before, but that didn't surprise her. The staff was trained to stick to the shadows, and unless they were wanted, they knew to keep their distance.

"Officer Petala," Burn said in her best commanding tone. Kaz started and looked up, confused by the voice. His head swung around to find the source, and his eyebrows shot up in comedic surprise.

"Miss Hyde," he nodded, quickly overcoming his fright. "What may I do for you?"

"We're going out. Please prepare yourself to accompany me to the shops. We'll likely be gone for several hours." She said this more for the benefit of the servants than for Kaz. He knew their real mission – and their true target. But servants tended to talk, and she knew that whatever they heard would make its way to Una and Baylor in the end.

"Very good, Miss Hyde," Kaz responded, playing the part with ease. "I'll meet you in the front hall promptly."

Burn disconnected the video with a tap of her finger, not bothering with the pleasantries of goodbyes. As she'd learned that morning, Ellis wasn't one to shower niceties on the help.

Grabbing a cloak from Ellis' ample closet, Burn

instinctively reached for her mask and goggles before pausing. Fingering the intricate designs on the girl's custom accessories, she realized that she didn't need them here. The air in the heavens was crisp and clean, and there was no reason to hide her face. Ellis was not a fugitive, and her identity didn't need concealing.

Leaving the objects where they lay, Burn exited the room, making her way to the front of the house. She wasn't surprised to find that Kaz was already there, sporting his all-black Peace Officer kit. Burn smiled at the sight, flashing back to the first time she'd seen him.

She had broken into his house, searching frantically for a place to hide, and he'd appeared. He'd melted out of nowhere, clad in pajamas and the remnants of sleep, clutching a pipe in warning. But instead of threatening to turn her in or calling his comrades on the force, he'd taken care of her – and he was taking care of her still.

He had changed in the intervening months, although not quite as much as she had. His dark brown hair still fell in waves over one eye, and his straight nose and strong jaw gave him the air of the perfect soldier. Yet the smirk had faded from the curves of his mouth, and the twinkle was less constant in the green of his eyes. He had lost the boyish charm, the innocence, the carefree swagger. He had found his purpose but lost his purity. It was a bittersweet trade, and Burn yearned for simpler times.

Still, innocence and purity wouldn't win them a war. For that, they needed cleverness – and a good deal of luck.

"You ready?" Burn asked, drawing her cloak closed along the soft skin of her neck.

Kaz smiled a devious smile and nodded, his excitement palpable. "Let's do this," he replied with a wink, throwing open the door and ushering Burn outside.

In the daylight, the tier had lost some of its magic. It was still remarkable, to be sure, but the scene was reduced to streets and buildings, with no glimpses of the lives inside. Without the thrill of watching and being watched, its glamor faded from magnificence to mere grandeur, from brilliance to petty radiance.

Burn took a moment to look up, away from the suns, staring at the ceiling of glass. After a life spent down below, where a glimpse of the dome was rare, it was strange to be so close. The sight must have comforted the people that called these tiers home. It was, after all, a constant. It protected them. It shielded them. It helped them maintain their power.

To Burn, it felt like a cage. Not so long ago, she'd been on the outside looking in. She'd craved the familiarity of Kasis, the presence of her family, and the solace of her mission. Yet she'd never missed the feeling of captivity that suffused its levels, working its way into every dark and dusty corner.

"What's on your mind?" Kaz asked, noticing her silence and following her gaze.

She'd been so wrapped up in her thoughts that she'd nearly forgotten his presence, and she jumped at the sound of his voice, ripping her eyes from the dome and casting them back on him.

"I was thinking of the wildlands," she said truthfully, speaking just above a whisper. A steady stream of people passed by, strolling lazily as they went about their carefree lives, and Burn didn't want to be overhead.

"Was it terrible out there?" Kaz asked, concerned. "I can't imagine what you've been through."

Burn had been quiet about her time in the desert. She'd told the Lunaria what they needed to know: that survival was possible and good people existed beyond their walls. But she'd saved some parts for herself, holding on to the beauty and horrors like her own secret story.

"It wasn't all bad," she said, beginning to walk down the wide lane. "Sure, you can't go out after dark and an egotistical maniac may decide to kill you on a whim, but how is that any different than here?" she asked acerbically. Kaz rolled his eyes at her sarcasm, waiting for her to continue.

"The truth is, I liked it out there. I felt free in a way I've never experienced here. Still, I knew I had to come back."

"So when this is all over," he said, motioning to the world around them as if it were coming to an end, "will you go back – if that's a possibility, I mean? When your work here is done, would you rather live out there than in here?"

Burn stopped walking, taking a minute to consider Kaz and his question. She had a feeling he was asking more than he was saying, and his inquiry was a difficult one to answer. It wasn't that she didn't know her own heart, know its longings and desires; it was more that she hadn't allowed herself to dream, to conceive of a day when their war would be over. She'd spent so long fighting that she couldn't readily envision any other life.

"You talk like it's inevitable, us winning. It's not," she finally said, beginning to walk once more. "If we make it out of this alive, then I'll worry about living. Right now, all I can think about is surviving. Which reminds me: Don't we have a job to do?" The playfulness returned to her voice as she finished, routing the conversation back to the present.

She could tell Kaz still had questions, but they would have to wait. Because they'd been placed in the heavens for a reason, and it wasn't to chat or eat or lounge around in a fancy house. They were there to work, and the job came before all else.

"Where do you want to start?" Kaz asked, resigning himself to the business at hand.

"How about here?" Burn suggested with a sly smile, motioning to the majestic house directly in front of them. "It looks like the perfect place for a break-in."

Chapter 7

The house belonged to Colonel Lanson Creer and his extensive family, composed of a wife, five children of varying ages, a mother-in-law, and a cat named Niff. It wasn't a random target. It had been chosen with care, placed on a list of over 15 houses for Burn and Kaz to tackle during their time in the heavens.

As a high-ranking Peace Officer, Creer was the perfect focus for their first foray into breaking and entering. What was known about the Shadow Assembly pointed to an overlap between the governing body and the Peace Force, with an undetermined number of officers making up the assembly's ranks.

The conversation Burn had overheard during the Peace Force Ball confirmed that fact. On that fateful night, she'd listened as Illex Cross revealed his plans to massacre the city's lowest tiers – and the assembly had applauded, promising him a place amongst their ranks if he succeeded. Burn shuddered even thinking about it. She doubted that the entire assembly had been present at the gathering, but those that were had been invited because they were connected to the force in some way.

That meant that the Lunaria's best bet was to direct their attention at the force's top players, in addition to select barons of industry, the owners of the city and controllers of its resources. The Lunaria needed a glimpse inside their lives – and their homes – to determine whether they were at the helm of the city's corruption or merely riding in its wake.

This wasn't Burn's first time as a trespasser. When you're in the world of blackmail – or on the run from the force – you do what needs to be done. As proven by her first run-in with Kaz, however, her attempts had not all gone according to plan. She was hoping this time would be different.

Kaz, on the other hand, was new to the criminal life, and despite his gift – and his earlier excitement – he now seemed nervous at the prospect.

"It's going to be fine," Burn told him as they idled casually outside the house, feigning indifference as a gaggle of carefree pedestrians ambled past. "I can hear everything inside, and you can move through the house like a ghost. Together, we make the perfect burglars." She smiled at him reassuringly, but he didn't look convinced.

"And don't forget Scar," Burn added as an afterthought – one she had nearly forgotten about herself. "Trust me, her gadgets make breaking and entering a breeze, and she can hack anything she puts her mind to. She's just a bracelet call away," she said, shaking her comms device in his direction.

Kaz let out a deep, drawn-out sigh, as if exhaling his

misgivings. "Fine," he said grudgingly, shaking his head. "Let's get this over with."

"That's the spirit," Burn replied, punching him playfully on the arm. "I'll just have a little look inside and we'll see who's home."

Taking a deep breath, she closed her eyes and opened herself up to the house. She directed her mind across its rooms, traveling through walls and up staircases in search of its occupants. Burn was thorough, meticulously combing for any signs of life. After a minute, she opened her eyes, letting them readjust to the light before turning to Kaz.

"The coast it clear," she reported almost giddily, with relief and nervous energy mingling in her chest. "Everyone seems to be out."

"Everyone?" Kaz asked doubtfully, scanning the house as if he could detect something that she hadn't.

"Yes, everyone. Well, except the cat – although I highly doubt that Niff will give us away."

Kaz awarded her efforts at humor with a wry smile. The look lasted only a second before it was replaced with firm determination.

"That's better," Burn remarked, turning her attention to her comms and pressing the button along its side. "Scar, are you there?"

A few tense seconds passed as they waited for a reply. Then Scar's voice appeared from the bracelet, scarcely loud enough for Burn to hear.

"It's about time," she said briskly. "I was wondering when you two would finally get around to doing your job."

Burn smiled. "It's good to hear from you, too, sis. Stand

by for updates. We may need your help once we're inside."

With Scar on standby, Burn motioned for Kaz to follow as she crossed the street and drew up to the Creers' front door. Rifling in her bag, she pulled out the familiar blue tube and slipped it over her index finger before pressing it to the lock. The system thought for a moment, considering the faux fingerprint, before unlatching the door with a click.

Burn crept into the house, and Kaz followed, his movements nimble and silent. Burn felt a pang of jealously for his gift and for the easy stealth it conveyed. Beside him, she felt too loud, too conspicuous, too visible.

"We should split up," she whispered, conscious of how shrill her voice sounded in the silence. "We can cover more ground if we divide up the rooms."

Kaz nodded in agreement. "I'll take this side," he said, motioning to the left half of the house, which was considerably larger. Burn raised her eyebrow at his quiet chivalry, but wisely decided not to comment.

"Signal me if you run into trouble, and I'll do the same," she told him. "If anything happens, get yourself out. Don't worry about me."

Kaz nodded again. He already knew the plan – although whether he'd stick to it was a different matter entirely.

"Scar," she said, turning her attention back to her comms, "we're inside. I'll let you know when you're needed."

Burn and Kaz departed in their respective directions, each peeling off the main hallway to explore the rooms beyond. Neither was entirely certain what they were searching for. It wasn't clear where the secrets would be held or where the skeletons had been hidden. Maybe on a tab, maybe an encoded list, maybe a name scribbled hastily in a margin. In these houses, clues could be anywhere – or anything.

Burn took her time with the living and dining rooms but found nothing of interest. Sighing, she pushed her way gently through another door, finding herself in the home's expansive kitchen – and also finding herself with company.

"Intruder!" a tinny voice shouted from along the back wall, sending a cold wave of shock through Burn's core. If there was someone inside, Burn should have heard them – so why hadn't she?

She instinctively jumped aside, ducking behind a long metal countertop. As she did so, she caught sight of her foe, and her confusion sharpened into pristine clarity.

"Scar, I think I'm going to need your help," she said, adrenaline pumping through her veins. A whirring noise had sprung to life across the kitchen, and with every second it drew nearer. "Any chance you know how to deactivate a HouseBot droid?"

"Of course," Scar shot back, annoyed that Burn even had to ask. A second of silence followed as Burn's tension mounted, but Scar didn't seem to understand the urgency.

"And??" Burn asked in exasperation, urging her on. "How do I do it?"

Scar sighed. "There's a small magnet in your bag," she explained slowly, as if speaking to an infant. "All you have to do is attach it to the bot's head. I can take it from there."

As Burn dug through her bag in search of the magnet, the bot rounded the corner, making a beeline for her position. Her hand closed around the magnet, yanking it from the bag, but it was already too late.

HouseBots weren't allowed weapons systems, but that didn't mean they posed no threat. As property of the rich and powerful, they were equipped with the latest in lethal programming, enough to deter any unwelcome guest. And this bot was enacting its role with alacrity.

Picking up speed, it whizzed toward Burn, intent on collision. Burn could envision it in her mind's eye: metal hitting flesh, bones breaking, her blood spilling out onto the kitchen floor. Yet her reflexes were sharp, honed by weeks in the desert training with Nara, and at the last moment she dove to the floor, rolling out of its path.

Burn had hoped that the bot's momentum would keep it moving, driving it into the wall in a ferocious crash, but she'd sorely underestimated its skills. Instead, it stopped on a dime, its state-of-the-art systems all too prepared for such a pursuit.

Burn's mind was awash with blows and parries, with a complicated dance of attacks and evasion. Yet she'd been taught to fight creatures of flesh and bone, not steel and circuitry. Dueling with a bot was a different game altogether.

She wanted to sever its mechanical arms, to rip the cords from its neck, to leave it silent in a heap of parts, but she knew she couldn't. No matter how much she craved its demise, that would only alert its owners to her presence. They would know someone had been there, and they wouldn't rest until they found her.

She had to do this without damaging her foe. The bot, on the other hand, didn't have the same constraints. Reaching out with its metal claws, it snatched a gleaming knife from a wooden block and turned it on Burn.

Then it was off, gathering speed as it barreled closer, hell-bent on skewering her. Burn's body took over, and she ducked out of its path, evading the knife by mere inches.

The bot ground to a halt, recalibrating. Burn seized the opportunity and dealt a well-placed kick to its top half, intending to send it crashing to the floor, where she could disarm it and wrestle it into submission. Except the bot didn't fall. It only wobbled slightly, its sturdy frame absorbing the blow. Burn's foot, on the other hand, throbbed uncomfortably from the impact.

The HouseBot spun to face her, and before her mind could catch up, she was already sprinting from the room, her legs a blur as she crashed through the door and into the hall beyond. She dashed into the living room, scouring her mind for another plan. Scar was shouting at her by then, demanding an update, but Burn tuned her out, focusing on the problem at hand. The bot was gaining on her, and she knew it was only a matter of time before it caught her.

As it turned out, though, catching her wasn't its main priority. With a soft whoosh, it released the knife, its mechanical arm aimed straight at Burn.

The sound of the weapon slicing through the air was her only warning. Dropping to her stomach, she shielded her head with her arms and waited for impact, but it never came. Instead, the knife embedded itself in the couch beside her, ripping into its overstuffed cushion rather than her own tender flesh.

Breathing a grateful sigh of relief, Burn pulled herself up and looked down at her hand. She'd been gripping Scar's magnet so tightly that its imprint was etched on her palm in angry red lines. She knew what she needed to do.

The machine sped toward her once more, and there was no time to run – so she climbed. Using the couch as her stepping stone, she jumped onto its cushions, scaling its back and hurdling onto the tall table behind it. Moments later, the bot reached the place where she'd been and extended its silver claws to grab her, but she was faster.

A war cry exploded from her lungs as she leapt into the air, slamming the magnet against its head before dropping to the ground with a thud. In one fluid movement, she rolled to her feet and took off the way they had come.

"The magnet's in place. Now shut this thing down!" she shouted to Scar, praying that her plan would work.

Behind her, Burn could hear the bot pivot in place, taking off in pursuit. She lunged back into the kitchen, slamming the door shut and throwing her weight against it. Yet as she listened, the bot's mechanical whirr slowed then stopped, its systems steadily succumbing to Scar's commands.

"One HouseBot deactivated, as requested," came Scar's smug voice.

"Are you sure?" Burn asked, more out of habit than anything else. She took a deep breath, then another, attempting to slow her racing heart.

"Absolutely positive," Scar replied with surety. "I'm wiping its memory circuits now. In a minute, it will have no recollection that you were ever there."

Burn closed her eyes in relief. After a few seconds, she opened the door and considered the inanimate object, its eyes dead and its body silent. With purposeful steps, she pushed it back into the kitchen, stationing it in the corner where it belonged. Once Scar had finished her work, Burn removed the magnet before trekking back into the hall.

She retrieved the knife from where it was lodged inside the sofa, considering the hole it had left. After a beat, she placed one of the room's many pillows in front, hiding the damage. Burn was just returning the knife to its place in the kitchen when Kaz burst through the door, his eyes wild.

"I was on the other side of the house," he panted, his breathing shallow. "I came as quickly as I could."

"Thanks, Officer Petala," Burn said, "but your assistance is no longer needed. As you can see, I've managed to neutralize the threat all on my own."

Scar cleared her throat loudly on the other side of the comms. "Sorry, *we've* managed to neutralize it," Burn corrected.

Kaz looked at her dubiously, taking in her rumpled state and the knife still clutched in her hand. "Right…" he said slowly, shaking his head. "Well, maybe it's best if we stick together from now on."

"What, you don't think I can protect myself?" Burn asked, her adrenaline still high from the fight.

"It's not that," Kaz said, choosing his words carefully. "But with me by your side, you might not have to. Wouldn't that be better?"

Burn wanted to protest, to decline his magnanimous offer and continue on her own, but she knew he was right. The Creers' droids would continue to awaken at her presence, but Kaz could move without their notice, gliding through the house unseen and unheard. With his gift, he could dispatch them, switching them off and clearing the way.

"Fine," Burn said, echoing his earlier response. "Let's get this over with."

Kaz smirked, the twinkle in his eyes back in full force. He was clearly glad to be of assistance, and he took up the mantle with delight, combing each room for mechanical observers before allowing Burn to enter.

Together, they swept the house, searching for a fragment, a clue. Burn would have settled for anything – any scrap that shed light on the shadows – but nothing appeared, and the more they searched, the more desperate Burn became.

Her hope flared to life when they reached the office, the promise of proof prickling at her skin. After Kaz's inspection, she leapt inside, crossing the threshold in one long stride.

The room that met her was static and cold, a place of silence, solitude, and study. Everything was still, save for a single revolving hologram tucked neatly in the corner. As the sole source of motion in the frozen space, it drew Burn's attention, pulling her toward it.

It was Kasis. The domed city moved in one fluid sweep, around and around like a dancer on a stage. Its tiers and levels were crisp and clear, and the streets were a picture of calm perfection. Yet there were no citizens, no Peace Officers, no lives trapped inside. Just like the room, it was silent, dead.

Without thinking, she reached out to touch the sloping curve of glass, expecting to feel the cool surface of the dome. Instead, her hand swept through empty air, dissecting the city. For a moment, she too felt hollow – merely a shell of herself suspended in midair. In an instant the feeling passed, and she pulled her attention back to the present.

Turning, she found Kaz examining the series of flat

electronic screens that covered the walls. They were placed in frames like paintings and showed inert images of artwork, yet this mask of beauty couldn't obscure their harsh nature.

Burn knew their real purpose. Underneath the façade of lush alien landscapes, they were a tool of the regime, a method for facilitating the Peace Force's plans. She could see them now, each painting replaced by a face, each frame home to a sergeant, a colonel, a captain. Without even leaving home, their leaders could conspire against them, issuing warrants and mandates from the safety of their tier. They could meet and plot and plan without anyone being the wiser.

"Do you think the Shadow Assembly could be using these to communicate?" Kaz asked, searching the room for a centralized hub.

"It's possible," Burn said, joining the hunt. "Although it's just as likely that they're Peace Force-issued. It's difficult to say for sure."

"Scar," Kaz said, turning to the expert, "where would you put a comm screen control panel if you had one?"

"Underneath the floor in the center of the room," she said with absolute certainty.

Burn was the first to reach the area in question, and she knelt on the cool wood, rapping her knuckles against its knotted surface. She listened as she worked, opening her mind to any anomalies.

It wasn't difficult to find. One tap and she could hear it: the soft, muted thud of something hidden beneath. Reaching into her bag, she pulled out a knife and wedged it under the board, prying it up with ease. Below, a small silver box no bigger than a book lay waiting, its computerized innards softly spinning.

"Found it," she reported with satisfaction.

"Attach the magnet," Scar instructed, seizing the situation. Burn did as she was instructed, and Scar took control, typing away on the other side of the comms.

As Burn waited for further direction, she straightened and rose, surveying the rest of the room. A few side tables, chairs, and a wide bookcase were all that was left, and she moved to investigate each, carefully scouring their surfaces for secrets.

Delicately pulling books from their shelves, she flipped through them, half hoping to find codes or names hidden amongst their pages. But nothing fell from their bindings and nothing lurked between their covers. Only words and sentences hid inside their folds, concealing nothing more than stories.

A few meager minutes passed before Scar's voice chirped through the comms once again.

"Done," she stated briskly, snapping Burn's mind away from the books. "There's nothing here that points to the assembly, but I've downloaded the data just in case. I'll sort through it tonight and see what I can find. In the meantime, you two should get going."

Burn closed her eyes, fighting back her frustration. A part of her, nestled deep in the pit of her stomach, had hoped that their first search would be their last, that they'd somehow find what they needed in a day and be out of the heavens the next. The logical part of her knew that their mission would never be that simple, but that didn't stop her from longing for an easy escape, for a clear path unmuddied by danger.

Still, she took her sister's advice, leaving the house and its cloying confines. Outside, she breathed in the fresh air, clearing her mind and freeing her chest from the weight of disappointment. Beside her, Kaz looked on, watching her expression transform from defeat to acceptance to resolution.

"What now, captain?" he asked, leading them away from the house. "Are you ready for round two?"

Burn chuckled, cheered by his eagerness. "My god, I've created a monster," she said, shaking her head in mock disdain. "One taste of a life of crime and you're hooked. Whatever am I going to do with you?"

"I think there's only one thing you can do," he said, waggling his brows. "Show me our next target."

Chapter 8

Burn had never thought much about marriage. Her own faux union with Hale out in the wildlands had been convenient – and even pleasant at times – but she'd never had the desire to make it real. Simply put, marriage wasn't a priority, not when the world was falling down around her.

Ellis' parents, on the other hand, thought about marriage a great deal. Not for themselves, of course, as their union was perfectly suitable, albeit devoid of any real connection. But their daughter, it seemed, was in need of a spouse, along with everything that entailed – status, power, security. Plus, it had the added benefit of getting her out from under their roof.

Naturally, Burn knew none of this. The idea of scouring Ellis' thoughts for ideas of matrimony hadn't occurred to her. It hadn't seemed relevant to the Lunaria's mission, and in all Burn's visions of the future, her worries and fears, marriage had never made an appearance.

It was a surprise, then, when Ellis' mother broached

the subject during breakfast one morning, several days into Burn's new life in the heavens.

"Remember, we have dinner with Ignis and Iris tonight," Una purred, looking up from her tab for the first time that morning.

Burn paid her no mind. Thus far, her parents' dinner parties had never included her, and she couldn't see why that would change now. She had no urge to go with them, and they knew she contributed nothing to their dialogues. Yet on this particular morning, Una zeroed in on her daughter, considering her with undue force.

"Ellis, honey, I've bought you a new dress for the occasion. We'll obviously have to clean you up – and do something with that hair. I want you to look presentable."

"I'll be joining you?" Burn asked, her hackles raised. Una hadn't spoken more than a handful of words to her since she'd arrived, and the attention felt unnerving.

"Of course, darling," she said, her voice cold and forceful beneath the sweetness of the words. "Don't you remember? Tonight's the night Ignis is going to propose."

Burn choked on a bite of eggs, the salty fare turning to sand in her mouth.

"I know, I know. It's all so exciting," Una continued, waving a hand to excuse Burn's improper outburst, as if she had chosen to start choking.

"Ignis is set for a promotion on the force," she said, speaking louder to cover Burn's coughs. "That boy is going to do great things, just like his father. You two will make the perfect couple."

Burn swallowed a large sip of water, trying to clear her

throat – and her mind – and buy herself a chance to breathe. This was not her life, she reminded herself. These were not her parents. And this would not be her marriage.

Yet the prospect still frightened her. Pretending to be Ellis amongst her parents was one thing. They didn't see her, nor did they notice when she slipped, when she fell back into the comfort of being Burn instead of the ruse of their daughter. But a lover would notice. A fiancé would spot a fake.

That thought ate at her throughout breakfast, plaguing her as she finished her meal and excused herself. It stayed with her even as she prepared for another day of espionage, the worry lingering in her mind as she dressed and donned her pack and departed with Kaz in tow.

"What's on your mind?" Kaz asked after some time, seizing on her silence.

Burn started, having long since forgotten that Kaz was there. His stealth made him easy to overlook, and she took a moment to focus on him before she spoke.

"Do you know an Ignis on the force?" she asked, trying to sound nonchalant as they strolled across a bridge toward the far side of the tier.

He thought for a minute, raising his face to the suns as he rolled the name over on his tongue.

"I can't say that I do," he finally replied, shaking his head. "Why? Is he another one of our targets?"

"Not quite," Burn started then stopped, not sure how to explain. Taking a deep breath, she decided to spit it out. "I think I'm supposed to marry him."

Kaz let out a loud guffaw at her pronouncement, clearly amused. Then, glancing at her face, he swiftly sobered.

"Oh, shit. You're serious."

"Of course I'm serious," Burn replied, crossing her arms over her chest. "My parents are taking me to his house tonight so he can propose. Unfortunately, I know nothing about him. I was hoping you had something – anything – so I wouldn't be going in blind."

"Sorry," Kaz said, adopting a look of pure pity. "I wish I could help."

"Are you at least coming with us? I could use some backup, especially if things don't go as planned."

Kaz shook his head, his expression deepening. "The Hydes gave me the night off. They said I wouldn't be needed. They probably think your *boyfriend* can protect you, what with his position on the force."

Burn groaned, her apprehension strengthening until it lay thick and viscous at the bottom of her stomach, coating it with unease.

"I'm sure it'll be fine," Kaz said, draping his arm around her in a reassuring gesture. "You won't be here forever. It's not like you'll actually have to marry the guy. All you have to do is get through tonight. If worst comes to worst, break it off. Una and Baylor can't force you to keep seeing him."

"They can do whatever they want. Who's going to stop them?" Burn queried, but his words soothed something in her, and some of the stiffness faded.

"Just stay calm. Listen. And think before you speak," he said, giving her a meaningful look. They both knew that patience and contemplation weren't her strongest assets.

"Alright, alright," she sighed, shrugging out of his grasp. "I'll play the good little daughter."

"Good," Kaz said with a smile. "Now that we have that settled, whose house are we hitting today?"

Their last few days had been a bust, and they'd turned up nothing new on the assembly or its members. Kaz, always a beacon of optimism, was sure that it was only a matter of time before they stumbled upon something of value. Burn was less certain. It felt like they were on the wrong path, going deeper and deeper down a dead-end lane, but she had no more ideas to save them. Their only hope was to keep going, keep working, and pray that fate would find a way to reward them.

The house they were scouting that day lay at the edge of the city, one tier down and a sector out from the Hydes' grand home. It belonged to a factory owner, whose livelihood rested on sourcing food for the rich and keeping it from the poor. Along with help from his friends on the force, he'd been known to manufacture food shortages, propagating the idea of scarcity in order to starve out the weak.

It made Burn furious. She'd seen it firsthand on the bottom tiers – people shivering, starving, living on scraps while he bathed in the lap of luxury. She ached to make her fury felt, to steal his excess and divvy it up amongst the poor. She knew she couldn't, that it would only lead to suspicion and arrest, but the idea still sang to her with soothing melodies of retribution and reckoning.

When they reached the house, Burn did her thing, mapping its interior and searching for signs of life.

"There are four people inside," she relayed to Kaz, dismayed by their presence. "Two servants and two children by the sounds of it."

"Guess I'm going in alone, then," he surmised, and Burn nodded, resigning herself to her role.

It wasn't the first time they'd faced such a hurdle. With his gift, Kaz could still salvage their assignment, trekking through the halls with silent grace. Burn could not, so she was relegated to the role of bystander, forced to remain outside to watch and listen and wait. She didn't relish the post, but she accepted it, doing what she must to move their mission along.

Kaz slipped inside with ease, taking with him Burn's pack and Scar's gadgets. Burn tracked his progress as he worked, acting as a sentinel, a lookout, a guard. But the house remained quiet, its occupants – and its secrets – undisturbed. It was yet one more dead end in a maze of many.

Night was just starting to think of falling when the pair returned home, dejected and drained. All Burn wanted to do was turn out the lights and collapse into bed, dreaming of better days. Yet as soon as she crossed the threshold, she was swept up in a whirlwind of attention.

Servants and stylists flocked to her, tearing her clothes from her body like vultures. Before she knew it, she was naked and shivering, then plunging into a warm lavender bath, then clinging to sanity as her hair and nails and skin were rubbed and polished to a shiny clean.

By the time she was hoisted out of the tub, she felt raw and tender, her skin pink and her blond hair hanging in knots around her shaking shoulders. But the torment was far from over.

Pairs upon pairs of hands reached out to touch her until they consumed her vision. Some spread a sweet-smelling cream across her skin, while others brushed the tangles from her hair. Still more flung a satin robe across her form or painted lines onto her nails or applied streaks of red to her flowing yellow mane.

Their attentions were constant, and they bombarded her with a barrage of treatments and products and paints masquerading as beauty. They tugged at her torso, squeezing her into garments designed to mold her body into one more pleasing to the eye. Her stomach was crushed, her breasts elevated, her hair tugged and teased. Then a dress of sizzling red was lowered over her shoulders and fastened across her back.

The flurry stopped in an instant, grinding to a halt as the artists considered their masterpiece. Another hand reached out, but this time it merely moved her, turning her to face the mirrors standing against the wall.

Burn didn't recognize the person staring back. Well, she never truly recognized her, but she'd grown accustomed to the face and the form. Now even those were gone, replaced by an alien angel with fearsome beauty and otherworldly grace.

Ellis' hair was piled in delicate curls on top of her head, streaked with brilliant color and falling in soft tendrils around her face. Her eyes smoldered in sensual desire, while her lips shone with lacquer the color of blood. Her ears sparkled with gems and her throat was wrapped in a silver collar that elongated her neck and drew attention to her chest.

The dress she wore was low and suggestive, leaving her shoulders and arms bare, along with a good portion of her back. The red silk clung to her form as it traveled down, stopping in a hard line below her knees. It fanned out behind her, trailing in her wake like a train and kissing the ground in quiet whispers.

Burn had only a heartbeat to gape before Una swept in, intent on passing judgment. She circled Ellis in silent scrutiny, raking her eyes across the girl like a sculptor searching for flaws. After a minute, she stopped. Her lips remained tight and her eyes hard, but she released a single nod of approval.

"This will do," she said by way of praise. Switching course, she addressed Ellis. "Come now. We must be going. You shouldn't keep Ignis waiting." Turning on her heel, she strode out of the room, with Burn falling in line behind her.

Within minutes, the family was in motion, making their way out of the house and onto the street beyond. Once again, the lanes were ablaze with stories, each house's internal dramas brought to life through the darkness. The images called to Burn, tempting her to look, to wonder, yet her attention was consumed by her own nervous state.

Burn was a mess of unease and anxious energy. She struggled to keep hold of herself as she plunged deeper into Ellis' world. She knew if she wasn't careful that she would drown, losing herself in the tides of someone else's life.

The Hydes' journey was short and brisk, with few words exchanged between them. Burn was surprised when they traveled down a tier, then another. They were almost to the border of the upper levels when they stopped their descent, with Una making a sharp turn onto a narrow lane. Then all at once they were there.

The home was a modest two stories, with nearly identical dwellings placed on either side. Compared to the Hydes' spacious tier, with its sparkling glass and radiant affluence, this one felt dim and cramped, a canvas of shadows and steel. It was still grand, to be sure, but it seemed slightly less in every way – less opulent, less brilliant, less alive.

Raising her hand, Una knocked, giving three assertive taps before stepping back. Burn waited, holding her breath, itching to see who answered. It felt like an eternity, but the door finally moved, swinging open in slow motion to reveal their host.

Burn's skin turned to ice at the sight and breathing became impossible. Her mind began to fill with fog, and wisps of panic clawed at her chest. It took all her strength to stand, to hold her ground, to resist the urge to flee.

She knew that face. On him, it was softer, younger, more muted, but the resemblance was undeniable. He had the same slick black hair, the same sharp face, the same dark eyes that seemed to stare straight into Burn's soul. And the same smooth voice.

"Welcome," said Ignis Cross, his eyes meeting hers as he spoke. "I'm so glad you could make it."

Burn wanted to scream, to curse the gods for their cruel joke at her expense. As if joining in the jest, her mind conjured the image she'd tried so hard to hide, placing the man next to his son in the doorway. Illex Cross, covered in blood, stared at her in utter hatred, the hole in his head still dripping from her fatal shot. Her stomach clenched in horror, and it took everything she had not to scream.

Illex Cross had been her own personal demon, and her father's before that. He'd thrown Arvense down the Pit. He'd plotted against Burn's kind. He'd attacked her and captured her and tried to kill her. But she had won. She had killed him. She had come out victorious.

Yet for some reason, fate would not leave her be. It laughed at her, bucking the naïve notion that she could ever truly win, that she could ever be free of the man – and of what she'd done.

As if he could tell what she was thinking, Ignis began to laugh. Beside him, the ghost of his father joined in, enjoying her pain. Then Una and Baylor followed until the street sang with mirth. In the back of her mind, Burn knew they weren't laughing at her. Someone must have told a joke, but she hadn't caught it. All she could hear was the blood rushing through her veins, beating out the seconds of her agony.

Una had to say Ellis' name three times before Burn rallied, snapped to attention by the glares.

"Honey, are you alright?" she asked, feigning concern.

Burn knew Una's tenderness was an act. She didn't know if she could hear it in her mother's mind or merely see it in her eyes, but Una's real message was a command: "Get yourself together. Now. Or else."

"I'm sorry," Burn said mechanically, scanning her mind for a lie. "I'm…just so excited about tonight. About being here. It's all so…surreal." At least that part was true.

Ignis laughed again. "I completely understand," he said, playing the gallant host. "It's exciting to have you here. But where are my manners? Please, come in." He stood aside, beckoning them into his home.

Burn didn't move. Her feet wouldn't obey her commands. She was sure that if she looked down, she would find them glued to the pavement, her painful red shoes sinking into the ground like it was quicksand. Yet Una would never allow such a thing.

Grasping her daughter's arm with considerable force, she propelled Burn forward, her eyes burning with the heat of things left unsaid. Burn could hear it clearly now, hear the words on the tip of her mother's tongue, her enhanced gift coming to life under the force of such feeling.

"You dare embarrass me? I will not have my family look weak because of you. You *will* behave."

A chill went down Burn's spine at the words. This was a dangerous game, yet it was one she had to play. There would be no running, no forfeit, no graceful retreat. She had to play, and she had to win.

Drawing herself up to her full height, she wrenched her arm from her mother's grasp and strode into the hall, taking in her surroundings. The home was small by the Hydes' standards. It contained no trophies of grandeur, none of the excessiveness of wealth. To Burn, it looked stark, clean, and glaring, with sharp lines and hard surfaces and bright white light.

It actually felt like Cross – too smooth, too polished. It even smelled like him, a piercing scent of pepper and oil and mint. It drove Burn's mind to places it didn't want to return, to images filled with blood and smoke and hatred.

Cross wasn't there, she reminded herself, repeating the words like a mantra. Cross was dead. Cross was dead. Cross was dead.

Her feet carried her down the long hallway and into a large open space, with a kitchen to the left, a dining room in front, and a living space beyond. Everything was white and black and shades of gray, with glass and steel and stone catching the light and casting it back.

Ignis led them to the table, holding out a chair for Burn before taking a seat beside her. Her heart was a mess of stutters and silence, so she merely smiled, forcing her face into a mask of thanks. He didn't notice the lie. He was too occupied staring at her lips. And her dress. And her chest.

He liked Ellis, that much was clear. Although the line between liking and lusting was blurred to nonexistence. Yet he smiled at her tenderly, the expression softening the sharp lines of his face until he almost appeared kind.

I killed your father, she thought, staring into his eyes. She wondered if he could see it there – the guilt, the anger, the pain. If he did, though, he didn't show it.

A sudden presence broke their silent study of one another and drew Burn's attention upward.

"Una! Baylor! It's such a pleasure to have you here," the woman crooned, traveling to each to bestow a peck on their cheek. "And Ellis, darling! Don't you look lovely."

Iris flitted to Burn's side and she rose, stooping as the woman planted a chaste kiss on her right cheek.

Burn was surprised by Iris. She wasn't beautiful in the traditional sense. Her skin didn't glow, nor did her mousy hair shine. She wasn't dressed in the latest fashion, but rather in a smart gray suit that accentuated her shrewd eyes, giving her an aura of quiet intelligence.

Burn could easily see her standing beside Illex, whispering into his ear. There was something about her that spoke of calculating control, of the ability to sway armies with a mere suggestion.

Had she planted her husband's ideas, fanned them, watched them spark and grow? And was she now doing the same with Ignis, swapping one man for another as her puppet, her pawn? Burn considered her with fresh eyes, curiosity taking root and overshadowing her alarm.

Done with her pleasantries, Iris sat, calling for a servant to pour drinks. Burn watched as a dapper man dressed all in black sailed forth from the kitchen, carafe in hand. Without a word, he began to round the table, filling each glass with a thick red liquid. Grasping hers, Burn sipped deeply, enjoying the feel of the alcohol as it set her throat on fire and cauterized her nerves.

"Feeling better?" Ignis asked in a low voice, a smile playing on his lips.

"Much. Thank you," Burn replied, emboldened by the spirit.

In the background, their parents talked, discussing mutual friends, the state of the heavens, the stories they'd heard of each other. It was clear that they were old friends, comfortable in each other's presence, and they talked amongst themselves with such gaiety that it lightened the room, bringing laughter to its halls.

Burn could see them in her mind's eye – the Crosses and the Hydes – planning their children's union, plotting out their lives. Ignis and Ellis' marriage had the distinct air of something arranged, a deal struck between parents, a tidy pact for a perfect little life. This was not Ellis' dream, Burn realized, but theirs. She was merely their plaything, their puppet, their doll.

Suddenly, Burn became acutely aware of Ignis. While

their parents had been talking, his eyes had never left her, and they positively smoldered as he regarded her.

Burn dipped into Ellis' memories, searching for this boy, but she came up blank, with nothing more than whispers of thought to cling to. So Burn took a deep breath and leapt.

"How is it on the force these days?" she asked, leaning toward him. "It must be difficult, what with all the unrest. I'm sure that can't be easy."

Ignis raised a dark eyebrow at her in surprise, yet the smile didn't leave his lips.

"You've never asked about my work before," he said playfully. "I was beginning to think you didn't care."

"I thought it was only right that I should take an interest. After all, isn't it about time we get to know each other more...intimately?" Burn was playing with fire. She knew it was risky, but the wine and the danger swam within her, making her bold. Or stupid.

Ignis chuckled, amused by her newfound bravado. "The force has everything under control. Those rebels pose no threat. We could wipe them out in an instant if they ever drummed up the courage to show their faces."

"You're awfully sure of yourself," she said, shaking her head – and fishing for more. "But aren't those rebels *freaks*? Aren't you afraid of what they'd do to you?"

"No," he said simply, shrugging in self-assurance. "We have enough weapons to deal with them. They're not immune to bullets, you know. Well, most of them aren't." He laughed lightly. "But we have other tricks to deal with the rest."

"What kind of tricks?" Burn's intrigue was on full display,

and Ignis noticed.

"Why are you suddenly so interested in the Peace Force?" he asked, bringing her up short. She realized she'd gone too far, stretched herself too much outside the boundaries of her role, but she couldn't take it back.

"I'm interested in you," she said plainly, attempting to redirect his attention. "I want to know what you do. I want to know that you're safe." Furthering the lie, she reached under the table, putting her hand on his knee.

"I like this new Ellis," he said after a moment, covering her hand with his. Then he began to squeeze, tightening his grip until her hand was trapped. "But your concern is misplaced. Fear for them. Fear for their safety, not mine."

He leaned in, drawing his mouth to her ear in a gesture she knew all too well. It was a mirror of his father, with his warm breath tickling her face.

"And if you ever lie to me again, you will come to regret it. I'm not so easy to fool as you seem to think." He took the time to nuzzle her ear in a gesture of faux affection before dropping her hand and pulling away.

Beside her, Ellis' mother crooned. "Young love. How sweet. Oh, to be a child again."

In her lap, Burn's hands shook, and she kept her gaze focused on her plate, unwilling to look up. Ignis could see through her. He could *read* her. Maybe it was a family trait, or something his father had taught him. Either way, it put her at risk, doubling the odds that she'd be discovered.

At some point, a bowl of soup had appeared before her, although she couldn't recall it being served. The others sipped at the aromatic broth and Burn did the same, forcing her hand to remain steady. It went down easily, but she didn't taste a bite, too distracted by her own thoughts to process the flavors.

"I remember when Illex and I were first married," Iris said between bites. "Such a lovely time. I wish he could be here to see this."

Burn choked on her soup, coughing into her cloth napkin to free the liquid from where it had congealed in her throat. Ignis leaned over to pat her gently on the back while the others politely ignored her, continuing their conversation.

"He would have been so happy to see Ignis settled, both on the force and in life," Iris remarked sadly, shaking her head. "It's all he ever wanted."

Well, that and the complete destruction of the *freaks* on the lower tiers, Burn thought tersely. She swallowed her words – along with another spoonful of soup – hoping that no one noticed the flash of hatred that briefly clouded her eyes.

Their meal continued like that for two more courses, the conversation light and fleeting as they demolished their engineered steaks and delicate chocolate tarts. Burn remained quiet throughout the whole affair, lending her voice only when it was needed. She made no more attempts to press Ignis for information, certain that he would rebuff them if she tried.

After dinner, the crowd filed into the living room for drinks, but Ignis stopped her, pressing his hand to her lower back. The move felt intimate, wrong, and Burn shuddered. Either he didn't notice or he didn't care because he leaned in closer, enveloping her in his grasp.

"You'll join me for a drink in the office, won't you?" he murmured, more a command than a question. "We have so much to discuss."

Una watched with satisfaction as her daughter disappeared down the hall, presumably to secure her fate. Soon, Ellis and Ignis would be yet one more generation of the powerful elite, effectively keeping control in the hands of the few.

Ignis paused outside a large wooden door. He released her for an instant to scan his finger on the lock, then just as swiftly grabbed hold of her again, guiding her into the darkness. At their presence, the lights snapped on, dousing the room in shards of blinding light.

Burn blinked at the sudden illumination, trying to get her bearings, but Ignis was faster. Without warning, his mouth was on hers, crushing it with the taste of wine and greedy longing. Surprise coursed through her at his touch, but she knew that she couldn't pull away, couldn't give him another reason to doubt her. So she leaned in, molding her body to his and hating herself for every second.

After an agonizing minute, he pulled away, chuckling. Looking up, Burn saw Illex in his eyes and heard him in the laughter. Her stomach lurched in disgust, threatening to send her dinner back up, but she clamped it down, focusing on her breathing.

"I knew you missed me," he drawled, trailing his hand down her side. "I don't know what game you're playing – lying to me so brazenly – but I assure you I will win. I always do."

"I..." Burn started before stopping abruptly. Except it

wasn't self-control that curbed her. It was the low vibration of her wrist cuff, signaling a message.

She was grateful for the interruption. She didn't know what she'd been about to say, but she had a feeling he wouldn't have liked it. And it wasn't her place to split up this union, no matter how much she might wish to.

Her curiosity clawed at her as she considered the message. Scar knew she was at a function, and she'd never risk Burn's cover unless she had to. If she was interrupting, it had to be for a reason. Burn's momentary relief soured into dread.

"I…need to freshen up," Burn continued, as if that was what she'd intended to say all along.

Without waiting for a reply, she leapt toward the door, yanking it open and spilling into the hall. She located the bathroom and dashed inside, locking the door with such force she was afraid it would break. She could hear Ignis follow, tracking her through the house, but she didn't care.

Huddling in a corner, she sank to the floor, the cool tile a soothing balm against her burning skin. Taking a deep breath, she tapped the side of her bracelet, playing the message that hid inside its depths.

"Burn," Scar's voice began, "something's happened. Hale…" Her sister trailed off, unsure of how to continue. Yet that one word turned Burn's heart to ice.

Hale. Something had happened to Hale.

"Hale hasn't checked in. We haven't heard from him for days, and we can't reach him on his comms. Burn," she paused, the weight of the message clear in her voice, "Hale's missing."

Scar said more, but Burn didn't hear it. She couldn't hear

anything. Suddenly, her world collapsed, squeezing in on her until it hurt.

Hale, her Hale, was gone. Her head fell into her hands as she dissolved, feeling every bone in her body melt until she was nothing more than skin and tears.

If the world was a kind one, Hale was already dead. If not, he was in *their* grasp, subject to their whims and their hatred. They would hurt him, torture him, bleed him for answers.

Hale would never betray the Lunaria, but he was strong. He could withstand a world of pain. And they would make sure he felt every bit of it – every slice of the blade or fall of the hammer, every broken bone and bit of singed flesh.

Burn could no longer breathe. The air had escaped from the room, filling her head with screams and fog. All she knew was that she had to get out.

Pushing herself up, she grabbed for the door, heaving it open. Ignis stood in the light, and he reached for her, but she slipped out of his grasp, following her broken heart to the front of the house and into the night. Voices rose behind her calling for her return, but she ignored them, stumbling away from the sounds.

When she finally lost sight of the house, she stopped, leaning against a wall to empty the contents of her stomach onto the road. Her body itched with the feel of Ignis' touch, with the taste of him on her lips, and she heaved again, spewing the memories onto the pavement at her feet.

It felt like her fault. She knew it wasn't – that the blame belonged to the Peace Force and its men – but at that moment reason had no place within Burn's mind. She was being punished, she was sure, and the universe knew every crack, every weakness, every failing. It was clawing at her scars and wringing every wound until it bled.

Somehow, she made it home. The Hydes' house rose within view and then she was there, safe within its walls. She collapsed onto her bed, the energy drained from her bones and puddling around her in pools of despair. Scar's voice once more echoed through her comms, calling to her, but she refused to come, clinging instead to the darkness and its promise of escape. And, after a while, it took her, welcoming her into its sea of blissful oblivion.

Chapter 9

Scar was beginning to hate the safe house. It was too crowded, too loud, too full of people and their ideas. She longed for the stillness of her own home, her own tier, where she had room to work and think in peace – and where no one had the gall to wander into her workshop and touch her things.

It wasn't all bad, of course. Whereas before the Lunaria had met several times a week to discuss plans and strategies, their debate was now constant, with the promise of freedom driving their discourse.

Those that could safely show their faces in Kasis were out, stoking the flames of resistance in the streets. For the rest of them, ideas were all they had, and they flew like weapons through the house. Not all of them hit the mark, but those that did were polished and sharpened until they arose as action in the world.

The importance of the news hub as a key component of

those plans came into stark relief one evening as the Peace Force used the platform for their own advantage, taking to the arena to spread their lies. On a news bulletin beamed onto every tab in the city, they took aim, centering the target once more on the Lunaria's backs.

"Good evening, citizens of Kasis," said a polished brunette woman in tailored military attire. Under her image, the name General Brika was displayed like a badge of honor, and Scar couldn't help but scowl. The woman's newly acquired rank, paired with her past support of Cross and his corrupt machinations, made Scar's opinion of her a good deal less than favorable.

"The Peace Force has recently learned that the Lunaria have been ramping up their efforts to undermine our great government," Brika continued. "It saddens us greatly to know that, even as we speak, they are out there spreading atrocious falsehoods about Kasis, the Peace Force, and our brave officers."

Inspirational music rose in the background, attempting to fabricate the emotions that the woman so obviously lacked.

"It was only last year that this band of terrorists viciously attacked our city's lowest levels, intent on wiping out its poor and defenseless residents. Their extremist actions left countless families mourning the loss of their loved ones and unable to find closure. Others suffered grievous wounds that left them incapable of providing for their families."

Images of the destruction following the ManniK Battles covered the screen, with buildings reduced to rubble, and blood and bodies blanketing the streets. Then the mood abruptly changed, transitioning from gruesome to maudlin in the space of a second.

"As is our duty, the Peace Force stepped in to clean up the streets, to help the wounded, and to care for those who could no longer care for themselves."

Staged clips of Peace Officers feeding broth to the elderly and infirm were interlaced with images of raggedy children smiling and injured citizens gratefully receiving care.

"With our help, those on the lowest tiers were able to rebuild their lives and find hope in a brighter tomorrow. Yet the Lunaria still lurks like a black cloud, blocking out the light of the suns. It is clear from their radical actions that they want nothing less than the total destruction of Kasis and its culture."

The camera zoomed in on Brika's lined face, powdered over with makeup and rouge.

"This is a warning to the Lunaria and all who associate with them: You will not win. We will not let you reduce our grand city to ashes. We will meet your terrorism with the full might of our Peace Force and the full support of the Kasian people. You will be destroyed, and Kasis cured of your disease. And you will be forgotten, your legacies erased, and your names lost to history.

"To the rest of our brave populace, hear me now: If you love your city, help us defend it. Stand up, speak out, and assist us in putting these traitors behind bars. If you sense that one of the Lunaria is in your midst, contact us immediately. We will respond with all due haste to protect you and your family. Be on your guard. These rebels are cunning. They will approach you with lies and half-truths. They will attempt to turn you against us. Stay strong. Believe in your leaders. We will defend you – and we will defeat them."

The broadcast cut off abruptly, leaving Scar's tab blank. Her face, too, was blank, a mask of stoic calm, but inside she was fuming. It was one thing to blame the Lunaria for the battles, to cast them as the enemy in a war they had not waged. It was another thing entirely to depict the Peace Force as saviors and crusaders for the weak. In truth, the only ones they'd ever saved were themselves.

As Brika's words replayed in Scar's mind, she felt a gentle presence at her back.

"Did you see it?" Nara asked, her voice full of righteous indignation. Scar nodded, staying silent as the woman took a seat before her. "It's bullshit," she said simply, and Scar couldn't help but smile.

"If only those 'cunning rebels' had a plan to strike back," Scar replied evenly. "That would wipe those smug smiles off their faces."

Nara's eyes twinkled at the prospect, and she gave Scar a look that was positively wicked. "I can't wait," she said with obvious zeal.

"Then it's a good thing you don't have to," Scar said, zipping up a bag and slinging it over her shoulder.

"Do you think it'll look suspicious – going in after tonight's broadcast?" Nara queried.

"No," Scar said with complete confidence. "It'll look like retaliation, like a spur-of-the-moment attack. They'll think they got to us and we couldn't help but react. It's perfect, really."

And it was, although Scar couldn't take all the credit.

When she and Nara had returned from her ill-advised scouting mission, she'd been unable to hide the news of her violent run-in with the law. Her injuries had seen to that. Although Crete, the healer, had fixed her up before many had seen her battered state, she couldn't stop the spread of gossip, and it had raged through the house like fire, setting tongues alight with news of the intrigue.

She'd been reprimanded, of course. An operative going AWOL was a dangerous thing, especially during such turbulent times. But after the dust had settled – and Scar had put on an appropriate show of repentance – the Lunaria had softened, suitably impressed by the intel she and Nara had gleaned.

What followed was a flurry of ideas, a mingling of minds, a cacophony of creative schemes. Their congress had lasted hours, fueled by an excited fervor and a decent amount of back-alley booze. The harsh liquor had loosened their tongues and fed their imaginations, facilitating a raucous dialogue that flowed like a river through the room. Rising from its depths, a plan had eventually emerged, sparkling like a brilliant cache of sunken treasure.

They were going to attack the news hub. They were going to hide behind the visage of violence, feeding into the Peace Force's view that they were a vicious mob, bent on destruction. They would prey on their enemy's prejudice, bend to their bias, embodying the skewed personas that their leaders had placed upon them.

The havoc they wreaked would soon be remedied. Within days, the Peace Force would have the hub up and running, confident that they'd bested their foes once more. Yet they'd never think to look beneath the surface.

Because the Lunaria's true aim wasn't destruction; it was control. While cornering converts in the streets had strengthened their numbers, they all knew that it wasn't enough. They needed a larger stage. They needed to hijack the hub.

That's where Scar came in. Under the cover of carnage, she would sabotage their systems, installing an untraceable virus to grant them remote access to the whole of the hub. With the power in their hands, they could direct the message, shining a blinding light on their leaders' darkest deeds.

"We're leaving in 10," came a voice from the hallway, and Scar turned to see Coal striding past, spreading the word.

Coal's face-changing ability was a crucial part of their plan, and the man was exhilarated at the prospect of partaking in the action. Ansel and his fire would be joining them as well, along with Dormaline, who had helped them through the ManniK Battles with her gift of walking through walls. A few newer recruits had also volunteered for duty.

A former tailor named Jade, who had a particular knack for combat, had quickly nabbed a spot on their squad, while Rakasa, who could manipulate air, was a later addition. A set of twins, Ino and Lux, added a bit of brawn to their ranks and rounded out the team.

Called to action by Coal, the misfit band gathered in the front room, equipping themselves for the mission. Despite the danger, there was an air of excitement between them, and they chatted freely as they donned their weapons and armor.

Nara stood beside Scar, and she winked as Scar's gaze traveled over her and her arsenal. In comparison, Scar's armory was empty, with no metal spears crossing her back, no bows slung across her chest, and no knives tucked into her belt. Yet her pack was heavy on her back, filled to the brim with her own brand of weaponry. The weight was a comfort, a reassuring presence in the same way as the others' guns and spears and ammo.

Beyond the door, the night called to them, promising adventure and a respite from the tedium of the safe house. Before their 10 minutes had even elapsed, they were out on the street, their heads covered and their steps light on the dirty pavement. Out front, Nara acted as their eyes and their guide, directing them toward the safest route through the slumbering city.

Their small band traveled swiftly through the empty lanes, sticking to back roads and dark corners. No one seemed to notice their presence, and no alarms sounded as they passed. It was as if the world was theirs for the taking, their own private playground to do with as they pleased.

Scar was amazed at how different it was from her own solo expeditions. Alone, she had felt free, unrestrained by the burden of others. Now, with those "others" by her side, she felt unstoppable. There was a strength in their numbers, a power in their presence. It was as if each of their gifts complemented the others, forming a whole that was greater than its parts. For once, the weight of victory didn't lie solely with her. It was a novel feeling for Scar, and she marveled at its complexity.

It wasn't long before they arrived outside the hub, bypassing its roving patrols with a little help from Ino and Lux. Stopping a block back from the building, they stowed themselves in the veiled spaces around corners, masking their presence. They paused to catch their breath and re-group, tightening their masks, checking their weaponry, and helping their cohorts do the same. The moment swelled with anxious tension as their adrenaline spiked, connecting them like a cord.

Then – all too soon and not soon enough – it was time to move in. Digging around in her bag, Scar produced several small cannisters, handing them gently to Ino and Lux. Both men smiled at the gifts, silently accepting the weight of the role they had to play.

It was a delicate dance they were attempting. If they timed it right, each move would flow into the next, cascading them gracefully toward their goal. If they timed it wrong, however, this night could be their last. Scar tried her best not to contemplate that as everyone readied themselves for action.

"We're all set," Ansel whispered through the comms, setting the events in motion. "Places, everyone."

Without speaking, they lined up along the street, with Ino, Lux, and Rakasa in the lead. Behind them, Jade and Nara formed a wall of defense, with Dormaline tagging on their heels. Bringing up the rear were Scar and Coal, with Ansel covering their backs.

Soundlessly, they departed, creeping closer to the hub. Scar's steps were light, but her heart raced thunderously in her chest, calling out like a siren in the night. She was amazed that no one else could hear it, that no one could see her nerves spark or her skin begin to crackle. By the time they stopped, just outside the reach of the Peace Force's guns, her body was positively humming.

Ahead of her, Ino and Lux gave one quick nod before lurching forward. With a nimble gesture, each man bowled his cannister across the street, the steel clanking against the pavement as the cylinders bounced.

The noise brought the guards to abrupt attention. They regarded the contraptions with wary unease, pointing their guns at the darkness and shouting. Before they could act, the cannisters erupted, spilling forth a noxious gas that stained the air white with its poison.

Rakasa moved through the space like smoke, swirling his hands in sweeping arcs. At his touch, the silvery air converged upon the men, attacking from all sides. Coughs and gasps echoed from the opaque cloud as the officers tried to fight it – and failed. One by one, they hit the ground with light thuds.

Right on cue, Jade and Nara surged into the ring, their eyes peeled for any errant officers who hadn't fallen for their trap. Carefully, they stepped over the sleeping forms and split, each targeting one side of the building.

With the front of the hub clear, Dormaline made her move, sprinting toward the solid wall with childish delight. Behind her, Rakasa cleared a path, parting the smoke to aid her progress. As she neared the wall, her speed only increased until collision appeared inevitable. At the last second, her skin seemed to shimmer and she vanished, surging into the building's core.

Outside, Ino and Lux had similarly disappeared, losing themselves in the viscous mist as they gathered the weapons from their slumbering foes. In the darkness, Coal, Scar, and Ansel were left to linger, biding their time as they waited for their signal.

Sounds of a scuffle echoed from the left as Nara found more men to challenge, and soon the same could be heard from the right. Inside, Dormaline was silent as she slipped through walls, cutting a path that no one else could follow. She was a phantom, at one with the building, following its corners and curves. Unrestricted, she might have crept to the core with ease, but without Scar's skills, the systems would have stumped her. Instead, she set her sights on the security chamber, on the video feed and its guardian, on the last remaining obstacle barring entry.

The girl was small yet eager, fearsome in her fervor, and well-equipped with a few of Scar's inventions. With the element of surprise on her side, there was little she couldn't do.

Sure enough, her small voice soon graced the comms line, confirming the all-clear. "The feed's been taken out," she said simply. "C team, you're free to move in."

Jade and Nara echoed the call, their areas now free from foes. Together with Ino and Lux, the women would remain outside, new guards taking the place of the old. For the most part, though, their roles had been played. The rest was up to Scar.

Flanked by Ansel and Coal, she dashed across the open space as Rakasa cleared it of smoke. They paused only once, stopping as Coal unmasked an officer and memorized his features. By the time they reached the door, that officer stood beside them and Coal had vanished, giving himself up for the cause. Thanks to Ino's scavenging, Coal was even clothed in Peace Force garb, clad all in black and disguised by the body of the enemy.

"Unlock the doors, D," Scar commanded, and Dormaline obeyed, taking command of the controls to release the exterior doors.

"Come on in," she said as the lock clicked, granting them access.

Coal instinctively took the lead, safe in his new form. Ansel and Scar trailed behind, both alert and on their guard. As they crossed the threshold, Scar withdrew another gadget, this one new and untested, and held it aloft before her, prepared for a fight.

The first few hallways were quiet and still, their brightness glaring after the hazy dimness of the tier. They bore no hint of color or life, no pictures or paintings or cheer. Everything was antiseptic, austere, almost medical, a rigid stage from which to sell rigid lies. Scar's hackles rose as a chill of unease swept down her spine.

They needed to get to the building's rear, where the broadcast room lay waiting. Yet they couldn't rush, couldn't make a scene, couldn't alert the guards inside to their presence. Instead, they crept along gently, endeavoring to soften their steps as they wove through the halls.

For a while, they were lucky. They progressed through the building with ease, their confidence growing with every step. This seemed like their night, their moment, and they delighted in every empty hall, every quiet corner. Yet luck, by its nature, isn't meant to last, and eventually theirs ran out.

"C team, you have company," came Dormaline's voice in warning as she watched their progress on a screen. "One officer, moving toward you. Be prepared to take him out."

The trio halted, positioned at the end of a long hall.

Without a word, Coal motioned for them to stay put as he took the corner and surveyed the space beyond.

"What are you doing here, officer?" came a new voice, brimming with control. "No lower-level guards are permitted inside. You know the rules."

"Yes, sir, I do," Coal stated in his best attempt at subservience. "I thought I heard something inside. I came to check that everything was alright."

Scar and Ansel looked at each other, a hunger in their eyes. It was clear that Coal's lies wouldn't be enough to save them. Scar raised her weapon – and her eyebrows – silently pleading to be the one to strike. Ansel frowned for an instant, clearly wanting the takedown for his own, then nodded, reluctantly agreeing to her request.

She snuck forward with glee, angling herself to peer around the corner. The officer stood several paces down the hall, out of range of her new contraption, and Scar felt her vexation mount. She needed him closer, and she willed him forward, her finger dancing eagerly around the trigger. As if sensing her need, the officer advanced, flexing his authority.

"There have been no issues here," he said sternly, upbraiding Coal for his impertinence. "Now return to your post at once or I'll report you to General Brika."

At the mention of the woman's name, Scar took aim and fired. A silver net flew from the steel barrel, wrapping itself tightly around his torso. Before he could react, a surge of electricity coursed through the threads. Beneath it, his limbs vibrated, then gave way, and he crashed to the ground, unconscious, his body still twitching from the current.

Scar dashed from the safety of her spot to admire her

work. A small puddle formed beneath the man, and she carefully crept around it, letting the current subside before reclaiming the net.

"Hmm, I may have to lower the shock levels a bit," she said, mostly to herself.

Behind her, Ansel snorted, hastily covering his outburst with a cough. He bent down, seizing the weapon the officer had dropped, and straightened, his face now blank.

"We should keep going," Coal said, warily keeping watch for more company.

Scar got up, stowing the net in her bag. With one last look at the man on the ground, she set off, following Coal deeper into the bowels of the building.

They stopped outside a set of imposing steel doors, the last hurdle between them and the heart of the hub. Scar moved to fetch her tools, but Coal was quicker. Before she even had the chance to grab her glasses, he'd changed his face once more, switching from the unconscious man outside to the one they'd just left.

It was an unsettling feat – although highly useful. He passed the fingerprint and retinal scans with ease, and in a matter of seconds the doors beeped and opened, beckoning them inside.

Beyond the doors, a world of cameras and backdrops waited. Ansel rubbed his hands in excitement, and sparks fell from his fingers. They rained to the floor in bright droplets, sizzling where they landed. This was his playground, his stage, his canvas to do with as he pleased. His eyes lit up at the prospect, sparkling with hints of his fire.

As Scar watched, Ansel began to burn. His hands were

consumed by flames, and they licked across his body in a lover's caress. With a flick of his wrist, he sent them sailing, painting the room with a savage palette of oranges and reds. It was beautiful in its ferocity, elegant in its destruction, and Ansel smiled as he conducted the whole affair.

Scar, on the other hand, zeroed in on the computerized bank blinking at her from a small, windowed room.

"Don't burn the place down while I'm gone!" she warned Ansel, ducking into the space and out of reach of his flames.

This was *her* playground. The screens and tabs and drives called to her, tempting her to touch. She wanted to lose herself in their depths, to dive into the wonderful world they hid and explore every corner of their code. Yet she knew she couldn't. She had a job to do and the briefest of windows in which to do it.

Zeroing in on one of the tabs, Scar picked it up and got to work. Her fingers flew across the surface as she typed, and she relaxed into the familiar comfort of its code. This was a language she knew well, and it flowed from her in easy waves, crashing against the fragile firewall. Within a minute, she'd fashioned an elegant hole, granting herself access to the network.

As flames began to rage in earnest just beyond the wall, Scar lit her own fire in a dark corner of the system. With efficient keystrokes, she planted an undetectable virus within the hub, granting herself access to its secrets and control over its functions, even from afar. It was magnificent, a feat of sheer brilliance, and she took a moment to revel in her skill before getting back down to work.

Just as she was putting the finishing touches on her

masterpiece, Nara's insistent voice broke through.

"C team, you need to get out of there," she commanded. "Backups are on their way."

"How long do we have?" Coal asked, jumping on the line.

"They've just left the Peace Station," Nara replied, her voice tight. "My guess is five minutes max."

The anxiety that had drained from Scar's system returned with a vengeance, sending a chill through her veins. With a few final taps, she finished her work, erasing any hint of her presence. Then she dashed from the room, coughing as she entered the studio beyond.

Ansel had done his job well in her absence, and the room was engulfed in smoke. A chemical smell lingered in the air, carrying notes of rubber and tar, and ashes rained from the groaning beams, coating the scene like snow.

"Ansel!" Scar yelled, shouting over the flames.

When he turned his head in question, Scar jerked hers toward the door. With a sigh, he held out his hands, calling back the fire he'd unleashed on the hub. It came to him like a loyal dog, retreating into his hands and disappearing beneath his skin. Within seconds, the fire had ceased completely, leaving only a sea of blackened rubble and whispers of smoke.

The team backtracked through the building, their prior caution forgotten as they raced against time. Scar could feel the panic mounting, buzzing between them as hallways and doors passed in a blur. They were almost to the entrance when the luck that had sustained them faltered again and failed in an instant.

A weedy guard stood before them, eyes wild, blocking their path to escape. He was armed and incensed, pointing his shaking gun toward their chests. They had only a handful of heartbeats to react before he leapt, spraying the hallway with bullets.

Scar threw herself to the side, landing awkwardly on her stomach and arm. The impact knocked the wind from her lungs, and she coughed, trying to breathe.

Looking frantically around for her team, she quickly spotted Ansel off to her left. As she watched, flames erupted from his hand in a fierce orange ball, but before he could throw them, a bullet bit into his forearm, eliciting a shocked moan of pain. The flames rapidly sputtered and died, and he clasped the wound, trying to stem the flow of blood.

Scar couldn't think. Her body felt like it was glued to the ground and she couldn't move, couldn't crawl away from the shooter or thrust herself toward him. Her mind raced and sputtered in equal measure, searching desperately for solutions yet finding none.

Suddenly, another figure appeared on the scene, materializing from nowhere to stand behind the officer. Unlike Scar, she didn't hesitate, didn't waver. Her movements were practiced and fluid as she held out a pen and slammed it into his neck, sending him crashing to the floor.

The sound of gunfire abruptly vanished, and Dormaline bent down to retrieve the weapon.

"Let's go," she said as she rose, gun in hand. The girl she had been was gone, and in her place was a woman, viciously determined, with fire in her eyes.

No one argued. Even Ansel, whose blood stained the

ground behind them, followed without a word, his face contorted in pain. They emerged into the cool night with blissful relief, glad to be free of the hub – although they weren't free of its dangers entirely.

"The force is almost here," Nara breathed, her gaze focused on Scar. "Follow me."

They set off at a sprint, fleeing into the shadows. The clatter of their footsteps echoed off the walls, cracking the stillness of the night, but they didn't slow. Nara led them in a complicated maze, twisting through deserted streets and flying over stairs.

Eventually they stopped, taking shelter in an alley several tiers down. Scar collapsed next to Nara, trying to calm her hammering heart, but Nara had other things on her mind.

"Did you do it?" she asked, insistent. "Did you manage to plant the virus?" All heads turned to Scar, awaiting her answer.

After a beat, a smug grin spread across Scar's face, and she nodded. "The news hub is ours," she declared triumphantly.

Chapter 10

Burn lay in bed, hugging her knees to her chest. Her dreams had been dark and muddled, and she felt tired and weak, weighed down by the burden of everything she knew. She didn't want to rise, to face the world – and deal with the consequences of her actions.

Una and Baylor would be furious. From their perspective, she'd behaved appallingly, running out of a dinner party without even so much as a word. Una, in particular, would abhor her. Ellis had returned with no fiancé, no ring, and no promise of a brighter future.

Burn knew she'd have to leave her room eventually, though. The maid had already been by twice to rouse her, but Burn had locked the door, keeping the world at bay. She longed to retreat back into sleep, to submerge herself in nothingness until Hale had been found.

Except Burn wasn't that kind of girl. She did not sit by while others worked. She did not lie back and leave the saving to someone else.

Pushing back the blankets, she hopped out of bed, heading for the bathroom. She spent a few extra minutes scrubbing her skin, ridding it of makeup and scent and the feel of Ignis' hands on her. When she finally emerged from the tub, she felt almost human, restored to her typical tenacity.

Picking the most comfortable outfit from Ellis' wide closet, Burn changed and threw back her long blond hair, preparing for the day ahead. Glancing in the mirror, she was surprised to see herself behind Ellis' eyes. It wasn't a physical change; her eyes were the same soft blue they'd always been. It was what her eyes held, what they showed: the anger and pain and determination coursing through her soul. That was Burn – and that was what would save her.

She left her bedroom and headed toward the kitchen, intent on grabbing a quick bite to fill her aching stomach, but Una, it seemed, had caught her scent. She pounced on Burn within moments, backing her up against a wall.

"So, you finally deign to show your face?" she asked, a wicked sharpness in her tone. "You could have ruined everything last night. Do you know that? You behaved like a child, leaving your father and me to make excuses for you."

"What did you tell them?" Burn asked flatly, with no hint of apology in her voice.

Una chuckled, the sound devoid of cheer. "We blamed your nervous disposition. Said it was just pre-engagement jitters, although I highly doubt that they believed a word we said." Burn opened her mouth to speak, but Una shook her head.

"You will apologize to Ignis and his mother," she

commanded. "You will beg for their forgiveness and pray that they accept it. And you will show Ignis just how deeply you care for him. You'll do what you must, and you'll return with a fiancé."

"I will do no such thing," Burn shot back without thinking, her contempt clear.

"Excuse me?" Una breathed, raising her eyebrows in disbelief at her daughter's impertinence.

Burn knew she shouldn't respond, but even if she'd wanted to, she couldn't stop the words from coming, from spilling out in a whirlwind of frustration and fury.

"You heard me," Burn said, enunciating every word. "I will do no such thing. I will not go to them. I will never beg at their feet. And I certainly won't give myself over to that man. He is a sadist and a brute, just like his father. He cares nothing for me. He simply wants to own me – and I will never be anyone's property."

Una's expression immediately shifted from outrage to confusion. The woman stared at her as if seeing her for the first time, and Burn shrank back, suddenly nervous. She cursed herself for speaking, for letting her emotions overrun her, but she couldn't take it back.

"How do you know anything of Illex Cross?" she asked, staring into her daughter's eyes. "You never met the man."

Burn's heart sank as she saw her mistake, but she kept her gaze even, searching for a lie amidst the panic. "Everyone knows the stories," she said, refusing to blink.

Una digested her answer, swirling it around in her mouth like a fine wine. Yet something in it still displeased her, and her expression soured.

Burn knew she wouldn't win. This wasn't a battle; it was an ambush. Una had no intention of letting go, of yielding to her daughter's dangerous desires. The more Burn fought, the tighter Una's grip would become until all wisps of resistance had been wrung from her bones. Burn's only hope now lay in retreat.

"I'm so glad we could have this chat, mother," she said, ripping herself from Una's grasp. "But if you'll excuse me, I have things to do." She turned, storming down the hall as anger pulsed through her veins, hot and piercing.

Unwilling to let her daughter have the last word, Una bellowed after her. "This discussion is not over. You will be brought to heel. Mark my words, Ellis, you will obey me."

Burn pretended not to hear, even as every word bit through her, penetrating her mind like a dagger. Instead, she continued on, yearning for escape. Reaching the door, she paused briefly to call Kaz on the comms mirror in the hall.

"Officer Petala," she said before the screen had even resolved, "I'm leaving."

Without waiting for a response, she strode outside and down the lane. She had no destination in mind, merely a need to get away. Her aggravation drove her, and she blew through the streets like a madman, with no care for the people or the weight of their probing stares.

"Ellis, stop!" came a voice from behind her, but she couldn't stop.

She did slow, however, tempering her pace so Kaz could catch up. Once he was by her side, she picked up speed once more, craving space and air and freedom. Craving separation from that horrid house and its monsters.

Kaz glanced at her expression and frowned, clearly concerned, but she couldn't bring herself to care. She had no desire to put back on her mask or to feign indifference. She was done pretending.

"What happened?" Kaz asked with genuine concern. He was breathing heavily, but he didn't slow, nor did he try to slow her. Instead, he matched her pace, falling into step with her canter.

"Well, let's see," Burn began, ticking off the items on her hand. "Hale is missing. Una suspects that I'm up to something. And, oh yeah, I spent last night pretending to be in love with the son of the man that I killed." It all seemed so ridiculous that she let out a hysterical laugh, unable to stop herself.

Kaz's eyes went wide. "You don't mean…" he trailed off, not wanting to finish the sentence for fear that it might be true.

"Illex Cross," she supplied for him. "Last night, I had dinner with his widow and his *charming* son, Ignis – my soon-to-be fiancé."

"Damn," Kaz muttered in some combination of shock and horror – two sentiments with which Burn wholeheartedly agreed.

"And while I sat there drinking their wine and *kissing* their son, Hale was out there being tortured – maybe even killed!" Burn ground to a halt as the panic welled up, blurring her vision.

But Kaz was there. Gathering her up in a tight embrace, he held her, silently lending his strength. After a minute, he loosened his grip, but he didn't let go.

"The Lunaria are searching for him as we speak. They will find him, Auburn."

"What if he's somewhere we can't look, like the Peace Station?" Burn asked. "What if they're beating him as we speak, trying to break him?"

Kaz sighed. "I'll look into it tonight. And if they've hurt him...well, you of all people should know how strong he is. He's going to make it."

Burn shook her head, but his optimism was a welcome balm, soothing the ragged edges of her despair.

"I need to do something," Burn told him, letting her tension fade into a steely resolve as she detached herself from his grasp. "I can't just sit in that house and wait. I have to help."

"Then let's help," Kaz said simply.

"What do you propose we do?"

"Our job," he stated firmly. "If we discover what the Shadow Assembly is up to, it may lead us to Hale. Hell, it may even help us take them down once and for all."

"Except we haven't found anything yet," she countered. "Nothing in any of these houses points to the assembly."

"There has to be a trace somewhere, a trail we can follow," Kaz assured her. "No one can operate invisibly, no matter how much money they have − or how many people they have in their pocket. There's always something that betrays them."

"Fine," Burn said, giving in with a sigh. "Who's on our list today?"

Kaz smiled. It was the question he'd been waiting for. He grabbed his tab from his back pocket and unfolded it.

After a few taps, he paused, contemplating the screen.

"It looks like Colonel Tellus is up next," he said.

"Colonel Tellus…" Burn mused, rolling the name over on her tongue. She'd never heard of the man, and she wondered what he'd done to set himself up so well, what questionable things had garnered him such an enviable rank. "Do you know him?" Burn asked as they began to walk once more.

"I know *of* him, but I can't say we've ever worked together. He mainly handles interrogations. He's developed quite a…reputation," Kaz said delicately.

"Torture?" Burn inquired, getting straight to point.

"The Peace Force would never use that term," he replied, his expression strained. "More like 'persuasion.' Whatever you call it, though, I've heard he's one of the best."

Burn shivered despite the morning's balmy weather. Her mind unwittingly flicked to Hale, wondering if he was currently in the hands of such a demon, bound and gagged and begging for death. Her stomach constricted at the thought, and she had to push it from her mind.

"Does he have a family, this Tellus?" she asked trying to prepare herself – and distract herself.

"Apparently his husband was also on the force – before he was killed in the ManniK Battles," Kaz stated, reading the dossier off his tab. "As you can imagine, he's not too keen on *freaks.*"

Burn snorted. "Then I bet he fits right in on the force," she spat sarcastically.

Kaz gave her a cautionary look. "He's dangerous, Auburn. I think I should handle this one on my own."

"Not a chance," she said, her conviction on full display.

Kaz looked at her for a long second. "I figured as much, but you can't blame me for trying."

Burn felt an ember of warmth blossom in her chest at his show of concern, and she took a minute to consider the man at her side.

Their relationship had evolved since their first encounter all those months ago. Back then, it had been brittle and fleeting, something built on hope and starlight. Neither had truly known the other, and it had collapsed almost as quickly as it began, crumbling into a pile of anger and regret.

It was different now. It was…more. There was a friendship, a trust, a knowledge of each other that bound them together. As they had changed, morphing into stronger versions of themselves, their connection had intensified. Before they had hidden, tucking parts of themselves away and pretending they were whole. Now they'd shed those masks and could see each other for who they truly were.

She loved Kaz, although not in the same way she once had. It was not the bright, blinding love of romance and passion, the kind that sweeps you up and carries you away on the wind. It was a much subtler thing, a whisper in the night, and it felt more real than anything they'd had before.

"Thank you, but I'll be fine," she eventually said, refocusing her gaze on the road. "Now let's get to work."

They walked for a while in comfortable silence, drawing farther from the center of the tier with each step. When they finally stopped, it was at the far end of the level, where the houses ran flush with the edge. Beyond the buildings, a sheer drop lingered in quiet menace, a blank swath of air with emptiness above and below and the dome stretching up in the distance.

The height made Burn's head spin, and she forced herself to focus on the house in order to ease the dizziness swelling in her veins. Tellus' abode was tall and wide, yet it lacked depth, like it was merely a façade of a building rather than a home. Concentrating on the shape of its rooms, she closed her eyes and listened, but all that greeted her was silence.

"It's empty," Burn said with satisfaction. "There's no one home."

Kaz grimaced for a split second before letting his face go slack, but Burn could see the disappointment in his eyes. If Tellus had been home, Kaz could have gone in alone. He could have spared Burn the danger. He could have kept her safe. But right now, she didn't want to be spared a thing – the danger, the thrill, the satisfaction of doing something other than standing by and waiting. She needed to work, to help, and he knew he couldn't stop her.

They let themselves in without issue. Inside, a coolness met them, sinister and wrong. It was as if the heat had fled in fear and left a frigid malevolence in its place.

Burn shivered as they pressed deeper into the home, exploring its curves and edges. They began at the top and worked their way down, scouring bedrooms and bathrooms and halls. They considered every file, every tab, every desk and drawer and closet, but they found no answers, no clues.

They saved the office for last. It was always the most promising room – and the most disappointing. It contained so much knowledge, so many books and tabs and facts, yet so little information.

Burn and Kaz took their time sorting through the

clutter. Tellus was not an organized man, and his papers and notes were strewn around the room in an incoherent mess. Still, they couldn't risk upsetting the madness for fear that the man would notice. So they carefully stooped to read the pages where they lay, thrown across chairs and tables and dotting the floor.

Halfway through their search, they stumbled upon a tab and patched in Scar, who got to work unraveling the system's secrets. She toiled in the background, a hushed soundtrack to their search, with the glimmer of hope growing fainter by the second.

Then Burn spotted something. It was a word or a phrase or a note in the margins. Something small and precise, something about the *freaks*. In her excitement, she lunged for it, but the chaos of the room would not let her pass by unscathed. It pulled at her, and before she knew it a vase was tumbling to the floor, knocked from its pedestal by her fervor.

It fell in slow motion, as if time were drawing out the torture. When it finally reached the floor, it let out a resounding crash, sending ceramic shards showering over Burn in a fearsome attack.

But she hardly felt it, even as the splinters drew blood from her arm. The shock and surprise that had stunned her were gone, replaced by something else entirely. Her attention was fixed, glued to the place where the vase had met the solid wood floor.

Except it wasn't solid. The sound had been wrong. The clatter it made had been too high, too resonant to be right.

Beside her, Kaz was reeling. He'd begun to pick up the shards of the vase, as if he could somehow piece it back together. Yet both of them knew that was impossible. It had shattered, split into a hundred tiny pieces that had scattered themselves across the room.

As Kaz scrambled, Burn got to her knees, crawling over to where the vase had hit, to the epicenter of the storm. Clearing away the dust and the remnants of paint and clay, she began to knock on the boards and listen, seeking the anomaly.

Three knocks was all it took to locate the source. Wiping the boards clean, she lowered her head to the floor, tracking the cracks and crevices with the tips of her fingers. She pressed lightly on their surface and dug into their sides, searching for a way in, a way through.

Her nails caught on a segment of board, a straight line in a forest of curves. Hope stuttered in her chest as she pried it up, revealing a cavern of darkness beneath. The shadows were all-consuming, eating away at the walls, the shapes, the floor. Burn could make out nothing other than a few silver rungs, which petered away into the abyss.

"Hello?" she asked the darkness, listening for its response.

Closing her eyes, she felt the space. The echoes bounced back to her with stories of a deep well, narrow and empty. It was an antechamber, an entrance.

Pushing farther into the darkness, she felt for signs of life, for anything that moved or breathed or bustled. Nothing came to her – no footsteps or words or whispers of thought. The only thing she could hear was a low hum, a constant drone so faint it was nearly swallowed by the depths.

Burn spun around, preparing to drop into the secret chamber and climb down its rungs, but a hand on her shoulder stopped her. Looking up, she saw Kaz kneeling beside her, considering the passage.

"I'll go first," he decreed, lightly pushing her aside to make room.

"But…" Burn began, but Kaz cut her off.

"You have a taser. I have a gun – and military training. I couldn't stop you from coming, but I can at least try to protect you from any additional danger."

"There's no one in there, Kaz," she informed him, refusing to move. "There's no danger."

"If I recall, that's exactly what you said before finding yourself in a duel with a HouseBot," he said dryly. "Danger doesn't just come in the form of other humans, Auburn. There could be traps or bots or any number of threats. You're not indestructible."

Burn felt a flash of resentment, but it rapidly faded, leaving grudging acceptance in its place. "Well, neither are you. So be careful," she instructed, giving in and moving out of his way.

Kaz did as he was told, slowly making his way down until he was lost to the darkness. Grabbing a small light off his belt, he flicked it on, illuminating the space with flimsy rays. It wasn't much, but it was enough to bring the walls into focus, confirming Burn's suspicions of the space.

It was a narrow pit, dropping down at least a story, if not more. The walls were slick and smooth, coated in a blackness that absorbed the light. At the bottom, Kaz stood alone – with no bots or traps or threats to attack him.

"I'm coming down," Burn shouted, embarking on her descent before he had time to protest.

She reached the bottom in less than a minute, dropping onto the solid floor and shivering. It was cold in the pit, and their breath mingled in the air, hanging around them in puffs of white. It was an unnatural chill, an artificial winter that smelled of ice and frost and chemicals.

Burn rubbed her hands as she turned, surveying the room. She and Kaz were crushed together, and there was barely space to move, but they rotated in unison, each studying the wintry walls before them.

The chamber appeared empty, simply four solid walls with nothing beyond them. Except that made no sense. Tellus wouldn't create such a passage without a plan, without a use for its clever secrecy. It was hiding something, and Burn knew exactly how to find it.

Closing her eyes, she placed her hands against the smooth surface of the wall. Listening intently for any change, she mapped its planes with her fingers, the chill biting into them with icy greed. She turned once, twice, again, before pausing on the final wall.

All of the walls were cold, but this one was different. It was a type of frozen that hurt to touch, that gnawed at her hands and threatened to burn them. Instead of drawing away, Burn embraced it, moving her head to rest along the slick surface.

"There's something behind this," she said after a second, tearing herself away. "There's a sort of humming inside, like a generator. I can almost feel the room, but I don't see a way through."

"Let me have a go," Kaz said, and the pair gradually rotated to give him access.

He squinted through the darkness, his eyes searching. His hands, too, roved across the space, feeling for any variance, any hint on how to access the portal.

"Aha!" he whispered after a minute, his hands tracing the outlines of a box. "I think we have something."

Pushing lightly with his fingertips, Kaz watched as a screen sprang loose from the wall, lighting the tunnel with a clear blue light. Instinctively, Burn reached for her biometric key and handed it to Kaz, letting him do the honors.

He slipped it over his finger and held it to the pad, but there was no accepting beep, and no door swung open before them. Confused, he tried again, but nothing happened.

"I think we need an expert," Burn said, fetching the magnet from her bag and attaching it to the screen. "Scar, we've found something – finally – and it looks like it's right up your alley."

"Tell me more," Scar said, intrigued.

"It seems to be a secret basement of sorts," Burn said, glancing at her surroundings. "It extends down into the next tier, with at least one room branching off the side, but we can't get in. Can you work your magic?"

"Do you even have to ask?" her sister replied, a note of heady excitement coloring her tone. She immediately got to work, tapping away at her tab as she infiltrated the room's security and began to break it down.

A minute passed, then two, and Kaz and Burn began to shiver in earnest. Eventually Scar's voice came back on the line.

"They must really want whatever's in that room to stay hidden," she said. "I've never seen a system like this."

"You can crack it, right?" Burn asked, the cold ebbing at her patience – and her extremities.

"You insult me, sister," came her tart reply.

A few seconds later, a beep sounded from the screen and the wall before them began to shift. As they watched, a flush section broke loose and slid aside, revealing an archway. Bright light spilled forth, and Burn and Kaz blinked as their eyes grew accustomed to the glow.

"Voila!" Scar exclaimed with satisfaction. "And you two doubted me."

"Lies!" Kaz said with a grin. "We'd never doubt you."

"Right," Scar responded with a snort. "Burn, put on your glasses," she commanded, getting down to business. "I want to see what's inside. If the security is anything to go by, this might be worth recording."

Burn did as she was told, snagging her glasses from her pack and turning them on. Once they were secure, she moved to enter the space, but Kaz put an arm out to stop her, shaking his head and placing himself before her.

With tentative steps, he crept into the room, his gun raised. Burn could make out some of the space now, but Kaz's body blocked the rest. What she could see was a penetrating blue light, which lit up the stark white cabinets that lined both walls, the sterile counters above them, and the cold stone floor beneath.

"It doesn't look like anything is rigged to blow," he deduced, turning back to her. "But be careful. Don't touch anything. There could still be traps."

Burn practically sprang into the room, her pent-up excitement bursting forth. She wanted to look at everything at once, to investigate every crack and crevice. Yet only a few feet in, she stopped, her gaze trained on the center of the room.

Resting there, framed by lights and accessorized by thick woven straps, was a table. An operating table.

Chapter 11

Burn's blood went cold. This was a lab – a place of experiments and research and *torture*. A place where people were brought to be dissected and studied. A playground where the cruel and contemptuous paraded their power.

If it were anywhere else, it might have been a doctor's office, a surgery, a clinic. But here, buried beneath the home of a Peace Force pawn? Here its purpose was clear.

"Are you getting this, Scar?" she asked, sweeping her gaze around the space.

"Clear as day," Scar said, appalled. "What the hell are they up to in there?"

"I don't know," Burn breathed, "but I plan to find out."

She threw herself into the investigation with a renewed fervor, wrenching open drawers and cabinets and tearing through their contents. She didn't care about being gentle. The broken vase would give them away in an instant, and she had no urge to keep her wrath contained. She wanted to rip the room apart at its seams, to take out every hint of emotion on the vials and scalpels and syringes.

"Burn," came a stern voice through the comms, and she stopped, her hands cupped around a pack of gauze.

"What?" she asked curtly, unwilling to stop her rampage.

"You're not going to discover much by destroying the place," Scar advised, acting as the voice of reason. "There's a tab in the corner, mounted on the wall. Get me access, and I promise you I'll find what they're hiding."

Burn grumbled but obeyed. She transferred the magnet to the tab and watched as the screen flickered to life, moving through pages as if possessed. Burn made a move to return to her search, but she paused, her attention caught by a hint of sound.

It was the humming she had heard, but it was stronger here, luring her toward the far wall. And there, wedged between the counters, was a door. It wasn't hidden like the last door, but it blended into the wall, with only a faint outline to betray its presence.

Burn felt around its edges, poking and prodding in search of a clasp. Finding none, she moved her fingers to the center, pushing firmly with both hands. Through some miracle, the door gave way at her touch.

The cold greeted her like a vengeful ghost, clouding her sight and sinking into her bones. Frost hung in the air and dripped from the ceiling, and she hugged herself for warmth. Behind her, Kaz followed. For once, he didn't insist on going first, although he stayed close, wary but vigilant, his eyes peeled for danger.

It was difficult to see through the haze of ice and

refrigerated air, but it was clear that this was the epicenter of the storm, the source of the chill. It was also the source of the hum, which flowed through the vents as they pumped the room with chemicals and cold.

Burn ventured deeper into the space, losing herself in the frozen mist and colliding with a set of tall white wardrobes. Squinting, she could just make out more wardrobes lining the walls, taking up space on either side of the room. There had to be at least 30 of them, each an arm's length wide, stretching from ceiling to floor.

She tried to pry one open, but her hands wouldn't obey. They clawed uselessly at the handle, unable to grasp or clutch or turn. When she finally managed to grab hold, she yanked on the cupboard, putting her body weight behind it, but the door remained shut. Another locked door, another set of secrets.

Giving up on the closets, Burn propelled herself forward. Her legs were beginning to lock from the cold, and she exaggerated her movements, shifting her limbs in a slow-motion dance. The stiffness was painful, and it crept like ice through her veins, threatening to trap her. Yet she knew she had to push on, had to discover all that was hiding in this den of the damned.

In the distance, she saw a shape, something long and low and lumpy. It called to her, dragging her through the space as she puffed her exhaustion. As she drew nearer, she recognized the outlines of a body laid out along a table and draped in white.

With shaking hands, she reached out to draw back the sheet, revealing the body beneath. Revealing the *man* beneath.

Raqa. Hale.

Burn instinctively dropped her head to his chest, desperately searching for signs of life. She closed her eyes and slowed her breathing, tuning out the hum and the cold and the sound of Kaz calling to her from somewhere in the mist. She listened with all her might, praying for a sound. And there, beneath his pale, sallow skin, was a heartbeat.

"He's alive!" she shouted to Kaz, a joyous disbelief floating weightless in her chest.

She wanted to cheer and cry and scream her relief, but she couldn't. The sight of him stopped her, tearing her heart to pieces with its cruel injustice. Tubes and wires poked out from across his body, while cuts, bruises, and incisions marred his skin – all new and vibrant and angry.

Burn couldn't help but think how small he looked. Hale had always felt colossal, like a presence you couldn't ignore. Now, beneath Raqa's ashen skin, he seemed so fragile, so breakable, so mortal. In that instant, Burn wanted nothing more than to protect him, to gather him up in her arms and shield him from this horror.

With fumbling fingers, she got to work peeling away the tubes and disconnecting the wires. She longed for him to wake, to open his eyes and see her, but he remained asleep, lost in an unconscious haze. She didn't realize she was crying until a tear froze on her cheek and cascaded downward, breaking into minuscule shards as it collided with Raqa's bony chest.

"It's going to be alright," Kaz said from beside her, his efforts mirroring hers. "We'll get him out of here. We'll get him somewhere safe."

Burn nodded, trying desperately to steady her frozen fingers. She winced every time she removed a tube, and her stomach clenched at every drop of blood that hit the floor. His battered body had taken so much torment, and she feared that her clumsy hands would be responsible for dealing the final blow.

They were almost finished stripping his body when Scar's voice came through the comms once more.

"Burn, I've found something," she said, her voice uncharacteristically tight.

"What?" Burn cut back, a syrupy fear clogging her throat. "Do you know what they did to him? Do you know why?"

"No. Not yet," she said. "I still have a lot of data to decrypt. I'm downloading it now. But I do know what's in those cupboards."

Burn didn't know if she wanted to hear it, if she wanted to understand the true horrors around her. Hale's present condition was enough of a shock. Anger already tore at her, hot and fierce, and she didn't know how much more she could handle.

"What is it?" she finally asked between clenched teeth. "What are they hiding?"

"It's people, Burn. They're filled with people."

Scar said it so quietly that it almost didn't register. When it did, Burn pushed herself off the table and onto the nearest set of doors, yanking them with all her might. She let loose a strangled scream as they resisted her efforts, unwilling to part at her touch.

"Are they alive? Who are they? Why are they here?!" Burn asked, panic rising in her chest.

"I think they're alive. Well, at least some of them, judging by their vital signs, although some aren't registering. The cases could be empty or…" she trailed off, unwilling to finish the thought.

Burn finished it for her. "Or they could be dead."

As if on cue, the doors released with a click, swinging open and revealing a line of frozen forms, blue and bruised and still as death. Burn walked along the rows, cataloging the faces, but none were familiar. Still, they pulled at her heart, their helplessness dragging her down into the depths.

She turned to Kaz, the panic making its way to her eyes. He had finished disentangling Hale and was trying to wake him, but the man wasn't responding. So instead, Kaz gently lifted him to a seated position before draping his arm around Hale's waist.

"Kaz," she all but pleaded, "we have to help them. We have to get them out."

Kaz raised an answering gaze and Burn paled. His eyes were filled with an immeasurable sadness, a lost and desolate look that said everything he needed to say.

"We can't leave them here," she begged, her voice steadily losing its conviction. "Isn't there something we can do?"

Kaz sighed, dropping his eyes from hers. "We've stayed too long already. We have to go. We can't save them."

"Yes, we can!" she shouted, her frustration mounting. "They'll die here."

"It'll be hard enough getting Hale out," Kaz said softly. "We can't bring these people, too. If you want to save him, we have to leave them behind."

It was an impossible decision, weighing one life against

others. How could she decide who lived and who died, who they rescued and who they left behind? Even though she knew it would be Hale they'd save – that it would always be Hale – she couldn't stomach the thought of condemning these people to such a grueling and grisly fate.

"Scar?" she asked, turning to her big sister for help. "Tell me you can do something. Unfreeze these people. Wake them up! Maybe they can escape on their own."

"Unfreezing them safely would take hours – and I can't guarantee that they'd make it," Scar said with the same regretful tone as Kaz. "I'm no doctor, and I don't know what's been done to them. If I try to alter their life support, it could kill them."

"Then…" Burn paused, trying to think of another solution, one where all of them could survive. "Wipe the data. Scramble whatever information they've been gathering on these people. Do something. Anything."

Silence engulfed the comms as Scar hesitated, choosing her words carefully. "I'll do what I can," she finally said, "but it's likely that the data's been backed up off-site. Without knowing where it's stored and having access to the system, I can't corrupt it. All I can do is delete the local files."

"Damn it!" Burn cried, infuriated by her helplessness. She had no more ideas, no clever plans or brave stratagems. She only had compassion, thick and unruly, and it was slowly tearing her apart.

"Burn."

The sound of her name made her stop in her tracks, made her thoughts freeze and her panic grind to a halt. Because it hadn't been Scar that said her name, and it hadn't been Kaz. It was Hale.

Turning, she stared at him, tracing the curves of his face. His eyes were open, albeit foggy, and he looked at her in dazed disbelief.

"I knew you'd come," he said, his words slurring together. "I knew you'd save me."

The barest hint of a smile crossed his lips before his head slumped and he fell into oblivion once more. Yet his words had done the trick.

Burn tore herself from the wardrobes and rushed to his side, needing to be near him. Somehow, she no longer saw Raqa, no longer noticed the traitor's face or form. It was just Hale – her Hale – and she knew exactly what she had to do.

"Do whatever you can, Scar," she commanded, her jumbled emotions coalescing into resolve. "Deal as much damage as possible. It might not stop them, but it will slow them down. In the meantime, we'll parse through the data. We'll discover what they're up to. We'll find a way to stop them and save these people."

She gave Kaz a nod and joined her arm with his around Hale's back, hoisting him to his feet. Hale stirred at her touch, and his feet began to move of their own accord, propelling him forward.

Together, the trio retreated through the lab and into the pit, awkwardly heaving Hale up the ladder and into the light. They collapsed onto the floor in the office, their hearts pounding and their bodies thawing in the glorious heat. Yet they knew they couldn't linger. Once they'd caught their breath, they set out once more, ambling through the house and its halls and tumbling back into the city.

Out in the open, everything seemed too bright, too warm, too public. Burn and Kaz began to sweat from the effort of supporting Hale, and they longed for the safety of shadows in a world consumed by light.

Danger lurked around every corner and down every street, parading as servants, citizens, and Peace Force patrols. Each of them was the enemy, the *other*, and each would be more than happy to be the dealer of their defeat.

It was clear that Hale did not belong. He was bruised and broken and weak, a slice of reality amidst the dream. They needed to get him to safety, off the streets and away from its spies. Yet safety was a tenuous concept in a world that was not their own. The best they could hope for was shelter, a sanctuary to shield them while they devised a plan.

There was only one place that fit their needs. Yet the Hydes' home was halfway across the tier, a dim beacon that danced like a dream in the distance. Getting there unspotted and unscathed would be a challenge, one that posed dire consequences should they fail.

They took their time preparing a route across the level before setting off, with Burn using her gift and Kaz using his. Together, they slid through the streets, arms lashed around each other and bodies entwined. They moved as one unit, sharing each other's strengths and bearing the weight of each weakness.

Their journey was achingly slow, yet they kept moving, dipping down a tier before rising again. The suns ticked relentlessly across the sky, measuring their trek in seconds, then minutes, then hours. By the time they caught sight of the house, dusk was nearly upon them, and the threat of twilight hung thick in the air.

Burn closed her eyes and listened, praying for the safety of silence. Yet beyond the doors, conversation blazed, burning like a light when all she needed was darkness.

"Una and Baylor are home," she said, turning to face Kaz and Hale. The latter had regained a steady consciousness, but she could tell it was taxing him. He needed to rest and regain his strength, and he couldn't do that on the street.

"What do we do?" Kaz asked, looking to her for a plan. "How do we get him inside?"

"*We* don't," she said with resolve. "*You* do."

Kaz shook his head, and Hale followed, the two men united in silent agreement. Burn shook her head right back, unwilling to accept their dissent.

"I'll cause a distraction, and you two get inside," she instructed, ignoring their imploring looks. "You'll only a have a minute, so you'll have to be quick. If you time it right, though, you can make it."

"Auburn..." Kaz started then stopped, cowed into submission by her glare.

"Take Hale to my room. I'll join you when I can." With that, she took off across the street, her strides long and her head held high.

Of course, she had no idea what she was going to do. She was running on fumes of conviction, and they were rapidly evaporating. Still, she knew she couldn't stop, couldn't turn, couldn't face herself if she failed. So she kept walking, tearing through the door and into the cruelness of the house beyond.

Her parents were there to greet her. Or, rather, to watch

her as she entered. They sat like statues in the living room, just like they had on the first night. Just like they had every night. Cold and poised, with masks of decorum. They stared at her with flat eyes, with indifference and detachment.

Their looks slowly changed as they took in her disheveled state, digesting the blood on her clothes and the sweat on her brow. Apathy gave way to shock then anger then outrage. Burn saw herself through their eyes, saw the tear-stained cheeks, the red-rimmed eyes, the mess of her hair and clothes. She saw their daughter, covered in someone else's blood. She saw their thoughts as they jumped to conclusions.

"What have you done?" Una cried, sitting up straighter. "Come here right now and explain yourself."

Burn tried to do as they said. She forced her feet to move, covering the ground between them, but something was wrong. The world lurched, rolling beneath her and trying to buck her off. She swayed in place as the light around her dimmed, threatening to disappear completely.

It suddenly dawned on her how long it had been since she'd eaten. She'd skipped breakfast and lunch and dinner, and her last meal had ended up on the street.

She tried to tell this to Una, tried to ask for water or bread, but the words didn't come. She took a step, then another, then the floor fell from beneath her and she was tumbling, down and down and down.

The last thought she had before she landed was one of pure satisfaction. She had made an excellent distraction after all.

Chapter 12

"I didn't think I'd be caring for two invalids today," Kaz said as Burn came to, the feeling of something warm and salty traveling down her throat and filling her with heat.

She tried to sit up, but Kaz stopped her, placing his hand on her shoulder.

"You need to rest. And eat," he said soothingly, bringing another spoonful of soup to her lips. "You sure took your role seriously. I have to hand it to you, though – fainting did cause quite the commotion."

Cobwebs clung to her memories as she strained to make sense of his words. "What happened? How did I get here? Where's Hale!?"

She sat up as the memory surfaced, searching for the man, but he was nowhere to be seen. The sudden movement made her vision dance, and stars appeared before her eyes, threatening to blind her.

"See?" Kaz said with grim conceit. "I told you that you

needed to eat."

Burn grabbed the bowl from his grasp, discarding the spoon and drinking it down in several long gulps. The heat burned her throat, and the liquid pooled in her empty belly, but it restored some of the sharpness to the world, clearing its fuzzy edges.

She noticed that the dimness of dusk had deepened to an all-consuming blackness, wiping away the features from the streets outside and replacing them with mere ideas, overseen by a clear night sky.

"How long have I been out?" she asked, taking it easier this time.

"About five hours," Kaz said, gently removing the bowl from her grasp and placing it on the table beside her.

"How did you explain it to Una and Baylor? The blood…" she shuddered at the memory and looked down at herself, surprised to find pajamas where her clothes had been.

"The maid got you cleaned up and changed," Kaz said, seeing her suspicion. "I told them that someone tried to attack you, probably a member of the Lunaria, but I shot him. He fell and you caught him. It was his blood on your clothes. But he managed to stagger off before I could get to you. I've let the Peace Force know, and they'll be on the lookout for a hooded figure with a gunshot wound."

"That was quick thinking," she said, giving him credit.

"Yeah," he said sheepishly. "Well, I told them that's why you passed out. The whole situation was too much for you, so you fainted. It seemed to satisfy them."

Burn let out a sigh of relief, but the feeling was short-lived. "Where's Hale?" she asked again, her attention drawn to him like a magnet. "Is he alright?"

"He's fine," Kaz assured her. "He's sleeping. I put him in your bathroom after everyone left so no one would find him."

Burn made a move to rise, to go to him, but Kaz stopped her, placing his hands on her arms.

"Let him be," he told her, a note of warning in his voice. "He's been through a lot. He needs his sleep."

"Kaz, what did they do to him?" she asked, her voice so quiet she didn't know if he'd hear. "What were they doing down there?"

His eyebrows furrowed and he looked away, obviously contemplating her question. He knew something, that much was clear, but he didn't know how to tell her, how to give her the facts without sending her sprawling.

"I think you need to talk to Scar," he finally said, handing her the comms. "She can explain it better."

Burn felt the unease trickle through her like a polluted stream, twisting her insides with its restless fervor. She scooped the device from Kaz's grasp and held it before her with both hands, staring into it as if she could see her sister on the other side.

"Scar, it's me. Are you there?"

Barely a second passed before Scar jumped on the line, obviously awaiting her call.

"Good, you're awake," she said with blatant mockery. "You know that was a foolish move, right? When we send troops into the field, we typically like it if they remain conscious. We don't need a damsel in distress. We need a spy."

Burn knew she deserved the lecture. She had been reckless with her safety – along with Kaz's and Hale's. She had put them in danger and could have cost them their lives. She had gotten lucky, and she knew it.

Still, she wasn't calling for a sermon. She needed answers, and Scar was the only one who could give them.

"I got it, Scar. Food good. Fainting bad," Burn said wearily. "Now tell me what you've found."

"Gladly," Scar said, as if she'd been waiting for that very command. "I've been decrypting the data I downloaded. It's taken me some time, but I've finally found something." She took a deep breath before diving in. "Burn, they're experimenting on mutants. They're testing us. They're *dissecting* us."

Burn's vision swam at her sister's pronouncement. "I thought their experiments ended," she said, unexpectedly breathless. "I thought they died with Wight and Cross."

Suddenly, she wasn't in Ellis' bedroom. She wasn't in the heavens and she wasn't in this form. She was at the bottom of the city, trapped and wounded and at the mercy of her captors.

They'd been testing MovriK on *freaks*, varying the dose and chemical makeup until it had the power to turn mutants into monsters. And she was to be their latest test subject.

Cross had dragged her there himself. He had handed her to Wight and told him to kill her, to *use* her. The mastermind behind the tainted MovriK, Wight had tried to do just that. But she'd been lucky. She had escaped. She had killed him – and then she had killed Cross.

She thought she had stopped them. She thought she had won. Yet it seemed that even death couldn't stop true evil.

"The MovriK experiments were only one of many," Scar

151

continued. "Their research has been going on for years, but they've ramped it up over the last few months – which explains the increase in disappearances."

"But why?" Burn asked forcefully, the anger and frustration fizzing in her chest. "Why are they doing this to us? What is it they're looking for?"

"They're searching for the source of our powers."

It wasn't Scar who had answered, but rather Raqa. His thin voice came from the direction of the bathroom, and Burn glanced toward it, her heart stopping in her chest.

His face was gaunt and hollow, with sunken cheeks and blue-rimmed eyes. Across his skin, blood lingered where they'd cut him and struck him and forced him to bleed. His skin shone translucent, with veins and bones on full display, and it hung baggy around his form, like a suit that didn't quite fit.

"What?" Burn asked, so stunned by his appearance that she gave no thought to his words. "What did you say?"

"They want to know how we got our gifts," he said again, raking his eyes over her face like she was air and he was fighting to breathe. "They're capturing us and studying us so they can understand us. So they can defeat us."

Hale leaned against the wall, his strength fading. Burn couldn't stop herself any longer. She jumped from the bed and rushed to his side, wrapping her arms around him as if she could protect him from the world.

"I'm sorry," she said as she held him, propping him up and squeezing him as tight as she dared. "I'm so sorry they hurt you."

And she was, although it was more than that. She was

sorry she'd left him, that she'd turned her back. She was sorry she'd walked away and left him and not told him how she felt. She was sorry that because he'd changed his face – and she'd changed hers – she'd thought they no longer fit together like they should.

She put all of that into her words, willing him to understand. Because none of it mattered – not the faces they wore or the roles they played or the things they'd done. Beneath it all, he was Hale and she was Burn and she loved him like the night loved the stars. And she needed him to know.

"You saved me," Hale said softly, his eyes traveling up to meet hers.

And in those eyes, she saw him – Hale. She saw his joy and his sadness and his pain. And his love. Love that matched her own and sent her heart soaring.

They stood like that for one suspended moment, their eyes locked and bodies entwined. But Burn could see that his strength was fading, that the light was dimming from his eyes. So she helped him to the bed and laid him down, settling him gently amongst the pillows and blankets.

He sighed as he relaxed, relishing the softness. His eyes closed for just a second before he fixed them back on her, his light in the darkness. He kept them there, trained on her face, as if the sight of her would heal his wounds and fix his soul.

Burn knew that wasn't the case. He needed a doctor – or a healer – but that was more difficult than it sounded.

"What happened?" she prodded, needing to know more in order to help. "What did they do to you?"

Hale sighed again. Beside her, Kaz sat on the edge of

the bed, bracing for the tale. On the other end of the comms, Scar was silent, but Burn could tell she was there, computing their words and cataloging the data.

"They didn't trust me from the start," he began in a faraway voice, his eyes and his mind now somewhere else entirely, tracing the threads of a story only he knew. "They hated that we *beat* them, that we managed to make it in from the wildlands and past their defenses. They were looking for someone to blame, and Raqa was an easy target.

"Of course, they didn't want to kill him. Or me," he corrected himself, shaking his head. "I was the only spy they had inside the Lunaria, and they still thought I could be useful. But they were guarded, cagey. They came to me with demands, and when I asked questions, tried to pry out more intel, they shut me down."

Hale sagged, and Burn couldn't tell if it was from exhaustion or defeat. He'd gone in with excitement, with a light in his eyes and a passion for the cause, but they'd broken him, beaten him down in more ways than one.

"I gave them the information we agreed on," he continued, closing his eyes. "It was small things. The location of a rarely used safe house. The identity of an operative who had perished, one they didn't know was gone. They put the people on their watchlists and conducted searches of the properties, but they came up empty.

"They wanted more. They demanded the location of the operatives who had gone into hiding. I told them that most of us had died and the rest had scattered, dispersed by the threat of the price on their heads. Yet they never fully believed it." Hale shook his head, rubbing at his eyes.

"I fed them other lies, too – about how defenseless we were, how weak. *That* they believed. Hell, they've always thought of us as pathetic. But, of course, that information didn't do them any good. It didn't get them any closer to ending the Lunaria. All it did was stroke their egos."

He fell silent for a second, and Burn could feel his frustration and disdain, his need to do something and his utter inability to help.

"It's OK," she told him, placing her hand gingerly on his. "You did everything you could, everything we told you to do. I…" she broke off, the emotion cracking through. "I thought it was a good idea. I thought it could get us some answers. I was wrong – and I am truly sorry. It's all my fault."

The pain she'd been feeling since she'd learned of his disappearance came bubbling to the surface, resolving itself into an aching guilt. She had devised the idea of using Raqa's body to infiltrate the Peace Force, and when the Lunaria had questioned her, she had convinced them to comply.

"I volunteered," Hale responded, an anger in his voice. "I put myself in this body. I believed I was strong enough to take them on alone. I was reckless, and it's no one's fault but mine."

A lengthy pause enveloped them. Kaz finally broke the silence, stirring from his stillness to move the story onward.

"How did they finally get you?" he asked, his voice gentle yet firm. "We didn't think that anyone could take *you* down."

Hale laughed, but there was no mirth in the sound. His eyes remained hard as he flashed back to that time, immersing himself in the story.

"Raqa made a mistake. The real Raqa," Hale said,

exhaling in frustration. "He let it slip that he was gifted. He probably bragged about his abilities. Thought the Peace Force would admire him for his way with technology, but they never saw him as anything other than a *freak*.

"They'd been gathering mutants, rounding them up," he continued. "I hadn't been able to figure out why, but I knew they were going missing, especially in the poorer areas of Kasis. I thought I was safe because I was valuable, but apparently that value was limited. As soon as I stopped being useful as a spy, they decided to make me useful in other ways."

He clenched his fists in his lap until his knuckles went white. It was clear that he was trying to suppress the anger, but it ate at him, worming its way into his mind and onto the tight planes of his face.

"We met like usual in an abandoned building near the bottom of the city. I fed them intel and they pretended to listen, but something was off. I could feel it. Then they told me they wanted to take me somewhere. They wanted to show me what they were working on. I suppose they weren't lying. I did get a front-row seat to their *project*." He let out another mirthless chuckle.

"There were four of them, all armed. When I refused to go with them, they came for me. Naturally, I fought back – and I won. Or I thought I had. Except they'd come with reinforcements. They managed to surround me. I fell, and they laughed. They said I'd been holding out on them, that I was an even bigger *freak* than they'd realized. That I would come in handy."

The muscles in his jaw tightened at the insult, and his eyes narrowed into slits. Burn could see he was losing the battle, losing himself. So she reached out and pulled him back.

"Where did they take you?" she asked, willing him to look at her. "What did they do to you?"

"They knocked me out," he said, refusing to meet her eyes. "When I woke up, I was in that room. It was so cold. I tried to get out, to break free, but they'd dosed me with something. No matter how hard I tried, my body wouldn't obey. So I lay there, staring at the ceiling, waiting for them to come for me."

Burn flashed back to him in the lab, cold and pale and helpless, and fury roared to life in her chest. She wanted to find the people that had done that, to hunt them down and make them pay. They had hurt Hale, and she wanted to hurt them in return, to make them bleed and scream and pray for mercy.

"I finally heard them coming, but I couldn't move. I could only watch as they studied me, their eyes filled with glee. They wore lab coats and masks, parading as doctors, but underneath they were demons. They hooked me up to machines and watched them beep as they cut me, draining my blood and marrow. They beat me and strangled me and drowned me. They watched with detachment as I nearly died again and again and again."

Hale began to shake, his body lurching at the memories. He tried to hold himself together, to carry on as the pain took hold, but he didn't have the strength. So Burn reached out and held him, giving him some of hers. Eventually, he drew back and embarked on his tale once more.

"They finally ran out of ways to test me. I was barely

conscious, on the verge of giving in, but I held on, listening as they talked. It felt like a dream, yet I know it was real."

"What did they say?" Burn asked, urging him on.

"They said that they were close, that I might be the key, although to what I have no idea. They'd been running the tests for years, they said, and it was finally paying off. All those humans they'd captured – and all the *freaks*."

"Wait, they didn't just take mutants?" Kaz asked, interrupting the story. "What use could they have for those that aren't gifted?"

Hale shrugged, shaking his head. "I don't know. Maybe they were the controls, the baseline. But I did hear those damn doctors say that they were finally beginning to understand us, to trace how mutants came to be in Kasis. They said their work would be the beginning of the end, that understanding us was the first step to defeating us. That the balance of power was shifting."

"Do you think they know how to strip us of our powers?" It was Scar's voice on the line, a ghost without a body, and the trio started, surprised at her presence.

"Is that even possible?" Kaz asked, aiming the question at no one in particular. "Can they take our gifts away?"

The room dropped into silence as the question lingered, chafing at their nerves. Even Scar remained silent as the theory took hold, propelling itself into her fears.

"Did they say anything else?" Burn probed, turning back to Hale, but the man had succumbed to the silence, dropping out of consciousness and into sleep.

Burn smiled sadly, unwilling to wake him. She watched as his chest rose and fell, listening to the steady melody of his breath. It soothed something inside of her to have him there, yet she knew it couldn't last.

"We need to get him to Crete," she whispered to Kaz. "He can't stay."

"I know," Kaz said with a sigh, running his hand through his hair. "We'll figure it out in the morning. Right now, you should sleep. We should all get some sleep."

With a small smile, he rose, padding to the door and slipping outside. Burn followed as far as the threshold, locking it behind him. Then she returned to the bed – returned to Hale – and climbed in, pressing her body to his. Before she knew it, she was drifting away, lost to the darkness and lulled into sleep by the rhythm of his heart.

Chapter 13

Scar felt anxious and she hated it. She wanted answers, but all she had was the night, stretching on like a chasm before her, its yawning maw intent on swallowing her.

She couldn't imagine herself without her gift. It was who she was and how she understood the world. It gave her context amidst the confusion and the power to create something from nothing. Who would she be if she were forced to live without it?

The question rang in her mind like a bell, too loud and too insistent. She tried to lose herself in work, to sink into the comfort of the data she'd recovered, but even that couldn't distract her.

Each file she decrypted was another life, another person who had fallen prey to the Peace Force. Or to the assembly. It wasn't clear who was running these experiments, who was directing the course of the future, but Scar had an inkling it was the latter.

Sure, Peace Officers were formidable, but the assembly's members were gods. All-powerful, all-knowing, all-consumed by their own importance. To gods, a mere life meant nothing – just a blip on the radar or a drop in the sea. While the Peace Force played, the Shadow Assembly reigned, doling out life and death without consequence or conscience.

Scar wanted to bite back, to fight back, but it was futile, like dueling with the wind. She couldn't see them, couldn't touch them, couldn't strike. They were an enemy with no face and no form, yet with claws that could kill.

Scar scrolled through the data on her tab, searching for their scent. Yet she was no doctor, no scientist, and the sequences stumped her, shoving her back each time she pushed on.

Frustration lingered at the edges of her mind, threatening to break free. It curled in smoky tendrils as she read, distorting the words and numbers until they lost all value. Then, all at once, her irritation broke free and she slammed her hand against the desk, letting out an angry cry.

"What does it mean?" she asked the screen, as if it had the power to reply.

"I don't know – but have you considered asking for help?"

It wasn't the screen that had spoken, although Scar's tired mind considered the possibility. Except the voice was too light, too playful to ever emanate from a machine. Turning, Scar spied Nara leaning lazily in the doorway, considering her.

"How long have you been there?" Scar asked, raising an eyebrow.

"Not long," Nara said with a shrug. "I saw you were still

up and thought I'd come check in. It looks like it's a good thing I did."

"I'm fine," Scar shot back, an instinct honed over many years.

"Right…" Nara said slowly, her insightful gaze still focused on Scar. "Because shouting at your tab is a completely normal thing to do." The sarcasm oozed from her words like lava, spilling over the edge and creeping steadily toward Scar.

"What would you do if you lost your gift?"

The question was so sudden that it caught Nara off guard, filling her face with confusion. In an instant, though, it cleared, replaced by her typical steady gaze.

"It would suck, but I'd live," she stated plainly.

"But your gift is who you are," Scar said, almost like a question.

"True," Nara said with a shrug, "but it's not all I am."

Scar grimaced. "OK…but what if it's all that I am? What if it's so tied to my identity that without it, I'd disappear?"

"You're an idiot," Nara told her, shaking her head.

"Excuse me?" Scar was taken aback, thrust out of her contemplation and into an icy pool.

"You are so clever, but sometimes you don't understand the simplest things," she said, taking a few steps toward Scar. "Even without your gift, you would still be you. Smart, driven, beautiful."

Scar couldn't blush, but the words sent a warmth to her cheeks, making her feel flushed. She watched as the woman approached, coming closer and closer with each word.

"Our powers are an extension of us, an enhancement of our natural gifts," she said, seating herself on the cot Scar had erected next to her workspace.

Nara was so close now that their knees were nearly touching, but the smallest of gaps lay between them, tempting Scar to close it, to reach out and connect.

"You don't need your gift to be amazing," she continued, leaning forward toward Scar. "You're already bright on your own. Your gift merely helps you shine."

Her eyes were so big and dark that Scar felt like she could swim inside them, losing herself in their depths. Nara stared back with the barest hint of a smile, her lips parted and her face laid bare. Yet still the space lingered between them, charged with a current of anticipation.

With one fluid movement, Nara reached out, breaking the barrier and pulling Scar's head to hers. She paused on the precipice, their noses touching and their breath entwined, before closing the gap, bringing her lips to Scar's in a crushing kiss that made Scar's mind go blank.

After a second, Scar drew her in closer, relishing the feel of Nara's lips and the warmth of her form. They stayed like that for some time, the world falling away at their feet until nothing was left but them. Eventually, they parted, giving in to their need for air, but they remained close, with hands and legs and feet pressed together in an intimate embrace.

"Why are you even worried about that?" Nara asked once they'd regained their breath. "Why are you afraid of losing your gift?"

Her hands moved gently over Scar's curls, tracing the mess of hair and wires, and she tucked a few strands behind her ear in a gentle caress. Scar wanted to lean into her, to keep the world at bay, but she knew she couldn't.

Sighing, she filled Nara in on the night's events. "Burn and Kaz found Hale, which you've probably heard. His captors had been testing him, *torturing* him. They were looking for something. And he wasn't alone. Whoever took him has been studying mutants for years. Our best guess is that they're looking for a way to remove our gifts, to make us like them. Only, I can't read the data. I can decrypt it, but it doesn't make any sense."

Nara contemplated that, drawing away as the gravity settled. Yet she didn't look concerned.

"You should ask Crete to take a look," she advised, tilting her head to indicate the tab.

"Crete is just a healer," Scar said, confused. "How would he be able to help?"

Nara rolled her eyes, giving Scar an exasperated look. "That's like saying you *just* fix computers," she said. "Have you ever even talked to the man? I mean when you or Burn weren't in need of medical attention?"

Scar shrugged.

"You really need to leave your room sometimes and actually talk to people," Nara told her. "His gift isn't that different from yours. He doesn't just heal people. He understands people – how their bodies work and how they break. He knows more than you think."

Scar considered her words. "I guess it couldn't hurt," she said, still not completely convinced.

Nara smiled, sensing her doubt. "You don't have to do everything alone, you know. There is a whole group of people here who want to help. You simply have to be brave enough to ask."

Scar had never been good at asking for help. In all fairness, she'd never felt the need. She was always the one who provided the assistance, the one with the knowledge and the know-how and the gadgets. Nevertheless, Nara had a point. Scar couldn't do this one alone.

"Where is he now?" Scar asked, standing abruptly and gearing up to go.

"He's in one of the rooms on the lower floor," Nara responded slowly, reservation tinging her tone. "But, Scar, it's the middle of the night. I'm sure he's asleep."

"We're at war," Scar said with a humorless smirk. "Sleep isn't a luxury we can afford." With that, she set off toward the stairs.

Crete was, indeed, asleep, and he did not enjoy being awoken by an insistent Scar and a reluctant Nara and a firm shake of the shoulder. Yet as soon as Scar explained their presence – and brought him his glasses and a cup of coffee – he perked up, eager to be of use.

Scar realized then that Nara had been right. She didn't really know the man. Sure, he had patched up Burn on more than one occasion, but she knew little of his life before the Lunaria, of how he'd come to be there and why he'd stayed.

"What did you do before you joined us?" she asked, taking Nara's advice and *actually talking* to the man.

Crete looked amused, no doubt wondering why it had taken her so long to ask – and why she'd finally chosen to do so in the wee hours of the morning. Still, he humored her, embarking on his story.

"I had a small practice on the lower tiers," he told them, smiling sadly. "I tried to help those who couldn't afford care.

165

I accepted anything they could give – canned food, broken gadgets, live chickens." He shook his head at the last one. "I did what I could for their injuries and illnesses, but my power only stretched so far. For some, all I could do was help ease the pain."

"How did you end up in the Peace Force's clutches?" Scar prodded, remembering how he'd come to them before the ManniK Battles.

Crete had been part of a prisoner transfer headed toward the Pit when Hale and his crew had intervened. Thanks to the Lunaria, Crete had been spared – along with almost 30 other prisoners. Yet Scar had a hard time believing that this gentle man would ever do anything that demanded a death sentence.

Crete's mouth thinned into a tight line. "It wasn't an active thing. I didn't hurt anyone or plan to. I wasn't a rebel. I was just a doctor."

"And they arrested you for that?" Scar asked, her voice doubtful.

"It's never that simple," he said, removing his glasses and cleaning them on his shirt. "An injured man came to me for help. He was in bad shape, his arm broken, his face bruised, his clothes covered in blood. He said there'd been an accident, and I agreed to treat him, but I knew he was lying."

"So why did you help him, then?" It was Nara's turn to ask. She sat beside the man on his cot, giving him the full force of her gaze.

"He was hurt, and I could help. So I did." He put his glasses back on and turned his magnified eyes to Nara.

"But he was on the run, a fugitive from the force, and they

came for him. They tore my surgery to shreds even though we were hidden in plain sight. They shot him, of course, but they grabbed me, intrigued by my gift. Except I refused to use it on them. So they starved me, forgot about me, left me to rot. Then one day they came for me, dragging me away to my death. Thankfully, the Lunaria got to me first." He smiled then, a genuine smile, and his face lit up with warmth.

"There's no shortage of people I can help here. Each day brings a new battle and new wounds. But I like being useful. I enjoy the work, and I believe in your cause."

"That's good to hear," Scar said, "because we need your help again." She pulled Tellus' data up on the tab, handing it to Crete.

"What can you make of this?" she asked. "It's data from the experiments being run on the gifted, but we can't read it. We need to know what they're doing, what they're planning. We need to know if they intend to take away our gifts – and how far they are from achieving it."

Crete considered her words, nodding in understanding. Then he lowered his head, engrossing himself in the data.

Scar watched him read, watched his fine eyebrows crease and his forehead wrinkle. He looked healthier than he had before, when their battles had consumed his strength and eaten away at his gift. Now there was meat on his bones, a fullness to his cheeks, a curve of muscle along his shoulders.

That was good, Scar thought. He would need his strength for what was coming. They all would.

Minutes ticked by in silence as Crete worked, jotting down notes and equations. Scar envied the way he understood the data, how easily it changed from figures to facts.

As he studied the tests, Scar studied him, wondering what he saw – although she didn't have to wait long to find out.

"You were right. Or at least partially," he said, making Scar's stomach drop. "These researchers are attempting to isolate the mutated genes that give us our gifts. They're trying to understand how we got them, but they're not trying to remove them."

"Then what are they doing?" Scar's voice was too loud, too insistent, but she didn't care. She wanted answers.

"It's difficult to say for certain. This is only the raw data, without the scientists' notes or any background on the tests. If I had to guess, though, they're trying to use our genetic sequences to alter their own."

"What does that mean?" Nara asked, shaking her head in confusion.

Crete sighed, bracing himself for what came next. "I think they're trying to give themselves gifts – and I think they're close to achieving it."

Scar and Nara blanched, each taken by surprise.

"But how?" Scar breathed, trying to understand his words, to process their meaning.

"This data goes back nearly a decade," Crete said, scrolling to the top of the file. "At first, they were just running general tests, likely in hopes of preventing future mutations. After a few years, though, they abandoned that line of research. Maybe they realized they couldn't stop the changes – or that they could use the mutations to their advantage."

"So they started trying to *manufacture* mutants?" Scar asked, spitting out the word like it was poison.

Crete nodded. "After that, their data focuses almost

exclusively on cataloging mutants' genomes. They didn't have many test subjects to start with, but in the last few years, the data pool has grown exponentially."

"That explains all the gifted citizens that are going missing," said Nara, a sharp edge cutting through her voice.

"And the increase in wrongful arrests among our kind," Scar chimed in.

"Most likely," Crete agreed. "But around that time, they also started inputting data from nonmutants."

"We thought those were the controls, the baseline by which to judge the mutants' data," Scar said, giving him Hale's theory.

"Maybe in the early years, but they'd already taken the samples they needed," Crete told her, shaking his head. "What they still lacked, however, was test subjects. Guinea pigs."

"Wait, you don't mean…" Nara said, a horrified expression passing over her face.

"I'm afraid so. They've been taking normal citizens and subjecting them to all manner of procedures in hopes of turning them into mutants. Unfortunately – or fortunately, depending on how you look at it – most of the subjects perished. Those that didn't came out…wrong."

Crete shuddered, and a chill swept through the room, filling it with apprehension. Images of gruesome experiments, of twisted bodies and misshapen limbs floated through Scar's mind, making her feel ill. She clamped down on the disconcerting thoughts, willing them to clear.

"But you said that they're close," she said, breaking the silence. "How can you tell?"

Crete paled at the question, returning his gaze to the tab and navigating to the end.

"Because their last test group survived," he said, his eyes going glassy, "and they all showed signs of having powers."

Chapter 14

An insistent knocking startled Burn awake. Glancing beside her, she saw that Hale was still asleep, although the rest had done little to heal his wounded form. In the early morning light, his skin looked sallow, and his bruises stood out stark against it.

The knocking came again, louder and more adamant. Burn could tell she had only moments before her guest would forgo pleasantries and simply let themselves in with a key. Locked doors only did so much in a house without trust.

"Just a minute," she shouted, panic swelling within her.

She turned to Hale and shook him, but he didn't wake. She shook him harder, but his eyes remained closed. Fearful, she checked his breathing, but it was even beneath his chest.

Launching out of bed, she tore loose the curtains that were tied to the bed's posts, wrenching them closed. With Hale obscured in his fabric coffin, she leapt toward the threshold, reaching the door right as it swung open before her.

"What the hell took you so long?" Una demanded, her face red with irritation.

"I'm sorry, mother," Burn said, lowering her head while consciously trying to block Una's view of the bed. "I'm still recovering from last night's attack. I didn't mean to make you wait."

She thought the mention of her faux assault would soften Una, but of course she was mistaken. Una scoffed, frowning at her daughter.

"Do you really expect me to believe that?" she spat, shaking her head in derision. "If what Officer Petala said is true, then that man barely touched you. Your weakness is your own. Don't try to blame it on others."

Una shoved Burn aside with surprising strength and strode into the room, moving straight to the windows. With practiced ease, she pushed the curtains aside, drenching the space in light.

"Your recent behaviors have been an embarrassment to this family," Una continued. "The way you treated Ignis and Iris – and the way you treated me. It has become increasingly clear that you have no respect for authority. You do not know your place."

Una opened the final set of drapes and turned toward the bed, setting her sights on its curtains. Burn's heart sped up, sensing the danger. She couldn't let Una open them, couldn't let her see the man within. Even if she didn't know who Raqa was, a man in her daughter's bed would certainly trigger an onslaught of questions – ones that she couldn't answer.

"And where is my place, *mother*?" Burn asked, drawing

Una's attention toward her. "Is it kneeling in front of some man like a piece of property?"

Una rounded on her. Before Burn could raise a hand in defense, her mother slapped her, knocking her head to the side as a sharp flash of pain blossomed on her cheek. Yet Burn remained silent, turning to her mother with a look of pure defiance.

"You can't control me," Burn said, and for once she was fully herself – not Ellis, not a Hyde, not a member of the insufferable elite. "I am my own person and I make my own decisions."

Una laughed. It was such an unexpected response that Burn froze, uncertain of what to do.

"Is that what you think?" Una asked, turning back to the bed. "I thought you were smarter than that."

Without another word, she yanked back the fabric shielding the bed – shielding Hale. Burn acted without thinking. In one quiet move, she reached for the lamp near the bed, raising it over her head. At the first sound of a scream, she would strike.

Yet the scream never came. Instead, Una moved on, drawing back the remaining curtains until the bed was laid bare, its sheets rumpled but empty.

Burn stared at the mess of blankets, certain that Hale had been there. Yet the bed was vacant. The entirety of the room lay exposed, yet no man could be seen within it.

"What are you doing with that lamp?" Una asked, turning to face her daughter. "Did you intend to fight me?" she scoffed.

"No, mother. Of course not," she said, placing the lamp

back on its perch.

Una stared at her, unconvinced. Yet a moment later, she smiled, shaking off the concern like it was nothing more than a bug on her gown.

"I have a little surprise for you," she said with an evil gleam in her eyes. "Well, technically I have two, but the first one is really for me and your father. And your future husband, of course."

Burn wanted to retort that she would never marry, that she would rather live the rest of her days within the Corax End than be sold as a bride, but something in Una's tone stopped her. She took an involuntary step back, putting more distance between them, but she should have known that no amount of space could save her from her mother's spiteful machinations.

As if on cue, two male orderlies dressed head to toe in white entered the room, their sights set on her. She looked to Una for an explanation, but the woman only smiled, exposing her teeth in a predator's grin. A bubble of dread rose in Burn's chest as the men advanced, their arms outstretched.

Burn backed away from their hungry clutches, retreating through the room until she hit the far wall. With nowhere else to go, she raised her hands to fight, but these men were quicker. In the blink of an eye, they'd captured her arms, pinning them to her sides and forcing her forward.

She raged against their hold, but their grasps didn't loosen, and they dragged her across the room, seating her in a chair by her mother's side. Their hands moved to her shoulders with practiced ease, and they held her down while she kicked and clawed and screamed.

"What the hell are you doing? Let go of me!" she cried, attempting to bite one of her captors on the forearm.

She just managed to rake her teeth across a curve of muscle before a hand rose up to strike. Burn had no time to brace herself as the fist made contact, knocking her sideways.

By the time the world stopped spinning, another white-clad figure had materialized beside her. This time it was a woman in a mid-length lab coat, and she held a syringe in one hand, a placid look plastered on her face.

"Hold still, dear," she told Burn in a sing-song voice as she brought the needle closer. "This will only hurt for a moment. I promise."

Of course, Burn did the opposite of what she was told. Squirming in her seat, she made every effort to liberate herself from her prison, but her guards held tight. The nurse tsked her disapproval, but she didn't stop her advance, and soon the needle was biting into the skin beneath Burn's shoulder.

Burn could hear it all – the release of the needle, the drug leeching into her arm, her veins carrying it through her body with every beat of her heart. For a few glorious seconds, nothing happened, and Burn prayed that the drug wouldn't work, that she would be mercifully immune to its poison.

Soon, though, a stiffness took hold in her limbs, and the more she tried to move, the more her muscles resisted. Her fingers and toes slowed then stopped, followed by her hands and feet, her arms and legs. Before long, her whole body refused to respond even as she strained with every fiber of her being.

Only her mind remained free. And her tongue.

"What have you done to me?" she asked from frozen lips as the orderlies released her.

"Oh, this?" Una asked, the picture of innocence. "This is nothing – merely the appetizer before the main course. The drug will wear off in a few hours, and you'll be back to your normal self. We just needed to make sure you'd be compliant for what comes next."

The words rang in her ears as she waited, braced for the worst. *What comes next.* Would it be torture? Mutilation? Some effort to break her, to shape her into the perfect daughter and wife? Although her body was frozen, it wasn't numb, and she'd be able to feel every slice, every strike. She was expecting pain, hot and angry and bright.

What she wasn't expecting was Ellis' father. Nevertheless, Baylor strode into the room, quiet and poised, with a simple smile and a wooden box.

"Hi, honey," he said evenly, as if all of this was normal, as if she hadn't been attacked and drugged and forced to submit. "Glad to see you're doing so well. We were worried after last night. You gave us a scare."

What was wrong with these people? They were deranged, unbalanced, unhinged. They treated her like she was property instead of family, something to be owned and wielded and bartered away.

"Go to hell," Burn whispered as Baylor came to a halt beside her.

"That's no way to speak to your father," Una said, coming around to face her. "Have you no respect for your superiors, Ellis?"

"Now, now, Una," Baylor crooned, patting his wife's arm.

"She's had a difficult few days. I'm sure she'll come around. And if not – well, she won't be our problem for long."

The threat hung in the air between them, and they smiled, relishing its power. Burn, on the other hand, seethed beneath the surface, fighting the drug's hold and failing. She struggled against the helplessness, the hopelessness, but it rose within her, coursing through her static limbs and rising through her chest, ready to choke her.

Beside her, Baylor knelt, fingering the box. He freed its metal clasp and reached inside, caressing its contents. Then, with gentle hands, he drew from its depths a small black gun.

Burn's panic turned to outrage then anxiety then fear. It clung to her like tar, hot and thick and dark, coating her body and muting her brain. Reason and logic fled, leaving only feelings and need and a burning desire to flee.

Baylor reached into the box once again, drawing out the ammo. Only, it wasn't a bullet he held. It was a chip.

"What are you doing?" she asked as the confusion descended, wiping away the fog. "What is that thing?"

"I warned you this would happen," he told her, shaking his head. "We asked you to play nice. We asked you to obey."

"I did!" she cried as he loaded the gun, placing the chip in its chamber. "I didn't go down to the lower tiers. I listened to what you said."

"No, darling, you didn't," he retorted calmly as if speaking to a child. "You put yourself in danger. You put this family in danger. You've been careless and reckless, and now it's up to us to ensure your safety. Tagging you is the only way to make sure you'll always be protected. We're doing this because we care."

In one fluid sweep, he brought the gun to her arm, placing it just below her shoulder. Moving his finger to the trigger, he pulled, and a blinding pain shot through her, tearing her arm apart. She let loose an agonizing scream as the chip lodged itself in her body, a foreign object in a foreign host.

Blood began to pour from the wound, and the nurse bent down to bandage it.

"You'll be sore for a few days," she said, her delicate voice a match for her delicate hands. "Try not to move your shoulder, as it will aggravate the wound. You should regain movement in a few hours. Until then, try to relax. The hard part is over."

Burn doubted that very much, but she had no more strength left to speak, no more energy to protest. She remained silent as the men lifted her and carried her to the bed. She said nothing as the orderlies left, as the nurse gathered her things and followed, as her mother closed the curtains, nearly yanking the fabric off the posts.

Yet silence wasn't one of her strong suits, and when her mother spoke, she couldn't help but reply.

"Now that we've dealt with you, my dear, it's time to pay a visit to Officer Petala," Una said with malicious glee. "The man has some explaining to do."

"No!" Burn cried as her mother turned to go. "This was my fault, not his. Kaz has done nothing wrong. Leave him be!"

"It's Kaz now, is it? I didn't know you two had gotten so close. That should make this all the more satisfying." With a little chuckle, she turned out the lights and left.

Burn remained still. She had no other choice. The drug

lingered in her veins, holding her down, fusing her to the bed. She needed to warn Kaz, to tell him what was coming, to command him to run.

"Kaz! Kaz!" she cried, pleading with the darkness.

And for once, the darkness responded. A muffled groan escaped from under her, a sound of pain and fury and force. Burn gasped at the sound, stunned by its nearness – until she remembered Hale.

"Hale? Are you there? Are you alright?" she whispered, praying for an answer.

From beneath the bed, a form emerged, sliding out in laborious lurches. Burn could tell that it pained him, that it took all he had and more to move, but he kept going until he'd freed himself. Standing, he wavered, swaying precariously before collapsing on the bed beside her.

"I'm sorry," he said from between clenched teeth. "I'm sorry I couldn't help you. I'm sorry I left you alone."

"It doesn't matter," she said, trying to turn her head and failing. "What matters is saving Kaz – then getting you both out of here."

Hale started to speak but she interjected. "There's no time. You have to call Kaz and warn him. Use my bracelet. Tell him to come. He should be able to get through the house unseen."

Hale did as she instructed, relaying her words to Kaz, and Burn waited with bated breath for a response. The silence ticked by, spanning one second, then two before a voice finally answered.

"I'm on my way," Kaz said in a huff, already starting to run, and Burn thanked the gods for this small mercy.

Within no time, he was there, slipping through the doorway like a ghost and appearing beside them.

"Shit. What happened?" he asked, leaning in to examine her.

"They injected a paralyzing agent then tagged me," she explained as quickly as she could. "I'll survive, but you two won't if you stay here. After last night's events, Una and Baylor are out for blood. They've already gotten their pound of flesh from me, but I bet your sentence will be worse. Take Hale and go. Now."

"Damn it! It's all my fault," Kaz cried, slamming his fist against the bed. "I came up with that stupid story. I got you into this."

"It doesn't matter," she said, her frustration rising to the surface. "Just get Hale out of the heavens and down to the Lunaria. Get him to Crete."

"What about you?" Kaz demanded, his voice turning grave. "I won't leave you here – not with *those people*."

"You have to," Burn shot back. "Hale can't even stand on his own, and you don't have the strength to carry us both. If I could call in reinforcements, I would, but we don't have the time."

"Fine," Kaz said with reluctance. "How do you suggest we get down? By now, Raqa must be on the Peace Force's watchlist, and the guards will be on the lookout. We'll be scanned for sure."

"With your gift, you may be able to pass by unnoticed," Burn whispered, gradually regaining some feeling in her lips. "If you do get stopped, tell them you found the fugitive sneaking around the heavens, and you're taking him to the

Peace Station for questioning."

"And if they don't believe us?" Hale asked. "What then? We can't exactly shoot them. It would draw too much attention."

"Take my pack," Burn advised. "Use Scar's gadgets. Do whatever it takes. Just get yourself home. Once you're safe, send the pack back to me. Use Coal. Disguise him as another officer. He should be able to pass by unquestioned."

The two men considered her plan, both looking uneasy. Yet neither put forth another idea. Burn could tell they were trying, racking their brains for another solution, but there simply wasn't a way to save them all.

"I still don't want to leave you," Kaz said, his voice tight.

"And I still can't come," she replied. "I may be able to salvage the mission. There's still more I can do here, but you two have done your parts. It's time for you to go."

Finally, grudgingly, they obeyed. Kaz grabbed her pack, slinging it across his back before moving to Hale. With a grunt, he hoisted the man up and helped him stand, guiding him to the door. Before they left, they turned, taking one last look.

"I'll come back for you, Auburn," Kaz whispered before turning to go.

"We both will," came Hale's strained voice.

A second later, the pair was gone, leaving Burn alone to fight back the darkness.

Chapter 15

Burn drifted in and out of sleep, her dreams plagued by the same monsters that haunted her reality. Una, Baylor, Ignis, the faceless assembly. They came for her like vultures, circling her corpse, and she lay there rigid, straining to move.

Gradually, though, her body began to awaken, slowly coming back to life. First her fingers, then her feet, then her arms. They felt too heavy, too solid, too clumsy, and moving even the slightest bit took energy she didn't have.

While she waited, she worried, casting her thoughts to Kaz and Hale. Were they safe? Had they made it down? Had they made it home? She knew she could do nothing for their cause, that their fates rested solely with them, but it didn't soothe the fear that had made a home in her heart, nesting like a bird.

Burn needed a plan. She was alone now, unprotected. She could be tracked and trailed and taken. She was exposed.

Yet her mission remained in place, and she was close.

She could feel it, sense it like a ghostly force. Invisible hands were moving pieces, playing games, and she could just about make out the strings. Finding Hale had been the crack that would open the door, laying their actions bare. Now she just needed to push.

She could no longer lurk in the shadows, scouting out homes and offices and lives – but perhaps she didn't have to. Perhaps the answer lay closer than she'd ever realized.

Baylor. If he was truly part of the assembly, maybe he could lead her to them. He could be her pilot, her path through the darkness, her guiding star. If she followed him, stalked his movements, maybe he'd lead her to the truth.

With her purpose clear in her mind, Burn sat up. It felt as if her body were made of lead, and she panted with the effort of moving, but it was impossible to stay still. With trembling legs, she stood, bracing herself on the bed. Then she began to walk.

Each step was an eternity, a trial, a test of her endurance, but she persisted, making her way across the endless stretch of room. Finally reaching the wall, she threw open the blinds, letting the light of the afternoon suns penetrate the depths. Exhausted and out of breath, she returned to her bed and picked up the comms.

"Scar? Are you there?" she asked.

"I'm here," Scar said in an instant, alert and on her guard. "What happened? I've been trying to reach you for hours."

"It's a long story," Burn told her, shaking her head and cringing at its stiffness. "I'll tell you in a minute, but first I need to know: Are Hale and Kaz safe? Did they make it back?"

A pause stretched between them, stiff and prickly, before Scar responded. "They're not here, Burn. But why would they be? What happened?" she asked again, more insistent this time.

Burn's heart constricted in worry. They should have made it back by now. She knew they could be fine, simply taking their time to descend, but something felt wrong, rotten, and she couldn't help but imagine the worst.

"Give me a sec," Burn said, and she broke off, severing her ties with Scar.

She tried to connect to Kaz, speaking low into the comms, but she received no answer. With a frustrated sigh, she turned back to Scar, the unease mounting within her.

"Burn?" her sister queried, shaking her from her qualms. "Are you there? Tell me what's going on."

Burn sighed and embarked on her tale. She tried to gloss over her pain, to skip the scenes that might make Scar's temper flare, but her sister knew her too well. Scar poked and pried at the story, resolving its rough edges and shoring up its details.

"You need to get out of there," Scar commanded once the tale had been told. "You're not safe. It's time to end this."

"No!" Burn said fervently, the heat rising to her cheeks. "I will not abandon my mission. Not when I've gotten this far. I know I can find out more about the assembly. I just need time!"

"You don't have time. You're unarmed and unguarded," Scar retorted. "The top tiers are no place for a mutant. Not now. Burn, the assembly is trying to give themselves powers. They may have already succeeded. You are outmatched on every level. Stop trying to be a god damn savior and come home!"

Burn paused, processing what her sister had said. The truth of it lodged in her bones, and a chill of apprehension rippled down her spine. She saw a hundred possible futures, each more gruesome than the last, and her resolve hardened, lending her strength.

Calmly, she spoke. "I can't come back. We need to discover exactly what the assembly is planning. If we quit now, we will never get another chance. They will win, and they will crush us to dust in the process."

"We'll come up with another plan," Scar insisted. "We'll find another way."

"It's too late," Burn told her. "By now they'll know we took Raqa. They'll know we saw their lab and their data. They'll know we're on to them, and they'll be preparing to strike back."

A loud sigh crackled through the comms as Scar made peace with Burn's stubbornness, coming to terms with the fact that she'd never be able to change her sister's mind.

"Fine," she grumbled in submission, "but at least wait until we return your pack. You can't go around unarmed. Hale and Kaz should be here soon, and when they arrive, I'll send someone back with your things. Until then, hang tight. Don't go searching for trouble."

"What if trouble is already in here with me?" Burn breathed, glancing around as if it might be lurking in the shadows.

"Don't. Do. Anything. Stupid," Scar stressed, speaking in a forced staccato. "I mean it, Burn. Stay put until we can get to you."

"Alright," Burn shot back, her own voice clipped. "I'll wait as long as I can, but you better make it quick. I have a feeling I won't be able to stay put for long."

She promptly signed off, turning down the comms and fastening it around her wrist. Some of her strength had returned by then, and she opened her wardrobe to change, throwing on a pair of linen pants and a silk blouse before rising to go.

She hadn't lied to Scar, although she hadn't told her the whole truth. She wasn't going to leave the house, to search outside it for answers, but she wasn't planning to stay still, either.

As soon as she'd determined that the coast was clear, Burn slid into the hall, her ears peeled for movement. The house was never silent, but it was calm, with mere hints of sound skirting the periphery. There were whispers of activity in the dining room and kitchens, the living room and her parents' bedroom, but otherwise the path lay open, beckoning her to explore.

Burn moved straight for her father's study, making a beeline across the house. Without her pack, she had no tools, no bypass, no plan to circumvent locked doors. But when she reached the room, she saw that it was already open, the door cracked in some small hint of a blessing. Without hesitation, she leapt, crossing the hall and closing the door behind her.

Despite the accumulated hours she'd spent trapped in the house, she'd never entered this room, and its starkness surprised her. Compared to the rest of the home, it was bare and cold, with no color to bring it life and no curtains to bring it warmth. It was gray and brown and dull, its tedium broken only by a wooden desk and a rickety metal chair.

Along the walls, empty bookcases stood like monoliths, their hungry shelves untouched by pages. Yet all around her, books lay in stacks upon the ground, rising in unbalanced towers that climbed to her waist.

Burn waded through the piles, skimming their covers and fingering their pages. Most were on business, machinery, math. A few spoke of art, promising poetry and passion. Yet none told of power. There were no tomes on dominance, no volumes on control – and no pages tucked between them, no plans hidden amongst their folds.

Burn reached the desk and sat, surveying the kingdom. It held no secrets that she could see. Then again, sight was not her forte. So she closed her eyes and breathed, scanning the room for the truth, for hidden passages or cellars, for secret doors or portals.

Instead she heard footsteps. They came not from a secret place, but from the hall, and they neared the door with alacrity.

Burn shot up, searching the space for a shield. Yet the starkness held no hiding place, no armor or protection. The desk was too slight, the books too narrow. There was nothing to shroud her from view.

She simply stood there, frozen, as if her stillness might protect her. The footsteps neared and stopped, and her heart pounded in response, pumping unease through her veins. Then a small beep echoed, and the door swung open.

"I saw that you were in here," Baylor crooned, holding up his tab. "You never seemed to be interested in my work before. Whatever could bring you in here now?"

"I was looking for you," Burn said, the lie slipping over her tongue like water. "The door was open, so I came in."

"Well, fancy that. I was looking for you, as well," he said with quiet amusement. "But ladies first. What is it that I can do for you?"

Burn gulped, cornered by her own lie. She raked her mind for another, sifting through the coals for an ember.

"I wanted to tell you that I understand," she began tentatively. "I know why you tagged me. I get it, but you don't have to worry about me. I've learned my lesson. You don't need to track me."

Baylor's amusement intensified. "I'm so happy you understand, but the matter's not up for discussion. What's done is done, and there will be no changing our minds. Now, your mother would like you to come to dinner. We're eating early today. Big plans tonight – for all of us."

Baylor turned to go, jerking his head for his daughter to follow. Burn cursed beneath her breath but did as she was commanded, trailing in his wake like a dog. They reached the dining room in no time, finding Una already seated and hard at work on her meal. She chipped away at the food with no obvious relish, her face blank and her eyes unreadable. Burn took her seat and studied her plate, its contents already prepared for her.

"Eat up," Una demanded, bringing a bite of rice to her mouth. "I'm sure you're starving after today's ordeal."

As if on cue, Burn's stomach growled, betraying her appetite. With a strained smile, Burn began to eat, taking her time as she savored the succulent meat stripped from the bones of a small, flightless bird and mounds of rice dotted with spicy flecks that set her tongue alight.

After a few bites, she finally found the courage to broach the question on her mind. "Why are we eating early?" she asked, trying to sound indifferent. "Dad mentioned that we have plans?"

"Your father and I have a meeting, although you won't be attending," Una said, her voice smooth despite its frost.

Burn perked up, her interest piqued. They had a meeting, a gathering of like minds. A gathering of the assembly? She couldn't help but hope, and it buzzed within her like a drug.

"Will you be leaving me here, then?" she asked, already forming her plan to follow.

"Of course not," Una said with derision, shaking her head. "You also have plans, although of a slightly different sort. Remember, I promised you a surprise?"

Burn's heart, which had been fluttering in her chest, turned to ice and dropped, crashing through her stomach and weighing it down. She'd thought her surprises were over, that the paralysis and her chip had been the whole of her sentence, but she should have known better.

"What kind of surprise?" Burn asked, unsure if she wanted to know.

"The kind that gives you a second chance," her mother said tightly.

The kind that will get you out of our lives for good, Una thought, and Burn was surprised at the sudden flash of words through her mind. Una's ferocity fueled them, and they lingered in her brain, coursing like a threat.

As if on cue, Una's water glass broke beneath her fingers,

shattering into shards that rained down onto her plate. Instead of looking upset, she merely looked amused, waving to a servant to clean up the mess.

"Will…Officer Petala be accompanying me?" Burn asked, trying to hide her interest. She needed to know what had become of him – and of Hale – and asking outright seemed like the obvious solution.

Una's scowl deepened, turning to a sneer. "Officer Petala is a coward. He has abandoned his post, most likely because of you," she spat. "But don't worry. We've already reported him to the Peace Force for desertion. He won't get far."

Burn's stomach turned, lurching at her words. Her appetite had vanished, and she laid down her fork, unable to eat. The fear that lurked at the edges of her mind increased until it obscured her vision, clouding her thoughts.

She couldn't lose Hale again – and she couldn't lose Kaz. Her heart raced at the thought of their capture, at the fear of what they could be facing, but she held herself in check, remaining still despite the strain.

"May I be excused?" Burn asked politely, folding her hands in her lap. "If I'm expecting company, I would like to freshen up."

Una smirked. "Fine. Go sulk in your room. But know that you can't stop what's coming. Greater minds than yours have planned for your future. We know what's best, and we won't let you ruin it."

Burn shivered, a thick chill oozing down her spine. She knew they were talking about Ellis, about their daughter's future and her marriage, but they may as well have been discussing Kasis, reveling in their control of its people. They thought they knew what was best. They thought they had control. Burn was going to prove them wrong.

"I look forward to learning about your plans, mother," Burn said with a hollow smile. Without waiting for a response, she strode out of sight, heading toward her bedroom. As soon as the door closed behind her, she was on the line to Scar.

"Scar, come in. I need you," she whispered urgently. "We're out of time. Staying put is no longer an option."

She expected Scar to jump on, to chastise her, to tell her to wait, but the line remained silent. No one answered. Burn had never felt as alone as she did in that moment. She had to act, had to move, but she couldn't. She needed help, but there was no one there to save her.

"I hope you get this message soon," she said to Scar, holding her comms bracelet in both hands before her. "Baylor and Una are on the move. I think they could lead us to the Shadow Assembly, but I can't follow, not without them knowing. Even if I could, I have no weapons, no backup, no way in."

In the distance, Burn heard a knock on the front door. A servant rushed to answer it, beckoning the figure in, and another servant was dispatched to fetch her.

"Ignis Cross is here to take me away. I don't know where we're going or what he'll do. I don't know how I'll get away."

The footsteps drew nearer, and Burn knew she only had seconds before they reached her.

"Scar, send help. Stat. I don't think I can do this alone."

A knock sounded on the door behind her, loud and even. Burn's heart hammered in her chest, sending sparks through her veins.

"Mr. Cross is here for you, Miss Hyde," the servant said. "Gather your things. It's time to go."

Her time was up.

Chapter 16

Raqa spilled through the door of the safe house, bruised and bleeding. It was difficult to tell the old injuries from the new, to see where the dried blood stopped and the fresh blood began.

He collapsed on the floor in the hall, his face pale and his eyelids fluttering. Scar, who had been tinkering with a prototype in the front room, was the first to reach his side, kneeling down and glancing over his injuries. She was afraid to touch him, to help him for fear of hurting him further.

"Somebody get Crete!" she yelled, knowing someone in the vicinity would obey. "This man needs help!"

A crowd gathered, intrigued and appalled and drawn to the drama. They clustered around her like flies, buzzing and circling and murmuring.

"Get back," Scar warned them, her eyes wide and hands raised. "This man needs his space."

That wasn't entirely true. Hale's fate would be the same

whether he had 5 feet or 10 or 20. It was Scar who needed the space. She needed to breathe, to focus, to think.

"Hale, what happened?" she asked, tuning out the crowd. "Who did this to you? Where's Kaz?"

And where's Burn's pack? She scanned the man's tattered clothes but saw no trace of the gadgets. The pack had disappeared, lost somewhere between the heavens and here. Lost along with Kaz.

Where had they gone, Scar wondered? Or, rather, who had taken them?

Hale didn't respond. He didn't even indicate that he'd heard her. The only noise he made was a low groan, a sound of such pain that the crowd cringed in sympathy. Scar, however, was undeterred. She moved to ask him again, to shake him until he answered, but before she got the chance, the crowd parted and Crete came rushing through.

"Stand aside," he cried, and this time they obeyed, cowed into compliance by his vehemence.

Yet Scar remained where she was, watching as Crete knelt beside her and took in Hale's state.

"This isn't good," he muttered to himself, tearing at Hale's clothing and revealing his wounds. "He'll require a good deal of healing. Even then, it may not be enough."

Crete glanced up, looking past Scar into the crowd. "Bring him to my room. I'll have to start at once," he stated, getting to his feet.

Scar followed, trailing in his wake through the swarms that had gathered. "I need to talk to him, Crete. I need to know what happened."

"If you haven't noticed, he's in no state for conversation,"

Crete shot back, a steely edge to his tone.

"Clearly," Scar retorted, matching her edge to his. "That's why I called for you. But I can't wait until he's fully healed for answers. Burn's life could depend on it."

"Well, Hale's life depends on me," Crete said, rounding on her. "Right now, he is my patient and my top priority. You will get your answers in time. If he lives, that is. Now I need you to stand aside. I have work to do."

He turned on his heel, stalking into his makeshift infirmary. Hale's body followed, held aloft by four men who had jumped at Crete's call. They placed Hale gently upon the cot before departing down the hall, whispering of his life in terms of ever-dwindling odds.

Scar moved toward the room, but Crete stopped her, his gaze firm. He shook his head once, denying her entry, before closing the door in her face.

Scar was fuming. She paced the hall, her anger mounting as she stewed in her own frustration. Eventually, her thoughts resolved into something resembling a plan.

With one last look toward the door, she set off, her sights fixed on her room. She might not have Burn's pack – or even a clear picture of where it had gone – but she might not need it. After all, Scar had her own arsenal of equipment, her own set of gadgets and weapons, and right now Burn had more need of them than she did.

Scar grabbed a bag and dumped its contents onto her cot. Scrambling, she seized whatever she could find, emptying her own stash until the room lay bare before her.

Scar knew her sister well, and Burn wouldn't stay still for long, not after what they'd done. Burn would want retribution, payback for the pain they'd caused to the people she loved. When it came to vengeance, her sister could be single-minded in the extreme.

She had mere hours, maybe less, before Burn would tire of waiting and pounce – if the decision was even up to her. Burn had the habit of tumbling into precarious situations by chance, of falling into the path of fate and colliding with catastrophe.

Scar didn't waste any time. As soon as she'd stowed enough gadgets, she went in search of Coal, scouring the house for the shapeshifter. Yet the man was nowhere to be found.

"Have you seen Coal?" she asked Jade, who was teaching combat skills to new recruits in the study.

Jade shook her head. "You could try the kitchen. I've caught him sneaking a snack on more than one occasion."

"Thanks," Scar breathed, shifting her attention to the back of the house.

Yet when she arrived, she found only Ino and Lux, their heads bent together over the table.

"Hey," Scar said, startling the pair, who immediately jerked upright. Their guilty expressions made Scar pause, and she glanced down to the loaf of freshly baked bread held aloft between them. Their hands were sunk into its soft interior, and crumbs of it still dotted their lips.

"We weren't doing anything," cried Ino, trying to block the crime with his body. Lux punched his brother lightly on the arm, his eyes going wide in a secret signal.

"I don't care that you're stealing rations," Scar told them, shaking her head. "I need to find Coal. Is he here?"

She glanced around the kitchen, as if he might be hiding in a cabinet or perching beneath a table. The brothers looked relieved that she wasn't there to upbraid them, and Ino let out a breathy sigh.

"I haven't seen him since this morning," he said with a shrug.

Scar turned to Lux, waiting for a reply. He stared at her for a second longer before giving in.

"He went out this morning with one of the teams," he told her. "They're searching for more recruits on the lower tiers. Won't be back until late tonight."

"Damn it!" Scar muttered, cursing Coal's need to be part of the action.

Most of the other Lunaria whose identities hadn't been compromised would be out there with him, combing the streets for converts to the cause. Which meant that no one here could help her reach Burn.

"I don't suppose you two are on good terms with the Peace Force?" she asked between clenched teeth.

The brothers grimaced, telegraphing their response.

Scar slammed her hand on the table, shocking them both. She had promised that Burn would never be alone, that she would always be there to help her. Yet now Scar couldn't even get her a few measly gadgets. They were worlds apart, separated by more than space, and there was only one thing Scar could think to do. It would be risky, possibly deadly, but she had to try. If she didn't, Burn would be helpless, left to the mercy of the heavens and its gods.

Scar's train of thought was abruptly interrupted by a tap on the shoulder. She spun around, ready to turn on the person who had touched her, but she stopped at the sight of Dormaline.

"Crete told me to find you," she said, her voice quick and light. "He said to tell you that Hale is awake. You have 5 minutes before he'll need to get to work again."

Only 5 minutes. It wasn't much, but it was something. Scar turned at once, leaving the kitchen and weaving her way back to Crete's room. While she walked, she considered the girl by her side.

"Is there any way you could get to the top of the city without being seen?" she asked, a ray of hope shining in her chest.

"No," Dormaline said gently, extinguishing Scar's light in an instant. "There are too many people. I'd be spotted for sure."

Scar sighed, but she didn't have time to dwell on the disappointment. They'd reached Crete's room, and Scar strode inside, her eyes focused on Hale. Yet the sight of him stopped her in her tracks.

It was Hale. The real Hale. He'd shed his faux skin in favor of his own, and he took up twice the space as before. Glancing around, Scar saw Eyana in the corner of the room, her head bowed in consultation with Crete. Scar turned her attention back to the cot and its larger-than-life inhabitant.

"What happened?" she demanded, skipping over pleasantries to get straight to the point. Scar had a sinking feeling that she knew the answer – that she'd known it all along – but she needed to hear it from him.

Hale looked wretched. Guilt was splashed across his face in hard lines, which blended with his wounds to paint a picture of pain. It was clear that Crete had brought him back from the brink, but his body was still damaged and still in need of extensive repairs.

"We did everything Burn said," Hale began, his deep voice sounding faint and drained. "We took our time getting down through the heavens. I was…useless. Could barely stand on my own, let alone walk. But thanks to Kaz, no one saw us."

It was the first time Scar had ever heard Hale speak civilly of the man. She could tell from that fact alone that this story would not end well.

"We reached the edge of the heavens, but the guards were on alert. There was no way to sneak past. Even if Kaz had been on his own, he probably would have been stopped. So we went for plan B. Kaz tied me up and paraded me out like a prisoner, like a prize he'd won and was eager to show off."

Hale broke off as a stab of pain struck. He tried and failed to suppress a groan, wrapping his arm around his midsection as if it could hold his body together.

"The guards didn't buy it," he continued, the words rough with pain. "The Hydes had already gotten to the force. They were on the lookout for Kaz. They tried to stop us – and we tried to run." Hale shook his head, staring at the cot as if the scene were playing out upon it.

"What happened?" Scar asked, trying to move the story along. "You had Burn's entire pack. Why couldn't you get away?"

"We tried," he said defensively, "but a smoke bomb and a stun gun aren't exactly enough to stop a small army."

Scar took offense at that, bristling at his words even though she knew they were true.

"Without me, Kaz would have been fine," Hale continued, ignorant of her annoyance. "He could have escaped, could have lost them in the streets, but he stayed by my side. We managed to distract them long enough to get out of the heavens, but we couldn't shake them. And I wasn't strong enough to keep going for long."

"Let me guess – they caught up?" Scar asked acerbically, indicating his fresh wounds.

Hale nodded rigidly, ignoring her tone. "They weren't happy, and they made sure we knew it. Fortunately, their orders were to capture, not kill. They didn't use their guns, but they had other ways of making us pay."

"Yet here you are," Scar said, attempting to draw the story to its conclusion. "How did you escape? And where is Kaz?" Her nerves were frayed, and she was in no mood for an epic. Plus, she could tell from Crete's insistent gaze that her time was rapidly running out.

Hale sighed deeply, bracing himself for the finale. "Kaz managed to get free and grab one of your devices. There was this bang, and the world went sideways. And then he was there, picking me up and telling me to run. So I did. I used the last ounce of energy I had to get as far away as I could. When I finally collapsed, I realized that Kaz wasn't there."

"Idiot," Scar breathed, an involuntary reaction to Kaz's stupidity. Hale looked at her, confused, and she clarified, "Him, not you. Although I can't believe you didn't see that coming. Of course Kaz would play the decoy so you could escape. He's always needed to be the savior. Just like Burn."

"I tried to go back. I really did," Hale told her, as if begging her to believe him. "By the time I got there, they were already hauling him off. He was unconscious but breathing. I heard the officers say they were taking him to the station for questioning."

"And you did nothing to stop them?" Scar asked, shaking her head.

"I was barely conscious!" Hale growled. "It took everything I had to drag myself back here without being caught."

Scar knew she was being harsh on him, that it couldn't have been easy to admit defeat – especially for a man like Hale. Still, she had to face the facts. Kaz was in the hands of the Peace Force, as was Burn's pack. Hale was out of commission. And Burn was alone and unarmed. Things weren't looking good.

"Look, they don't know that Kaz is gifted," Hale rumbled, his voice growing deeper from the pain. "They won't put him through what they did to me. All they know is that the Hydes don't like him and that he ran when his comrades accosted him. It's not enough to tie him to the Lunaria, even if you factor in my presence. And if they do connect the dots…well he's not the kind of man to turn on us."

That was the nicest thing Hale had ever said about Kaz. Yet Scar didn't have the capacity to care. Her thoughts were consumed by Burn, riddled with worry and unease.

"That's enough," came a voice from beside her, and Scar looked up to see a worn and weary Crete looking sternly at her. "Your time is up. You've gotten what you came for. Now allow me to get back to work. As you can see, Hale is still in need of my attentions."

Scar did see. Even their short talk had taken its toll, and Hale sat limply in the bed, devoid of his usual vigor. It was clear that he had nothing left to give her – no strength and no story – so she rose, nodding once to Crete and Hale before departing.

She only had a moment to regroup before her pocket buzzed. Scar grabbed her tab and unfolded it, expecting it to be Burn. Instead, a message flashed like a warning across the screen.

Her heart sank. She'd been too wrapped up in Hale's story to notice the sound of Burn's call. Scar immediately pressed play, cursing herself for her failure.

"I hope you get this message soon," came Ellis' soft voice, sped up by anxious tension.

Scar's heart dropped even farther, falling through her stomach to her feet. She listened to the message once, then again, its words pounding through her like a drum. Her sister's last plea lodged itself in her mind, scattering her thoughts to the wind.

"Scar, send help. Stat. I don't think I can do this alone."

And Scar wouldn't let her. If no one else could help her sister, then it was up to her. There was only one small problem: She was a wanted fugitive. Getting to the top of the city in broad daylight wouldn't be an easy feat.

Ducking back into Crete's room, she swiftly located Eyana, giving the woman a jerk of the head to indicate that she was needed. Eyana followed without question, intrigued by Scar's behavior.

"I need a favor," Scar said, getting to the point.

"What kind of favor would that be?" Eyana asked, her

silky voice thick with amusement. "Or, better yet, *who* would that favor be?"

Scar smiled at the woman's question, ready to respond with one of her own. "Have you ever heard of General Brika?"

Chapter 17

Burn and Hale had made this transformation look easy, but the truth was that it hurt like hell. Maybe it was different for her, a girl with metal in place of skin. Or maybe they were stronger, more accustomed to such pain. All she knew was that every inch of her body was burning, its cells on fire.

She couldn't watch as her body bubbled beneath Eyana's fingers, morphing from metal to skin, but she could feel it. It was as if each wire and plate pierced her, retreating somewhere deep inside as she donned someone else's shape. It was agony, yet she held it in, biting down to stop herself from screaming.

Prickles of pain remained after Eyana's touch had gone, but they gradually faded, leaving her confused and out of sorts. This form felt too soft, too vulnerable, too exposed. Scar missed her steely skin, her impenetrable exterior, yet she knew that this was the perfect cover.

Thanks to her citywide broadcasts, General Brika had

become the face of the force. Not only was she known throughout the city, but she was feared in equal measure. No one would dare touch her, and no one would think to question her presence.

Well, no one would think to question her presence *outside* the safe house. Inside, however, her appearance raised some concerns. Per usual, Scar hadn't exactly been forthcoming with her plan, and the sudden presence of a Peace Officer caused some minor misunderstandings amongst the Lunaria. Within no time, though, she was dressed and packed and ready to go. Ignoring the gasps and stares, she donned a mask and goggles and stepped out onto the street, pausing as the smog enveloped her.

It had been weeks since she'd been out in the daytime, and the chaos of the world was a shock to her system. Everywhere she looked, people shuffled past in dreary desolation, their heads down and their eyes averted. Scar had to force herself to move, to step into the crowd and fuse with it. It was like jumping into a polluted sea, and it swept her away, dragging her this way and that as it swelled.

All around her, the buildings and streets looked the same as they always had, carpeted by a sickly yellow haze that muted the edges, yet the atmosphere was toxic, wrong. It felt oppressive and heavy, swollen with resentment and dread, ready to burst. She could sense that something was coming – something violent and destructive, something big.

Scar did her best to navigate through the streets, heading up and away from the masses. Her uniform helped, as did her new appearance. One glance at her and people stepped aside, their faces tight with barely repressed rage.

Yet no one wanted to throw the first stone, to light the match that would set the city ablaze. The Peace Force still had their hold, although every day it slipped, loosening ever so slightly as eyes opened and minds rebelled. But their presence could still be felt.

Pairs of officers armed to the teeth parted crowds, flaunting their authority. They fed on the fear and loathing, their chests puffed out and their weapons at the ready.

When they spotted Scar, they nodded, dropping their heads in deference. Scar nodded in return, cool on the outside but burning within. She hated this spotlight, this beacon. She longed for the safety of the shadows, the nameless, faceless dark. Even here, where the sunlight barely grazed the buildings, it was too bright. Too many eyes could see her.

Still, the guise did the trick. Scar was able to ascend through the city without issue, making good time despite the cloying crowds. The glances followed her, tracking her every move, but the world didn't touch her, didn't dare draw near.

As she rose, the mood around her shifted, lightened, just like the tiers themselves. There was still tension, of course, but of a different sort. These people liked their things, their lives, their privileges, and they wanted to keep them intact. They wanted to maintain peace – not for the principle of peace itself, but so they'd never have to endure the nuisance of war. Up here, Brika was revered rather than reviled. The scowls turned to smiles, the stares to friendly nods. She even received a greeting or two, kind words that caught her off guard and made her falter.

Scar realized, belatedly, that she didn't even know Brika's first name. She must have heard it somewhere, but it hadn't stuck, hadn't seemed important enough to remember. She mulled it over in her head, seeking the name that went with her face, but nothing came to mind.

The exercise distracted her from her aching legs and burning chest. The climb was long and tedious, and her weeks spent locked away in hiding had stolen some of her stamina. When she finally reached the gateway to the highest tiers, she was breathless and panting, and she paused to regain her composure before mounting the final hurdle.

Three guards leaned lazily against the barrier, separating her from the stairs beyond. The soldiers looked placid and bored, though Scar could tell it was an act. The way they gripped their guns and scanned the scene made them anything but innocuous, and the silence lurking like lead between them betrayed their vigilance.

Scar tried to steady her hands, to slow her breathing and slacken her steps. It wasn't easy. Every instinct told her to flee, to retreat, and her nerves were alight with prickles of panic. Her hand kept creeping closer to her pack, an unconscious reflex in the face of a foe, and she had to stiffen her spine to keep her head high despite her desire to crumble.

Yet none of the officers noticed. They merely saw a face, a form, a body that they could place and label.

"General Brika," said the nearest guard in greeting, straightening himself in a show of respect. He was tall and lanky, and the move served to stretch him to an unnatural height until he towered above her, blocking out the light.

Scar put on a smile, a tight thing with no mirth and no real meaning apart from civility. She had seen the woman use the expression on her broadcasts, with her hands clasped before her and her eyes dead to the world.

"Afternoon, soldiers," she said, her voice deep and velvety smooth. "Anything to report?" Scar knew her time was ticking down, but she couldn't waste this chance to get a lay of the land.

"Everything's been quiet here, ma'am," came the reply, this time from the broad-chested officer on her right. "Just the usual faces," he said with a wink and a smile.

Scar gave him a knowing grin in return. Even though she wasn't in on the joke, she could guess what he meant. The assembly was gathering.

"I'm surprised you're not up there already," said the third officer, this one pale and unassuming, cocking his head in question.

Scar rounded on him, drawing closer than was comfortable. "I had business to attend to on the lower levels, *officer*," she spat, looking down her nose at him.

"Yes, ma'am. Sorry, ma'am," he replied, bowing his head in submission.

"Good," Scar replied, taking a step back. "And speaking of business, I heard what happened with Officer Petala today."

Scar left that hanging in the air, like an invitation to say more, to expand on the story with a tale of their own. As expected, they took the bait.

"We heard that Officers Caellum and Nestra were the ones to spot him – and then lose him," the giant of a man relayed, chuckling at their incompetency. "If Petala would have come down here, we would have had him in a second."

"Yeah, we would," the broad man chimed in. "No chance

we would have let him escape."

"But they did catch him in the end," Scar continued, urging them past their boasting. She needed them to get to the point – and quickly. Her other *business* was calling, and she couldn't be late.

"They almost didn't," the mousy man said with a shrug. "I don't even understand what he did. The Hydes gave no details, only that they wanted him taken in. Then he shows up with a fugitive in custody? It all seems suspicious to me."

Scar couldn't disagree, although the whims of the rich hardly ever played by the rules of justice. Still, that wasn't something she could say out loud.

Instead, she merely said, "The Hydes had their reasons. But what of Officer Petala? He arrived at the station in one piece?"

The tall officer chuckled again, a habit that made Scar's skin crawl. "More or less," he said blithely. "I heard they roughed him up a bit for the trouble he caused, but he's locked up now."

Scar nodded in understanding. Kaz was in the Peace Station, after all – and he was still alive. At least they had that to hold onto.

"Well, I better not keep everyone waiting," Scar said, plastering on the same dead smile. "If you'll excuse me, I'll be off."

Without waiting for their reply, she pushed past them into the heavens, climbing the stairs to the next tier. The guards didn't move to stop her, but they watched her go, following her movements with their eyes. As soon as she was out of view, she paused, sighing in relief. Then she stiffened as a realization took hold.

She didn't know where Burn was. Her message had said that Ignis Cross was taking her – but taking her where? Burn hadn't specified a location, and the panic returned as Scar realized that her sister could be anywhere.

Then another thought blossomed, its petals peeling back the alarm that had settled over her. Burn was tagged. Burn could be tracked – and not just by her parents. Anyone who knew the basics of intercepting positioning signals could find her. Thankfully, that was one of Scar's many specialties.

With her tab in hand, Scar began her search, scouring her surroundings for a signal. It didn't take long to find. Tagging people was not a common practice, even in the heavens, and there were few signals to compete with. Once Scar had found them, all she had to do was hunt through their histories to see which had been activated earlier that day.

In all honesty, Una and Baylor had done her a favor – although she highly doubted that Burn would feel the same. Still, without their help, she may have had to comb the tiers for traces, wasting valuable time. Instead, she made a beeline for the highest tier, following her sister's signal like a trail.

She had to admit, it felt good. In this form and in this place, she felt unstoppable, with the suns shining freely and the people parting before her. It was a rush, one that strengthened and solidified her resolve. She was going to save Burn. Then together, they would save the city.

Ignis Cross was his usual charming self. He led Burn to the

outskirts of the highest tier, his arm wrapped around her in an act of possession. Dressed in a tailored suit with his dark hair slicked back, he was the spitting image of his father, and the same cold arrogance rolled off him in waves.

They walked in silence, the air around them charged with a crackling energy that fizzled across Burn's skin. She tried to see what Ignis was planning, tried to push inside his thoughts, but her power had faded, and his mind remained a mystery. So she decided to ask.

"Where are you taking me?" she inquired plainly, with no guise or guile.

She didn't really expect an answer, so she was startled when he replied, "We're going to the edge of the world."

"Why?" she prodded, looking for more.

"Well, if I told you that then I'd spoil the surprise," Ignis said, his voice thick and oily. "I do hope you like surprises."

Burn did not like surprises, especially from the likes of him, although telling him that seemed unwise. Instead, she attempted to move the conversation in a more useful direction, leaving behind the small talk in favor of something larger.

"Speaking of surprises – I'm surprised that you're not at the meeting," she said casually, as if she couldn't care less about it all. "It sounded rather important."

In truth, she wasn't all that shocked. Based on what she'd overheard at the Peace Force Ball, Illex had been vying for a seat on the assembly for years without success. It was highly doubtful that his son would have surpassed him and captured what he could not. Nevertheless, Burn wanted to see his reaction to the words, to gauge what he knew – and what information she could glean from him.

Ignis, however, wasn't about to give anything away. "Still so interested in my affairs, I see," he drawled, keeping his eyes focused on the road.

"Would you rather I not be?" she asked lightly. "Do you prefer a woman who doesn't care about your work – or the workings of Kasis?"

"No," he said thoughtfully. "I would prefer a woman I can trust, and I have a sneaking suspicion that I'm not going to find that with you."

Burn tried to laugh off his words, turning them into a joke. "Well, that sounds terribly boring. I like to keep things interesting. Life is too short to spend it in the dark."

When Ignis didn't respond, she continued, "Don't you want an equal by your side, someone who can help lift you up instead of merely indulging your whims?" Her mind flew to Una and Iris, to the real sources of power behind the powerful.

"Who are you working for?" Ignis asked calmly, and Burn nearly choked on her breath, stunned by the abruptness of the question.

Gathering herself, she stowed her surprise and replied, "What do you mean? I'm not working for anyone."

"It was just a hunch," Ignis replied almost lazily. "It was based on something my father used to say. 'Never trust anyone who asks too many questions.' And you've been awfully curious as of late. I took a guess – and your reaction confirmed it. So answer the question: Who are you working for?"

Burn's world sharpened into pristine clarity as the danger of her situation took hold. "That depends," she said with forced bravado.

"On what?" Ignis asked.

"On you," Burn said simply. "You can consider me your enemy, and I'll have no other choice than to oblige. Or you can see me as an ally, and together we can bring this city to its knees before us."

She knew she was being melodramatic, that her all-or-nothing approach was risky, but Burn could sense that her time in the heavens was coming to an end, that her charade was cracking and wouldn't hold her aloft for much longer. So she preyed on his ambition, feeding into his lust for power. If he was anything like his father, then that quest for control consumed him, steering his actions and guiding his judgment.

Her ultimate goal, of course, was to flee, to escape from his grasp and find the assembly. Even now, she scanned for them, dividing her attention between him and the tier, between his words and the sounds of the world.

She knew she couldn't outrun him, couldn't best him in a battle of strength, couldn't slip away with his arm clasped so tightly around her. Instead, she did what she could, pumping him for information while waiting for her opportunity to escape.

"You've changed," Ignis said, shaking his head. "You used to be so sweet, so docile, so...simple. What the hell happened?"

"I grew up," Burn said bluntly. She'd thrown of the guise of Ellis completely by then, and she no longer felt like pretending. "I was sick of living someone else's life, of being some watered-down version of Una, just a pawn in her games."

Ignis appeared amused by that, cocking his head. "So you've decided that they're the enemy? And so am I?"

"No," Burn said, her voice rising slightly. "The *enemy* is the lack of choice. It's futures being planned for people before they're even born. It's lives being decided based on parentage and status. It's people forced to live and die in the shadows because they're never given the chance to see the suns."

"That's an intriguing notion of *enemies*," Ignis said, pursing his lips. "Although *lack of choice* is a difficult foe to fight against."

"Not if you know who's perpetuating it," Burn said sharply.

"Are we still speaking of your parents, or is this about something more?" he asked, stopping to turn her body toward his. The gesture was threatening in a way that Burn couldn't quite place, and she tore her gaze from his, casting it around her.

She hadn't realized that they'd reached their destination. She'd been so consumed by their game that she hadn't noticed as the edge of the tier drew near, the dome and the drop coming into stark relief beside them.

A striated steel railing was the only thing separating them from the end of the world. Beyond it, a descent of five tiers lurked, threatening to make Burn's head spin. Refocusing on Ignis, she tried to force her heart to slow, telling herself that the danger lived only in her head.

"Of course we're still speaking of my parents," Burn lied, her voice steady despite her nerves.

Ignis didn't look convinced. "Is that why you've been working with Officer Petala?" he asked, throwing the accusation at her like it was a fact. "You feel *sorry* for the people down below, those poor unfortunate souls?"

Burn raised her eyebrows in a look of indignation. "What are you talking about?" she asked, feigning innocence. "All Officer Petala did was protect me. Yet for some reason my parents saw fit to punish him for it."

Ignis laughed. "Do you think I'm an idiot? You seem to be forgetting who I am: a respected Peace Officer. I am well aware of what's been happening in the heavens – and what's been happening with you. Oh, yes. Your parents keep me apprised of your *activities*. I know everything," he said, tightening his hold on her.

"First, a prisoner breaks free of a lab, despite being heavily sedated. Then you and your *protector* return with blood on your clothes and a laughable story about an attack that no one can corroborate. The next day, your precious officer is spotted in the presence of that very prisoner. I sincerely doubt that any of this is a coincidence."

Burn stiffened beneath his grasp, his words turning her bones to solid stone. With his hands on her arms and his eyes boring into hers, she couldn't help but fall back in time.

Suddenly, she was in a ballroom, with Illex's hands around her and his face too close to hers, a haughty twinkle in his eyes. She could feel his touch, his breath, his arrogance as he spun her around the room, making a show of civility as he threatened everything she held dear. Even his voice echoed in her mind, dragged from the depths like a ghost of his presence: *Let's be honest with each other, shall we?*

Except she hadn't been honest then, and she had no intention of starting now. She would not cower before this

215

man, would not give him the satisfaction of her submission. Illex hadn't been able to break her, and neither would his son.

"I think you're searching for a culprit," she began, refusing to blink. "But I assure you, you're looking in the wrong place."

"You are a stubborn little creature, aren't you?" he said, a malevolent smile growing on his lips. He drew closer to Burn, moving one hand up to rest just below her neck in a lingering threat.

"If you hurt me," Burn said defiantly, "my parents won't rest until you've been hunted down and made to pay."

Ignis' smile widened until it spread across his face, his teeth glinting in the light of the suns.

"My dear, your parents are the ones who arranged this whole encounter," he said, his voice positively venomous. "They sent me here to ascertain your true allegiances."

"What are you talking about?" Burn asked, swallowing back the bubble of panic that swelled in her chest.

"Don't you get it?" he asked, looking down at her as if she were a simpleton. "This is all their plan, their idea. They're tired of your tedious antics. They want you gone – whatever that takes."

So much for being invisible, Burn thought, cursing her inability to act meek. She scrambled for a way out, a way to break his grip and flee, but dread clouded her mind, obscuring every clever idea.

"Then why would they have me tagged?" she finally asked, picking out the only question drifting through her thoughts. "If they intended to get rid of me, why bother tracking me?"

"Maybe they had more faith in you than I did," Ignis said with a shrug. "Or maybe they thought you could be brought to heel. Either way, they wanted to keep tabs on you, to keep you in line. It's a shame their little investment will be such a waste in the end."

Burn balked, the blood draining from her face at the implication.

Ignoring her silence, Ignis continued, "Of course, if you had turned out to be innocent, I was going to marry you. I think we could have had a good life. You clearly would have kept me on my toes. And as for passion...well, I haven't forgotten our last kiss."

Shame and fear rolled through Burn's body as he spoke, and she struggled to keep her face blank.

"You speak as if you've already determined my guilt," she retorted, keeping her voice even. "But how could you? You have no proof."

Ignis' smile held. "Your shameless attempts to pry information from me have been proof enough. Pair that with your skittish demeanor and evasive responses and I have everything I need."

His hand tightened around her throat in a show of open hostility even as his gaze remained cool and even. Burn's reflexes awoke and her body sprang into action, changing course from game to duel, from wit to war.

She brought her knee up with considerable force, ramming it between Ignis' legs and feeling it connect with a crunch. His grip on her loosened as he let out a grunt of pain, and she seized the opportunity to tear herself away. She readied a punch, hoping to break his nose, but he recovered in time, dodging the strike – and smiling. He was enjoying this, which only served to infuriate Burn further.

Ignis was close, with mere inches between them, leaving her precious little room to maneuver. With one arm protecting her face, Burn threw up an elbow with the other. She felt it connect with his solid jaw, and his head snapped back with satisfying speed. In an instant, though, he was on her again, trapping her body beneath his as he pinned her against the railing.

His hand once again latched onto her neck, squeezing hungrily. Burn twisted beneath his grasp, attempting to free herself, but he held firm, steadily crushing her windpipe until she could no longer draw breath.

"It is a pity," Ignis said, his voice rough. "You're such a pretty little thing – and surprisingly clever. It feels like a waste to kill you. We could have been a powerful team. Although I'm actually doing you a favor, you know. If I turned you over to the Peace Force, your death would be slow and painful, but I promise I'll be quick. It'll be over before you know it."

Burn couldn't believe it. She'd escaped from the father only to die at the hands of the son. Yet it was oddly fitting in a way. She'd taken Illex's life, and now his son would take hers. It was a twisted circle of death, a warped cycle that no one could break, least of all her. Violence begot violence and hate begot hate until the world was consumed by bloodshed and pain.

The city began to fade out of focus, smudging around the edges as the colors drained away. Burn tried to kick, to wriggle, to flail, but he held her tight, pressing down until her body bent back over the edge. She held her eyes open, staring at the confines of the dome and the clouded sky beyond. Even her hearing was fading now, reduced to the sounds of his skin on hers, her throat closing beneath his hand, her heart struggling to beat.

Another sound floated across the scene, but Burn was too far gone to care. Ignis must have heard it clearly, however, because his fingers loosened ever so slightly, allowing a sliver of air into her lungs. The burning in her chest eased as she sucked in more short sips, and the world began to brighten before her.

"Officer Cross," the voice came again, irate and insistent. "Let that woman go this instant. That is an order."

His grip on her loosened further, and she ripped herself away, reveling in the freedom. The cool air scorched her swollen throat, and she coughed and gasped, trying to steady herself as the ground spun beneath her. Despite the pain, a pure, joyous relief coursed through her at her escape, at the fortuitous appearance of this female figure.

Then she looked up, and her breath caught in her tattered throat. Her relief melted to watery dread as she beheld the face of her savior.

"Explain yourself, soldier," General Brika commanded, her beady eyes raking across Ignis in a look of utter contempt.

"This woman is a traitor, ma'am," he said, his voice flat and empty. "I've been commanded to terminate her at the earliest possible opportunity."

"Who issued this command?" Brika asked tersely, sparing only a momentary glance at Burn.

Ignis didn't reply. There was something in his gaze, a

confusion that made his eyebrows knit together and his mouth open in uncertainty.

"I asked you a question, officer," Brika said, her words gaining force and volume each time she spoke.

"Aren't you supposed to be at the meeting?" Ignis asked instead of answering, tilting his head and considering her with narrowed eyes.

Burn tried to move, to inch away as they spoke, but her legs wouldn't obey her. Her body felt weak and useless, and all she could do was stand there, watching her fate unfold.

Brika tucked her hands behind her back, strolling closer to Ignis and Burn. Her face contorted into a sneer as she shook her head at his insolence.

"How dare you question me, *Cross*," she breathed, his name a snarl on her lips. "My schedule is none of your concern. Now kindly hand over the prisoner so I can ensure that justice is served."

Ignis didn't move. There was something calculating in his gaze, suspicious, as if he didn't fully trust the woman before him. Within an instant, his caution turned to resolve.

Ignis lunged for Brika, but she was faster. Whipping a small rod from behind her back, she pressed a button along its side and the device lengthened into a steel baton. In one swift movement, she clubbed him upside the head, sending a tinny clang echoing through the air.

Ignis clutched his head, moaning in pain, but he refused to collapse, keeping himself upright by sheer force of will. Brika let out an exasperated sigh, clearly perturbed by his resilience. She approached him again, weapon raised, but this time he acted first.

With a low growl, he ran at her, tackling her to the ground in a mess of limbs. They grappled for a minute as each tried to win the upper hand, but neither could hold on for long.

Burn should have run. In fact, she started to, but all she managed was a few short steps before a voice stopped her in her tracks.

"Burn, help!" Brika shouted from beneath Ignis' body.

And with those two words, Burn knew: This wasn't General Brika.

Chapter 18

One heartbeat passed, then two as the pieces came together in Burn's mind. This person knew who she was. They'd called her by name – and they'd called to her for help.

They had to be Lunaria. It was the only answer that made sense. The Lunaria were the only ones who knew her true identity – and the only ones who would dare attack a Peace Officer in broad daylight.

It appeared that Scar had gotten her message after all. She'd asked for help and Scar had sent it. Now it was her turn to repay the favor.

Burn spun around, assessing the situation. In the instant it had taken to process the words, the fight had turned in Ignis' favor. Brika lay on the ground, arms splayed, while Ignis climbed to his feet, breathless and irate. The woman's baton was clasped in his hand, and he raised it above his head, preparing to strike.

Burn's mind was blank, but her body knew what to do.

Sprinting forward, she slammed into Ignis, propelling him away from Brika and toward the railing at his back. Their momentum carried them on, and the pair rammed into the steel fence set against the world's edge.

For a single dizzying moment, Kasis tipped on its axis. Burn scrambled, grabbing hold of the railing and digging her heels into the pavement. She ground to halt – but Ignis wasn't so lucky. The force of her attack drove him farther, flipping him over the balustrade and into the open air beyond.

Burn's panic burst in an explosion of surprise and alarm. She clawed at the sky, her hands searching the air for a piece of him. Her fingers skimmed the fabric of his pants, but before she could grab hold it slipped through her fingers, dropping out of reach.

She watched with horror as Ignis fell. He tumbled through the sky in slow motion, floating gracefully toward his death. She couldn't help him, couldn't save him, couldn't look away. Her eyes followed his path toward the ground, toward the mess of buildings and streets rising up to greet him.

He hit with a sickening thud. The sound rose through the city to meet Burn's ears, her own personal symphony of death. It shuddered through her bones and into her soul, filling her with paralyzing shock. No matter how hard she tried, she couldn't pry her eyes from the scene, from the image of his body contorted on a roof, bent and broken and wrong.

It was Brika who dragged her back from the edge. Her strong hands turned Burn around and guided her away. Burn was shaking, and Brika's hands flew out to comfort her, to hold her in place when all she wanted to do was fall.

"It's OK, Burn," she said with a shake of her head. "It's

OK."

It wasn't, of course. Burn would never get used to taking a life, to snuffing out that flame. Even though Ignis had threatened her, attacked her, tried to kill her, it still weighed on her, dragging her down with guilt.

Like father, like son, Burn thought darkly, and the idea made her laugh. The laughter climbed her ruined throat, coming out in raspy squeaks. She sounded deranged, but she couldn't bring herself to care.

A sudden slap to the face snapped her out of it. Burn reeled back, clasping her hand to her cheek. She looked up at the stranger, a realization dawning.

"Scar?" she asked tentatively, squinting her eyes as if it would bring her sister into focus. Because only Scar would be brazen enough to hit her simply to get her attention.

Brika cocked her head and smiled. "Hi, little sis," she said, and Burn's mouth dropped open in disbelief.

"How...why...what the hell are you doing here?" Burn demanded, waving her hands to emphasize the question.

"You're welcome for saving your ass," Scar said in her typical sardonic style. "Now if you don't mind, I believe we have a meeting to attend."

Scar was right, of course. In the chaos, Burn had nearly forgotten about the Shadow Assembly and their gathering. She'd been too preoccupied with staying alive to pay much heed to anything else. Now that she was free, however, and the path before her clear, her mind refocused on the task at hand.

"There's only one problem," Burn said slowly. "I'm tagged. If I go anywhere near that meeting, Baylor and Una will know."

Scar raised a brow. "I hate to break it to you, but I think your cover has already been blown. Throwing junior off the edge of the city is going to look suspicious no matter how you frame it. There's no coming back from that."

"Obviously," Burn said, rolling her eyes. "Although we have some time before they discover what we've done. What *I've* done," she corrected herself. "Still, it would be preferable if they didn't know we were coming. I don't exactly have Kaz's affinity for stealth. I need all the help I can get."

"Speaking of Kaz..." Scar started then stopped, already regretting that she'd brought it up.

"What?" Burn said, jumping on her fragment. "Scar, what happened?"

"Well, Hale is fine. He's back at the safe house with Crete," Scar began, "but Kaz is in Peace Force custody at the station. Your *parents* tipped off the guards. Some officers managed to nab him after he crossed into the lower tiers."

"Damn it!" Burn growled, the words tight and painful in her throat. Without thinking, she brought her hand up to her neck to touch the tender skin.

"It's better if you don't talk," Scar advised, observing her sister's movements. "When I got strangled, it hurt like hell for the better part of a week."

"Scar!" Burn snarled in accusation. "When were you strangled?! What did you get yourself into?"

"It doesn't matter now," Scar said with a wave. "We should really get to that meeting."

"And my chip?" Burn asked, pointing to her arm.

"Oh, that's simple," Scar replied, taking out her tab with

a confident smile. "I've already tapped into the signal. All I have to do is spoof your location so the chip transmits fake coordinates. Your parents won't have a clue where you are."

"Are you sure it'll work?" Burn asked, more out of nerves than any real doubt.

"Of course," Scar said in a huff. "It's not a long-term solution. Eventually we'll have to take it out, but this will work for now."

Scar's fingers flew across the tab, her eyes alight. It was an odd look on Brika, an intense sort of fervor that seemed unnatural on the hard lines of her face.

Burn wanted to thank her sister. Scar had made it clear that she wouldn't change herself for anything, even if that meant a life spent sequestered in a safe house. Yet here she was, with someone else's face and someone else's skin. She'd given herself up for Burn, trading who she was for who she needed to be. A fierce, protective love blossomed in her chest as she watched her sister work, but she knew Scar would only balk at the emotion.

So when Scar turned to her and told her everything was set, Burn merely nodded and smiled and said, "Let's go."

There was, however, one lingering dilemma standing in their way: Burn had no idea where they were going. Ignis had betrayed nothing of the meeting's whereabouts during their heated banter, and they were too far from the city's center to detect its action.

Nevertheless, Burn opened her mind, letting it graze over the houses and streets as they walked. The heavens were alive with energy, but it held a new menace, a sinister edge that lurked in the shadows. Burn strained to hear past it, to pick up any trace, but the voices melded into one, coalescing into a jumbled hum.

Her mind began to ache from the exercise, her temples pounding as her thoughts stretched across the tier. Most of the trails led to dead ends, to small groups and insignificant gatherings, but one stood out, a guiding light amidst the darkness.

Burn stopped abruptly, closing her eyes and reaching through the ether, following the whispers. They were faint, barely a breath on the wind, but they were there, calling to her in hushed tones. There had to be 50 of them at least, crowded together in a single space, waiting. She could make out no words, only sounds, but it was enough to guide her.

"This way," she told Scar, opening her eyes and picking up the pace.

Scar followed without a word, her disguise scaring away anyone who dared glance their way. The voices grew louder as they moved, beckoning Burn on. It was like a chain had been tied around her waist, coaxing her toward the source with a gentle tug. Words and phrases came to life in her mind, confirming her suspicions and spurring her forward.

Her heart beat like a drum, pounding the rhythm through her body, and her throat stung with the prick of a thousand pins, but she couldn't slow. The assembly was closer than they'd ever been, and Burn could feel them in her head, their moods laced with jagged anticipation.

As the voices neared, Burn slowed then stopped, her gaze catching on the source of the commotion. It was a house, mere blocks away, and it positively pulsed with activity. She had never seen it before, never had a reason to take notice, but she noticed it now. It was magnificent, rising up like a castle of steel and stone, with few windows granting a glance inside.

Burn began to inch closer, but a hand flew out to stop her, pulling her behind a low section of wall. She glanced back at Scar, who pointed toward the door. Burn followed her gaze, directing her attention to the home's imposing entry.

Out front, a group of guards stood defending the entrance, protecting its occupants from people like them. Burn could make out four figures, vigilant and attentive, their bodies rigid with the weight of control. The soldiers tried to be discreet, parading past like any other patrol, but they weren't fooling anyone.

"Any ideas?" Burn asked, rifling through her mind and coming up empty.

"Yes," Scar replied after a pause, "but we'll only have one shot. Are you sure you can't listen from here?"

Burn sighed. "I can hear bits and pieces, but it's muted. Besides, my mission is to discover their identities so we can expose them. I need to get a visual, and I can't do that from outside."

"Of course you wouldn't make this easy," Scar said in exasperation, diving into her pack. She resurfaced after a second with a pair of glasses, holding them out to Burn.

"Take these," she commanded, her tone all business. "They'll record what you see, just like the pair you had. If you do manage to get a visual, even from afar, we should be able to break it down and identify the members. Just don't lose them, alright?"

"Why don't you wear them?" Burn asked. "You are

coming with me, right?"

Scar shook her head. "I think the real Brika is already inside. I can't risk being seen. If the assembly learns that we can impersonate them – become them – there's no telling what they'd do. It's safer for me out here."

Burn nodded in understanding. "What's the plan?" she asked, the adrenaline beginning to pound through her veins.

"You'll need to take down the guards," Scar told her, reaching into her pack once more. "I'll be here in case anything goes wrong, but this part's up to you."

Gingerly, she handed Burn a small metal cylinder. "Take this," she instructed. "Get all the guards together, aim at their heads, then press that button," she said, pointing to an indent along the side.

"How…" Burn began, but Scar cut her off, anticipating her objection.

"How will you get them together? Simple. Do what you did last night."

A few minutes later, her pockets filled to the brim with Scar's eclectic gadgetry, Burn walked briskly toward the entrance. She made no move to hide herself, to duck behind buildings or slink through the shadows. For once, she wanted to be seen. She needed their attention.

And she got it. When she was less than a block away, the soldiers took notice, tracking her movements with their eyes. As soon as it was clear that her course wasn't changing, they stood at attention, gripping their weapons in warning.

"Halt!" a ginger officer cried, holding out his hand to stop her. "This is a restricted area. We must ask that you retreat immediately."

Naturally, Burn ignored the man. Instead, she walked closer, wringing her hands in an outward sign of anguish.

"I need to see my parents," she said, making her eyes wide and wild. "They're inside. I need to talk to them. Something happened. Something bad."

She rubbed at her neck to highlight her bruises, drawing the guards' attention to her distress. She knew she looked every bit the damsel. Her hair was unkempt, her clothes torn, her body battered and shaking.

"Please stay back," the officer said, his voice softening into a gentle plea.

Once again, Burn ignored him. "Someone attacked me," she explained, her voice trembling and threatening to give way. "He tried to kill me. I fought him off, but he may have followed me. He could be here any minute. Please, you have to help me," she begged, folding her hands before her.

To her immense relief, her ruse was working. The other officers had turned to face her, and with every word they moved closer, their attention captured by the pretty victim in their midst. Her breath came in shallow gasps as she glanced between them, measuring their positions.

"Please stay calm, miss," the officer told her, removing his hands from his gun and holding them out before him. "No one's going to hurt you. Tell us what happened and maybe we can help."

The guards were too far away. Even as they moved in, she could tell they would never be close enough, never come together in the way she needed. So she took Scar's advice, doing what she had the night before. She fainted.

The world fell away in a flutter of air and fabric as she

dropped, hitting the pavement with a thud. The impact jarred her aching body, but she suppressed the groan, keeping her eyes shut and her body still.

Burn could hear them crowd around her, hear their gasps and footsteps and whispers. Without looking, she knew each man's position, and she waited, biding her time until they were all in range.

"Miss? Miss, are you alright?" a voice asked, insistent and anxious.

Burn let out a low moan, gripping the device in her pocket. Then, without warning, she jerked her eyes open, took aim, and pressed the button, releasing the net on the unsuspecting guards.

Silver threads wrapped themselves around her targets in a wicked embrace, trapping them where they stood. Burn watched with a mixture of shock and surprise as the wires crackled to life, filling the air with an electric charge. The officers, confused and dismayed, squirmed under the web, trying to break free, but they didn't have the time. Mere moments elapsed before they sank to the ground, their muscles giving out beneath the force of the current.

Burn didn't hesitate. She pushed herself up and took off at a run, veering toward the door. She paused only briefly to get a sense of the world beyond it before pulling it open and creeping into the hall.

Inside, the building lost all resemblance to a house. It was cavernous and unfurnished, a hollow shell with no hints of home. The outside was a façade, she realized, a disguise that cloaked the building in normality.

This was the heart of the Shadow Assembly. Burn knew

it at once. The walls resonated with power, and the rooms beyond whispered seductively of control. The hall she had entered spanned the length of the home, its ceilings stretching up several stories to graze the sky above.

Past the hallway, several doors dotted the wide expanse of wall, leading to small chambers and rooms. Yet Burn had no interest in those. Her attention was pulled to the end of the space, to a yawning cavern lurking behind the final door.

It was the epicenter of sound, the source of the voices that had pulled her to the building. They continued to tug at her even now, forcing her feet to move with silent steps down the hall.

One man drowned out the rest, his low, slow voice tickling the corners of Burn's memory. She strained to grab hold, to remember where she'd heard it, but it kept slipping from her thoughts, dancing just beyond her reach.

Burn paused outside the door, holding her breath out of habit. She knew she couldn't enter. She would be spotted, captured, charged if not shot. For the second time that day, she wished she had Kaz's stealth, his ability to move unseen through the world, but on that point she couldn't dwell. Thinking of Kaz in a Peace Station cell threatened to crack something within her, and right now she needed to remain whole.

Swinging her attention around, Burn searched for a way to peer inside, but the hallway was stark, plain, and lifeless. There were no hidden passageways or secret compartments, no ways to see past the wall. Burn backtracked a few steps, reversing course until she reached the nearest door. After a quick listen, she eased it open and squeezed inside, folding herself into its dark embrace.

At her entrance, however, a light flared to life above her, casting its rays around the meager space. After Burn's eyes had adjusted, she took in her surroundings, noting a small desk crammed into a corner to her left and two chairs set beneath a shuttered window at the back. To her right, a chiseled stone wall butted against the assembly room beyond, adorned with two bleak cabinets that rose up like monoliths before her.

Burn leaned her head against the cool stone, closing her eyes to let her mind fill with words.

"...following the events at the news hub," said the same male voice. "We are told that normal operations will resume later today. Increased patrols have been posted around the building, and new security systems have been installed inside. If anyone tries to break in, they will meet with a swift and violent end. Of course, efforts are still underway to find the perpetrators..."

Burn pulled away from the wall, studying its surface and moving her hands along its bumps and ridges. Her eyes roamed hungrily, starting at the floor and working their way toward the towering ceilings, which arched above her like a cathedral. Her gaze came to rest just above the second cupboard, where a small grate marred the perfect lines of stone.

Burn didn't dally. Moving one of the chairs, she climbed onto its seat, straining to reach the top of the cabinet. Yet her hands merely scraped the surface, unable to gain purchase on its smooth wooden slats.

Stepping gingerly onto the chair's back, she barely managed to get a handhold before the chair flew out from beneath her, clattering to the ground in a flurry of noise. Dangling from the cupboard by her fingers, Burn cringed at the sound, silently praying that no one had heard.

With a grunt of effort, she dragged herself up, clearing her wrists then her elbows then her torso before swinging her legs over. The cupboard swayed precariously as she worked, but she paid it no mind, unable to stop for fear that she'd fall.

Once she'd managed to clamber up, she paused to get her balance before angling herself toward the grate, her fingers outstretched. The metal did not come free easily. She had to yank at the small grid of squares, nearly toppling off her pedestal before it finally broke away.

Steadying herself, Burn took a deep breath and dove into the shaft. It was a tight fit, with her hands stretched out before her and her hips sliding along the sides, but she managed to squeeze herself inside. Wriggling deeper, she brought her feet through the hole, encasing herself between the thin sheets of steel.

Moving was a slow and tedious process, with her legs crunched beneath her and her sweaty palms slipping as they clawed uselessly for purchase. Eventually she managed a clumsy crawl, propelling herself forward and around a rigid bend.

The sounds of speech grew ever louder, tumbling through the tunnel in tinny waves. They pressed on her from all sides, spurring her toward their source.

Ahead, another small grate poked through the metal, showering flickers of broken light into the dim surroundings. Burn pushed toward it, inching along in awkward lurches. Her shoulders cramped from the effort, but she ignored the discomfort, stationing her head against the checkered grill.

Only then did she realize she'd forgotten to don Scar's glasses. The spectacles sat in the pack around her waist, several feet away from her hands. Cursing beneath her breath, Burn writhed and wriggled, contorting herself into a myriad of shapes as she struggled to retrieve the gadget. Finally, she managed to drag them to her face, pinning her arm beside her as she looped them around her ears.

True to form, Scar's glasses were more than just a camera. As soon as Burn slipped them on, the world came to life before her, adding visuals to the soundscape in her mind. Without direction, they zoomed in on the scene, presenting the assembly in perfect clarity. With their aid, Burn had a perfect view...of the back of everyone's heads.

She hadn't thought this through, she realized as her stomach sank. She'd placed herself behind the crowd, with a sightline to the aging male speaker but no one else. Burn contemplated her lack of foresight as she listened to the man drone on, filling the room with numbers and statistics that meant nothing to her ears.

All at once, though, her worries slipped away as she remembered where she'd heard that voice. For the second time that day, she was thrust back in time, back to the Peace Force Ball, back to General Cross.

In an instant, the air vent disappeared, replaced by a thin veil of fabric. Suddenly, she was hiding behind a curtain, her hands shaking and her heart racing as the assembly came forth, filing into the room. Then a man spoke – this man – drawing the attention of the crowd with the silky rhetoric of *history-defining moments* and *the continued success of their great city.*

That had been the lead-up to the ManniK Battles, the preface to the fire and bloodshed that had nearly scoured the lower levels clean. And this man had been at the helm. Sure, Cross had orchestrated the affair, capturing the subjects and conducting the tests, but this man had been the one to pull the strings.

He had tempted Cross with promises of power, using him as a puppet, a pawn. He had waved the assembly in front of him like a prize and threatened elimination should he fail. Even if it was Cross that had led the troops to the edge, it was this man who had made them fire.

Burn's chest sang with righteous anger as she gazed upon his face, taking it in. The man was old, with folds of crepey skin hanging around his jowls and white hair slicked back from his temples. He wasn't what Burn had imagined, not lively or virile or strong. He seemed to sag beneath the weight of himself, oozing a weary sadness.

Burn had expected more from the Shadow Assembly. She had thought the face of evil would look more…well, evil. This man just looked pitiable, standing in robes that bore the reek of a long-lost era.

"And so," he droned, "the Lunaria have done us little damage. Our intel suggests that their resources have been depleted and their leaders rendered useless. Their efforts to convert more people to their cause have resulted in few new members, and the stories they've spread of us have done little to alter the public's perception, no matter how much truth they contain."

A polite ripple of laughter swept through the crowd at

his poor attempt at a joke, and Burn found her fists tightening in response. The Lunaria's resistance was no more than a hindrance to these people, no more than a bitter annoyance they could easily cast aside. But many a man had fallen over foes he did not deign to see, Burn reminded herself. The assembly would be the same.

"We are well-placed to end the Lunaria once and for all," the man continued, nodding at his own words. "In fact, dissidence will soon be a thing of the past. No longer will we have to face the petty unrest and pointless uprisings that currently plague our efforts at advancement. Within no time, the whole of Kasis will understand their place – and what will happen if they choose to forget it."

A smattering of applause erupted at his statement, growing louder before dying at the sight of his upheld hands.

"Save your applause, for I am not the one who deserves it," he said, grinning in a show of faux modesty. "It is long past time to hand the stage over to the one who does deserve your praise. Please put your hands together for our fearless leader."

That got Burn's attention. The discomfort and worries dancing at the periphery of her thoughts vanished in a blink, her focus trained wholly on the stage.

She had thought that this man was their leader. He'd played the part before the ManniK Battles – and seemed to be doing the same now. Yet as he stepped aside, Burn noticed another figure rising from the crowd and making their way toward the stage.

A figure with bright blond hair tinted by a streak of brilliant purple.

Chapter 19

Una Hyde ascended to the stage amidst a raucous round of applause. Burn's heart hammered in her chest as the woman she had come to know as a mother turned, unleashing her cool smile on the crowd.

The waves of clapping rose to a cheer, echoing off the stone walls and into the vent where Burn lay, unable to move or think or blink. The only thought she could pull together amidst the haze was that somehow it all made perfect sense.

"Thank you, thank you," Una said, her hard voice needing no amplification in the expansive chamber. "And thank you to Speaker Amos for the wonderful introduction." She nodded over at the aging man, who inclined his head in response.

"It's been some weeks since we've been able to meet, and so much has happened. I am delighted to be able to share our progress with you today."

A rancid foreboding churned in Burn's gut, and her skin

went cold at the words. Her breathing dwindled into shallow pants as she locked her gaze to the stage.

"Our experiments have finally paid off," Una declared, raising her hands in triumph. "We have at last been able to manufacture mutants!"

Burn had known it was coming, but she still felt her stomach sink, with an eerie stillness settling like fog across the banks of her mind. It was the quiet before the storm, the tranquility before the tempest, and it glued her to the spot, forcing her to listen.

"Our latest batch of test subjects not only survived but thrived, with each manifesting an incredible power that had only been seen thus far amongst the dregs of society. Of course, we couldn't risk these subjects being discovered, so we had to eliminate them," Una said with derision, "but the data they've provided will live on in us forever."

The excitement in the room was palpable. It felt as if an electric current buzzed through the air, alighting on each attendee and growing stronger through their glee.

"That's not all," Una taunted, her smile growing into a beast of a thing, all teeth and no humanity. "Although why tell you when I can show you?"

The crowd was voracious now, ravenous for more. They pawed at the ground like jackals, whipped into a frenzy by the lure of control. It was driving them mad, which was exactly what Una wanted.

She moved with deliberate slowness, drawing out the show. Every step felt like a threat, every turn of her head a warning.

Una strolled across the stage, then down the stairs,

ambling toward the side of the room. She stopped before a marble statue, eyeing it with hunger, its godlike form a toy in her ambitious eyes. Turning to the crowd, she smiled before wrapping her silky hands around its neck.

She picked it up with ease, as if it were made of cotton and clouds, and held it above her head. Then she flung it across the room. It collided with the opposite wall in a shower of stone and dust, raining down on the assembly like a gift from the gods.

Silence fell with it, a blanket of shock, before realization took hold. Una had a gift – and not just any gift. She'd taken Hale's strength, bled it from his body and injected it into her own.

Burn's limbs were shaking, her muscles tight and her brain on fire. Fury flared, hot and thick, as she looked down on her mother, whose elation infected the crowd.

Una did not deserve this gift. She had not suffered for it, had not slaved. She didn't know heartache or desolation or pain. She hadn't lived in the shadows, seen her loved ones die, watched helpless as the world succumbed to the dark.

But that was what *they* did. They took what they wanted with no care for the cost. Even nature was no match for their arrogance. They'd changed their genetics, altered their evolution solely to stay on top.

Their egotism grated on Burn. It also scared her. The assembly and their cronies had always been powerful, but this was something else entirely. With the key to biological advancement in their grasp, there was no telling what they'd be capable of.

"As you can see," Una continued, making her way back

to the stage, "we have reached the deployment phase of our strategy. As one of the first recipients of the serum, I can confidently report that there have been no side effects to speak of. Following injection of our unique concoction, results can be seen within a matter of hours."

The audience looked enraptured by her words, drinking them in as if they'd been dying of thirst. Burn, too, was held in thrall, still unable to move as the dread took root in her stomach and branched out through her limbs.

"Within the next few weeks," she continued, "we will have enough doses to distribute to the entire assembly. Not only that, but we hope to have enough for the entire Peace Force, as well. Soon we will be unstoppable, with a gifted assembly and a gifted army at our backs."

A deafening cheer rose around the room, a self-congratulation for their clever little coup. In her vent above them, Burn fumed, her mind spinning across a hundred possible paths and into infinite futures.

This would spell destruction, not only for the Lunaria but for Kasis as they knew it. The balance of power, already skewed so far against them, would tip forever in favor of the rich, stranding everyone else in the realm of disaster. Their only advantage thus far had been their gifts, but with enemies endowed with powers – and endless resources to match – the rest of society wouldn't stand a chance.

Una continued speaking, but Burn couldn't hear it. Her thoughts were too loud, too all-consuming to make space for more. Despite that, something inside her was always listening, combing the world for threats. It was a reflex, unconscious and instinctive, and it suddenly sent a warning through her veins.

Someone was coming. More than one someone, in fact. Several pairs of feet approached, striking the ground with military precision. Another set of guards, perhaps? Or maybe a few more *examples* for Una's triumphant display?

Burn didn't want to stay to find out. She knew they wouldn't look for her there, wouldn't think to check the vents for spies, but anything could give her away – the lights in the room behind her, the misplaced chair, the open grate. If they so much as peeked inside, she'd be done for.

Yet she'd only managed to discover half of what she'd come for. She knew their plans, but she hadn't seen their faces. Burn had already overstayed her welcome, but she couldn't help craving more. Each detail was a drug, and she needed her fix.

Burn spared a final glance out the vent before pushing herself awkwardly away, backtracking down the passage in a feet-first fashion until she reached the bend. Turning herself around in a mess of limbs, she continued to pull herself along until her head emerged at the other end.

As she had feared, the lights were still on above her, drenching the room in their honeyed glow. Outside, the suns had set, meaning the well-lit room would be a beacon to the guards. Burn hauled herself out head-first, clambering clumsily to the cupboard below.

Hers was not a graceful descent. She gingerly eased her body down, clinging to the cabinet's top through sheer force of will. With a groan of anticipatory pain, she dropped, landing harshly on her feet before losing her balance and tumbling over.

She collided with the chair she had knocked askew, and it dug into her back, eliciting a sharp squeak of pain followed by a hushed curse. Burn looked down at herself, assessing her body for injuries, and found a blinking blue light coming from her comms bracelet. She had a message.

"Burn, it's me," Scar said, her voice low and breathy. "I got your message. I'm coming up to get you. Only, I may look a little…different. You'll understand when I get there. Just stay put – and don't do anything stupid."

It was an old message, then. That would have been helpful to get when Ignis had been bearing down on her, although she supposed she had been a bit preoccupied at the time.

Burn hastily deleted the communique, yet the light continued to blink. She pressed play before she had a chance to think.

"What's going on in there?" Scar asked in a tone that was part exasperation and part impatience. "I'd appreciate an update. Or at least a line saying you haven't been caught. I really don't want to have to rescue you twice in one day."

Burn sighed. "Scar, I'm here," she reported over the comms. "Don't worry, I haven't been caught. Yet."

Scar didn't find her sister's antics amusing. "You should get out of there," she said in a tight voice. "I've dosed our friends out here with a little sleeping gas, but that won't keep them down forever. Plus, someone is bound to notice their absence."

"I know, I know," Burn bristled. "But I haven't been able to get a look at their faces. I've only gotten eyes on two of the members, although I have discovered what they're planning. Scar, it's…big."

"That'll have to be enough," Scar shot back. "We need to go."

"Alright," Burn conceded, knowing her sister was right. "Just give me a few minutes. I need to make sure the coast is clear."

She really did intend to leave, but once she'd slipped back into the hall, something stopped her. It was more than curiosity; it was a need to finish what she'd started. After all, she'd never get this chance again – the chance to see her enemies, to observe them, to understand them.

Instead of heading toward the door, Burn turned, focusing her attention on the room at the end of the hall. Maybe there was something she'd missed, a way to see inside – a crack, a crevice, a keyhole. Maybe if she eased the door open, no one would notice.

Burn didn't get the chance to test her theory. The footsteps she had previously noted began to travel toward her once more, snapping her out of her trance. She'd been stupid; she saw that now. She needed to leave, to get as far away from this place and these people as she could. Her time in the heavens had come to an end.

Except leaving was looking less and less like an option. Burn was too far from the door, and the footsteps were drawing near. They lurked just around the corner, threatening to expose her with each stride.

"Scar, I might need a way out of here," she whispered to her wrist, keeping the comms line open in case things went sour.

Burn took off, sprinting as quietly as she could toward the door, but she could tell she wasn't going to make it.

Halfway there, she stopped, seizing on another plan. It was a good thing, too, because a second later two Peace Officers rounded the corner and spotted her.

"Thank the gods!" she said, her voice a mask of faux fury and panic. The men looked startled to be addressed in such a way, especially by an intruder who had no place in their halls, but that was exactly what Burn wanted. "I need to speak to my mother, Una Hyde," she ordered them.

"I'm sorry, miss, but Una is unavailable," the larger of the two men stated, staring at her skeptically. "How did you even get in here? Our guards were told to let no one inside."

"Don't you know who I am?" Burn asked. "I am Ellis Hyde, and I have just been attacked." She leaned her head back to expose her neck, which had developed an angry red welt that she could feel with every move. She switched from anger to misery in an instant, wiping at her eyes irritably as if her emotions were betraying her.

"Please," she begged, "if I can't see my mother, at least let me stay here until I know he's gone." She bit her lip in a pretense of distress, hoping it would enforce her pleas.

She did not actually want to be taken to Una – and she didn't expect them to do it, either.

Which meant it was a surprise when the shorter guard turned to his colleague and whispered, "Can't you see the girl's upset? We should at least let Una know she's here."

After a second's deliberation, the larger man nodded, letting out a sharp "fine" before stalking to her side.

"If my mother's busy, please don't interrupt her," Burn said, trying to backtrack. "She hates being disturbed. I can sit out here until she's done. I could use a little quiet after everything."

"Nonsense," the shorter guard said, coming to stand beside her. "If someone's after you, your mother needs to know. It won't do any good to put this off."

He began to escort her toward the cavernous room, and her heart picked up speed, practically leaping out of her chest as it told her to run. As soon as she thought it, though, the guard's arm snaked around hers, holding her in place.

His other hand went directly for the knob, with no warning knock to precede it. Burn stared in shock as the heavy door opened before her, creaking as it revealed a sea of people – and a sea of faces all turning in her direction.

This was the Shadow Assembly. Burn considered them as they considered her, each taking in the other. She almost smiled at the sight, knowing that her mission was finally complete. She had seen their faces – and caught them on camera – and soon the Lunaria would expose them.

At least she could hold onto that in the darkness. At least her impending death wouldn't be in vain. But she was getting ahead of herself.

While she'd been detained in the hall, Una had resumed her seat in the crowd, relinquishing the stage to the elderly speaker who'd possessed it at the start. Once she saw Ellis, she rose from her chair, her face a canvas of hard lines and quiet anger. While the rest of the room grew bored of staring and returned their attention to Amos, Una cut through the space like a knife, her sharp glare targeting the trio.

"Would you mind telling me what *she* is doing *here*?!" she asked the guards with fire in her eyes. The men sputtered and spat, but she paid them no mind, continuing her tirade without them. "Follow me," she commanded. "We'll discuss this outside."

Once she'd steered them back to the hall and shut the doors behind them, Una stopped playing nice, letting loose the monster that lurked forever inside her.

"How dare you interrupt our meeting!" she cried, baring her teeth at the men. "I've never seen such insolence. I will make certain that both of you are stripped of your positions immediately. Now go! I don't want to see your pathetic faces for a moment longer."

The men did as they were told, scampering back through the halls and leaving Burn and Una alone in the silence. With an exaggerated sweep, her mother turned her attention to Ellis, going eerily still as she considered the girl.

"Now, daughter," she began with forced calm, "how is it that you find yourself here? And where, pray tell, is Ignis?" She made a show of looking around the empty hall.

Burn gulped, the movement sending a surge of pain down her ravaged throat. The image of her mother squeezing the sculpture's neck blazed to life in her mind, beating back her words and leaving her mouth dry. She fought against the fear and tried to remember her lies.

"Ignis tried to kill me," she whispered, her hand moving toward her neck. "I don't know what I did to upset him, but he just attacked me. I fought him off and managed to break free, but he's still out there somewhere, searching for me."

It would do no good to tell her mother how their fight had really ended – and it wasn't lost on her that Ignis' actions were at the behest of her parents. Still, she had to hope that Una wouldn't be brazen enough to kill her daughter here, in the halls of the assembly. She might be evil, but it was a calculated thing, a measured malevolence that steered clear of rash decisions.

"Hmm," her mother murmured, her eyes narrowing. "How did you know where to come?" she asked, a sharp edge of accusation coloring her tone.

It was a good question. If it hadn't been for her gift, she wouldn't have known where to find them. Yet she could hardly tell that to Una.

"Ignis told me," she said. "He pointed it out on our walk, before…" she cut off, as if she couldn't say the words out loud. "He probably thought I'd be dead soon and it didn't matter what he said."

Another silence descended as Una weighed her lies, tasting them on her tongue. However, the stillness of the scene was swiftly broken by Scar's insistent voice. Burn had turned down the comms so only she could hear it, but the sudden noise still made her flinch.

"I think I've found a way out, but you'll have to be quick," her sister said. Burn fought to keep her face blank as a ray of hope pierced her chest. "All you have to do is get to the doors. I've hacked into the system that controls the locks, and as soon as you're out, I'll flip the switch and strand them all inside."

Only one problem, Burn thought tersely, eyeing her mother, who stood between her and the door. She racked her brain, searching for a way to alert Scar to her dilemma.

"Mom, why would he do something like that?" she started. "I mean, if he wanted to *get out*, I wasn't going to *stand in his way*," she said, praying that Scar could read between the lines.

Unsurprisingly, Scar was able to see through Burn's crude attempt at a code.

"There's a pin in your pack that's laced with a paralyzing serum," she said hurriedly. "I got the idea after Una dosed you. If you can prick her, it might give you enough time to escape. But whatever you do, don't pierce your own skin."

Scar had to make things difficult. It wasn't as if Burn could rifle around in her pack under Una's nose and pull out a pin. She would have to be subtle – and quick – and hope to the gods that she didn't paralyze herself in the process.

"How did you get through the guards?" Una asked, raising an eyebrow in suspicion.

"I told them I was here to see you!" Burn cried, feigning offence. "I told them what happened, and they brought me in. I didn't do anything wrong!"

As she spoke, she unzipped her pack and stuck two fingers inside, feeling for the minuscule weapon. She traced the edges of several coins and a few metal cannisters before landing on the pin's bulbous head. Concentrating on not breaking eye contact with her mother, she gingerly drew the pin from the pack and brought it down to her side.

"You see, I don't believe you," Una was saying, shaking her head. "Ignis is an upstanding man and a respected officer. He would never attack a woman without cause."

"But mom!" Burn cried, throwing her arms around the woman's neck in a rush of emotion. "I swear I didn't do anything."

Una was too stunned by the sudden embrace to fight it. Burn seized the opportunity and slid the pin decisively into her neck, withdrawing it in the blink of an eye. She heard Una gasp as the pain pricked her senses, and Burn drew back, feigning concern.

"What's the matter? Did I scratch you? I'm so sorry!" she said before Una had the chance to speak. She didn't know how long it took for the drug to work, and she watched for any sign in the woman's face.

At first, nothing but a simmering anger shone through. After a beat, however, her eyebrows began to crease. Then her legs began to wobble.

"What have you done?" she asked, horrified and affronted. "What the hell have you done?"

Burn smiled a wicked little smile. "Payback," she said before turning around and sprinting toward the door.

Behind her, Una collapsed as her legs gave out beneath her. Yet her tongue still functioned, and she screamed for help, rousing her cohorts and inciting them to action. Burn listened as the door to the assembly room opened, as people took in Una's state with gasps, as they noticed Ellis and set off in pursuit.

"I'm almost clear," she panted to Scar as her legs worked, rapidly tiring from the effort. "Get ready to lock the doors."

The exit was in Burn's sights, bright despite the growing darkness. As soon as she was in range, she reached out, throwing the doors open. The second she was free, she slammed them shut, bracing against the impact of bodies on wood.

"Now!" she screamed to Scar.

The bolts slid into place a millisecond before the assembly reached her. Their furious attempts to knock down the gates echoed in Burn's mind, full of scratching and pounding and shouts. Despite it all, the doors held, keeping them at bay.

Burn gingerly separated herself from the building, half afraid that it would give way without her. Yet it remained in place, holding the herd within their pen.

Burn turned her attention away, searching for Scar, but she was nowhere to be found. She took a few steps down the lane, only to stop at the sound of her sister's new voice, which echoed from behind her.

"That should hold them for a while," she said, coming around the corner with a self-satisfied grin. "I don't want to brag, but that really was a stroke of genius."

"Genius or not, we need to get out of here," Burn said, her heart still beating frantically inside her chest.

"Whatever you say, sis," Scar replied, throwing up her hands in surrender.

Burn was about to join her, to abscond into the night, but a shuffle of cloth and a click from behind her made her freeze. She whirled around, her hackles raised, but she barely had time to take in the scene before it changed.

A guard knelt, gun in hand. He raised it toward the women. He took aim and fired.

A crack split the air, shattering the evening into brutal shards. Burn could hear the bullet fly, hear it bite through the stillness, hear it sink into soft folds of flesh.

She turned too late. By the time she rounded, Scar was already on the ground, her hand clutched to her stomach and her face contorted in pain. Blood welled up from the wound and spilled over, leaking between her fingers and pooling at her side.

Burn didn't think. She couldn't. She simply reacted, moving with lightning speed as her sister lay writhing before her. She felt nothing – not her hands reaching into her pack, not the coins gripped tightly in her palm, not the flex of her muscles as she let the bombs fly.

Later, she would marvel at the speed of her reaction, at the precision of her reflexes, but in that instant, none of it could penetrate her shock.

What did make it through was the explosion she triggered. She was standing too near the guards, too close to the radius of the blast. The force of the eruption sent her sprawling, heaving her into the air before yanking her down. She landed with a thud on her stomach, clutching her head in her hands.

For a minute, she couldn't hear a thing. The silence mocked her, filling her ears with muted pounding and an endless shrieking whine. Steadily, though, her hearing returned, conveying sounds of whimpers and fire and pain.

Burn scrambled to her feet, dashing through the smoke to her sister's side. She landed on her knees, not noticing the pain, and bent her head to Scar's cheek.

"Stay with me, Scar," she pleaded, tears pricking at her eyes. "You can't leave me. You have to hold on."

Scar let out a quiet, wheezing sound, and Burn realized it was a laugh.

"Just get me out of here," she said, her eyes closing beneath the strain. "I want to be me again. This damn woman is far too breakable." With that, Scar gave in to the darkness and went still.

Chapter 20

Something wild overcame Burn, something desperate and unhinged, and she scooped Scar up like a child, holding her as she ran. She didn't know how she bypassed the guards at the border. Maybe she fought them or gassed them or shocked them. Maybe the sight of Brika, broken and bleeding, convinced them to cave. Or maybe they were simply called away, up to the assembly trapped on a tier above. Whatever the case, she made it through, escaping her privileged prison for the haze of the world below.

No one stopped her. No one helped her, either. Most were too busy scurrying home, dodging the dusk and the curfew. Those that noticed her plight sank into the shadows, pulling back from her clear display of need. To them, it was someone else's problem, someone else's life. To Burn, it was all that mattered in the world.

Her body carried her when her mind could not. She had no sense of direction, no space in her brain unclaimed by fear.

Her legs moved as her awareness dissolved, evaporating into a pearly mist of panic and dread. The only thing she could think was that Scar was dying, her sister was dying, and Burn was the only one who could save her.

She burst into the safe house like a terror, screaming for help. They found her there, on the ground, wrapped around Scar like her body could save her. The Lunaria's shock swiftly turned to action, and they mobilized the medics, tearing away Scar's limp form.

Burn tried to follow, to go where Scar was going, but gentle hands stopped her, their owners whispering soothing words that never made it past her ears. Burn had never felt so empty. Her heart was broken, and its razor-sharp pieces tore through her body, ripping her apart from the inside.

It was Meera who came for her, who picked her up, who cleaned away the blood. Burn let the woman move her, let the water flow over her, let the hands remove her ruined clothing. None of it helped. None of it could stem the flood of fear or the images that replayed like a nightmare in her head. Or the guilt – the all-consuming guilt.

Scar had come for her. She'd changed into Brika because Burn had needed saving. She'd put her life at risk because Burn had asked, and now she might die because of it.

Burn didn't know how much time passed. The seconds leapt and stuttered and stalled, with Burn's heart beating in tandem. The only constant was Meera's hands, which stroked Burn's hair in a rhythmic caress. It wasn't enough to soothe her, but it calmed her tremors and beat back the demons, if only for a while.

After a time, Crete appeared. At the sight of him, Burn

straightened, her eyes consuming every inch of him in search of a sign, a signal of Scar's fate. Yet his form revealed nothing but fatigue.

Crete was gaunt and hollow, and he leaned on the wall for support, barely able to shuffle the few feet toward them. Meera jumped to his aid, ushering him to a chair, but all Burn could do was watch, the dread welling up until she could barely breathe.

Beside her, Crete was all corners and edges, his bones poking through his skin like they wanted to break free. It was the worst she had ever seen him, and her worry ratcheted up until it thrummed through her in painful pulses.

"I've done all I can," Crete said, each word taking strength he did not have. "I wish I could do more, but Hale's healing left me weak." As if to emphasize his point, he paused, his breathing labored. He closed his eyes, swallowing once before continuing. "We've been able to stop the bleeding, but Scar's condition is still critical. She lost a lot of blood, and I'm unable to gauge the extent of her internal injuries."

Burn's mind was spinning too fast to respond. She didn't know what to ask or how to put her worries into words. She was afraid if she opened her mouth, all that would come out would be a sob or a scream or another stretch of empty silence.

Thankfully, Meera understood her distress and said what she could not. "When will we know more? And what can we do to help?" she asked, her voice gentle yet strong.

"All we can do is wait," Crete said, his eyes fluttering open and shut. "If she makes it through the night, the chances are good that she'll survive. In the morning, I should be able to do more. Right now, it's up to her." His energy depleted, he slumped in his chair, succumbing to unconsciousness.

Meera heaved the man to his feet and took off in the direction of the sleeping quarters. There, Burn presumed she would help him into bed, tucking him in and whispering soothing words, just as she would soon try to do for Burn herself.

Only, Burn didn't want to sleep. Despite her exhaustion, she knew sleep would never come. She needed to see Scar, to watch over her, to be there when she woke up.

Burn rose, heading for the infirmary, but something stopped her. Turning to the wall, she saw her face reflected in the small oblong mirror and froze. Ellis stared back, pale and scared. Her blond hair was tangled, and her big eyes were a window to her tortured soul. Tears streaked her rounded cheeks, and her full lips quivered, trembling in time to the rest of her form.

This was not what Scar needed. If she woke – *when* she woke – she needed her sister, not this stranger. She needed Burn. And Burn needed to remember who she was.

The tears and the trembling stopped as Burn realized what she had to do. With a plan in place, she took off down the hallway, away from the makeshift hospital.

Burn wove through the halls with purpose, skirting people and ignoring their questioning glances as she searched for Eyana. It took three rooms for Burn to spot her, and three more strides before she found herself at the woman's side.

"I need you to change me back," she commanded, startling the woman out of her meditation.

Eyana's large dark eyes opened and traveled up to Ellis'

face, considering her. Despite her surprise, she had a lingering calm, like an aura of tranquility. It buffeted Burn's sides, beckoning to her to surrender, but she held it at bay, clinging to the disquiet as if it could save her.

"Are you certain?" Eyana asked, her voice low and velvety smooth.

"Yes," Burn said without hesitation. "Ellis has done all she can. It's time to bring back Auburn."

Eyana's lips quirked into something that wasn't quite a smile. "Very well," she replied, nodding once. "Take a seat and we'll get started."

It was agonizing, a sharp slicing feeling that split her open and turned her inside out, but Burn didn't scream. Instead, she seized on the pain, letting it fuel her and guide her back to herself. She was Auburn Alendra. She was a daughter, a sister, a friend. She was a rebel. She was a leader. She was home.

The process took longer than it had before, and Eyana was clearly straining. Her power – though great – was waning without access to the wildlands. It was difficult to watch, and even worse to undergo. Eventually, though, the pain subsided, changing from a constant rage to a subtle ache to a mild discomfort. Then it was gone, and Burn was back.

She felt unsteady on her feet, but she didn't care. Rising, she fumbled into the hall, searching for a mirror. Locating one on the wall, she lunged for it, her fingers closing around it just as her legs tangled beneath her and brought her down.

Burn landed on her back with a thud, barely managing to spare the mirror from destruction. A shock of pain pulsed through her from the impact, but it couldn't penetrate her mind. All she could think was that she was back. Auburn was back.

She stared at herself in the gleaming surface, tracing the lines of her narrow chin and her raised cheekbones before coming to rest on her wide dark eyes. She had been adrift for so long, grasping for something she couldn't quite see, and now it was right in front of her.

Burn breathed a sigh of relief, letting go of Ellis and her life, of the ties that had bound her and the rules that had constrained her, of the society and the family and the lies. They had eaten at her slowly, methodically, wearing her down until she was a ghost of herself. Now she was finally free.

Getting to her feet, Burn felt her legs grow steady beneath her. She cast the mirror aside, no longer needing its strength, and turned to face Eyana in the dim hallway.

"Thank you," she said sincerely, the sound of her own voice a reassuring melody to her ears.

Eyana simply nodded, her exhaustion apparent. Like Crete, she looked tired and worn, her face a map of shadows and fatigue. Burn wished she could help them, lending her strength in place of theirs, but only time could heal them, and it was steadily slipping through their fingers.

"Get some rest," Burn advised, leading Eyana back into her chambers and turning off the light.

With a new intensity, Burn headed to the infirmary to set up vigil. Heads turned in her direction when she passed as the Lunaria took in the familiar visage of their friend and ally. Murmurs of support and gratitude followed her through the halls, creating a cushion of whispers that muffled the dread.

The Lunaria saw her as a symbol. In her absence, the world had grown that much darker. Now that she was back, the flame of hope was flickering. Burn could feel it in the air. These people were ready to fight. They were ready to end this.

Burn accepted their fire and stoked it, holding on to the passion as she entered the infirmary. Yet what she saw nearly extinguished it for good.

Scar, still hidden under the veil of General Brika, was pale and still, with the shallow movement of her chest the only thing separating her from the grave. Her bloody uniform had been removed and replaced by loose garments, which were hiked up to expose the mess of bandages encircling her tattered torso.

The room reeked of blood and antiseptic, a harsh combination that stung Burn's nostrils and made her eyes water. Next to Scar, bags of fluids hung on poles, with tubes snaking downward into her arms. She looked so small, so breakable, and Burn's heart seized at the sight.

It felt like the air had been sucked from the room. Burn's head began to spin, and she looked away, needing a reprieve. Yet she wasn't destined to find one there. Because lying beside her sister, with his eyes shut and his body still, was Hale. Her Hale, freed of his disguise and returned to his strong, resilient self.

The sight of him was bittersweet, soothing some wounds while reopening others. Unlike Scar, Hale was a canvas of bruises and cuts, a watercolor of purples and browns with angry slashes of red. Each exposed swath of skin boasted its own collection of gashes and bumps, like a roadmap of his torment.

This room held her heart, and it hovered on the brink between life and death. Hale on one side, Scar on the other, both fighting to survive. And she stood in the middle, helpless. The camaraderie she had felt, the fire of resistance, sputtered within her. Even with all the allies she could muster, this fight was not up to her.

As if called by her need for a friend, Nara appeared in the doorway. Burn's eyes remained on Hale, but she recognized the woman's movements, her catlike grace and her sweeping gaze. She stood tentatively in the doorway, uncertain, before crossing the threshold. But instead of appearing by Burn's side, she walked straight to Scar, positioning herself like a sentry.

"How is she?" Nara asked, her voice tight.

Burn could hear the concern – and feel the affection behind it. She smiled despite herself, pleased that Nara and Scar had found each other. It was a comforting thought, that love could exist even in the darkest corners.

"Crete says she could pull through – if she makes it through the night," Burn said, struggling to keep her voice steady as her worries threatened to drown her. "But she's strong," she continued, as much to herself as to Nara. "She knows we need her, and she'll fight like hell to get back to us."

"I should have been here," Nara replied, clearly in her own world with its own creeping guilt. "I should have been the one to come get you, not her." Remorse sang through her words, biting into Burn's fears and forcing her around. She drew up next to Nara, standing shoulder to shoulder with her partner in arms.

"Scar saved my life. She risked everything for me. If it's anyone's fault, it's mine," Burn whispered. "But guilt won't get us anywhere. Laying blame on ourselves won't help her heal."

"Then let's find the people who did this," Nara bit back, her sorrow transforming into rage. "Let's lay the blame at their feet and make them pay."

"Oh, they've paid," Burn countered, flashing back to her actions. "Believe me, they've paid." The memory of the explosion and its aftermath tinted her thoughts red, and she shuddered, caught off guard by her own callous vengeance.

Nara, however, seemed mollified. "Good," she declared with a nod. "But if she dies, the rest of those fuckers are going down."

"Agreed," Burn said in solidarity, nodding in return.

The women settled themselves in for a long night, stationing themselves in chairs they'd stolen from the hall like sentinels keeping watch for death. Burn's exhaustion overcame her, and she drifted in and out of sleep, with her troubled dreams granting little respite from the strain.

Ever the guard, Nara remained awake, her wide eyes trained on Scar as if she could see the wound inside of her and watch as it healed. For all Burn knew, she could. Or perhaps the intensity was merely a form of love, a savage need to be there for every moment, to mark every change.

In between her restless fits of sleep, Burn shifted her attention from Scar to Hale and back. No matter how hard she tried, though, she couldn't detect their thoughts, couldn't make out their dreams, couldn't tell how much they suffered.

All she heard was the steady whoosh of breath, in and out, and the quiet thump of hearts as they beat out the time. But even those simple sounds were soothing in their cadence, a calming assurance of life, and they invariably lulled her into sleep once more.

After a time, the sound of a soft voice pulled her from her dreams, and Burn struggled to swim to the surface, to free herself from sleep. She felt groggy and out of sorts, and her body was stiff from a night spent upright. She groaned as she came back to herself, opening her eyes to the light.

The scene before her hadn't changed. Burn blinked as her eyes adjusted, taking in Hale's immobile form, Nara's seated figure, and Scar's bandaged body. Only, something about the sight was different, and Burn struggled to put a finger on it. Then she saw it: Scar's eyes were open.

Burn was across the room in an instant, nearly knocking over the chair in her haste. She gripped Scar's hand with bated breath, waiting for her sister to speak. Per usual, Scar wasn't one to disappoint.

"Damn it, Burn," she groaned, her voice weak but clear. "I thought I told you to change me back."

Burn couldn't help but smile, with hot tears welling behind her eyes. "I love you, too, sis," she said, her voice cracking with emotion.

Scar squeezed Burn's hand, giving her sister her patented wry smile. "I know."

Chapter 21

With Scar and Hale both on the mend, Burn's attention naturally turned to war. They were, after all, mere weeks away from the culmination of the Shadow Assembly's schemes, and unless they acted first, their enemies would be unstoppable.

The odds weren't entirely against the Lunaria. They knew their enemy's plans and they'd seen their faces. However, those factors had yet to do them any good. They knew what they were up against, knew the arrows in their enemy's quiver, but they still needed to acquire a shield.

"What resources do we have at our disposal?" Burn asked the war council, whose grim faces were growing grimmer by the minute.

They were a raggedy group of soldiers and spies, mostly leaders who had never wanted to lead. They had convened to hear Burn's report from the heavens and to watch the footage she'd risked her life to film. Now they considered their options, weighing ideas against casualties and plans against the cost of human life. And getting nowhere.

"We have some new recruits," Nara started, "but nothing close to what we'd need to win. Especially against a gifted army. Most of them are gifted themselves, but they're untrained in combat. We're teaching them what we can, but it may not be enough."

"What about weapons?" Burn asked, hoping for good news on that front, at least. Once again, though, she'd set herself up for disappointment.

"Our stockpile has dwindled," said Innoxia, a longtime member who'd helped them survive the ManniK Battles with her gift for manipulating the dead. "We were left severely depleted after our last few run-ins," she continued. "Plus, the increased pressure from the Peace Force has scared most of our suppliers underground."

Burn groaned in frustration. "That's not going to be enough. Not enough people, not enough weapons, not enough time. We're outmatched and outgunned, and unless we find a way to change that, most of us won't live to see another month."

"We've fought them back with less," said Ansel, shrugging. "During the ManniK Battles – and in the tunnels from the wildlands. We had a fraction of the people we have now, and we still came out on top."

"This isn't like anything we've faced before," Burn replied, her voice hard and unyielding. "We aren't fighting an arm of the monster. This time, we are facing the monster itself. And we're gonna need a bigger stick."

"I have an idea."

The voice rang out from behind Burn, and she slowly turned to meet it. Seated on a rickety wheelchair, still wrapped in her makeshift gown, was Scar, finally returned to her familiar form, metallic skin and all. Behind her, pushing her through the hall – and leaning heavily on the chair for support – was Hale.

Both seemed tired and worn, and it looked like years had been drained from their faces. Somehow, despite his strength, Hale looked gaunt, with deep purple smudges beneath his eyes and an ashen pallor to his skin. Beside him, Scar looked smaller than she ever had.

Yet there was a gleam in their eyes, a fire. Burn recognized it – and knew it all too well. It was conviction, certainty, passion. It was a need to fight, to give as good as they'd gotten. It was the spark of rebellion.

"Shouldn't you be resting?" Burn asked, one eyebrow raised.

"Fuck rest," Scar spat, shaking her head. "I'll rest when this is over. Right now, you need me."

Burn let out a frustrated sigh. She should have expected this, should have known that her sister would never acquiesce to life as an invalid, no matter how broken she was. Scar had a stubbornness in her veins, the same stubbornness that ran through her own, and she'd never consent to being kept from the action. She needed to fight, and her injury only fueled her fire.

"What about you?" Burn asked, turning to Hale. While she delighted in his presence, she hated to see him like this – sapped of his fortitude and trembling from exhaustion. It broke her heart every time he met her eyes.

"I'm staying," the large man said simply, his voice strong despite his frailty.

"What is it with you people?" Burn asked in annoyance. "Don't you know that you're supposed to take it easy? You nearly died. What will it take for you to go back to your room and lie down?"

Hale shook his head softly, sinking into one of the empty chairs.

"Scar's right," he said with a shrug. "We're no good to you in there. We might be injured, but we're not dead. We can still help. And by the looks of things, you need all the help you can get."

Burn just stared in shock. If she wasn't mistaken, Hale had actually agreed with Scar. It was a god damn miracle.

Still, Burn wanted to protest, wanted to wheel both of them back to the infirmary and hold them down until they slept, but she was no match for their combined obstinacy and ego. Plus, they had a point. The Lunaria were at an impasse, and Scar and Hale had two of the best minds among them. So she relented, giving in to their need to help despite her own reservations.

"Fine. Stay," she sighed, gesturing for Scar to take the floor. "What's this genius idea of yours?"

Scar's face contorted into an evil grin. "Well, technically it's *our* idea," she said, glancing over at Hale, "and the assembly will never see it coming."

Hale smirked in reply, and Burn's stomach did a nervous flip. This was either going to get them all killed, or it was precisely the plan they'd been searching for. She truly hoped it was the latter.

Getting shot sucked. Scar felt like she'd been trampled by a herd of wild animals, and a permanent exhaustion had settled over her system. Worse still was the way people treated her – like she was helpless and breakable and at risk of suddenly disappearing.

She was finding, however, that revenge really was the best medicine. While she might not be able to fight, she could plot and plan and choreograph the action, devising a foolproof method to win back the upper hand. The pieces had already been put into place, after all. All they needed were the finishing touches, the ingenious elements that would take their plan from clever to diabolical.

Scar was surprised to find that Hale had a passable eye for strategy. His penchant for impulsive reactions had long ago convinced her that his usefulness was confined to the battlefield, but their forced interactions within the infirmary had begun to change that theory. Maybe Burn was having a calming effect on him, or maybe his rational side had always been there, just buried beneath the thick crust of his ego. Either way, it was nice to have a partner with whom to plot.

It only took a matter of days to set the stage. With her own strength compromised, she had to rely on others for the supplies and information she needed. Their efforts weren't efficient, by any means, but they were adequate, and she was able to gather enough volunteers and equipment to give the Lunaria a fighting chance.

When the night finally came to put their plan into action, Burn and her crew suited up while Scar and Hale watched enviously from the sidelines. Well, Hale watched enviously while Scar just watched, content in her role as mastermind and puppeteer. She didn't need to be on-site to control the action. All she needed was eyes on the battlefield – and with the tweaks she'd made to the Lunaria's goggles, she had all the eyes she could wish for.

Staring at her tab, she could already see 20-odd views from inside the house as her army of spies prepared to depart. Beside her, Hale fidgeted uselessly as he watched the events unfold.

"I could go with them," he said for the hundredth time, his eyes straying longingly toward the door. "I'm almost healed, and my strength is returning. I could be an asset to the team."

Scar sighed, already bored of his whining. Crete still hadn't cleared them for active duty, and Hale knew it. Yet that didn't stop his incessant grumbling. Thankfully, Burn chose that moment to stick her head into the room, effectively curbing his carping.

"We're all set," she said, looking every bit the spy in her all-black attire. "Are we good to go?"

"Almost," Scar said, reaching behind her to grab something from beneath the sheets of her bed. Turning, she held out the weapon to Burn.

Her sister took it, staring at the strange piece of equipment as if trying to read its secrets. It was a jumble of parts in the general shape of a gun, with a squat barrel leading up to a bulbous head. Burn was right to be confused; it was a one-of-a-kind creation, a Scarlett Alendra original.

"In case of emergency," Scar said, letting her eyes drop

to the weapon before glancing back at Burn. "Oh, and you're gonna want to wear these," she added, handing her a pair of matte black earmuffs.

"What is it?" Burn asked dubiously, eyeing the strange contraption.

"It doesn't matter," Scar said, brushing her sister's concerns aside. "Just point it at the bad guys and shoot."

To her credit, Burn didn't question her further. She merely strapped the weapon to a holster on her belt before turning back to Scar.

"Wait for my signal," Scar instructed, her voice hardening until it was all business. "Don't make a move until I tell you to. And don't get caught. Or shot. We're counting on you."

In reply, Burn bent down and gave her sister a gentle hug, the move so quick that Scar didn't have time to react. In a matter of seconds, she was at the door once more, smiling confidently as she lowered her goggles over her eyes.

"See you both on the other side," she taunted before sliding away.

Training her eyes on her tab, Scar watched as her sister corralled her crew and slipped into the night. With Burn and Nara acting as lookouts, the elite team swept through the city like shadows, unheard and unseen. Even their comms went silent, with only a soft patter of footsteps to mark their progress.

Their target was the Dead Zone, the colloquial name for Kasis' manufacturing heart. It was home to nearly all of the factories and workhouses, the assembly lines and mills, the shops that spit out sludge and goods in equal measure.

Within the confines of the sector, workers toiled out their days under the thumbs of the elite, growing sicker as their bosses grew richer.

Fittingly, the Peace Force called it the Golden Borough. It was the source of Kasis' wealth, the heart of Kasian industry. And the heart of its pollution. It was the hell to the assembly's heavens, the golden goose for their coffers, and it was about to get its comeuppance.

Many of the Lunaria, including Hale, had worked within the Dead Zone, toiling away their lives within its borders. It was where they'd found the spark of rebellion, where it had blossomed into a flame. Naturally, they knew its passages and pitfalls, its guard towers and guardless paths. They knew their way inside, and they knew how to get there undetected.

Scar's eyes flicked between the feeds, each camera alighting on another angle of the misery. She could feel the despair, the aching tragedy of the prison. There was no beauty within its confines, only stark metal, welded together in the shape of walls and gates and walkways. It was an abyss for the senses, an endless leeching void. Yet at its center was the Peace Force's jewel – and the key to the Lunaria's survival. Within its dead heart lay the city's main source of weaponry, the facility in which all of the force's arms were fabricated. And they were going to blow it up.

Scar watched as the building came into view through the haze. Its severe steel chimneys sliced into the darkness and dyed it even darker, with their puffs of noxious smog consuming everything in their wake.

The building itself was quiet, still, but it was imposing nonetheless, standing like a fortress of stone amidst a world of clouds. Surrounding it was a heavy knotted fence that buzzed in warning. Within the gates, a small army waited, their senses alert for any disturbance.

The Lunaria spread themselves out in silent waves, breaking up to position themselves along the border. Their movements were light and quick, fueled by impatience, excitement, and a healthy dose of dread.

Scar surveyed the scene from a patchwork of angles, piecing together the building's defenses. Peace Officers armed with deadly tech strutted in even lines, faceless and menacing. Their footsteps tolled like a bell through the darkness, marking the passage of time. More guns jutted from the smattering of windows, peeking between bars to aim at the night.

Scar was so focused on assessing their arsenal that the sound of Burn's voice made her jump. Beside her, Hale grunted his amusement, chuckling at her show of discomfort.

"Everyone's in place," Burn said, hushed yet insistent. "Scar, you're up."

She'd been waiting for those words. Shifting her attention to a secondary tab, Scar's fingers danced as she played her part, setting the events in motion. She smiled as she spun her web, its cords a masterpiece of woven code. It was elegant, stunning, a work of inspired art, and it would rend the world in two.

With a tap of her finger, her beautiful beast came to life. Throughout the city, in every home and office and factory, in every back alley and every Peace Force den, screens snapped on and began to speak.

It was simple, really. With the bug she'd placed in the

news hub, she had control of the Peace Force's network – and now she had control of the message. An image of Una Hyde appeared on screen, torn from the video Burn had taken. She smiled at the crowd before her, drinking in their cheers.

"This is your assembly," said a voice – Hale's voice. "And this is how they plan to kill you."

"Our experiments have finally paid off," Una stated, just as she had mere days before. "We have at last been able to manufacture mutants!"

The scene jumped ahead, beating out an ominous strain. As it rose to a crescendo, Una located her prey and stalked to its side. With a flick of her wrist, she sent the statue flying, and it broke into shards in a cacophony of sound. The crowd's cheers resounded like a war cry, which melded with the music to form a dissonant hum.

Once more, Una's face consumed the screen, her look of triumph menacing in its ferocity. "Soon we will be unstoppable, with a gifted assembly and a gifted army at our backs."

At those words, the scene changed, morphing into one of fire and blood. It was Peace Force footage, salvaged from the news hub's banks. In it, screams of fear rose like smoke through the streets, accompanied by acts of torment and terror. It was the ManniK Battles, seen through Peace Force eyes. It was officers killing without mercy, slaughtering civilians and rebels with abandon.

"These are your leaders," Hale said as the video switched to a shot of the assembly, their faces turned in anger toward the camera. They'd been looking at Burn, denouncing her for her interruption, but on screen their sneers and stares read like fury, like pure, unadulterated loathing.

"Tell them what you think of their plans. Tell them in the streets. Tell them with your gifts. And when you're ready to join the fight, we'll be waiting."

With that, the video ended. Instead of going black, however, the message began again, looping like an infinite call to war, like an endless cry for battle.

It wasn't long before the city responded, sounding their own cries in return. Within minutes, the world exploded into a thousand echoes, as if one enormous beast had finally woken from its slumber. It growled its displeasure in the streets, seeking a soul to devour. It chanted and whispered and raged. It lit up the night with sound.

Pleased with the reaction, Scar turned to Hale with a smirk. "Let's see what you've got," she said, her voice taunting as if in challenge.

Hale smirked right back, meeting her gaze with fire in his own. Turning his sights to his tab, he took control of his army. "Phase one is complete," he growled through the comms. "Stand by for phase two."

The first stage flowed effortlessly into the next, as the guards stationed outside the factory were called away from their posts, repositioned by their masters like puppets on a string. Some were cast to the news hub to fight the invisible force that threatened their authority. Others were dispersed throughout the city, scattered on the wind to tackle the seething beast knocking at their gates.

Soon, a skeleton crew was all that remained, a bare bones defense to guard the hoard. Yet even the barest of bones posed a threat when armed with such an arsenal. Good thing the Lunaria had an arsenal of their own.

It was only a pity that the Peace Force had adopted gas masks in the wake of the recent attacks. It would have been simple to put these men to sleep and sneak past them. Instead, they'd have to do this the hard way.

"Send in Innoxia," Hale commanded, clearly enjoying his role. "Everyone else, get ready to strike."

From behind her sister's eyes, Scar watched as Innoxia materialized, a lone wolf set adrift from the pack. Except she wasn't alone.

Lurching forms bled from the darkness, lured to the front by her call. Their movements were unnatural, uneven, unsure. They loped and pitched and staggered. They were ragged, broken, and bent. Some lacked eyes, others arms, others faces.

Innoxia's crew was an army of the dead, their skin rotting and their flesh torn in tattered strips from their bones. In some cases, bones were all that remained, stitched together by sinews and scraps of moldering muscle.

The best amongst them, the recently deceased, gripped guns or knives or axes, trudging along like a semblance of an army in an almost believable fashion. Others merely ambled, their shocking state the only weapon they could manage.

Innoxia hadn't had much choice in her fodder. Despite the prevalence of death inside Kasis, corpses didn't tend to linger. They were mourned, then carted off, then burned. There wasn't room for death in a city so confined, and no space for sentiment beneath their dome.

These enduring few were the exceptions to the rule. These men and women had slipped through the cracks, even in death. They had lain in wait, on racks and tables, drawers and freezers, with no one to save them from the cold.

It had been Burn's idea to retrieve them, to give use to the useless and life to the lifeless. She'd been to the morgue before, ventured inside its confines to stare at the face of death. It had been part of her trials, part of her introduction to the Lunaria, so she knew well the treasure inside its walls.

Yet those walls were protected, watched by the same guards and the same guns that lay before them now. They'd needed a soldier, a spy, a man on the inside. With Kaz still locked away in a cell, they'd turned to the next best thing: Detective Grayland.

Grayland had served under Scar's father, Arvense. Despite their place on the force, the pair had been hopeful, idealistic, naïve. They'd tried to use their power for good, and Arvense had paid the ultimate price. Since then, Grayland had kept his head down and his feet on the ground, never straying too far from the company line – except when it came to Burn and Scar.

They were his family, his charges, his duty, and when they called, he answered.

Grayland wasn't a bad man. He did what he could to protect the people. But it had taken Burn's trip down the Pit for him to realize his purpose. He thought he'd lost a daughter, a confidant, a friend, and it had torn him apart. It had also made him question what was and consider what could be.

When Burn had resurfaced and reached out for help, he'd jumped at the chance to act, to assist, to follow in Arvense's path. He'd come to see the true face behind the force and understand that he wanted no part in their plans.

As a detective, he hadn't fought in the force's battles. He hadn't killed the defenseless or rounded up the freaks. He couldn't have saved them, either, nor could he have changed the course of the war. He couldn't even do much now, couldn't find Kaz or free him. Yet he could help them raid the morgue – and he had.

Gradually, over the course of two days, Innoxia had done her thing, animating corpses and guiding them through the city. With Grayland's help, she'd put in place her army, their dead faces unseen amidst the sleepwalkers shuffling through the streets.

Now those same dead figures trudged forward, their lifeless eyes trained on the gates. In a stroke of luck, the doors still stood ajar following the soldiers' exodus, beckoning them inside as if welcoming them into the fold.

"Burn, it's time," Scar whispered through the line, rolling the wheel closer to collision.

Burn knew precisely what to do. Grabbing a gadget from her pack, she tuned it to the enemy's frequency and pressed down hard, disrupting their comms with a single strike. Unable to coordinate or call for backup, the armory's guardians would be cast adrift, alone in the sea with no hope of help.

"Once that's done, you're free to move in," Hale instructed Innoxia. "While the guards are distracted, Ansel will sabotage the electrical box, causing an outage on the fence. That will allow the rest of you to sneak in through the side undetected."

They knew the plan by heart, but Hale's words spurred them to action. As the dead advanced, the living took their places, poised against the fence to make their move.

When the first of the guards spotted the intruders, he shouted his alarm, bellowing across the broken comms. No one came to help him, and no one saw him die. Two more fell in the same manner, their passing unhindered by resistance. By then, though, their shouts had drawn attention, and more men came to inspect the commotion.

Screams of fear and shouted orders echoed lightly through the air, followed naturally by the discharge of weapons. The corpses fired back, their aim suspect without the steadying force of muscles or eyes. Still, the onslaught did its job, forcing the enemies back against the walls and giving the Lunaria room to maneuver.

One of Scar's screens lit up as Ansel played his part, crafting an inferno in which he was the spark. A moment later, the fences fell silent, drained of their power. Burn moved decisively toward the toothless barrier, drawing out Scar's laser, which sliced through the links like a hot knife through butter.

Their path clear, the rest of the Lunaria moved as one, trickling through the portal and into the yard beyond. They lined up without a word, snaking through the space in a human chain. Nara and Burn stood apart from the rest, alert and armed, their lookouts and leaders.

Dormaline rose from the ranks, shimmering with excitement. The young girl melted from solid to ephemeral and back, like a ghost caught forever between worlds.

"Is it time?" she asked, her voice trembling. "Can I go?"

"Yes," Hale grunted from afar. "It's time."

Dormaline didn't need to be told twice. She sped off toward the building with alacrity and disappeared within its grimy wall, sliding into the heart of the darkness.

Then they waited, the seconds ticking by like hours as Dormaline worked. Around the bend, Innoxia's troops were faltering, their already ravaged bodies dropping beneath the onslaught of the Peace Force. Innoxia did what she could, reanimating the dead from amongst the soldiers' ranks, but even their hearty forms couldn't hold out forever.

Inside, Dormaline didn't dally, and she soon emerged with an arsenal in her arms. The Lunaria jumped into action, ferrying the weapons down the line until they reached the end of the row. By then, Dormaline had vanished once more, slinking back for another load.

This exercise repeated time after time, until every member had as many weapons as they could handle, strapped around their bodies and waists, piled into packs and bags, and held like children in their arms. By that point, Innoxia's defenses had dwindled, shrinking until only a handful remained. Ansel tried to help, tried to use his flames to beat back the throng, but his skill set was needed elsewhere.

Scar's fingers went white as she gripped her tab, anxious for her friends from afar. She itched to help them, to do more than merely watch, but her powers were limited, her wings clipped by the distance.

"Ansel, get to the building and do your thing," Hale ordered. "The rest of you, prepare yourselves for a fight."

The Lunaria turned as one to face their foes, transforming from an assembly line to the front line in an instant. They marched with purpose toward the building's entrance, following Hale's orders without question or reserve. Scar watched them go, watched the view change from calm to chaos, from stealth to struggle.

Instead of diving headfirst into the melee, the Lunaria fought from the shadows, using their gifts to rain madness on the scene. The air around the guards began to pitch and swell as Rakasa took the stage. Scar peered from behind his eyes, seeing the world dim as the sector's smog coalesced, drowning their rivals in darkness.

Shedding their loads, Jade, Ino, and Lux surged into the storm, disappearing beneath its viscous waves. From the sidelines, Burn and Nara kept up their vigil, protecting their troops by picking off any errant foes.

Meanwhile, Ansel worked, pairing accelerant with stolen explosives to lay a devilish path of destruction. His intrinsic understanding of combustibles fueled his efforts, and within no time he'd rejoined the crew, a smile on his lips and a fire in his eyes.

"Everything's in place," he reported. "Let's get out of here."

Ino and Lux emerged within moments, trotting to Ansel's side. Yet there was no sign of Jade. Burn called her name, but the comms stayed silent, an ominous quiet suffusing the line. Rakasa began to lift the darkness and Nara was preparing to pounce when the woman finally appeared, limping but whole.

Ino and Lux ran to assist her, each taking an arm to help her along. Together, the group made it to the temporary safety of a small guard booth, which rested halfway between the plant and its gates. As they paused to catch their breath and regroup, the remaining wisps of Rakasa's fog vanished, leaving the area clear – and revealing an advancing horde.

It was a secondary battalion, drawn from inside the factory walls. The troops kicked aside the moldering dead, which littered the ground in mounds, and paid no heed to their fallen friends. Detached and determined, they took aim and fired.

The Lunaria were protected behind their bunker, yet they had no way out. Bullets bit through the air like hail, carving up the night and keeping them stranded. Ever the martyr, Ansel moved toward his fuse with his hands outstretch, but Burn reached out to stop him.

"If you light that, this whole place will burn," she cautioned, her voice low and insistent. "We need a better way out of here, a way that won't get us killed."

Burn waited for ideas – and Scar waited with her – but the ideas didn't come. Sighing, Scar resigned herself to the inevitable.

"Burn," she said, grabbing her sister's attention, "I think this qualifies as an emergency."

At first, Burn merely stood there, confused. Then understanding dawned. Reaching around her belt, she unlatched Scar's weapon, easing it out with caution as if it might explode in her hands.

"Are you sure about this?" Burn asked, eyeing the weapon doubtfully.

"Yes," Scar replied, filling her voice with vigor. "Just make sure your ears are covered. And once you shoot, be prepared to run."

Burn shook her head, but she didn't protest. Knowing better than to argue, she did as she was told, securing the earmuffs before pointing the weapon toward her foes. Then, taking a breath, she fired.

A massive wave of sonic force burst forth, cascading into the approaching throng. It tore them from their feet, pushing them upward and backward with a wall of pure power. Screams of surprise and confusion mingled with the gun's sonic shriek to rip the night in two.

Despite her warning, Scar hadn't thought to cover her own ears, which rang from the output of power. She didn't hear Burn's panicked warning or discern the Lunaria's gasps, but she saw them turn and run and keep running. And, as they looked back on the scene, she saw the reason why.

Not only had the blast struck their foes, but it had hit the factory, as well, wrenching away its walls and sending them sprawling. They fell in every direction, like an avalanche of stone and steel, seeking to consume them.

Hale recovered first. Shouting into the comms, unaware of his own volume, he told Ansel to burn it, to light the fuses and run. Ansel complied, bending down to send his fire toward the wreckage. It snaked through the debris and raining rubble, splitting into channels to attack the armory from all sides.

It engulfed the building in moments, licking its uninjured sides and lapping at its windows, which shattered from the heat. Just as Scar's hearing returned, a shuddering boom echoed from the scene, followed by three more in rapid succession. Then, with unearthly grace, a ball of flames, bright and hot and angry, erupted from the shivering shell, rising like a beacon in the night.

Chapter 22

There was a quiet sort of peace inside the Lunaria's den, a tranquility that balanced on a knife's edge between the fear of war and their ceaseless preparations to face it. Burn knew that the peace wouldn't last, that the battle would steal their serenity in the end, so she clung to it while she could, relishing their present safety and the small victories they'd managed to claim.

The attack on the armory had been an undeniable success. With it, they'd secured enough weapons to equip a significant portion of their battalion, while destroying any hope the Peace Force had of outmatching them. Scar's sonic blaster and Ansel's incendiary measures had ensured that the plant was effectively eliminated, with no chance that it could return to its former glory.

Not only that, but their ranks were growing by the hour. Their broadcast had made people brave, given them the courage to fight and an enemy to fight against. It had pushed them to accept what they'd been ignoring for years, thrusting their fears into the spotlight and making them impossible to ignore.

Even the Peace Force was feeling the anguish. After the Lunaria's transmission, desertions amongst their officers had increased tenfold. People akin to Kaz and Grayland, who had thought they were working toward a cause, found they could no longer stomach the atrocities they were enabling.

Those that had maimed and arrested and killed at their superiors' behest were finally taking the time to look up, to stare into the demons' eyes, and not all of them liked what they saw. It wasn't what they'd signed on for, not the peace they'd intended to promote, so they parted ways with their past lives, becoming fugitives in the process. Their exodus wasn't enough to bring the force to its knees, but it was a start in leveling the battlefield between them.

Still, the Lunaria's actions had set fire to Kasis, and the blaze raged with fury outside their door, bringing retribution in equal measure to their reward.

The Peace Force hadn't been able to stop Scar's broadcast, a fact which made Scar and her smugness insufferable. Instead, the hub had gone dead, its feeds switched off to curb the spread of the Lunaria's seditious facts. With their main propaganda machine compromised, the Peace Force had taken to shouting their pronouncements through the streets.

They'd reworked their curfew sirens to broadcast their new edicts, which further constrained movement and life within the city limits. "Terrorists" could now be shot on sight, giving officers free rein to kill at will and license to label anyone as a threat. Weapons of any kind were forbidden, and anyone seen carrying one would face the force's power.

Movement through the levels and tiers had been heavily curtailed, with officers stationed on stairs and walkways to interrogate anyone who dared travel. Gifted citizens, who had long faced scrutiny, now experienced outright hostility. They were forced to register with the Peace Station and undergo rigorous testing to ensure their powers didn't pose a threat. Those that failed were jailed and forgotten, yet more casualties of the Peace Force's war.

If that wasn't enough, they'd also begun to "regulate" the utilities, with rolling blackouts now common in the lower levels and water service cut to mere hours a day. They said it was a necessary measure, a way to conserve their resources, yet they themselves faced no such strain.

They acted as though these restrictions would somehow restore order. Understandably, they did not. Instead, they created a powder keg, a roiling unrest that threatened to explode at any moment.

Throughout the lower and middle tiers, protests, riots, and mobs sprang up in the streets, triggered by a word or a gesture. People were shot down where they stood, armed with nothing but a fist and a foul word. Those that couldn't react in time were trampled or torn apart or tossed over railings to see if they could fly.

War was inevitable. It lurked on the horizon like a storm cloud, blotting out the suns. Its cold fingers could be felt in every corner of the city, creeping ever closer and consuming its warmth. The only question was when. Did they have days or weeks or hours? How long until their world began to burn?

Of course, the Lunaria wanted to attack first. They were done living their lives in reaction. This time, they planned to have the upper hand.

Yet there were difficulties in scheduling a war, unforeseen hurdles in organizing a fight. Their ranks were growing, but they were green, inexperienced and untested. They required guidance, training, and a decent dose of reality. They needed to understand fear, and they needed to know how to face it. It wasn't something they could teach in a day.

The Lunaria also needed a plan. They couldn't exactly march to the top of the city, stride up to the assembly's gates, and expect to win. This was going to take ingenuity, resourcefulness, imagination. It was going to take a god damn miracle.

They didn't have forever. In a matter of days, the entire assembly would have the serum. They'd have powers – the best powers – hand-picked from amongst the gifted like weapons chosen for war. In a few weeks, the Peace Force could have them, too. If they let it go that far, the Lunaria would have no chance at survival.

They did what they could in the time they had left. Nara trained their new recruits, tightening their movements and shaping them for battle. They used their powers in ways they'd never dreamed of – to hurt, to maim, to kill. They worked themselves raw, dueling through the day before passing out at night.

The rest of them planned and plotted, strategizing as if their lives depended on it – because they did. It was clear that not all of them would make it. Their friends, their allies, their lovers were fleeting, and each could vanish in an instant.

Burn knew that better than anyone. Her dreams were haunted with those she'd lost, with the lives she'd taken and those taken from her. She mourned them – and she grieved the fact that she'd be forced to endure it all again. She'd have to claim life and stand by as lives were claimed in return.

She held on to the people in her life while she could. Scar and Nara and Meera and Hale. She felt a hole where Kaz should have been, but she knew she couldn't save him. If he wanted to escape, he would have to do it alone. Burn believed that it was possible, that he could slip out and disappear within the station that had once employed him, but that didn't stop her chest from aching. She wanted her raggedy family whole, even as it threatened to crumble beneath her fingers.

"What will happen if we win?" Burn asked Hale one morning while they lay tangled together beneath the sheets.

Hale's face was angled toward the ceiling, and Burn studied the new lines around his eyes and the permanent furrow that had made its way onto his brow. He must have felt her gaze because he turned to study her in return, his face smoothing into something that resembled contentment.

"I don't know," he responded, shrugging with his arm still draped around her. "We rebuild, I guess. We make something better, something that will last."

Burn had been so focused on fighting that she'd never truly considered what they were fighting for – and what it would mean to succeed. It seemed foreign, this idea of winning, and something nagged at her as she considered it. She couldn't tell if it was hope or dread or some combination of the two, but it settled uneasily in her stomach.

"What makes us any better than them?" Burn asked, trying to put her fears into words. "Why are we qualified to decide other people's fates? Who's to say that we won't be the same as the assembly, that we won't strive for power at the expense of the powerless?"

Hale sighed, his warm breath tickling her face. He began to stroke her hair with his fingers, untangling the knot inside of her with his gentle caress. She hadn't realized how much she had missed this – how much she had missed him. How much she had missed herself.

"The very fact that you're asking those questions means we'll be better," he told her, his hand now moving down to her back. "We all want to do what's right. Sure, it will take some time to figure out what that means, but we have an opportunity. We have a chance to listen to the people, to hear them, and to turn their thoughts and their ideas into action. We're bound to make mistakes. We can't please everyone. But we can work to erase the boundaries that keep people apart. And, in doing so, I think we can create something beautiful."

"When did you become so wise?" Burn asked, snuggling deeper into his grasp. She heard the rumble of his laughter and felt it vibrate through his chest.

"Well, I've always been quite clever," he said, a hint of mischief in his tone. "It just took you a while to see it."

Burn hit him playfully on the chest, secretly amused by his smugness. He acted hurt, like she had wounded him, but the upturn of his lips gave away his mirth. He leaned down to kiss her and their lips brushed, and for a few minutes Burn heard nothing but the sounds of their breath and their hearts beating together as one.

All too soon, though, the world fell into place around them. Burn could already detect movement throughout the house as its ever-increasing occupants clambered for control of its limited resources. Pots and pans clanked as the kitchen came alive, while people jostled for access to the showers. Toward the back of the house, in the large room they'd commandeered for combat practice, some of the new recruits were already training, their grunts and blows forming a familiar din in the background.

Burn could even hear Scar toiling away with her tools and gadgets, adrift in her own little world with its own little atmosphere. Like Hale, Scar had been recovering steadily, and she no longer needed the chair. Burn could tell she was still in pain, that the damage from the bullet still plagued her, but she was too proud to admit it. She'd never let something as trivial as a gunshot wound hold her back from her work.

Scar had been focusing her attentions on bolstering her stockpile of contraptions, as well as fine-tuning her sonic blaster. While the damage it caused had been useful, the weapon's unpredictability and surplus of power made it dangerous in battle. Scar was working to concentrate that power, to harness the force into one destructive beam. With her patented veil of secrecy, however – and her inability to test the device at full power – no one was quite sure how well her tinkering was going.

Tearing her mind away from the activity of the house, Burn centered herself and groaned.

"I promised Nara I'd help with the new recruits," she said, trying to muster the willpower to rise.

"How are they looking?" Hale asked, cocking one

eyebrow as if he already knew the answer.

"Rough," Burn responded, shaking her head. "I had to put out three fires yesterday, and we're missing part of a wall. At this rate, there won't be a city left by the time we're done protecting it."

Hale smiled, and the expression sent a prickle of warmth through her chest. "Well, I believe in you," he told her, rising to a sitting position. "And I believe in them. They may be untrained, but they're motivated. They all have their reasons to fight – and people they want to fight for. I think that could be enough. I think we might stand a chance."

Burn shook her head at his optimism. "And I think you're going soft on me," she said, leveraging herself off the bed. "It's gonna take more than motivation to beat the assembly. Even with all the mutants in the city on our side, we'd still face an uphill battle."

Burn pulled on a pair of loose black pants and a burnt orange tunic as Hale considered her words.

"True," he said, acknowledging her fears, "but it's not impossible. Winning a battle requires more than just might. You need cleverness and ingenuity – and we have some of the best minds in the city."

"Are you talking about yourself again?" Burn teased, leaning over to give him a goodbye peck. He grabbed her around the waist and held her tight, unwilling to let her go.

"Of course," he said, smiling. "And you. And Crete and Scar and Nara and all the rest of us. We'll figure something out. I know it."

Burn sincerely hoped that was true. Tearing herself from Hale's grasp, she gave him a wink before slipping into the hallway. Everywhere she looked, there was a quiet fervor, an intense yet controlled frenzy. Everyone was working or studying or training. Some pored over maps and grids while others loaded weaponry or stockpiled water or handed out rations.

Burn swung by the kitchen, grabbing a piece of toast from Meera before making her way to the back of the house. By the time she reached the training quarters, most of the trainees were already there, warming up their bodies and preparing their powers for action. Nara stood against one wall, her arms crossed as she studied the recruits. Burn joined her in silence, turning to face their students.

Theirs was a strange band of misfits. Aside from her time in Videre, Burn had never seen so many of the gifted in one place, and the combination of powers and people made for a strange and unbalanced ecosystem.

Those without gifts kept to themselves, their intensity focused on combat. They seemed to feel the need to prove themselves, to show they were worthy of the fight. Burn sensed no envy amongst their ranks, no resentment toward their peers, merely a longing to make a difference and the knowledge that they'd need to work harder to achieve it.

The gifted, on the other hand, were a diverse and disjointed bunch. Their powers ran the gamut from subtle to intense, and each recruit seemed to believe they were a force unto themselves. Teaching them to coordinate, to feed into and off of one another, was proving more difficult than they had anticipated.

As Burn watched, she saw Ava, a woman with shades of blue for skin and hair, produce shards of ice from her palms and fling them like spears into a nearby wall. Kornak, a middle-aged man who had been clinging to the top of said wall, tumbled from his perch and landed with a thud on the floor below, clearly angered by the disruption. Beside them, a girl named Fia sat with her legs crossed and her eyes closed as timid sparks of electricity fizzled across her skin.

Two of the mutants were locked in a fierce contest of skill, which Burn prayed had its origins in friendly combat. Astor, who boasted a fine layer of gray hair across every inch of exposed skin, raked his hideously sharp claws toward his foe. He moved with the speed of a wolf, and Burn noted that his teeth were equally intimidating.

Yet his opponent, Raina, wasn't deterred. She matched his speed with catlike grace, her lithe body bending into unnatural shapes, as if it were composed of rubber instead of bone. She ducked and dodged and darted with ease, finding every opening and slipping through.

Ash, a boy barely out of his teenage years, sat like a bird in the rafters, considering the action, and Burn could only guess how he'd gotten there. Tucked into a corner, watching them all with eerie stillness, was Ecco, a figure who blended almost perfectly with the wooden planks of the wall, her skin shifting to mimic whatever she touched.

Nara sighed, rubbing her eyes with her fingertips as if the sight hurt to behold.

"The Peace Force won't know how to use their powers, either," Burn said, trying to reassure her friend. "They might be just as lost as we are."

"Yes, but they already know how to work together, how to fight as one," Nara replied, turning her gaze to the ceiling.

"All we have is a bunch of individuals, separate entities who might never coalesce into an army. Without that kind of team mentality, our enemies will pick us off one by one until there's no one left to oppose them."

Burn grimaced, sensing the truth in Nara's words. Suddenly, an idea surfaced, and she grabbed hold, fanning it into the outlines of a plan.

"Then let's show them what a team is, what it means to have each other's backs," she said, smiling.

"What did you have in mind?" Nara asked lowering her gaze and training it on Burn.

"Do you remember how we fought together to get back into the city?" Burn asked as images of their last encounter with the Peace Force ran riot through her mind. Nara nodded as she caught the thread of Burn's thoughts and latched on.

"Well, I say we give them a taste of that action," Burn said, looking around at the disorganized crowd.

Nara's grin widened into a toothy smile. "Let's do this," she said, grabbing two fighting sticks and tossing one to Burn.

Without speaking, the women sauntered toward the center of the room, positioning themselves back to back and twirling their weapons before them. Their apprentices parted at their entrance, retreating uncertainly into a jagged circle.

"Attack us," Nara commanded.

"And don't hold back," Burn added with a smirk. "Let's see what you've got."

At first, no one moved to challenge them. There was a general hesitancy in the air as the assembled fighters weighed the duo's sincerity. Some chuckled, some balked, some watched with unease. Yet as the seconds stretched on and the women didn't move, the authenticity of their offer became apparent.

Surprisingly, Ash, the boy in the rafters, was the first to attack. He dropped lightly to the floor in front of Burn, his legs bending to effortlessly absorb the impact. One of his cohorts in the crowd tossed him a stick, and Burn held hers out, inviting him to fight. He mirrored the gesture in a mark of acceptance.

Burn waited for him to strike, following his eyes as he contemplated his options. Finally resolving on a course of action, Ash feigned left then moved to strike right, but Burn caught him, blocking his blow. Shoving him back, she sent a blow of her own to his legs. He leapt over the baton with sprightly grace, launching into the air – and disappearing into its clutches.

Glancing up, Burn watched as Ash dangled from a beam for a moment before dropping down in front of Nara. Burn felt the woman's muscles tense in preparation for a fight. Instead of turning, however, Burn remained stationed at her friend's back, sensing each movement as if it were her own.

Unlike Burn, she made the first move. Raising her weapon, she brought it down from above, but the boy stopped it just in time, using both hands to fight back the force of her attack. Nara took advantage of the opportunity and delivered a kick to his midsection, which sent him sprawling into the crowd.

Shocked gasps mingled with nervous titters of laughter from the surrounding throng. Someone helped the boy up, and the crowd closed back around him, consuming him. Burn and Nara waited, circling in anticipation for their second opponent.

It wasn't long before another figure jumped into the ring, poised for a fight. This time it was Fia, the girl who could harness electricity, and the power danced in minute arcs across her palms as she considered Burn.

Rubbing her hands together, Fia geared up to strike, but Burn was ready for her. The girl threw out her hands, unleashing a bolt of jagged light, and Burn ducked and rolled, expertly avoiding the energy. Behind her, Nara turned and met the current with the wood of her baton, which lit up white from the shock.

Before it had the chance to reach her hands and singe her flesh, Nara flung the weapon toward the girl, whose surprise stopped her in her tracks. The rod cartwheeled end over end through the air before colliding with Fia's head. She stumbled backward into the crowd, and their collective arms reached out to grab her.

Now weaponless, Nara looked like an easy target. Astor, the wolf man, leapt to challenge her, his claws out and his teeth bared in warning. He lunged to grab her with both hands, clearly intending to graze his talons across her abdomen, but she was quicker. She dove to the side, narrowly missing his grasp, and his claws closed around empty air.

This time, Burn was the one to come to the rescue. Bending low, she turned, sweeping his legs out from under him in one graceful stroke. Astor hit the floor with a thunderous crash, the shock stunning him into submission. Burn lashed him across the chest with her baton, pinning him down. Sensing he was outmatched, he surrendered, leveraging himself up and stalking back into the pack.

Before Burn could compose herself, something sharp and cold slashed through her shoulder, nicking her skin and drawing blood. It was a warning shot, a well-placed threat, and the sudden pain made her gasp, although she didn't drop her guard. Instead, she spun, finding herself shoulder to shoulder beside Nara, their sights trained on Ava. In each of her cold blue hands she held an icicle, their points sharpened to razorlike tips.

There was something cold in Ava's eyes, a calculating intensity that sent a shiver down Burn's spine. Her teeth looked too white against her permanently frozen lips, and she ran her tongue across their edges in a menacing sneer. A slight twitch of her eyes was the only warning she gave before sending the ice spears flying, flinging two more in rapid succession.

Burn spun her stick before her, twirling it as rapidly as she could to knock the first two shards askew. Beside her, Nara moved with superhuman precision to pick the others from the air, as if she could see where they were going to be before they got there.

Ava flung her hands to the sides, producing two more slivers of ice, but before she could throw them, Nara sprang to her side. With a downward strike of her open hand, she knocked one of the weapons from Ava's grasp, halving her ammunition. Sensing Nara's need, Burn tossed her the baton and she caught it, bringing it down on the woman's other wrist to render her weaponless.

Circling behind their foe, Burn put herself into position

and waited. Ava sent a kick toward Nara's knee, thrusting downward with all her might, but Nara dodged the blow. Burn took advantage of the woman's momentum, dealing a kick from behind that sent her tumbling forward. Ava just managed to catch herself, turning the fall into a roll that brought her to her knees.

From Ava's cerulean hands, a longer shard of ice appeared, clearly an answer to Nara's staff. It swung out before her, striking Nara in the gut and shattering into a thousand crystalline pieces, which sparkled in the air like diamonds before dropping. Ava moved to strike Nara again, this time with bare hands, but by then Burn was at her side. With a punch to the jaw, she laid Ava out, knocking her to the ground where she remained, dazed and disappointed.

Burn stuck her hand out as an offer of truce, and the woman took it, allowing Burn to pull her up and lead her back to the circle. Nara, who had quickly recovered from the blow, strode to Burn's side to await their next opponent. Yet no one came forward to challenge them. Burn and Nara looked around at the shocked faces for a few silent seconds, letting their actions sink in and the implications take hold.

"Look around you," Burn instructed, seizing the reins of leadership and steering her subjects home. "The people in this room will be your greatest assets in battle. Sure, your weapons, your armor, your gifts are important, but they won't save you. They can't watch your backs, they can't protect you when you're down, and they can't help you get back up. But your team can."

Nara stepped forward, picking up naturally where Burn had left off. "Alone, you are nothing. If you fight alone, you die alone. If you go into that battle solo, separate from those around you, then you will be going in blind. The Peace Force will spot you in an instant and destroy you in the next."

Their trainees looked suitably chastised, with their gazes trained on the floor and their expressions bleak. A few still stared defiantly at the pair, certain they were the exception to the rule, but Burn knew their bravado would never last. It was an act, a façade, a way to camouflage their fear and convince themselves they were equal to the challenge.

"We go in as one team with one mission," Burn continued, turning as she spoke to address everyone in the room. "We work together. We fight together. And, if it comes to it, we die together. There is no me, no you, only us. The moment you accept that is the moment you become a fighter, a rebel, an ally. That's the moment you become one of the Lunaria. And that's the moment we become a force to be reckoned with."

A buzz rippled through the audience, a sharp, excited feeling that verged on inspiration. Contrition gradually tightened into determination as the recruits began to accept their role. Slowly, they stood up straighter, glancing around as if truly seeing each other for the first time. It wasn't much, but it was enough.

"Good," Nara stated, taking their silence as submission. "Now let's get to work."

Chapter 23

Scar's room was a graveyard of ravaged tech, with scavenged parts and pieces stripped to the bones and mountains of circuit boards, cables, and batteries climbing toward the ceiling in uncertain towers. She had so many ideas, so many avenues to try, but so little time in which to try them.

Scar wanted to save the world, to find that one weapon that would stop the assembly in their tracks. It was a fanciful dream and she knew it, but she had to try. The alternative was all-out warfare, battles in the streets, innocent people caught in the crosshairs. It was Burn and Nara fighting on the front lines and dying for the cause. It was Scar losing the family that she'd only just managed to piece together.

She thought she'd found family once, but it had been savagely ripped from her grasp, trampled by the same people who threatened them now. An image of Symphandra, still and lifeless on the battlefield, floated into her mind unbidden, and Scar shut her eyes against it. Her hand traveled instinctively to her heart, to the dented metal that served as a reminder of that nightmarish day.

As her mind skimmed memories of fire and fear, the images gradually changed, morphing from ghosts of the past into fears of the future. Instead of faces of those she'd lost, she saw those she was afraid to lose, their expressions blank, their eyes cold and dead, their bodies rigid. She saw the Peace Force and the Shadow Assembly standing above them, victorious.

It was her own name that dragged her back from the depths. Someone was repeating it over and over, and the sound gradually guided her up from the chasm and into the light. She opened her eyes to find Nara sitting beside her, her hands in her lap and her eyes trained on Scar. They were gentle yet concerned, and they probed lightly at Scar's sad expression, as if Nara could see beyond it into the thoughts beneath.

"Are you alright?" she asked as Scar blinked away the remnants of her daydream.

"I'm fine," Scar lied, unwilling to talk about the vision that haunted her thoughts. Nara looked unconvinced, but she didn't pry. "How's the training going?" Scar asked, eager to change the subject.

Nara let out a long sigh. "They're getting better, but that's not saying much," she said, dropping her head into her hands. "We've taught them teamwork, formations, movements, but it's all just the basics. They're still not soldiers. Maybe if we had a few months, I could do more. They're promising, but they're never going to be ready in time."

"What about their powers?" Scar asked, slightly more

interested in this line of questioning. Her analytical side was always looking for more data, more variables to input and compute and file away for future use.

Another sigh, this one smaller but just as resigned. "They're good...for Kasis," she said haltingly. Scar gave her a critical look, inviting her to say more, and she grudgingly complied. "It's just that out there, in the wildlands, people are powerful. I was powerful. Our gifts were unstoppable. In here, we're muted, stifled. We're only half ourselves, a fraction of what we could be."

"You think that if we had that kind of strength we'd win?" Scar asked, following Nara's thoughts to their natural conclusion.

"Yes," she replied without hesitation. "Imagine if we were all stronger, sharper, more in tune with our gifts. You saw what happened to Burn. She blossomed out there. So did Hale. If we could harness that power, then the Shadow Assembly wouldn't stand a chance." She shook her head wistfully as the visions disappeared, crushed by the weight of reality.

Scar, however, wasn't so easily deterred. The idea of using the air in the wildlands to supercharge their gifts was intriguing, and it sparked something in the back of her mind.

"Do you think we could fabricate it? The air out there, I mean?" Scar asked, genuinely curious now. "If gifts can be manufactured, why wouldn't it be possible to genetically enhance them the same way they're enhanced outside the dome?"

Nara looked skeptical. While Scar was a dreamer, she was more of a realist, and Scar could tell she thought it was a longshot.

"I don't know," she began, shaking her head. "We only have a handful of days until we need to be ready. That sounds like it would take years."

"We have the assembly's research," Scar reminded her. "Maybe Crete can use that to synthesize some sort of serum, like a booster for our powers."

Nara still wasn't convinced, but Scar felt energized, as if the idea itself were giving her life. Instead of waiting for Nara to come around, Scar vaulted off the bed and out the door, intent on finding Crete. A few seconds later, Nara was at her side. She understood Scar well enough to know that once she set her mind to something, there was no stopping her. So she held on, riding the current of Scar's fervor to see where it would lead.

Scar came to a sudden stop outside Crete's room and administered a few rapid knocks to his door. As she waited, her foot tapped against the floor, beating out her impatience. After an agonizing minute, Crete finally answered, yet he made no move to invite them in. Instead, he stood there, looking tired and worn.

It wasn't the type of tiredness that came from his healing, the gaunt hollowness that ate at his skin like sickness, turning him concave. This was something else, a mental exhaustion, an intellectual fatigue. Scar recognized it all too well, noting it in the dullness of his eyes and the hunched curve of his shoulders.

"I have an idea," Scar stated, getting straight to the point. She didn't want to waste his time, and she hoped he would pay her the same courtesy. "We need to know if it's possible to formulate something that would boost our powers, similar to the air outside the dome. It could be permanent or temporary; it doesn't matter. We simply need something to give us an edge, to improve our gifts enough to outmaneuver the assembly."

Scar expected Crete to speak, to confirm or deny the possibility, to react to her idea in some way, shape, or form. Yet he just stood there, blinking. A long sigh was all the reaction she received, and a sharp ping of irritation rang within her mind.

"Crete!" she said, snapping her fingers to get his attention. "Can you help us? We need…"

But what she needed was apparently unimportant, as Crete cut in testily, "What do you think I've been doing in here? Relaxing? Killing time until the assembly attacks us? Twiddling my thumbs while waiting for someone else to get injured?"

Scar was taken aback. She'd never heard Crete speak that way before, never heard him lose his temper. It was refreshing in an annoying sort of way, and Scar's respect for him leveled up a notch. Still, she didn't have time for his dramatics.

"What have you been working on, then?" she asked, not comprehending his obvious desire to be left alone.

Crete's eyes narrowed as he tried to determine if she was mocking him. Clearly deciding that her inquiries were in earnest, he sighed and rubbed his hand across his bald head.

"If you truly want to discuss this," he said, his voice resigned, "then you better come in." Standing aside, he ushered them into the room.

The space they entered was a frenzy of papers and charts. Old and new tabs displaying delirious amounts of data were strewn across the space, connected by twisting cords like some byzantine maze. They blinked and beeped and flickered, and even Scar found herself overwhelmed by the sight.

"I've been going through every piece of data we have, every fragment of research we were able to collect," Crete explained, sitting atop a cot covered in papers. Scar and Nara took his lead, stationing themselves in shabby chairs against the opposite wall.

"I've done everything I can to find an antidote, a way to reverse the effects of the assembly's serum," Crete went on, shaking his head. "But without knowing each person's genetic makeup and the particular gift they've chosen, I can't even begin to formulate a response. And even if I had access to all that information, I still don't know if I could help."

Crete seemed to be trying to explain that there was no hope, that they had no real recourse against the assembly or their newfound powers, but Scar remained undaunted. After all, until now he'd been going at it alone. She was certain that with the addition of her brainpower, they'd be able to find a solution in no time.

"What about the air in the wildlands?" she asked, returning to her original idea. "It makes the gifted stronger. It builds on our innate powers. Is there a way we can use that to our advantage?"

Once again, Crete displayed no notable reaction to her idea. Her mask of patience was beginning to slip, sliding closer and closer toward irritation. She hung on for a few more seconds, grasping at the edges until Crete finally deigned to speak.

"We have no samples from the air out there, no way to reconstruct its chemical makeup," he said tiredly, pushing his glasses farther up on his nose. "We might have been able to reverse engineer it by taking samples from the natives, but it's been too long since they returned. Every day they become more like us."

"Then let's get a sample of the air!" Scar said. She could feel the wires in her hair begin to spark in agitation, irritating her further.

Nara spoke up for the first time in several minutes. "How do you propose we do that?" she asked. Without waiting for a response, she continued, "The dome is being watched from all angles. The tunnels that haven't been filled in are being guarded by the best security teams. We won't be able to set foot within a mile of the dome without the Peace Force knowing."

"What about Dormaline?" Scar ventured, trying to salvage the plan. "Can't she slip through the glass and grab a sample?"

Nara looked at her sadly. "The forcefield is too powerful, and the glass is too thick. She'd never be able to make it through safely."

"And even if you managed to get a sample," Crete chimed in, "there wouldn't be enough time to create a safe and stable solution. Plus, what about the side effects? The disorientation, the headaches, the temporary euphoria. Those wouldn't make for the best soldiers."

Everything they said made sense, but Scar didn't want to hear it. There was something to her idea; she just knew it.

All she had to do was think.

Except nothing came to her. She stood up to pace, feeling like a caged animal in such enclosed quarters. The other two looked on in pity, exacerbating her feeling of confinement.

Sensing her frustration, Nara tried to soothe her, to tame the wild beast that was itching to escape. "We can still win," she said, her voice soft and encouraging – and patronizing. "We might not need some clever plan to beat them. Maybe we can take them on as we are. Maybe it'll be enough."

This time, Scar wasn't the only one who balked. Across from her, she saw Crete's face transform into a look of pure skepticism.

Nara noticed their expressions, and her own hardened in response. "I've done everything I can to prepare these people," she said. "They know how to attack, they know how to kill, and they've accepted the fact that many of them may be killed in return. I can't teach them much more than that. And unless we stumble on some miracle, this is how it's going to be. We'll set the date, we'll go in, and we'll do what must be done. And maybe we'll make it out alive."

Nara looked so defeated, so resigned to her fate that Scar's heart constricted in her chest. She knew Nara had come back to Kasis to prove something, to show the world – and herself – that she was more than her past, but she didn't need to die in order to do it.

Images from Scar's horrific daydream threatened to re-appear, but she beat them back. She couldn't bring herself to believe that this was it, that their only option was to attack in hopes of catching their enemies off guard and praying it would be enough. There had to be something else, something more, something they were missing.

A sticky silence descended over the room, coating its inhabitants in an oppressive blanket of unease. Around them, Crete's devices beeped out a dissonant melody as they scoured reams of data searching for a key. Scar's brain searched alongside them, combing through her own mechanical thoughts for a hint of a solution.

It was the dullness in Nara's eyes that finally sent her mind into overdrive. The captivating light that usually illuminated her deep, dark gaze was flickering, threatening to go out with each second that ticked by. Scar couldn't take it. Something inside of her screamed that she needed to fix it, that she needed to ignite the darkness and bring that spark back to life.

The air in the wildlands could help them. Of that much she was certain. Yet Crete's arguments were solid, as were Nara's. There was no way to synthesize it in the time they had left – but what if they didn't have to? What if they could utilize the real thing? An idea glinted in the depths of her mind and she fanned it, feeling her excitement rise as it sputtered into existence.

The force of the idea propelled her, and she began pacing once more, using the momentum to fuel the inspiration. Crete and Nara noticed but said nothing, a fact which Scar profoundly appreciated. Her plan was delicate, fragile, and any word or movement may have broken it into a thousand pieces, sending it floating away on the wind before it even had a chance to take shape.

As it was, though, the idea took root and blossomed, and a hint of a smile rose to Scar's lips. Part of her was afraid to speak the suggestion out loud lest it fall to pieces around her, but she knew it needed to be said.

"Let's break down the dome."

Understandably, Crete and Nara looked aghast at the suggestion. Neither spoke, but she could tell that their first instinct was to vehemently disagree.

Undeterred, Scar continued. "It doesn't have to be the whole dome," she said, attempting to allay their fears. "We only need to break through a section of it, big enough so the air in the wildlands can get through and saturate the city."

"Are you mad?" Crete asked – a question which Scar took quite personally. She stopped herself from biting back a bitter reply, knowing that she needed to listen to their qualms before overcoming them. However, that didn't stop her from throwing him a warning look.

"No. I'm perfectly sane," she said, trying to keep her voice level. "Think about it. If we have direct access to the air, we can be confident of its effects – no trial and error required. We can be certain that it will boost our powers and make us stronger."

"If we do that, won't the assembly reap the benefits, as well?" Nara asked. "Won't their powers be magnified, too?"

"That's the thing," Scar said, her smile widening. "I don't think it will affect them, at least not to the same extent it does for us. Their powers come from a serum, not from the radiation and the pollution. Therefore, their gifts shouldn't react in the same way." She turned to Crete, hoping for confirmation.

Crete squinted as he processed the thought. Then he, too, took to his feet, searching his tabs for some piece of data, some hint of intel to back up her suspicions. He cast aside a stack of papers to get at a machine beneath, pursing his lips as he navigated through its contents.

"The assembly's gifts resemble ours in a myriad of ways, but they're not identical," he said, still tapping the screen. "They've had to corrupt the mutations on a cellular level in order to get them to bind with their own genetic material. If they've changed the structure enough, then you may be right. The air may have no impact on their gifts."

Scar turned to Nara as Crete continued his search. Nara's eyes met hers, and this time they held a glimmer of hope, a beautiful drop of optimism that lit up her features. Scar had the sudden desire to lean over and kiss her, to fan that flame until its heat devoured them both, but she knew that now was not the time. If this worked, though, if this idea panned out, then they might just have a lifetime to burn together.

Crete's head jerked up, drawing Scar's attention. "You're right," he said, somewhat astonished. "They've tampered too much with the original cellular structure. In removing their gifts' origins, their ties to the atmosphere, they've effectively removed any chance that they could be impacted by the air. Which means that if we managed to carve a hole in the dome, we're the only ones who would benefit."

A flutter beat to life inside Scar's chest, a feeling she recognized as excitement. The wires in her hair seemed to sense her delight and they sizzled, showering tiny sparks across her shoulders. Only, she couldn't celebrate quite yet.

"We'll still have the side effects to worry about, though," Nara said, clearly hating to add another wrinkle to their plan. "The disorientation, the headaches. It may even render some people unconscious. Plus, the effects on our gifts aren't immediate. It can take days or even weeks for people to acclimate."

Damn it, Scar thought. Nara was right. She remembered her own reaction to the air – the lightheadedness, the laughter, the confusion – and she grimaced.

"Could we break through it before we attack, give our powers time to adjust?" Scar asked, scrambling for ideas to salvage the plan.

Nara looked dubious. "Any attempt to break through the dome will set off the Peace Force's alarms," she said, drawing on her background as a thief. "They'll know the second we try anything, and they'll have repair crews on site in minutes to fix it. We won't have time for the air to do anything other than drive us batshit crazy."

A splinter of annoyance pierced Scar's consciousness, steadily bleeding her optimism dry. "Who cares?" she asked, scraping the bottom of the barrel in hopes of dredging up something useful. "Let's find a way to break through. Maybe our masks will protect us, and the Peace Force and the assembly will be driven mad. It would still give us the upper hand."

Crete, whose head was still bent over his tab, piped up absentmindedly to ruin her last vestige of hope. "Peace Officers wear masks, too," he reminded her. "But it doesn't matter. They won't protect anyone from the air out there. Our filters weren't made for that."

It wasn't fair, Scar thought as her irritation rose to new heights, drowning the logical sectors of her brain and plunging them into darkness. There were too many obstacles, too many barriers to their success, and even with her unparalleled ingenuity, they couldn't break through them all. She'd been arrogant to think they could.

Scar moved to leave, suddenly finished with this useless conversation and its countless dead ends. She wanted to be alone, to lick her wounds in private, to go back to creating weapons that might actually grant them a chance at success.

"Stop!" a voice commanded as Scar reached for the door. She paused mid-motion, already resenting the interruption. She turned stiffly to face Crete, who stared at her with something resembling inspiration.

"What?" Scar demanded, too drained to deal with more pointless banter. "Do you have something to help us?" she asked, making her exasperation clear. "Do you have some way to avoid the disastrous effects of the air?"

"Yes, I think I do," he said with all seriousness. "I think I can create a serum to combat the effects of exposure – and speed up our acclimation."

"Won't that take time?" Scar asked, taking up the dissenting role. "Won't that take longer than we have?"

"No. I don't think so," Crete replied. "If my calculations are correct, I should be able to do it in a matter of days. The air only affects us the way it does because it's foreign and our bodies see it as hostile. If I'm able to tamp down that response, I think I can cut out those effects completely while simultaneously cutting down the time it takes for our gifts to react."

"Are you serious?" Scar said, not wanting to get her hopes up only to have them crushed once more beneath the harsh weight of reality. "Do you really think you can do it?"

"Yes, I do," he said simply.

"That still leaves us with the problem of breaking through the dome," Nara interjected, still acting as the voice of reason. "There are two layers of impenetrable glass protected by a formidable forcefield. You can't simply shoot at it and expect it to break."

"Well, that depends on what kind of weapon you're using," Scar replied as the cogs in her mind began turning once more. "You're right about the forcefield. We'd need to bring it down in order to attack the dome itself. But once it's gone, my sonic blaster should be strong enough to punch a hole right through."

Nara looked skeptical. "Scar, we all saw what happened the last time someone used that blaster. It brought down an entire building. How can you be certain that it won't bring down the entire dome – and the city with it?"

"OK, it may need a few tweaks," Scar admitted, "but it's strong enough to break through. Trust me."

"So that gives us protection from the air," Crete said, listing off their strengths, "and a way to access it. All we have to do now is find a way to take down the forcefield."

Nara smiled a clever little smile, one that lit up her eyes with a mischievous twinkle. "Leave that part to me," she said, her confidence blossoming beneath their burgeoning plan. "My troops may not be up to taking on an entire gifted army, but this they can handle."

The three Lunaria members looked at each other, a realization dawning amongst them. After years of struggling against their oppressors, they finally had a plan in place to defeat them, a promising avenue that could realistically lead to an end to the turmoil. It seemed too good to be true.

Scar smiled as a lightness took hold in her bones, dragging her thoughts skyward until it felt like she was floating. It was euphoria, excitement, hope. It was beautiful. And, of course, it couldn't last.

It was Crete who brought her back down, grounding her with a simple question. "So, which one of us is going to present this to the war council?"

Chapter 24

The air was full of goodbyes in those final days. No one said the word out loud, but it hung in silky ribbons throughout the safe house, forming a subtle part of each interaction and working its way into every stolen look.

No one knew who was going to make it, how many of them were going to live to see the light on the other side. They could all feel the battle drawing near, and its presence conferred an urgency to their lives, a need to embrace what they'd been given and hold on for every second that they could.

Burn wasn't immune to this force of nature, and neither was Scar, no matter how much she liked to believe otherwise. They were both caught in its pull, in the glamorous pain of endings, and it lingered between them, unspoken. They had both known loss, and there would no doubt be more before the week was over. Victory did not come cheaply, and – no matter how prepared the Lunaria thought themselves to be

– its price would be paid in blood.

"What will you do if I die?" Scar asked bluntly one evening, finally bringing the subject to the surface.

Burn balked, taken aback by her sister's laissez-faire attitude toward death – along with the implicit assumption that she would be the one to die. Burn had fought her sister tooth and nail, urging her to stay behind during the forthcoming brawl, but Scar had steadfastly refused, maintaining that she was more useful on the battlefield than back at base.

"You won't die," Burn said, brushing her sister's words aside. "I won't let you."

Yet her words were empty, and they both knew it. Scar wasn't one to leave such blatant pandering alone, so she pressed on.

"I mean it," she said, unblinking. "When all of this is over, if we've won but I'm lost along the way, what will you do?"

"Do you really want to know?" Burn asked, her irritation mounting. Scar nodded, her blank face unreadable, and Burn growled in exasperation. "It would crush me!" she declared, throwing her hands up in front of her. "What is the point of creating a better world if you're not around to live in it with me? I know that sounds selfish, but you are all that I've had for so long. It's been you and me against the world. And if you go, you'll be taking part of me with you."

Scar considered that while Burn composed herself, reining in her errant emotions. She knew her sister was only trying to understand her, to form a picture of a future without her in it, but how could Burn ever come close to explaining that heartache? She had thought she'd lost Scar once, and she couldn't imagine enduring it again.

"What about you?" Burn asked, flipping the question back on Scar. "What will you do if I die?"

"You're too stubborn to die," Scar said with a shrug.

Burn let out an unladylike snort. "And you're not?" she asked, knowing full well that Scar's obstinance rivaled her own. "Come on. You're not getting out of it that easily. I answered, and now it's your turn. What will you do if I die?"

"I'd keep going," Scar said simply.

Burn's face crumpled at her words, and her heart folded along with it.

"I mean, I'd keep going through the motions," she clarified, seeing the distress on Burn's face. "I'd keep living, keep working, keep breathing, but nothing would be the same. There would always be something missing. Life would always be a little bit muted."

Burn raised an eyebrow, curious where this newfound sentimentality was coming from. Scar noticed and sighed.

"You've always helped me make sense of the world," she explained. "Even when we were kids, you saw things in a way I never could, and you'd always try to explain them to me. It made me feel connected – not just to you, but to the world around us. I mean, there are still times when people confound me to no end. They can be so…erratic and inconsistent. It's infuriating."

Scar took a second to reorganize her thoughts, getting herself back on track before continuing. "You've helped me feel like I'm a part of things. If anything happened to you, I'm afraid I'd disconnect entirely."

"That's not going to happen," Burn told her. "You'd still

315

be part of the Lunaria, part of something bigger. You'd have Nara, Hale, Meera. They care about you. They care about *us*. They're family. They've chosen to stand by our side, to fight by our side, and they won't leave you once the fighting's done."

Scar shook her head. "You've always been better with people than me. What if I scare them away?"

"Listen," Burn said, meeting her sister's gaze and holding it, "if you haven't scared them away yet, I don't think it's possible. But stop worrying about things that will never happen. We're going to make it. Both of us. And then we'll have the rest of our lives to figure out this world together."

Scar looked so serious, so grave that Burn wanted to reach out and hug her, but she knew her sister's feelings on that front. Instead, she racked her brain for something to take Scar's mind off the uncertainties of the coming battle.

"We have two days until the Lunaria plans to attack," she reminded Scar. "What should we do with all that time?"

Scar didn't take the bait, so Burn continued, "Have you ever wondered who would win in a fight – Nara or Hale?"

That got Scar's attention. "It has to be Nara, obviously," she said with certainty.

Burn gave her a dubious look. "Well, there's only one way to find out for sure," she said, waggling her eyebrows before springing out the door.

Their remaining days of freedom passed in a blink, and soon the battle was at their doorstep. Around them, the world had only grown darker, with more arrests and explosions and outright attacks in the streets. The reports of Peace Officers with powers were growing by the day, and, if the Lunaria did nothing, it wouldn't be long until Kasis devolved into chaos, with pure martial law governing its sectors and tiers.

It could still come to that – if the Lunaria failed. If their uprising proved unsuccessful, their lives would be on the line, and they all knew it. Those that didn't fall during battle would be rounded up and executed, flaunted as a brutal example of the fate that awaited brutal crimes.

Even those that didn't take part, the gifted who preferred to stay on the sidelines, would be made to feel the Peace Force's power. They'd be gathered like cattle and shoved into camps. They'd live out their days as prisoners, as test subjects, as slaves. Who knows? The lucky ones might even be bred for their powers, used as mating stock to create more potent gifts for the assembly to steal.

At least before, there had been a semblance of autonomy. They might not have had much, but they worked hard. They kept their heads down, toed the line, and prayed it would be enough to keep them off the assembly's radar. After this, though, there would be no going back. There would be no separation, no independence, no safe place to hide.

They stood at a precipice, and either way things were about to change. The history books would record the coming days whatever the outcome, with the victor claiming the right to skew the story in their favor. Yet their story would be told.

Burn was a mess of emotions, which she tried to bury behind a brave face. She wanted to be a bastion of hope, a stalwart leader with no space for uncertainty. She managed it in most instances. Within the war council, she was an advisor, steadfast and determined. For her troops, she was a guide, brave and resourceful. And to the Lunaria, she was a figurehead, an idea more than a person, a symbol to stand behind and fight beside and believe in.

When she was alone, though, the fear took hold. She felt too young, too inexperienced, too breakable. She remembered every time she had failed. She saw every person who had died, every person she had killed, every time she could have saved them. In those moments, life and death ate at her, the former's transience and the latter's permanence gnawing at her gut.

She had thought by this point that she'd be numb to it, that the threat of death and the gravity of dealing it would lose their sting, but they hadn't. Maybe that was a good thing. Maybe it meant she wasn't like them, her enemies, those that seemed to kill without thinking. It meant that life still meant something to her, even if it was attached to someone she despised and a cause that despised her in return.

Still, when it came to it, she was prepared to do what had to be done – and so were those around her. This was not going to be a friendly battle. There would be no gracious losers, no acceptance in defeat. It would be bloody, violent, deadly. It would end in destruction. For all Burn knew, they could end up obliterating the city itself, leaving nothing behind and no one to rebuild. What good would their fight be if there was no one left to fight for, no one to benefit, no one to carry on once the fighting was done?

Crete's serum provided the key to a peaceful resolution – or as peaceful as they could get, given that their enemy was bent on war. Since there was no way to test the serum's efficacy within the confines of the dome, however, their strategy was banked heavily on faith. They'd verified that it wouldn't kill them, of course, but beyond that its properties remained a mystery.

Crete maintained that it would stop the air's effects completely, cutting out the days of lightheaded befuddlement that would be dealt upon their enemies. As for how their powers would react, his predictions were less certain. It was possible that the Lunaria would feel the boost within minutes, as if they'd been wandering in the wildlands for weeks. Or the change could be more gradual, with their gifts shifting over hours or days, increasing incrementally until reaching their peak.

Everyone hoped it was the former. They didn't have the luxury of days, and each hour that passed on the battlefield would mean countless more lives at stake. Each battalion, each company, each soldier scattered throughout the city would depend on the serum's success to survive.

The Lunaria weren't planning a singular strike. After all, to topple a government, you needed to attack more than just its head. So the Lunaria would divide and conquer, splitting themselves off to tackle targets throughout the city.

Their overlords in the assembly had sequestered themselves within their castle, tossing out edicts and laws from the safety of their fortress. It was convenient that they'd gathered themselves together, that they'd saved the Lunaria the trouble, but it also posed the greatest threat.

Equipped with powerful mutations, the council would be a force unto themselves, an army with unknowable weapons and incalculable strength. Even with the limited time they'd had to grow accustomed to their powers, they would still be formidable. As Una had proven all too well, a little vigor went a long way in the hands of fanatics.

Naturally, Burn had volunteered to take them on. Backed by the Lunaria's most steadfast fighters, she would be ascending into the heavens – and she would be blowing them up. Or at least blasting a hole in the side.

Scar had assured her that the sonic blaster would work, that it would effectively carve a hole into the side of the dome without bringing it down on their heads. If used correctly, it would discharge a blast that would cut through the glass, sucking in the air and circulating it around the city.

The weapon did come with caveats, however. It only held two charges, two chances to break through their cage, and if its power cell was damaged, it would be rendered useless. Burn would have to time her attack precisely, to wait until the forcefield was down before dealing her blow.

That's where the other teams came into play. With the top tier covered, Nara and Scar, together with a band of new recruits, would be diving downward, taking their talents to the middle tiers to sabotage the power plant that fed the forcefield. No one expected them to target the dome and, therefore, no one would be expecting their attack.

That wasn't to say that their job would be easy. They needed to make their way past the plant's considerable defenses before tackling the mechanics of the forcefield itself. Then there was the matter of backup, the Peace Officers who would inevitably be called in as reinforcements. The Lunaria could cut their communications, of course, but that wasn't the goal. They wanted to draw the Peace Force out, to lure them away from their stations and separate their ranks. They wanted to tear them apart in order to tear them down.

More of the Lunaria's teams would be stationed at critical sites throughout the city, with a larger swarm outside the Peace Station itself. Operatives posted at access points to various levels and tiers would ensure safe passage for allies and innocent civilians while limiting movement for their enemies. A somewhat less formidable force, graced by the likes of Meera and Cali, would patrol the outer edges, picking off the errant few who tried to slither past unnoticed.

It was a complex puzzle of people and places, with endless moving parts. Should one unit fail, the others might follow, tumbling in rapid succession until none remained standing. Yet if they succeeded, victory might just be theirs for the taking.

The wild card was how many Peace Officers had been turned, how many had acquired gifts and were now prepared to wield them. Despite the Lunaria's attempts, no one had been able to ascertain the number with certainty, with the answer still lying in the muddy chasm between *some* and *all*. Going up against them blind was a risk, but it was one they had to take.

When Burn's thoughts turned to the Peace Force, they naturally fell upon Kaz. She felt his absence keenly, and it weighed on her, piercing her thoughts at the most inopportune times.

With him on the Lunaria's side, they'd gotten a glimpse into the Peace Force and a chance to pry inside their walls, but that wasn't what Burn missed. Kaz had been a partner, an ally, a friend. Burn had grown accustomed to his lightness, his humor and passion, to the childlike way he saw the world and his unerring faith in her. Somehow, he was able to find moments of beauty in the world even when it was shrouded in darkness.

The Lunaria could have used a dash of his optimism in those final days. Burn could have used it, too. Despite the distance and the barriers, she listened for him, casting her mind out through the city toward her enemy's lair.

Yet no matter how hard Burn tried, she couldn't puncture the veil that shrouded him. She listened until her head hurt and her brain pounded with the voices of hundreds, until the world around her slipped away and she found herself slipping with it. She disappeared beneath the waves of the city until Kasis threatened to drown her, but someone was always there to pull her out, to drag her back to the shores of reality.

"Burn, it's time," a gentle voice said, drawing her once more from the brink.

Burn followed the voice, using it like breadcrumbs to trace her way back to the world. Eventually, her eyes fluttered open, and she found Hale seated beside her, his soft gaze trained steadfastly on her. She tried to focus on it, on him, to capture one more blissful moment of peace before the world turned to chaos, but it slipped through her fingers like sand. All too soon, the tension and the worry and the dread invaded her consciousness and she looked up, taking in the troops before her.

They looked like an army. They stood tall, heads high, chests out. Adorned in armor, they clutched their weapons with ferocity, psyching themselves up for the fight. Yet behind these trinkets of battle, their warriors were a mess. Some stared ahead with steely gazes, some prayed behind closed eyes, some feigned levity, some cried. Some shook so violently that Burn feared they wouldn't be able to walk, let alone march like soldiers into war.

Burn's gaze fell on Meera, and her heart constricted. She looked so small in her armored shell, unsuited for the cruelty of war, yet the kindness still lingered like a light in her soul. She whispered words of comfort to her ragged crew, but they fell on deaf ears, bouncing to the floor to lay forgotten at their feet.

These people were not meant for combat. They were tradespeople, shopkeepers, factory hands. They had lives and families and friends. Yet here they were, prepared to fight, to give everything they had for the cause. They were afraid, yet they were willing. They knew the stakes and they accepted them. In Burn's opinion, that made them stronger than any army.

She looked out at the brave faces around her, preparing herself to lead. Of course, not all of their force was present. The Lunaria's ranks had long since swelled past the number that would fit into a single house, no matter how expansive its footprint. Instead, their people were spread across the city, sequestered in houses and hidden amongst tiers. Some were already in place, waiting for their signal, while yet more cleared the way.

Despite the distance, Burn could sense them, like independent parts of a larger whole. Naturally, they were all connected by comms, with a link to each team and tier, but it was more than that. They were connected by something else, something greater, like a spirit that dwelt within all of them. To Burn, it felt like a force, unbreakable and brilliant like the sun, which eclipsed their differences and united them.

Burn stood and made her way to the front of the room, with a hush falling in her wake, quieting the anxious chatter. The Lunaria seemed to know what she was planning, and they respectfully opened the floor for her remarks. Her heart hammered in her chest as she considered them, filled with equal parts pride and panic, and she took a deep breath before beginning.

"Thank you," she said simply. "Thank you for choosing to be here. Thank you for deciding to fight. Thank you for giving us your trust, your faith, your lives." Burn paused, making eye contact with the people she was proud to be fighting alongside.

"It is easy to do nothing," she continued. "It's simple to stand by and watch. It's painless to stay silent, to do what you're told, to accept the status quo. Here in Kasis, our people have done it for centuries. Our parents, our grandparents, and their grandparents before them. They did what they had to to survive.

"But you've chosen a different path. You've seen things they could never have dreamed of, and they've made you brave. The Peace Force has tried to break us, but they've only succeeded in making us stronger. They've used us as lab rats, as toys, as pawns in their games. They have tried to drug us, to kill us, to wipe us out because they're afraid, but we are still here!"

At that, a wave of cheers went up around the room, and

Burn smiled, pleased that her words were hitting home. She let the shouts die down before pressing on.

"Survival is only the start. The assembly has grown accustomed to taking what they want without consequences. Now, they've even taken our powers so they can use them against us. It's time to show them that their arrogance comes at a cost. It's time to show them the true price of their tyranny."

Burn could feel the heat rise in the room as her rhetoric stoked the fire of rebellion. She could see it in the Lunaria's eyes, hear it in the snippets of passionate thought that broke through the gates of their minds. These people wanted to fight. They wanted to follow her. They wanted to finish this.

"Victory won't come easily," Burn continued, tempering her words with caution. "Their power has bought them protection, and they'll draw on every resource they have. This battle won't be bloodless. Our ranks won't come out unscathed. But, then again, neither will theirs." Burn cocked an eyebrow, and hungry chuckles rolled across the room and over her comms.

"I believe in you," Burn said, looking out across the sea of faces. "You're willing to stand up and face the people who have kept you down, who have endeavored to make sure you stay silent. Well, today you go out there and make yourselves heard! You are the change we need in this world. You are heroes, and you're about to make history."

Burn could feel the room come to life around her, as if her encouragement were feeding the crowd. The spark of indignation, of passion, rose until the flames of it burned bright between them. It didn't extinguish the fear, which still roiled beneath the surface in uneasy waves, but it usurped it, taking pride of place at the helm of the Lunaria's minds.

"We all have our parts to play, our own roles to enact in this battle," Burn continued, sensing that the end of her address was near. "While I might not be there fighting beside you, I will be with you. We all will. Because you are not going in alone. Remember that in the darkness of battle, when your strength is gone and your weapons run dry. Remember that when all hope seems lost. We are in this together. Our strength is your strength. Our gifts are your gift. Together, we are powerful. Together, we can bring these bastards down."

A surge of pure determination pulsed through the crowd. Burn could feel it rising within herself, as well. It was heady, this camaraderie, this solidarity, and it leeched into her veins like a drug, conferring energy and confidence with every heartbeat.

Burn didn't know what was going to happen. Despite all their planning, she couldn't foresee the outcome. All she knew was that they were ready – ready to fight, to face their oppressors, to die if fate deemed it so. They were ready for the end.

Chapter 25

Burn had never seen Kasis so still. The city was eerie in its silence, a mausoleum waiting for its dead. Shops were shuttered, stalls abandoned, homes deserted. Lights flickered and went out, casting a menacing pall across each sharp corner, each jagged staircase. The gray smog that swirled in the air threw ghostly shadows before them, painting their reflections like contorted creatures against every wall.

The city was not abandoned, however, merely scared into silence. The purr of factories still warbled in the background, and a brave few carried on with their lives, willfully ignorant of the coming storm. Yet a lull blanketed the lanes, a peculiar serenity that whispered warnings of predators and blood.

The Peace Force had stopped shouting their propaganda through the streets, but it still lurked around every corner. Posters plastered with the Lunaria's faces graced every wall, with Burn and Scar, Hale and Ansel each featured heavily. They'd been deemed terrorists, fugitives, criminals. They'd been assigned a value and shouldered with blame, and they'd been offered like lambs to those starving for justice.

Still, the citizens had rebelled in their own small ways. Fresh graffiti marred the walls and the placards, telling the Peace Force what its people truly thought of their rules. Rude drawings and even ruder words decorated the streets like a statement of fact, screaming *we are here* and *we will not be silenced.*

Even muffled by the cottony clouds of fog, Burn's steps sounded too loud in the still afternoon streets. Without the noise of crowds to mask them, the Lunaria's movements were painfully apparent, with each whisper echoing like a shout and each clatter of weaponry clanging like a gunshot. Burn's senses were on high alert, and she heard every skitter of stones, every rustle of cloth, every rodent scurrying through the dregs and dirt. Each new noise carried the fear of discovery, the fear that their enemies had found them at last, but each time it would fade, sinking to linger in the background.

The Lunaria's advanced scouts had done their jobs well, effectively clearing the streets of patrols. They'd struck swiftly, cleanly, efficiently, dealing death with a handful of blows and providing each unit with a path to their goal. Plus, with a little ingenuity from Scar, the Peace Force was none the wiser. The patrols appeared alive and active in the system, moving through their rounds like ghosts, mere echoes of themselves.

There were still some unforeseen obstacles, however, which sprouted up like weeds to trip them. For Scar and her squad, it took the shape of a small army of PeaceBots, resurrected from the depths of the scrap heap and outfitted with new armor and new programming. It was a desperate measure by the force, a frantic bid to fill the city with their presence. Of course, the droids were still no match for Scar. Now they lay in lifeless pieces along the road, a testament to her sister's cunning and a lesson on what happened to those who stood in her way.

Burn's weeds were of a different sort. Tall iron gates had risen up in the streets, their ugly oxidized bars blocking the Lunaria's path. They were meant to deter residents from the sectors that didn't want them, and to funnel their travel through guarded avenues and metered access points. It was yet one more way to control the masses, to herd them like cattle and trap them down below.

Yet the gates couldn't stop the Lunaria. Scar's lovely little lasers made sure of that. Within minutes, the Lunaria had sliced their way through, strolling unhindered between bent and broken bars, which smoked in lazy tendrils.

The higher they climbed, the more the tension rose until it sang around them in one shrill note. Every step they took, every street they passed brought them closer to their enemies, closer to the battle that would decide it all. Adrenaline coursed through Burn's veins as countless possible futures played across her vision like a preview of what was to come.

Soon enough, though, those previews had to become reality, expanding until a full-fledged drama played out across the screen. The setting was a tier below the heavens, the mid-afternoon light bright and constant and the streets ominously quiet. The characters were in place, with the Lunaria on one side and a Peace Force battalion waiting just beyond their line of sight, standing rigid at the entrance to the heavens. And the time was now.

"There are 30 guards on this side, with another 30 a few blocks down," Burn informed her squad, picking out their enemies' movements through the barest hints of sound – and Scar's heat sensor, which currently showed an angry ball of red in each location.

Burn pulled out Scar's comms jammer and tuned it to the officers' frequency. While the other teams were the decoys, the lures to draw the force from their lair, Burn's team required stealth. They intended to be ghosts, to float into the heavens unannounced and take the assembly by surprise. They intended an ambush.

With the comms link broken, Burn pocketed the device and readied herself for battle. She felt like a walking armory, with fearsome weapons glinting their menace from across the expanse of her body. Scar's bulky sonic blaster was strapped to her back, with two handguns on her legs and a knife belt around her waist. Between her shoulder blades, her familiar wooden batons had been replaced by a single steel rod. When a button was pressed along its side, the blunt metal transformed, lengthening and sharpening until both sides had the power to kill.

Her colleagues boasted similarly destructive arsenals, a lethal collection of sharp edges, blunt sides, and propulsive force. They were long-range and short, old and new, savagely brutal and wickedly clean. Each warrior had selected the weapons that would best suit their talents and gifts, those instruments with the highest likelihood to kill.

The simple fact was that they didn't know what they'd be fighting. They had no clue what creatures awaited them, what threats lurked beyond the borders. Besides Una, the assembly's powers were a mystery – and the Peace Force's status unknown. With a shroud of uncertainty before them, the Lunaria had to be prepared for anything.

Burn gestured for her troops to spread out, and a rustle rippled through the air as they took their places. They were quiet but not silent, their listless energy palpable, and Burn prayed that no one had chosen a gift like hers, that no officers had picked perception over power. She doubted they had. Keen senses, though useful, weren't practical in battle. They were quiet, demure, modest – and they were easily underestimated.

"Let's move in," Burn commanded, motioning her troops to war.

They moved as one, separated by space yet connected by purpose. Feet tapped along the pavement in gentle clacks, breath came in ragged bursts, and bodies shook in unison as they devoured the ground, cutting away at the final seconds of calm until the enemy was finally in sight.

Before the force could even reach for their guns, Burn's troops let loose their first volley, felling a third of the ranks where they stood. By the time the officers recovered, the rebels had taken off, ducking into the adjoining alleys in a lethal game of cat and mouse.

The soldiers took off in pursuit, their fervent requests for backup falling on deaf ears. The streets were wide, the air clean and clear, the afternoon lit bright by the stalwart yellow suns. The Lunaria were easy to spot – and easy to follow. They drew the troops from their posts, luring them into a wide square, where shining glass mirrored their movements and pristine statues stood poised to laugh at the carnage.

Burn found herself hunkered behind a bubbling fountain on the side of the square, its cheerful stone children unaware of the coming horrors. She cast her senses out, tracking each officer as they descended. They entered in droves, filling up the square until it all but buckled, its corners ringing with calls for bloodshed.

Beside Burn, Ansel knelt behind an overturned cart, his fire licking his palms with a greedy thirst. Meeting his eyes, she nodded once. Ansel smiled, his friendly flames growing hot and angry in his grasp. Winding up, he let loose, lobbing the blazing balls over the soldiers' heads and into the buildings beyond. Burn heard men shout and glass shatter. She listened as the flames roared and the officers turned in shock to face them.

That's when the Lunaria struck. Popping out from the safety of their burrows, they fired, taking down yet more of the enemy battalion. Alongside the bullets, shards of ice tore through the air, finding glass more often than flesh, and arcs of electricity crackled, branching out in jagged lines in search of targets.

Gradually, a breeze began to rustle, and fragments of glass tinkled like prophetic chimes along the pavement. The breeze strengthened into gusts, and Burn hunkered behind her statue as the wreckage of broken things flew through the air, swirling about in spiraling cyclones. But this time the Peace Force was not the target. This time, the Lunaria were under attack, and their assailant was one of the gifted.

Burn flinched as a sturdy tin awning cut through the air, cleanly decapitating a laughing stone child. The head dropped beside her, smashing into pieces that ricocheted off her like rain wrung from a stone sky.

As soon as the cyclone subsided, the Lunaria leapt, peeling out from behind makeshift forts and crawling from under wreckage. By then, the second set of guards had arrived, called by the sound of gunshots to shore up the Peace Force's ranks. Yet Burn's troops weren't deterred. In fact, they seemed energized, brought to life by the whirlwind. It meant that their enemies were gifted. It was time to fight fire with fire.

A cascade of flames erupted from beside her as Ansel unleashed his fury. Along the opposite line, officers began to fall, felled by some invisible force. Burn squinted, just making out the ripple of Ecco's camouflaged skin before another man dropped before her. Somewhere farther along the square, Ava propelled shafts of icy air with eerie precision, meeting the officers' guns and freezing them in place.

Burn took that as her opportunity to join the fray. Stowing her gun, she reached for the metal rod, its cool bulk reassuring in her hands. She pressed the button along its side, watching as it extended and sharpened, its blunt ends transforming into sinister points. Twirling it in her hands, she smiled a savage smile before jumping into the anarchy.

The first officer she met seemed surprised by her appearance, stumbling backward before cementing himself in place. Out of instinct, he raised his gun to fire, only then realizing that his weapon had been frozen to his hand, creating one block of solid ice. Instead of panicking, however, he transitioned his attack, changing tactics from bullets to blunt force.

His frozen arm swung in Burn's direction, obviously aimed at her head. Burn ducked, dropping to all fours to avoid the blow. Without a target to stop it, the icy append-age arced through the air unhindered, dragging the officer off balance and spinning him around in a graceful pirouette. Burn seized on his imbalance, slamming the side of her rod into his head with all the strength she could muster.

She moved to finish him off, intending to run him through, but he held up his hand before him, blindly shield-ing himself with the ice. The metal tip of her spear scraped uselessly against the surface, and Burn's mind stuttered in a second of confusion. Her enemy saw his chance, sending a blow to her midsection that knocked the air from her lungs in one agonizing breath.

Burn swiftly righted herself, gritting her teeth against the pain. As the officer prepared for another attack, Burn took charge, aiming her weapon at the soft spot between shoulder and chest. Gathering herself, she thrust her spear toward him, bypassing his defenses and sinking it into his skin.

He let out a wordless cry of pain, but Burn tuned it out, yanking the blade free from its organic sheath. She heard the sickening sounds of muscles tearing and skin parting, yet she couldn't stop. As he reached up to clutch at the wound, she rammed her blade into the soft flesh of his belly, eliciting a gut-wrenching cry. She pulled back, and he dropped to the ground, his blood-soaked body going still.

Burn wiped the residue from her blade, focusing on the weapon and not the damage it had caused. Stowing her emotions, she looked up, scanning the battlefield for anoth-er enemy to challenge. Conveniently, however, this time the enemy found her.

A torrent of water slammed against her back, knocking her to the ground beside her fallen foe. The water pooled around her, mingling with the soldier's blood to drown the scene in pink. Burn felt the water trickle beneath her armor, cooling her heated skin and washing away her worries.

Steps sloshed through the puddles toward her, painting Burn a picture of her opponent's position. Instead of moving, she stayed still, feigning paralysis until the steps drew closer. When the figure came to a halt beside her, Burn saw her opportunity. In one fluid movement, she sprang to her knees and whirled, knocking her foe to the ground with a rapid sweep of the legs.

The lanky woman sent up a spray of water as she fell, collapsing onto the sodden street in a pile of limbs and armor. Burn vaulted on top of her, bringing her steel staff up to the woman's neck to pin her down. At first, the woman tried to push the bar away, struggling to match Burn's considerable strength, but she quickly changed course. Bringing her arms up to Burn's torso, she launched dual streams of water at her chest, propelling Burn backward.

The officer took a wheezing breath, pushing herself up as Burn did the same. Within moments, they were facing each other again, a steely determination settling over the scene. The woman's hand twitched and Burn leapt to the side, narrowly avoiding a burst of water aimed at her abdomen.

This wasn't the first time Burn had faced such a gift. Her thoughts naturally flashed back to Imber and their duel, to the wildlands, to the way he'd attacked and she'd parried. To the way she'd won.

Thanks to that fight, Burn knew intrinsically how to

move, how to dance away from the tides as they pelted toward her. It helped that this woman was a novice. She had the power, but she lacked finesse, and it showed in the way she fought, in her clumsy strikes and sluggish recovery.

Burn advanced on her opponent, dodging a series of rapid bursts. Once she was within striking distance, she slashed, opening a rift in the skin of the woman's thigh.

"Go to hell!" the officer screamed as she dropped to her knees, cringing as her battered leg struck the ground.

Burn didn't feel the need to reply. Instead, she let her spear do the talking. She brought it down, intending to end it with a blow to the head, but the woman twisted, grabbing the weapon and pulling Burn down.

The pavement lurched from beneath her feet, and she landed with a thud on her forearms. She had just enough time to roll onto her back before the woman leapt astride her, pinning her down. Before Burn could react, a wave engulfed her head, drenching her with an endless deluge.

She couldn't breathe. She tried to suck in air, but there was water in its place, a deadly stream that was steadily drowning her on dry land. Burn couldn't see, couldn't think, couldn't move from beneath the waterfall.

Water. Water *and* air.

Seeing those two gifts side by side was eerily familiar, but Burn couldn't quite remember why. As far as she knew, the assembly had never taken Rakasa, and they didn't have access to Imber in Videre. Yet they weren't the only mutants that had been blessed with those particular powers.

Something registered in her mind, and a cold flash of realization rushed through her. All those months ago, when she'd found herself locked in a Peace Station cell, two men had battled to the death in the cell beside hers. Hopped up on ManniK, they'd been driven mad and forced to fight as a ream of officers watched, cheering on the combatants and betting on their lives.

Burn had heard it all. She'd heard the rush of water, the whistling of wind, the crash of bodies breaking against concrete. And she'd seen the aftermath – two men floating lifelessly in a flooded cage. Yet that hadn't been the end of their suffering. Burn could see it now, see their bodies being carted away to a lab, see them split open, see them studied. They must have been dissected like lab rats, poked and prodded until their limbs went stiff. And just like the force had stolen their lives, they'd also stolen their gifts, cutting them out of the dead and claiming them for themselves.

The images made Burn sick. They also made her angry, and that anger made her strong.

She wrenched her hand from beneath her attacker and moved it to her belt. Caressing the familiar lines of her knives, she drew one from its sheath. With a decisive swing, she brought the blade up and blindly slammed it into the body before her.

The water cut off in an instant. Burn remained trapped beneath the woman, but she could feel her sway, her body lingering on the cusp between life and death – and she could see why. Her blade had found a home at the base of the soldier's throat, and the woman clutched the wound, struggling painfully for breath. Soon enough, her eyes went dim and she collapsed, hitting Burn like a ton of bricks. Blood still pulsed from the wound, trickling out in hot waves as Burn lay panting against the pavement.

After a handful of heartbeats, Burn wriggled out from beneath the body, pausing to reclaim her weapons before assessing the battle. There were casualties on both sides, but the Peace Force was strained, with their ranks making up most of the victims. Some still fought, but the war was waning, tilting too far to ever be level. Sensing this, some officers fled, some forfeit, and some fought, brawling until their last breaths.

Burn dispatched two more ungifted soldiers as she made her way across the square. The officer with the gift of air was still fighting, still holding out hope for victory, so Burn set her sights on him. Before she could get there, however, he turned, conjuring up a howling gust just for her. She braced herself, glancing around for something to grab, but her preparations were in vain.

As the man marshalled the wind to war, the puddles beneath him gradually changed, morphing from rippling pools to solid ice. Out of the corner of her eye, Burn could just make out Ava crouching to the ground, sending her chill through the channels. Yet their enemy was oblivious. With his concentration trained on Burn, he didn't notice the change – at least not until his feet slid from under him and he landed with a thud on his back.

Burn darted toward him, expertly dodging the patches of ice that dotted the square. In seconds, she was by his side. A breeze began to swirl around his left hand, but she stomped down hard, hearing his wrist crunch under the force of her boot.

Burn struck before he could summon another gust,

ramming her spear into his chest. He seemed surprised by the sudden appearance of a metal rod in his body, and his hands went to investigate the object before slowly going limp. Satisfied, Burn retrieved her weapon and looked up.

The battlefield had fallen quiet. Burn turned, searching for another enemy to challenge, but none appeared. They had won. Burn breathed a sigh of relief as the first of many knots loosened in her chest. She wasn't cocky, though. She knew that this was merely the preamble, the lead-up to the larger fight. They'd done well so far, but their luck could change in an instant.

As if on cue, she stumbled and fell, landing hard on her hands and knees. Confused, she looked back to see what had tripped her, only then spotting the body on the pavement.

Even in death, Ecco's skin remained camouflaged, and her stillness made her nearly indistinguishable from the ground. Burn closed her eyes as a wave of sorrow washed over her. This woman would not be the last to die. Burn knew that all too well. Yet it didn't make Ecco's death any less poignant.

A hand appeared before her and she took it, grateful for the offer of strength when it felt like hers was failing. She rose to her feet, coming face to face with Hale. The strong-man had been at the rear of their company, protecting them from behind, but it was good to have him back at her side. Burn gave him a nod in thanks before turning to her team.

"Lunaria, assemble," she commanded, watching as her soldiers fell into line. Ava was one of the first to appear, and Burn gave her a close-lipped smile. "That was clever, what you did with the puddles," she said, garnering a shy smile in return. "I can't wait to see what else you have up your sleeve."

"Thanks," Ava replied, clearly pleased. "I didn't know if it would work. I was sure he was going to spot me, but he didn't even notice. Did you hear the noise he made when he fell?" She giggled. "He let out this high-pitched squeal, like a little girl."

The way Ava's eyes lit up made Burn fear for her. There was a hunger in her gaze, something awakened by the battle. She was enjoying this, and she wanted more.

"Be careful," Burn warned. "They won't all be that easy to bring down."

As grotesque proof of her point, the bodies of the dead suddenly began to move. The officers they had so recently dispatched lurched out from beneath the debris, their bodies broken and bent. Some looked almost normal, while others were clearly wrong, with heads and arms and feet twisted at unnatural angles. Others had weapons protruding from their skin, the spears and knives and arrows evidence of their untimely end.

Burn scanned the field, her eyes locking on Innoxia. The woman noticed Burn's expression and shrugged.

"I thought they might come in handy," she said by way of an explanation. "You never know when you're gonna need a body."

Somehow, Burn knew that wouldn't be the strangest thing she saw all day. She shook her head, refocusing on her troops.

"You did good," she said, "but that was only the beginning. We have a lot more work to do, and from here on out it will only get harder. We were lucky here. The Peace Force only had a handful of gifted soldiers. Up in the heavens we'll meet the real demons, and until we break through the dome, we *will* be outmatched. You will need to be clever and resourceful. You will need to be brave. Are you with me?"

A cheer went up amongst the Lunaria in a chorus of affirmation. It wasn't as bold as the excitement back at the safe house, not as laden with unfounded optimism, but it was real and true. They had started something, and now they intended to finish it. Together.

Regrouping, they rose like spirits into the heavens, solemnly creeping toward their target with a line of the dead at their helm. There was a silence between them that touched on calm. There was no need to speak, and nothing more they could say to prepare each other for what was coming. For the moment, it was enough to be in each other's company, to be surrounded by love in its myriad forms.

Soon enough, though, their fellowship had to be broken. A few blocks from the assembly's lair, the group split, heading in various directions to surround the building and the considerable force that guarded it.

Burn could hear the assembly inside, hear the buzz of chatter and the hum of tension. They knew the city was under attack. They'd gotten reports from across their realm, from the Peace Station to the power plant to the streets. It was clear that war was at their door and the Lunaria would soon come calling. Yet they remained sequestered in the safety of their cell, unwilling to protect the city if it meant putting themselves in danger.

These people hid behind walls and bodies, believing they were better than these sentries, that their stolen skills should be saved for a battle worthy of their talents. Burn scoffed at their arrogance, more than happy to give them such a fight.

She still hadn't heard from Scar and Nara, a fact which chafed at her rapidly fraying nerves. Burn had relayed her own progress to the other teams and received similar reports in return, but she hadn't heard the one thing she needed: that the forcefield was down. She assumed they were still working, still fighting their way to the core, but the dome remained protected, impenetrable. So Burn readied herself for a fight.

She could have left. She could have stationed herself at the edge of the dome, just waiting for the signal to strike. She could have broken from her crew, leaving them behind to fight this battle without her. Yet it didn't feel right. She needed to be there at that moment, in the thick of it. Burn couldn't explain why, but something inside of her screamed that she stay, that she see this through to the end.

They couldn't wait for the dome to be broken to attack. It would have been simpler if they could, but that would give the assembly time to plan, to coordinate, to shore up their defenses. It would nullify the element of surprise. They needed to strike now.

The problem was the guards, who were more than likely gifted – and the fortified bunker, which separated the assembly from the need to fight. Bypassing both required resourcefulness and a good deal of radical thinking. Thankfully, the Lunaria boasted an abundance of each.

With her troops poised in position, teetering on the edge of elation and dread, Burn gave the signal for the first wave to advance. A listless silence descended, expectant and full. Slowly, a noise registered in the back of her mind: boots clacking against pavement and guns jostling against armor. It was a sound Burn knew all too well, the sound of officers, of enemies, yet her breathing didn't falter.

The assembly's guards spotted them and rose to attention, alert and wary, eyeing their brethren with confusion. They were Peace Officers, to be sure, decked out in Peace Force gear with Peace Force guns at their sides. Most of their faces were bare, revealing them as friends and allies. Yet a hint of suspicion lingered, souring the scene.

"Halt!" a beefy guard commanded, and the line of soldiers did as they were told. "Why have you left your positions?" he asked in apprehension. "State your business here."

"We haven't been able to reach you on the comms, sir," a familiar deep voice said, pulling at something in Burn. Unlike the others, the man's face was obscured by a helmet, and she couldn't see his features. "It appears the rebels are interfering with our signals," he continued. "We were sent as backup in case those traitors try to get through."

"Oh, they're gonna try," the first man said, practically sneering, "and we're gonna make sure they fail."

The leader of the second band laughed in derision. "Well, we just want to be part of the fun."

The burly man squinted, considering the troops. Burn's heart stuttered as the pause lengthened, the sticky silence floating in the air like a viscous mist. Finally, after what seemed like a small eternity, he shrugged.

"Fine," he said, "but stay at the back. My men get first crack at the rebels. You can tackle whatever's left after we're finished – if there's anything left at all." Another round of chuckles ensued as the second battalion took their places, stationing themselves behind the first.

A restless stillness rose amongst the guards as they waited for their enemies to arrive. Only, their enemies were already there, hidden in plain sight behind them. Quietly, the dead men raised their guns and fired.

Innoxia had been right – a few spare bodies really did come in handy.

All around the perimeter, Peace Officers dropped as they found themselves with bullets in the back. Those that didn't fall turned to face their former friends, outraged and bewildered in equal measure. Their shock turned to terror as more bodies rose, plucked from death to play for the enemy.

Hale stood amongst them, an avenging angel caught amidst the dead. Still dressed in his Peace Force garb, he blended with the soldiers in the fray, but Burn recognized the way he moved and fought, the way he dodged and killed. He was a warrior through and through, and this was his stage.

Half of the battalion dropped before they realized what was happening. The other half took shelter or fled or tried to fight. Some of the gifted used their powers to make the undead pay. Yet more seemed to forget they had gifts at all, relying solely on weapons clutched tightly in shaking hands.

It was enough. With the chaos they created, a clear path to the building opened, granting them access where none had been before. At the sight, a trio of Lunaria members split off, seizing the opportunity to advance. Together, Ansel, Ava, and Fia darted through the passage, keeping their heads low and their eyes on the prize.

By then, the assembly knew they were there. In time, they would be lured from their domain into the streets – and into the battle. Except the Lunaria didn't want to wait. They wanted war on their terms and their timeline, so they hastened the departure.

Ava and Fia positioned themselves beneath two of the building's sparse windows, which sat high on the reinforced walls. With a nod, they each raised their hands to the glass and took aim. Ava drew back and fired, releasing two frozen spears, which crashed through the window with ease. Beside her, an arc of electricity jumped up, smashing the panes of the other.

Behind them, Ansel was ready, with two fireballs in hand. As soon as the glass shattered, he jumped into action, letting loose his barrage of flames. Soon, smoke began to curl up in languid swirls, marring the perfect sky with sooty tendrils of gray. Satisfied, the trio moved on, repeating the process again and again until the building smoldered in earnest.

Watching the scene from afar, Burn itched with impatience. She wanted to fight, to join the battle, to make the assembly pay. Instead, she sat there, listening. Inside the building, she heard movement, restless and agitated, interspersed with heavy coughs. She heard the assembly rush from their rooms, their distress apparent. She heard them beg for relief.

"Everyone on your guard!" Burn shouted, spurring her troops to action. "The shadows are coming to play."

Hale, Ava, Ansel, and Fia retreated from their posts, joined by the remainder of the dead. Together, the rebels formed a circle of force around the base, a wall of energy and strength that pulsed with power. They stood tall, united, a single army aimed against a single foe. In front, the ragged corpses of officers lingered, forming a pseudo shield to protect their new masters.

Suddenly, the fortress blew open with unnatural force, ripping the doors from their hinges. Smoke billowed from the cavern in blackening waves as figures filed from its depths, resolving into an army.

Chapter 26

The assembly boasted a strange band of warriors. They did not have the advantage of youth, but rather the wisdom of age. Some had served on the force for decades, climbing their way over bodies and colleagues to eventually emerge at the top. Others had been born to privilege, bred for carnage and cruelty, trained from a young age to kill. They knew how to hold on to power – and they knew how to wield it.

Burn's heart quickened as she considered them. Despite their demure appearance, her mind fired out warnings of a threat. Confidence rolled off them in waves, an utter certainty that they would win, that the Lunaria posed no threat to their dominance.

Glancing at them now, Burn wondered if they were right. Their numbers were practically equal, but where the rebels' gifts were random, the assembly's were deliberate, a curated collection of skills. From among their lab rats, they had chosen the strongest powers, the ones best suited to battle. They'd been planning this for years – and the Lunaria had just presented them with the perfect opportunity to play.

Their gifts weren't the only weapons they wielded. The assembly was armed with the latest in deadly tech, with guns clasped in their hands, bombs in their belts, and blades of varying lengths at their sides. Most wore armor, light and fitted, although several didn't seem to see the need. One man wore nothing more than a sleeveless tunic and pants, not even bothering with shoes.

A minute ticked by in slow motion, and still no one moved. Then, unhurriedly, two men made their way to the front, positioning themselves like shields before their charges. The first was the shoeless man, his chiseled features set into a scowl, and his long, dark hair accentuating his cold, dark eyes.

The other man was softer, less menacing, but similarly unprotected, boasting shoes but little else. Burn was startled to find that she recognized him. This was Lanson Creer, the colonel whose home she had searched during her first day in the heavens. She had battled his HouseBot and won, and now she was about to battle him. It seemed fitting, somehow, almost cyclical, and Burn smiled in spite of herself.

Despite their lack of protection, the men showed no fear at forming the front line. They stood tall, braced with a chilling conviction that made Burn's skin tingle. The remaining Peace Officers, those that had survived the Lunaria's trap, took that as their cue, falling into place behind them and beginning to march.

Their pace was unhurried, almost leisurely, and they fanned out to meet their opponents on all sides. The Lunaria raised their guns in response but didn't fire, waiting patiently for a signal to act.

Burn couldn't sense what they were planning, couldn't see inside their minds. She yearned for the insight of telepathy, for access to their thoughts. She needed a boost, yet she could still hear the buzz of the forcefield singing shrilly in her mind, separating her from that power. For the time being, she had to work with what she had.

Aiming her gun at the shoeless figure out front, she took a steadying breath and fired, thereby signaling for the others to do the same. Within an instant, the sounds of gunfire echoed across the tier in a cacophony of thunderous cracks.

Several things occurred in rapid succession, with the start of each indistinguishable from the end of the last. A shield composed of pure power erupted from Creer, growing from his hands and rising in tides of shimmering blue to cover the assembly and their minions. The Lunaria's bullets met the wall, slowing then stopping then dropping to the ground.

Burn's bullets, however, hit their target. Aimed at the shoeless man who brazenly stood outside the boundaries of the barrier, they flew straight, striking him in the head, the chest, the heart. Yet the man didn't drop. Instead, he smiled, not even flinching as the bullets bounced off his skin, ricocheting in every direction.

Realization dawned on Burn, clawing her chest raw. She knew that gift, and she'd known the man who had wielded it. Shaw. He'd fought beside her in the ManniK Battles, saving countless lives with his impenetrable skin – but ultimately losing his own. His body had lain there, tied to a post, trapped on the field of the dead. The assembly must have taken him, stolen his power, and warped his legacy into this, into yet one more arrow in their stolen quiver.

As Shaw's impersonator stalked toward the Lunaria, the assembly and their pawns raised their weapons to fire. Somehow, Burn knew their bullets would make it through, that the shield that sheltered them would in no way hinder their attack.

"Take cover!" she shouted to her unit as the bullets began to fly.

Most of the shots struck the ragged lineup of the dead, but some made it farther, finding homes inside living flesh and bringing Lunaria down. Burn managed to evade the bullets that pelted the scene, taking shelter behind a low stone bench. Her breathing was reduced to shallow panting as the adrenaline and fear compounded, making her mind go blank.

"Scar, we could use some good news," Burn whispered through the comms, trying desperately to reach her sister. But just like before, only silence met her ears, disconcerting in its emptiness. "Nara?" she tried, hoping her friend would respond where her sister did not. "Does anyone copy? We're under fire, and we could do with a little boost, if you know what I mean."

Burn took a breath, then two, but still no one responded. That meant it was up to her – not to take down the forcefield, of course, but to stall until their team made contact. The realization sliced through her fear like a dagger, wrenching her back to the present. Suddenly she knew what she had to do.

"Hale, you'll need to take down our dense little friend," she commanded through the comms.

Hale's resonant voice rumbled back, "I was thinking the same thing – but how do you propose I go about it?"

"Do you remember Shaw and the ManniK Battles?" she asked, garnering an affirmative grunt in response. "Well, I suggest you take their lead. You might not be able to pierce his skin, but that doesn't mean you can't crush it. Tie him down and go for the throat. If it worked on Shaw, then it'll work on him."

"I'm on it, boss," Hale shot back, "but I'm gonna need a distraction."

"We'll have you covered," Burn promised. Turning her attention to the rest of her party, she expanded on her plan. "They're strong because they're united. Apart, they'll be easier to tackle. Our job is to divide and conquer."

"That won't be easy," said Fia, her voice quickened by nerves. "They're safe behind that field. They won't leave it willingly."

That was true – in part. The assembly wasn't likely to forsake their positions, yet they weren't entirely safe, either. Just like the forcefield surrounding the dome, Creer's shield buzzed with its own kind of energy, humming in Burn's mind like a swarm of angry bees. She could sense its power as it flowed up and over, pulsing in muted waves above its masters. It was strongest at the source, at the point where hands met shield in a rustle of blue, where it droned on in one ceaseless note. As it stretched, though, its song weakened, petering out until it wobbled in a faltering staccato.

"His power isn't stretched evenly over the field," she said, relaying her findings. "The sides are the weakest. We'll attack from the edges – and from above. All we need is one casualty.

Innoxia, the rest is up to you."

"Copy that," Innoxia replied, grasping her role in an instant.

"Good," Burn barked. "Fire on my mark. Three, two, one."

The world erupted in a shower of fire and ice as Ansel and Ava lodged their shots to the sky. On the peripheries, bullets echoed as they berated the barrier, steadily eroding its strength. Nearby, Burn caught the crackle of energy, which sparked as it arced, searching the surface for a gap.

Burn didn't see the man fall, but she saw him rise. One second, the gray-haired assembly member was on the ground, felled by an unseen force, and the next he had righted himself, a dead sheen glazing over his formerly bright eyes. He clasped a gun in his right hand, and no one noticed as he raised it.

"Get ready," came Innoxia's voice through the comms. "Things are about to get ugly."

A moment later, one more shot split apart the day, rending it in two. In an instant, the shield shuddered, then blinked out as Creer dropped to the pavement. The assembly spun to face the traitor, openly aghast. In another moment, he was back on the ground, his body riddled with bullets that had never been meant for him.

The Lunaria didn't dawdle. They jumped on the assembly's surprise, firing into the circle with fervor. The assembly's anger was tangible – and even audible, with growls and roars and bellows breaking free from their ranks.

Shaw's gifted double did his best to shield his friends from the onslaught, but on his own he could only do so much. Outside of his protection, the armor did its job safe-guarding some, but it couldn't save them all. Slowly, more were lured to Innoxia's side to sew turmoil from within.

Burn's plan was working. Scared out of the center court by the dead lurking within it, the assembly peeled off in twos and threes, no doubt hoping to employ their gifts to bring things to a brutal end. But out in the wings, the Lunaria were waiting.

As the madness raged, Burn found her sights locked on Una, who remained entrenched in the center of the scene. Burn itched to challenge the woman, to be the one to bring her down, but she knew that she was no match for Una's strength. She had speed and stamina, yes, but her gift was of little use in such a matchup.

There were, however, enough additional adversaries to ensure that she didn't lack a partner. Spotting a scrawny man equipped with a dangerously sharp sword, Burn immediately switched to combat mode. Darting from the safety of the bench, she readied her spear and silently snuck behind him, preparing to strike. He sensed her presence and began to turn, but by then she'd already plunged the point of her weapon toward his shoulder, ripping an angry gash in the muscle of his arm.

Instead of dropping his weapon or crying out in pain, though, the man merely looked at the wound with curiosity. Confused, Burn lowered her gaze from his face to his arm, which was steadily stitching itself together until no hint of the injury remained.

"Oh, hell no!" Burn cried, cursing her luck. She could have been faced with anything – someone who could control light or bend metal or shoot acid from his hands – but this was going to be a problem.

Her opponent smiled in response. "You're Auburn Alendra, right?" he said, shaking his head. "I've heard about you."

"Sorry, but I can't say the same," Burn replied, dodging a wild swipe of his sword. "But I guess it's hard to gain renown when you hide behind anonymity."

"I'm Corporal Dane," he said, giving a mock bow before attacking once more. This time, his sword struck Burn's spear, sending a clang up her arms as she parried.

Burn was unaccustomed to dealing witty repartee alongside killing blows, and the multitasking slowed her reflexes, making it considerably more difficult to foresee his moves. Dane, on the other hand, seemed unhindered by the banter.

"You and your sister are the talk of the Peace Station," he said, pausing for her reply. When she didn't rise to the bait, he continued, "Don't you care what they say about you?"

"Couldn't you just pretend I care?" Burn asked, trying to concentrate on her attacks. "It would save us both some time." She managed to bypass his defenses and deal a blow to the side of his neck, opening a horrid red slit in his skin. Just like before, however, Dane didn't even seem to feel it, and it closed before Burn had a chance to strike again. Clearly, killing this man would require some creativity.

Dane wasn't discouraged by her cheek. He continued on as if she hadn't even spoken. "We think you're impressive – both you and your sister. I mean, you've gotten so far with so little. Raqa told us how quaint your gifts are. Eavesdropping and building trinkets? At least Scarlett's gift could come in handy. But yours? How have you even survived this long?"

Burn could feel her cheeks going red as her blood began to boil. She knew he was trying to provoke her, to get her to drop her guard and do something stupid, yet his words stuck in her mind, fanning her anger. Deep down, she knew she wasn't useless, but right now she felt it. Each strike of her spear left no lasting mark, and each parry sapped more of her strength.

"You know how I've survived?" she growled, twirling her spear in her right hand. "It's thanks to people like you. You write us off because you can't see our value. You don't understand us, so you label us as worthless. You underestimate us – and that is our greatest power."

As Burn spoke, she deftly drew her gun with her left hand, aiming it at Dane's thigh. By the time he noticed, it was already too late. Burn had pulled the trigger, releasing her bullet into his body. And this time he felt it. Falling to his knees, he dropped his sword and brought both hands to the wound, crying out in pain.

Burn knew he would soon recover, but she didn't need long. Dropping her own weapon, she lunged to the ground, grabbing his sword. It was heavier than Burn anticipated, but she kept moving, rising to her feet in a graceful sweep. Dane threw out his hand to grab her, but she evaded his grasp and spun to a spot behind him.

A roar broke free from somewhere deep within her as she gathered her strength. Raising the sword up high, she brought it down with all the might she possessed, swinging it toward his neck until it met resistance. The blade, however, was sharp, new, and clean, and in the battle between steel and flesh, steel came out the victor.

Dane's head dropped first, followed by his body. Burn stood blinking at the carnage, waiting for him to rise, yet he remained immobile.

"Whose gift is quaint now, you son of a bitch?" she whispered to the dead man, happy to have the last word. For good measure, she kicked his head away, sending it bouncing into the battle beyond.

Burn threw the sword aside, reclaiming her spear. The weight felt familiar in her palm, and she took a breath to steady herself before jumping once more into the fray.

Her next opponent was, thankfully, far less talkative – and far easier to dispatch. Within the span of a few breaths, she managed to disarm him, ripping his gun from his hands and turning it on him. This time, one shot was all it took.

Straightening, Burn barely managed to dodge a spear of ice that had gone astray, the slick and slender weapon nearly impaling her against a wall. A muffled "sorry!" erupted from an adjoining battle as Burn regained her bearings.

It was only then that she noticed the difference in the air. It was…quiet. Not the battle, which raged on around her, with cries and screams aplenty, but the air itself. It had lost something, like an echo, and it felt flat and thin in her mind.

The forcefield. It was down. The realization shocked Burn's system, thrilling her to the core.

They'd done it. Scar and Nara had brought down the barrier, exposing the dome. They'd completed their part of the plan – and now it was up to her.

Burn dashed through the street, propelled by her excitement. She swerved around combatants and ducked under errant blows, skirting the chaos that threatened to stop her.

As she ran, she saw friends locked in battle, fighting for their lives. Her heart went out and she yearned to halt, to help, but she knew she couldn't.

Burn tried to ignore the dead, but the bodies pulled at her, tempting her to look, to recognize, to mourn. She noticed that they'd stopped rising, stopped defying the laws of life and death. A few feet down the road, Burn saw the reason why. Innoxia sat, eyes open, propped against a wall. Her hand lay limp around her stomach, where acid still sizzled, eating through her skin and into the organs beyond.

Burn closed her eyes against the sight, fighting back burning tears. Innoxia had been with the Lunaria through so much, from the ManniK Battles onward. She'd always been willing to fight, to lend her talents to the cause. And where others had found her gift odd, even wrong, she'd found acceptance with the Lunaria. She'd found a family.

Burn turned away, refocusing her sights on the dome. She had to continue, had to make it to the edge. Every minute wasted was another life claimed, another ally lost to the whims of war. All eyes were on her – and all hopes for success rested on her shoulders.

Out of the corner of her eye, Burn saw Hale, still locked in combat with the man who stole Shaw's skin. Blood trickled from a cut above Hale's eye and he was limping, hindered by some unseen injury. His opponent, on the other hand, still appeared unscathed. Burn's hands tightened into fists, but she knew she couldn't help him. In a battle between such rivals, she'd only be a burden.

Burn turned a corner, then another, dragging herself from the epicenter and into the margins. Even these streets were soaked with the bedlam of blood, but it was easier to tune out, to turn down the sounds and focus on her prize. Burn used her senses to guide her, feeling her way through the city as it clattered and crashed around her. And under her.

Without warning, the pavement beneath Burn's feet betrayed her, quaking in rolling shocks before splitting in two. Burn lost her balance and fell, her body tumbling into the yawning maw of the growing crack. Her hands lashed out, scrambling against smooth stones and slick surfaces in search of purchase, but they found none. Below her, a drop of several stories lingered, waiting, calling – and she was slipping, sinking into its grasp.

At the last moment, right before her hand gave way and her body slid into the darkness, a whistling sound broke through, like the clear chime of a bell sounding through fog. A second later, a shard of ice punctured the pavement next to Burn, embedding itself in the stone. Without a thought, she grabbed it, gasping from the cold. It shocked her system, bringing her back to life, and she leveraged herself up and into the world.

She lay on the ground, panting, waiting for the tremors to subside, but they didn't. Instead, they grew around her, growling, threatening to tear apart the world and drag her down. Burn scrambled up and away, seeking safety amidst the treacherous terrain.

As she leapt, dodging cracks and cave-ins, she spotted the culprit. He was a large man, his face decorated with scars and a scowl, and his eyes were trained on her. He knelt against the ground, his hands caressing its stones and his will causing them to break.

Burn sighed, preparing herself for a fight – but some-one beat her to the punch. As Burn watched, a flutter of tiny icicles flew through the air, puncturing his hands. From behind a corner, Ava appeared, her palms dancing with dag-gers of ice. With another throw, the man was torn from the ground and pinned to the bricks behind him. In an instant, his whole body was frozen by an icy gust, which cemented him in place. Without his link to the pavement, the tremors weakened, then stopped, the ground reverting to its familiar solid stasis.

"Thanks for the save," Burn shouted across the chasm to Ava, genuinely grateful for her help.

"Any time," Ava responded with a nod. "I've got this," she continued, waving to the scene – and the man frozen to the wall beside her. "Go do what you have to do."

Burn didn't need to be told twice. She'd been delayed long enough. It was time to finish this.

Lurching into an uneasy jog, she neared the side of the dome, watching as the buildings fell away to reveal its softly sloping curve. It had never looked so beautiful, its surface clear and tangible against the setting suns. Out here, she could almost believe that the world wasn't burning, that the carnage and chaos had merely been some dreadful dream. Yet she could still hear the gunshots, the screams. She could still taste the fear.

She closed her eyes for an instant, sending out a si-lent prayer to the fates, pleading for the safety of her allies. Opening them once more, she reached around for the blast-er, unhooking it from her back. It was heavy, bulbous, and awkward, and it felt strange in her hands, but its power was undeniable. She moved her finger to the trigger, heaving the weapon toward the dome. Then her world exploded.

Burn hadn't pulled the trigger; she was sure of it. Yet suddenly her feet no longer touched the ground. She was thrust into the air, a weight pressed against her chest, propelling her back. She had an instant of weightlessness where the tier seemed to stand still around her before everything crashed into place – including her. Her back slammed against something solid, and she heard her body crack, breaking from the impact.

Air seemed to evade her lungs as she gasped for breath. Every sip was a struggle, and splinters of pain pierced her chest, threatening to steal the light and force her into oblivion. She tried to move, to wriggle free, but a pillar of stone restrained her, crushing her beneath its bulk.

Someone approached, unhurried and slow, as if enjoying her pain. Burn tried to raise her eyes to the figure, but her head was too heavy, too tired, too full. Instead, she watched as the feet drew near, pausing in silence before her.

After an agonizing moment, a familiar voice rang through the wreckage. "You thought you could get past us?" Una asked, her voice mocking. "We're everywhere. We see everything. Who do you think you are that you could fool us?"

Burn let out a dry little laugh, which quickly transformed into a racking cough. She could taste blood, and she spat, sending a sprinkling of red onto the dusty pavement.

"Don't you recognize your own daughter?" Burn asked, finally raising her head to the woman. Something told her to stop talking, to keep her mouth shut, but that part of her brain was muted, drowned by pain and exhaustion. "You think that nothing gets past you, mother dearest, but you didn't even notice when your own daughter was replaced with a fraud. Your arrogance has blinded you. Face it: You're just as clueless as the rest of us."

Una lurched forward, grabbing Burn's hair in her hand and forcing her face up. They were mere inches apart, and Burn stared into her eyes, unblinking. She should have been afraid. She should have been terrified. Yet she only felt numb.

"What did you do to Ellis?" Una asked, a new coldness in her tone.

"Like you care," Burn bit back. This woman didn't deserve the comfort of knowing that her daughter was alive and well, albeit locked away in a cell. "Ellis was only ever a pawn in your game, another tool you could use to gain power. She deserved better."

Una's hand flew out, slapping Burn across the face in a stinging rebuke. "What do you know about family?" she asked, shaking her head in disdain. "Yes, I know who you are – Auburn the orphan. Our little rebel leader who raised an army and started a war all because her daddy died. Tell me, is that your idea of family?"

"If that's what you think this war is about, then you're more clueless than I thought," Burn spat.

"Well, then maybe you should enlighten me," Una crooned. "What is it that you're fighting for so futilely? What could possibly be worth this destruction?"

Burn thought for a moment before replying, "Freedom."

Una laughed. "You're not slaves, darling. You're just poor.

You've always had freedom."

"No, we haven't," she said. "We have never been free. This dome is our cage, and you are our captors. You use us as you please and toss us out when you're done. You built a world of fear so you can look like the saviors. But you've never felt our pain. You've never watched a loved one die, coughing up the grime you force us to breathe. You've never been attacked in the streets simply because of the way you were born. You've never been thrown into a cell and forgotten, forced to starve while your friends battle to the death next door. You call me a criminal for fighting to change the system, but you're the real villain of this piece."

Una's eyebrows rose in mock amusement, and she gave a slow, taunting clap. "Bravo. That was quite the speech. I can see why your precious Lunaria tag along in your wake. But this time you've led them to their deaths. Honestly, I should be thanking you. You've brought us a plethora of new gifts to harvest. After we finish dissecting your little friends, the assembly will be unstoppable. Part of me wants to keep you alive so you can watch as they're rounded up and shot. Unfortunately, I can't risk you running around underfoot, trying to ruin things. So it's time to say goodbye."

Una brought her hands up to Burn's neck, just like Ignis had done mere weeks before. The soft pressure turned painful as she began to squeeze, enjoying Burn's look of panic. Burn closed her eyes, preparing for the end, but a soft whooshing noise forced them open.

"Gah!" Una cried as a sliver of ice pierced her shoulder. She instinctively dropped her hands from Burn's neck to tear the icicle from her skin.

Burn coughed and wheezed, her eyes watering as she forced air into her lungs. Meanwhile, Una spun, searching the scene for her attacker. Once more that day, Ava appeared, her clothes ragged and her hair a mess, but her face radiant with righteous anger. Burn thanked the gods for her beautiful blue savior.

Una growled, leaping toward Ava's side. Yet Ava was quicker, dodging out of the way and evading her opponent's clutches. She sent two more icy shards sailing toward Una, but the woman sidestepped both, reaching out to pound one into a thousand glittering pieces as it sailed by.

Burn saw her chance. Seizing on Una's distraction, she began to wriggle free from the pillar, cringing as the weight pressed against her broken form. It wasn't easy to move the column or keep from crying out, but Burn did it, gradually emerging from her solid stone prison. Around her, the sounds of ice shattering and stone splitting filled her ears, but she kept her attention focused on the task at hand.

Eventually, Burn pulled her torso free. Panting from the effort, she pushed with all her might to liberate one leg, then the other. As she rose, rocks and dust streamed off her tattered armor, and the world spun around her. She gripped the wall for support, knowing that if she fell, she might never rise again.

Taking a deep breath, she bent over to retrieve the blaster. The movement sent a scream of pain through her midsection, but Burn bit down, muffling her moan. Straightening, she aimed the weapon once more at the target.

"I wouldn't do that if I were you," came Una's cold voice from the other side of the street, drawing Burn's gaze. What she saw made her heart stutter.

Ava knelt before Una, a gun to her head. Her eyes were wild, with anger and fear churning behind them, and she pressed her lips together in a hard, defiant line. Despite her terror, she held her head high, refusing to bend.

"Put the weapon down or I'll shoot," Una said, her self-satisfaction apparent. Burn knew she wasn't bluffing. She would shoot Ava without a second thought. Una had no qualms on that point. The only question was if Burn backed down, would Una do the same? Burn had a sinking feeling she wouldn't. Ava's chances of survival were slim – and the girl knew it.

Something changed in Ava's face as that realization settled. It was a calmness, a determination, and it quieted her unease, descending like a tranquil peace. Slowly, she raised her eyes to Burn's, her look glowing with resolve.

"No," Burn whispered, sensing Ava's plan. She didn't need telepathy to know what the girl was thinking. Hell, if she'd been in Ava's shoes, she would have done the same. But Burn couldn't bear to see another ally fall – not like this.

This time, however, it wasn't up to her. Ava gave a tiny shake of her head, glancing meaningfully at the blaster before focusing back on Burn.

"This is my part to play," she seemed to say, "and that's yours. Don't fuck it up."

"Fine, you win," Burn shouted, dragging Una's attention back to her. She put her hands up in surrender, holding the blaster gingerly in her right hand and lowering it to her side. Una smiled, obviously pleased, lowering her gun in response. That was all the time Ava needed.

Reaching out both hands, she grasped Una's legs. With a cry, Ava sent out her icy tendrils, which encased the woman in their grasp. The ice climbed her body, starting with her feet and working its way toward her chest. Yet her arms remained free. Clearly struggling, she raised the gun to Ava's head and fired. A split second later, her hands froze over, and Ava dropped into a pile at her feet.

Burn shuddered, her hands shaking, but she remained where she was, glued to the spot. Tearing her eyes from Ava's body, she trained the gun on the dome and fired. And nothing happened.

She tried again, squeezing the trigger with all her might, but the gun remained silent and the dome remained whole. It was only then that she spotted the crack in the power cell. Her heart, which had been sputtering in erratic bursts, slowed as her body went cold and her hope drained to nothing.

"Scar, it's broken," she said through the comms, her voice quiet and low. "The blaster is broken. The power cell cracked and...I can't break through the dome." She didn't expect Scar to answer. She hadn't before, so why would she now? Burn just needed to say it, to cast her despair to the ether, to set it free.

Yet her sister was full of surprises.

"You had one job!" Scar's irate voice burst through, biting into Burn's self-pity and bringing her back to the present. "Do I have to do everything myself?" she growled. "Just stay put. I'm coming to fix it."

A cracking sound broke the stillness of the scene, and Burn looked up, searching for the noise. Her gaze fell on Una, who was steadily shattering her prison, sending icy blocks crashing to the ground around her.

"Uh, Scar?" Burn said, her voice suddenly shaky. "I don't think staying put is going to be an option. I have company."

Scar sighed. "Well, then it's a good thing I never took out your tracker."

Chapter 27

Scar and Nara's mission had gone sideways before they'd even arrived at the power plant. The attack from the Peace-Bots had left them frazzled, and their luck had only gotten worse from there.

"Everyone, stay close," Nara said as they crouched low in the shadows outside the structure, waiting for their opportunity to strike.

Their crew was smaller than the others, but it was well-stocked, boasting a fine selection of mutants with an array of powers – and a lot of guns.

The wall-climber, Kornak, had been one of their first recruits, quickly followed by the wolf-man, Astor, and contortionist, Raina. Ash had volunteered as well, lending his light feet and leaping talents to the team. While they hadn't managed to nab Jade or Rakasa, whose gifts were needed elsewhere, they had gotten lucky with Ino and Lux. Their brawn rounded out the team nicely, and their jaunty humor kept things light while they waited to strike.

The plant itself was far smaller than the munitions facility – and half as well guarded. Most people considered the dome their salvation, not their cage, meaning they'd never thought twice about its forcefield. That's not to say the building was without its protections. A towering brick wall stood firmly in their path, and the plant was accessed by a solitary steel gate staffed by a handful of officers.

Their plan was simple: Kornak and Astor would scale the wall and Ash would vault it. Then together they'd take out the guards and open the gate, ushering their crew inside. But, as was usually the case, the reality was a tad more complicated.

Nara gave the order to proceed, and the three men took their positions. Ash was the first to reach the top, his powerful legs taking him straight to the peak, but Kornak and Astor scrambled up soon after. Together, the trio dropped beyond the wall into the enemy's camp.

Then everything went quiet. Too quiet.

"Kornak? Astor?" Nara asked after a minute. "What's your status? Do you copy?"

Scar expected Nara's words to crackle through her comms, but her device stayed silent, enforcing the eerie calm.

"Something's wrong," Scar whispered, shaking her head. "Our comms are down. It's like they're using a jammer," she said, confused. The last time she'd encountered them, the Peace Force hadn't had that technology – and, to be honest, she didn't think they were smart enough to discover it overnight. Pulling out her tab, she intended to bypass the obstruction, but its dead screen stopped her in her tracks.

"Can you fix it?" Nara growled in frustration. "I need to know what's happening."

Scar winced. "It's more than just our comms. It looks like they've wiped out our tech, too." Which meant that not only was she rendered tab-less, but that many of her weapons would be worthless, as well.

"How could they even do that?" Nara asked, her annoyance clear.

"Likely a localized electromagnetic pulse," Scar said with a shrug. "But since that's far beyond the Peace Force's wheelhouse, I think we're dealing with something closer to home. I think someone in there is gifted – and I think they know we're here."

At that moment, a battered and bruised wolf fell through the front gate, the iron door swinging open behind him.

Nara closed her eyes, breathing out an angry sigh. "Well, it looks like we're going in blind."

And that was precisely what they did.

Falling into line behind Nara, the group crept quietly toward the entrance, their guns and their hackles raised. For all they knew, a small army could be lurking just beyond the wall, waiting for them to appear. Yet as they crossed the threshold, nothing jumped out to greet them. Well, nothing but Ash.

The boy descended from the dimness, out of breath and bleeding. "There were more guards than we expected," he gasped, clutching his side. "We took down a few, but they kept coming. Kornak is trying to hold them off, but they'll be here any minute." He swayed precariously, then crumpled, hitting the ground in a dead faint.

Nara growled even louder. "Take cover!" she shouted. "And someone shut that damn gate. We don't need any more company."

Raina jumped into action, helping Astor to his feet and closing the gate behind him. There wasn't time to cross the yawning expanse of open ground, so they scrambled, scattering across the field in search of cover. Scar barely managed to duck behind a sturdy steel storage tank before the enemy's troops descended, their guns blazing.

The shootout seemed to last an eternity, steadily lengthening into an endless barrage where neither side could seize the upper hand. Ino and Lux were fair shots, and Nara was a master. They gave as good as they got, picking off soldiers with precision. A novice at war, Raina did what she could from the sidelines while Astor tried to revive Ash from his stupor.

Scar, meanwhile, rooted through her bag, searching anxiously for something to help. After a beat, her hand landed on a cool metal tube and she smiled, yanking it from her pack.

"Close your eyes – and get ready to run!" she shouted as she pulled the pin and lobbed it.

To her surprise, her aim wasn't half bad, and the cannister clinked across the yard in errant bounces before lighting up the space with a blinding flare. Even with her eyes shut and her hands clasped over her face, the light seeped through, filling her sight with stars.

Nara, Ino, and Lux didn't seem to have that problem – or, if they did, they didn't let it stop them. As soon as the light dissipated, they were off, darting across the pavement to challenge their opponents head-on, trading guns for spears and knives and fists. Astor followed soon after, bounding across the space on all fours, while Raina remained behind with Ash.

With a few well-placed strikes and slashes, they efficiently disarmed their foes. Astor helped in his own way, forgoing weapons for claws and teeth, which bit through his targets with ease. Still, they were outnumbered three to one, and the tides soon began to turn as the officers regained their wits and their vision.

Scar rustled through her bag more frantically now, searching for another score. She threw aside her pen, which had long since lost its spark, and the net that was equally dead. Weapon after weapon clanked to the ground, discarded, until her hands grazed the bottom of the pack. Then something struck her – literally.

She didn't see it coming, but it hit home nonetheless, filling her head with a clanging pain. She dropped to the pavement, barely conscious, and grasped for something to save her. Her hands seized on a cool metal cannister just as her opponent grabbed her leg and began to pull.

He dragged her along the rough expanse of street, stones digging into her stomach and her head lolling against the pavement in painful thuds. Scar couldn't think, couldn't fight, couldn't imagine what he was planning. It took all she had to hang on.

Maybe he intended to use her as bait. Maybe he wanted company when he killed her. Maybe he simply craved more space to do the dirty deed. Whatever it was, he never got his chance.

A shot rang out and the man before her twirled, knocked off balance by the bullet and his desperate attempts to evade it. The metal embedded itself into the thick muscle of his arm, and he howled, emitting a sound comprised of rage and pain. He dropped Scar's leg as he spun, giving her enough time to roll herself over and aim.

The man's shock doubled when he found himself tangled in a web of wires, which encircled his ankles and feet, bringing him down in a wriggling heap. What the net lacked in electricity, it more than made up for in surprise. The impact knocked the air from his lungs and the gun from his grasp. Scrambling, Scar threw herself on top of the weapon, claiming it as her own.

Jumping to her feet, she watched as the world spun – and the man spun with it. She was out of his clutches for the moment, but he was fierce and angry and bent on revenge, and the net wouldn't hold him for long. Scar might have had terrible aim, but at that range, missing was a hard thing to do. Taking a breath, she fired.

Scar closed her eyes as the ground swayed, threatening to rise up and claim her, but a hand pulled her back, steadying her on her feet. Glancing over, Scar found Raina's lithe limbs holding her in place and her kind eyes searching her for wounds.

"Thanks for the assist," Scar mumbled, straining to think through the fog.

"I couldn't very well let you fall," said Raina, attempting to lighten the mood.

"I meant the shot," Scar replied, gesturing to the man on the ground. After all, it had been Raina's bullet that allowed her to escape. She owed the woman more than she could say.

"Oh, that," Raina said, forcing a smile. "That was nothing. Burn always told us we should have each other's backs. I was only following her orders."

The mention of Burn stirred something in Scar. The dizziness remained, a painful reminder of her recent encounter, but her mind kept working, kept spinning, kept repeating her mission. She had to turn off the forcefield. She had to do it for Burn.

Glancing up, Scar noticed that the path to the plant was clear. During her brief absence from the fight, Nara and her gang had somehow managed to even the odds. They were now busy challenging the final few guards, diverting their attention away from the doors. If they moved quickly, Scar and Raina would have a clear shot to the entrance – and hopefully to the power source beyond.

Out of nowhere, something fell from the sky, and Scar hastily spun to fight it. Yet it was only Ash, looking as unsteady as Scar felt. They were a battered trio, in no shape to continue, but they pressed on anyway, determined to succeed.

Ash covered the distance to the door in two large leaps, but Scar and Raina took the hard way, scurrying across open ground in a flurry of uncertain steps. Mercifully, nothing jumped out to attack them, and no bullets bit through their path. Before long, they'd joined Ash at the door, and together they entered.

The halls inside were quiet and dim, almost sleepy in their stillness. The only tangible sound was the buzz of generators, droning on in a ceaseless call. Without a map, Scar was blind, but their hum spurred her on, drawing her steadily toward the building's core.

Scar's instruments were still dead. Her tab was blank, her comms silent, her weapons lifeless. If her hunch was correct, it meant the culprit was still alive, still conscious, and still blocking their devices from somewhere inside, obstructing their efforts from afar.

They proceeded slowly through the halls, guns drawn, peering around every corner before taking it. They didn't speak, guarding their own voices out of fear of detection. Their silence kept them safe – at least for a time. Yet this far behind enemy lines, safety could never be guaranteed for long. Someone would always come calling. Or, in their case, some*thing*.

A soft whirring noise was their only warning. Burn would have sensed it, would have gotten out of the way in time, but Scar didn't have her skills. By the time she located the source of the sound, the attack had already begun.

Small slits opened in the ceiling, peeling apart to reveal the barrels of small guns. Scar shouted a warning, a jumbled mess of surprise and fear, before the hiss of shots began. She ducked and dodged and rolled in an intricately awkward ballet, ultimately reaching the safety of the far wall. She plastered herself against its surface, panting and wheezing, waiting for the barrage to end.

In another second, it did, leaving an ominous tranquility in its wake. Raina and Ash both lay on the ground, unmoving, their bodies twisted in a pantomime of escape. Yet there was no blood, no gore, merely silence. And darts.

Scar sighed, cursing the building and its secrets. It had not managed to kill her cohorts, but that hadn't been its goal.

It had merely put them to sleep, drowning them in dreamless oblivion to be collected and questioned and jailed. Checking herself for injuries, Scar plucked two darts from her pack – and one from the armor over her chest – pocketing them for later use.

She spared a few precious seconds to remove the darts from her allies and drag their bodies to the wings, out of sight of wayward guards. Then she set off, her pace sprightly yet wary. Now she scanned not just corners, but walls, ceilings, and floors. Each posed their own threat, their own trials and traps, and each might prevail in stopping her.

Yet somehow, they didn't. Two more hallways tried, but both failed, leaving her alive and conscious at their ends. One used gas, the other trap doors, but Scar outwitted both in classic Scar fashion. Soon, she arrived at the core, at the heart of the labyrinth, where the generators' buzz enveloped the air, drowning out her steps.

No one heard her enter. The doors parted silently before her, whooshing open at her touch and closing at her back. Beyond them, rows of generators lay in neat little lines, shouting with effort as they shielded the dome.

Scar ducked behind one of the monoliths, peering around its back to process her surroundings. The space was tall and broad, a rough, stagnant warehouse composed of dangling chains and steel beams. It was dim, cold, and dry, unwelcoming and unfriendly, and it stank of fuel and its derivatives. And it was deafening.

Scar could barely piece together thoughts, let alone a whole plan. Her head wound wasn't helping, but she pressed on nonetheless, needing a strategy to guide her through the haze.

It would be simple to turn off a generator, to break it beyond repair, yet that would do little to further her cause. One generator on its own had little power in this synergistic system, which functioned as a unit rather than a medley of parts. To bring it down, she'd have to target the machine as a whole, going for its heart instead of a limb.

That heart, the system that kept it all online, lay at the back of the wide expanse of space, held aloft by a sturdy iron platform and guarded by three men, alert and armed, ready to defend their realm. Yet they hadn't seen her. Somehow, she'd managed to slip in unnoticed, slithering to her spot unobserved. The ease of it sent a chill down her spine, setting her nerves alight.

Her confusion swiftly settled into understanding when a fourth guard turned the corner beside her, emerging mere feet from where she hid.

Once again, however, it seemed that luck was on her side. Scar slid soundlessly around the generator, her back pressed against its rumbling sides. She stalked around one corner, two corners, three, pulling up behind the man and his gun. By the time he turned, he was already falling, a dart lodged deep within his neck.

Scar lowered him softly to the ground, relieving him of his gun – and then his armor. Donning her disguise, she crept deeper into the room, past rows of noise and peace and noise again. She kept her head bowed, her curls tucked away, her identity hidden. When she drew alongside the other guards, they didn't even notice the change.

"Back already?" one inquired, a mocking lilt to his tone.

"What, are you scared of those little freaks? Think they'll bite you in two?" His cronies laughed, amused.

Scar didn't speak. She merely raised one finger to her lips, then pointed with a shaking hand toward the door.

The change was immediate. Gone were the smiles and laughter, replaced by a calm determination and an eerie quiet. Two of the three descended to flank her, their gazes and their guns trained on the door. They didn't notice her hands – or the darts held in her grasp. At least not until those darts entered their necks, dropping them in quick succession.

The third man seemed alarmed by this sudden turn of events. His surprise gave her an instant to escape before the shots began. Instead of hitting her, they struck iron and steel, adding short, resounding clangs to the soundscape of the space. Then, suddenly, the world went still.

The generators buzzed in unison around her, but the sounds of gunfire ceased. The peace was disconcerting, and Scar removed her helmet, peering toward the platform to find no one peering back. The man had vanished.

Just as quickly, he reappeared beside her, knocking the gun from her hands. But instead of firing he merely stared, his eyes traveling to the metal peeking beneath her armor and the wires sparking in her hair.

"Fascinating," he said, entranced. "How much of you is machine and how much human?" he asked shamelessly, stepping closer. "Are there circuits in there? Gears? Sensors? What makes you tick?"

"I'm not a robot. I'm a person," Scar spat, drawing up to her full height before him. "And I'm going to need you to turn off these generators."

The man scoffed, and Scar shrugged. It had been worth a try. Yet even her brazen demands couldn't distract him from his new obsession: her.

"I wonder what would happen if you got a shock to the system," he said, his eyes lighting up with excitement. "Would you stop? Would it kill you? Or would you survive?"

The pieces came together in Scar's mind. "You're the reason our comms are dead – and our tabs. You're the human EMP," she guessed, shaking her head.

"Guilty," he said proudly, wiggling his fingers. "Isn't it marvelous? It's so…versatile. Of course, the force didn't think I was useful enough to be on the front lines, so they stuck me here, in this cell of a space. But if I bring them the head of Scarlett Alendra, there's no telling how they'd thank me. A promotion, of course. A medal, a commendation, a seat on the assembly. The world would be mine for the taking."

"I think you overestimate my value," Scar jeered, buying time so she could formulate a plan. This man certainly liked to talk. Maybe she could use that in her favor.

"Perhaps," he said calmly, "but this gift is powerful. Its previous owner couldn't see that, but I can. I could bring this city to its knees before me. I could make them all beg."

"That sounds like a terrible plan," Scar said bluntly, inching toward her weapon, which lay discarded between their feet. "Making yourself a terrorist won't make them respect you. It will only make you a target."

"I'm not a terrorist. You're a terrorist!" the man cried like a petty child who couldn't get his way. "I'm merely talking about a show of power, a display of force."

Scar laughed, prying the sound from her throat. "What

power? You turn off a few radios? Power down a few tabs? Face it – you're not a god. You're a light switch."

"Oh really?" he cried. "Watch this!" With a wave of his hands, he sent a ball of energy crashing into a nearby generator, killing it stone dead. In the process, his weapon dropped from his grasp, clattering to the floor by his feet.

Scar seized her chance. She lunged for her gun then rolled away, heading for the stairs. Waves of energy rippled behind her as the officer tried to test his theory and turn her off, but she evaded the blasts, pushing forward in an all-out sprint.

The system's core was in sight, the bank of tabs blinking and bright, but something made Scar stop. She took a breath as the soldier aimed, then she leapt through the air toward the heart.

The blast hit her with a flash of cold, enveloping her and her surroundings. She dropped to the ground as the machines died down, broken by his blast. He cursed as he realized his mistake.

To Scar's surprise – and his – she rose from the silence, unaffected, and fired. He dropped without another word, falling to the pavement with a thud.

Awoken by his demise, her comms crackled on. Checking her tab, she found life where none had been before. Yet the generators remained silent, a casualty of a direct hit rather than a widespread pulse. To be safe, Scar took her time disconnecting a series of wires and parts, even setting a small fire for good measure.

That's how Nara found her – descending the stairs in the wake of a blaze. Her eyes went to the soldiers on the ground, to the generators, to Scar, her eyebrows raised in disbelief.

"You did all this by yourself? Without gadgets?" she asked, incredulous.

"Don't sound so surprised," Scar responded in mock offense. "I'm scrappier than I look."

"Right," Nara said, nodding sagely.

"Fine, I got lucky," Scar admitted, "but the important thing is that we did it. The generators are off. The forcefield is down. Now it's up to Burn to save us."

She shrugged out of her guard costume in favor of her rebel attire, with Nara watching her intently. As soon as she was done, Nara closed the gap between them, drawing Scar in for a soft, lingering kiss. Scar didn't pull away.

"You really are full of surprises," Nara said, her hands still wrapped around the back of Scar's neck. "But next time, you leave the fighting to me. I promised Burn I'd keep you safe."

Scar's heart warmed at the sentiment, and she drew Nara in, letting her lips drown out the memory of the fight and the lingering pain beating through her skull. They stayed like that for some time, the world dropping away around them. Yet even Nara's skillful ministrations couldn't hold back reality forever.

"Scar, it's broken," came Burn's quiet voice through the comms, shattering the beautiful silence. "The blaster is broken. The power cell cracked and…I can't break through the dome."

Scar's skin went cold at the words, and her warm heart froze over once more.

"You had one job!" she growled, annoyed. "Do I have to

do everything myself?" she asked, partly to Burn and partly to Nara. Sighing, she went on, "Just stay put. I'm coming to fix it."

But even that was apparently too much to ask. "Uh, Scar?" Burn replied in concern. "I don't think staying put is going to be an option. I have company."

Scar sighed, basking slightly in the glow of her foresight. "Well, then it's a good thing I never took out your tracker."

Chapter 28

Scar and Nara stalked through Kasis like shadows in the night. The growing darkness helped, as did the utter chaos around them. Every street and alley was now a battleground, a war zone, a grave.

Scar had intended to go solo, to ascend to the heavens alone, but Nara wouldn't allow it. She said it was her job to protect Scar, to watch over her, to make sure she returned in one piece. Scar had secretly been pleased. Aside from Burn, she'd never had someone to look out for her, to make it their mission to defend her. It was comforting in a way she couldn't quite explain.

Yet she didn't have time to dwell on the novel feelings taking shape within her. Once more, the world needed saving – and once more the job had fallen to her.

They'd left the rest of their party behind to clean up the mess. Or what was left of their party. Ash and Raina would be fine in time, although others hadn't been so fortunate.

Kornak hadn't made it past their initial push, and Lux had dropped shortly thereafter, falling victim to a bullet that hadn't been meant for him. He had saved his brother's life, and, in the process, he'd forfeited his own.

Scar had seen the pain in Ino's eyes and felt it ripple from him in waves. She knew that feeling, that loss. From now on, there would always be a part of him that was missing, a hole he could never hope to fill. Right now it was jagged and raw, something so sharp it seemed like it could kill, but time would sand down its edge, leaving a dull throb that would forever linger.

Of course, if Scar couldn't get to the heavens and fix the blaster in time, none of it would matter. There would be no time to heal, no time to mourn. Soon they'd all be joining Kornak and Lux as yet more *freaks* lost in a failed rebellion.

Soon after their departure, Nara had taken the lead, insisting on playing both lookout and guard. She handled Scar with such care, like she was crucial, indispensable – and she was. But what Nara didn't realize was that she was indispensable, too. At least to Scar. So as Nara led the way, Scar followed, ready to defend the woman with her life.

It wasn't a hollow sentiment. There were times in their ascent that it truly looked as if one or the other would fall, but Nara had her weapons and Scar her gadgets, and together they prevailed.

Still, by the time they reached the Peace Sector, only a few tiers up from where they'd started, they were both out of breath, bruised and bleeding. They picked their way across the tier, clinging to its fringes, unable to risk being sidetracked by the battle.

From the reports that filtered through their comms, they knew the Lunaria had been lucky, with less than a third of the Peace Force possessing powers. Yet those that were gifted knew how to fight – and so did the rest of their battalions.

The Lunaria were once again outnumbered and outgunned. It wasn't surprising. They had known from the outset that things would never be equal, that this job required an abundance of faith. And currently, that faith was all that sustained them.

Their troops were tired, broken, and worn. Even from the outskirts of the sector, Scar could sense their desperation, their despair. The battle had spread even to these farthest reaches, and the faces that greeted them were hollow and pale. Yet they were determined to keep going, to keep fighting, to hold out until help appeared.

Scar and Nara skirted bodies and blows, doing their best to keep to the shadows. It was slow going, with untold obstructions in their path, but they slogged on, wading through the remnants of battle. Here and there, fires raged and shots sounded and people cried. The air was thick with smoke and haze and the smell of gunfire, burnt and sulfurous, like hell itself had come to life in Kasis.

It no longer resembled the city that Scar knew. This was something else, something worse. Gone were the familiar shops and carts and swarms of people. Now it was a land of broken things, of shattered glass and twisted metal and fractured spirits. Scar swallowed the emotions that struggled to break free, but the heady taste of them remained on her tongue, stinging of fear and guilt and heartache.

The sudden clang of metal striking metal effectively

banished them from her mind, leaving behind a solemn and dangerous calm. Scar looked down to see her shirt torn along her forearm, yet the skin beneath was smooth, unmarked, a beautiful, gleaming silver.

Even though the blade hadn't drawn blood, Scar was still furious. She didn't need to be injured to want vengeance; an attack on her person was more than enough of a motive. Unfortunately, it looked like Nara had already staked her claim on Scar's attacker.

The woman crossed the short stretch of street to the man's side, challenging him to a deadly duel. The gruff man, bearded and burly, seemed assured of his success, sizing up Nara's lanky body and laughing her off with a grunt. Nara remained unfazed, having long since grown used to such reactions. With a few rapid strikes, she wiped every trace of derision from his red and sweaty face.

Nara was amazing. If the world wasn't currently falling down around them, Scar could have watched her fight for hours, mesmerized by her speed and surety. There was a precision to her strikes, a graceful agility to her evasion, which marked her as something different, something unique. As it was, though, there were certain other matters that required Scar's attention – mainly the two soldiers that had just entered the lane and trained their sights on her.

They moved in unison toward her, two lions cornering their prey. Both were young, thin, and nimble, with barely a scratch to their armor. All in black, with their faces obscured by masks, they could almost have passed for twins. The only difference was their hair – one with blond the other black.

"How did you get so far out here?" the blond one

drawled, drawing closer. "Were you running away from the battle? Was the scene too much for you? Because we can make it all go away." He spoke to her slowly, as if she were a child, and her hackles rose in response.

The men had split, and they flanked her, with one lingering on each side. They stood with legs apart and hands twitching, their bodies poised for combat. Meanwhile, Nara had dealt with her first foe but discovered two more, leaving Scar to handle these men on her own.

Without looking, she pulled a weapon from her belt, fingering its cool metallic surface as she glanced between her rivals. They glanced back, curious but immobile, waiting for her to strike, and she couldn't help but oblige. In one unbroken motion, she activated the pen and lunged.

Scar was surprised when, instead of sparks, a laser erupted from the barrel. The blond man seemed surprised, as well. Scar had a hunch that lasers weren't something the Peace Force often faced, and, as such, weren't something they were trained to tackle. The only problem was that Scar wasn't trained on them, either. She hadn't packed it as a weapon, but as a way to bypass gates and fences. Using it on humans was new and untested.

Her hand sliced through the air toward him, eliciting a cry of pain. Looking down, she noticed a long gash along his arm, his singed flesh softly smoking. Scar gulped down the bile that rose in her throat at the smell of his burnt and smoldering skin.

The black-haired man took advantage of her pause. Drawing up behind her, he dealt a kick to the small of her back, sending her tumbling toward the arms of his partner.

Despite his injury, the blond man caught her. Scar wriggled against his hold, but he snarled and held fast.

The laser still glowed in her grasp, but her arms were trapped, her hands glued against her sides. Seeing no other options, she threw her body forward, into the man's embrace. The laser found a sheath in the muscle of his leg, and he groaned, thrusting her away.

Instead of freedom, however, she simply found the arms of the second solider. His hands came down to hers, ripping the laser from her grasp. It flickered as it fell, then went out, extinguished by the pavement. Scar lunged, expecting to hit cold ground but finding only air as two muscled arms wound around her chest.

The dark-haired man reeled her back, showing her no mercy. In an instant, she was against him, her back crushed to his front and her chest protesting the pressure. By then, the blond man had recovered his strength – and discovered his anger. Closing the gap between them, he punched while the other restrained her. Together, they covered her body in blows.

Scar couldn't see or hear. All she could do was feel as each strike landed and each shock of pain spiked through her. She couldn't stop them. Her world closed until it was only them, there, in that instant. Nothing else existed.

When the beating stopped, she didn't understand why. She simply dropped to the pavement, the taste of blood in her mouth and the slick warmth of it dripping down her hands. Yet each second that passed brought with it more perception, more awareness, more understanding of the scene.

Nara was still fighting, still winning, still beautiful, but she was not the one who had saved her. That honor fell to another. As Scar's vision leveled out, she recognized the gray hair and kind eyes that belonged to Meera.

Meera was not a fighter, but she hadn't let that stop her. She had insisted on joining the battle, on doing her part to bring the Peace Force to an end. And as Scar watched, she proceeded to do just that.

Despite her age, Meera was spry and strong. She fought with an anger that had been building inside of her for decades. It had mounted at each injustice, each slight, and now it was singing within her, calling for action.

Meera held a gun that looked far too large for her short frame, yet she had no trouble wielding it. As Scar watched, she slammed the butt of it into the dark-haired man's face before kicking him to the ground. Before Scar knew it, she'd shouldered the weapon and shot, dealing him a quick and violent end.

In Scar's blurred vision, Meera looked like an angel, bent on revenge. But sometimes even angels fall. The blond man, whom she'd somehow managed to send sprawling, rose to his feet beside Scar. Meera turned her gun on him, but he was faster, and before Scar could even think to react, he'd fired.

"No!" Scar screamed as the shot struck home, burrowing into Meera's chest. The woman fell back with the impact, striking the ground in a clatter of limbs and making no move to rise.

Scar's vision went white with fury. A moment later, she found herself at Meera's side, the handle of her laser slicked with blood and the blond man lying still behind her. She had killed him, yet she couldn't even remember how.

"Meera?" Scar cried, her heart thundering painfully in her chest. "Meera?!" She bent down beside the woman, fumbling with shaky hands to sit her upright, but Meera was already fading. "No, you can't go," Scar told her firmly. "You can't leave us."

She didn't know what she was saying. All she knew was that Meera couldn't die. Scar wouldn't allow it. Meera was the closest thing to a mother she and Burn had. She had always been there to guide them, help them, teach them things a mother should have taught them. She had even led them to the Lunaria, to their mission, to their home.

In fact, most of the people fighting beside them could trace their presence in the Lunaria back to her. She had brought them all together, instilling one purpose, one aim. She wasn't its founder, but she was its keeper, its curator. In short, Meera was their soul – and now their soul was dying.

"Stay with me," Scar pleaded, a wetness on her cheeks. "Please stay. We need you. *I* need you."

Meera's blood was leaking onto her lap, trickling steadily into deep pools of red. Scar tried to stop it, pressing her trembling hands to the torn flesh, but it didn't seem to help. Meera's eyes grew hazy and her heart slowed, beating in tentative taps. Her lips rose in a sad smile as she gathered her strength to speak.

"It's time, sweetheart," she whispered. "It's time to let go."

"I can't," Scar choked, unwilling to say goodbye.

"It'll be alright," Meera crooned, her own face slick with tears. "You don't need me – but this city needs *you*. So stop sitting around and go save it."

Scar's lips trembled and her throat constricted. There wasn't time to say everything she wanted to say, to thank Meera for everything she had done, to perfect her goodbye. Instead, she said one thing.

"I love you." The words felt foreign on her tongue, but also right, a fitting end to a radiant life.

Meera smiled and sighed and was gone.

Scar held her until Nara roused her with a touch, telling her it was time to go. They didn't speak as they walked, as they left Meera behind on the battlefield. Nara gave her that – the silence to process her grief, the space to feel, the time to adjust.

Around them, a war still raged, but now it seemed to leave them alone, as if it too understood her loss. They slid through the Peace Sector and up through the tiers, alert and aching. Scar had forgotten her pain, her injuries, and as she walked, she nearly forgot herself. All that mattered now was her mission.

Scar hadn't heard from Burn since her last frantic communique, although Scar could tell she was on the move. It appeared she was running, evading someone's clutches by sheer force of will. On Scar's tab, the red dot that was her sister skirted the edges of the city, never straying too far from the dome.

There were no more elevators up to the highest tier, and no stairs that would lead them to its farthest reaches. Their only option was to ascend into the battle, to place themselves within the chaos and hope to make it out alive. It wasn't ideal, and both Scar and Nara knew it.

Every corner they turned posed a risk – not just the risk of death, but the risk of finding others dead. Their colleagues, their family, their friends. Scar tried to harden herself to the sight, to expect it, but she was never prepared.

She also wasn't prepared for the sudden appearance of Kaz, his gun raised and his eyes alight from battle. It took each figure a moment to process the other before an immense relief took hold.

"How the hell are you here?" Nara asked, shaking her head in confusion before closing the gap for a one-armed hug. "We thought the force had arrested you."

Kaz snorted. "They did. They basically labeled me a traitor and chucked me in with the rest. It was so crowded in there, there was barely room to breathe."

"So how'd you get out?" Scar asked, intrigued.

Kaz's green eyes sparkled, and he seemed energized despite his rumpled, blood-stained clothes. "It's thanks to you, really. I've been trying to use my gift to escape since the moment they caught me, but they were watching too closely. The Lunaria's attack gave me the perfect diversion. Plus, I managed to spring a few other *traitors* in the process."

"You engineered a prison break?" Nara asked, amused.

Kaz shrugged in faux modesty. "A few cells full of mutants with a grudge against the force? I thought they'd come in handy – and they did. We fought our way out of the station, then kept on fighting. But I split off to make my way to the top. I figured that's where the real action would be."

"You figured right," Scar said, suddenly realizing the time they'd wasted on pleasantries. "In fact, we might need your help."

As they climbed, Scar and Nara filled Kaz in on the specifics of their plan, and he was more than happy to assist. After weeks trapped in a cell, the prospect of action seemed to thrill him. The fact that it was dangerous and potentially deadly did nothing to deter him.

Together, the trio glided through the last few tiers before finally emerging at the heart of the heavens, where fire and smoke and screams mingled to paint an infernal scene. Scar had thought the gore of the war below had numbed her, but she'd been wrong. This was something else entirely. This was barbaric, gruesome, relentless. This was hell.

Nothing could have prepared her for the injuries she saw. Bodies lay ripped in half, limbs torn, skin burnt beyond repair. The smell that lingered was repugnant, an acidic mix of cooked meat and singed hair and smoke. Scar's body started to shake, to shudder at the sight, but she clamped down, balling her hands into fists and focusing on her steps.

As Scar navigated through the madness, Nara and Kaz roamed before her, taking up the mantle of guards. Their movements were slow, deliberate, obstructed by mounds of rubble and sections of angry flames. It felt as if their whole world was at war, as if Kasis might burn to the ground around them, leaving nothing behind but ash. If this continued, there would be no one left to remember, to pick up the pieces and rebuild. In fact, soon there would be no pieces left to salvage.

Scar mapped Burn's progress around the dome, searching for a point to intercept her. As she did so, she tried to hold the worries at bay, to hide behind her mask of omniscience, yet the seeds of doubt took root. The truth was that she didn't know if she could fix the blaster, especially without her tools, and each step brought her closer to the test. What if she couldn't mend it? What if this was it? What if they were destined to fail?

Suddenly, a twirling ball of sparks sprang from around a corner, shocking Scar out of her stupor. It took a few seconds for her to recognize the figure, to make out the shape of a head and limbs as the woman somersaulted through the air and bounced along the pavement. By then, a second figure, taller and broader and considerably more irate, had stomped into view, unaware of his new audience.

Fia unrolled herself from the tight little ball and dodged just as the man's fist descended. Scar watched with rapt fascination as his hand changed from smooth skin to rough stone, crushing through layers of pavement and into the steel structure beneath. It wedged itself there and he struggled to free it as Fia let loose a bolt of jagged light.

As Scar watched, the skin on his torso rippled, transforming into the same rock-like texture as his hand. The electricity struck his stone collarbone and fizzled to nothing. His chest rapidly reverted back to skin, and he hauled his hand from the ground, aiming to strike again.

Fortunately, he didn't get the chance. From behind her, Scar heard the thunderous crack of a gunshot. The bullet traveled faster than the stone man could react, and his skin had no chance to change. The shot struck him squarely in the back, and he froze in shock before falling to the ground with a thud.

The world was quiet for an instant before Fia bounded over, out of breath and sweating. "Thanks," she said, pointing her smile toward Kaz. "That guy was a beast to bring down.

Definitely one of the nastier mutations I've seen today."

Scar didn't have time for this. Now that her path was clear, she made a move to go but stopped as an idea emerged.

"You," she said, pointing to Fia. "Come with us." With that, Scar took off at a trot.

The group exchanged bewildered glances, clearly perplexed by her command, but they didn't fight her. There was too much fighting already. Instead, they merely shrugged and followed in her wake. The idea of a plan, of someone who knew what they were doing – and, more importantly, where they were going – was intoxicating, and they latched on quickly, ready for the ride.

As it happened, though, it was a rather short ride. Their journey took them through two more achingly elegant streets before they stopped, positioning themselves like roadblocks alongside the dome. Then they waited, their bodies tensed for a fight as the dot that was Burn drew closer. They didn't know what was chasing her – or what would soon be chasing them. All they knew was that it was dangerous, and they'd have to act fast if they hoped to make it out alive.

As the seconds ticked down, Scar folded up her tab and stowed it, aiming her gaze at the road. She listened intently, but all she could hear were the distant sounds of war, calling to her in one unending cry that all but begged her to hurry.

The stillness of the scene broke in an instant as Burn's bedraggled form came into view. She was a mess. Her crimson face was streaked with blood and sweat, and her hair stuck out in every direction. She wasn't just panting but straining for breath as each step took her closer to exhaustion. Her expression screamed with pain, her eyes wild and her teeth exposed in an anguished grimace.

When she spotted Scar, though, everything changed. Burn's pace quickened and a light blossomed in her eyes as a desperate hope took hold. In her hands, she cradled the blaster like a child, and Scar's chest tightened at the sight.

A long, angry crack ran along its side, threatening to shatter at any moment. The cell inside was dead, drained of its power and rendered useless by the fissure.

As Scar watched it draw closer – and her sister with it – she mentally dissected the machine, cataloging its parts in search of a solution. Every component lived inside her head, and she traced their connections, her fingers gliding through the air as she examined each invisible joint.

When Burn spoke, breathless and panicked, Scar barely heard her. It was only when Nara jostled her shoulder that she finally came to, picking up the thread in the middle of Burn's tale.

"...is coming!" she shouted, gesturing for them to flee. "We have to go!"

Then they were running. Scar's pack jostled against her back as she dashed through the darkening lane, the suns tipping precariously over the horizon and into the night.

"I can't exactly fix the blaster like this," Scar shouted, already out of breath. "We have to stop. I need to determine the extent of the damage."

"Fine!" Burn bit back. "But not here."

Scar's annoyance quickly mounted – as did her fatigue. A stitch had sprouted in her side, and her head pounded along with her steps, making the world feel fuzzy. Her injuries screamed their aggravation, commanding her to stop, yet her pride prevented her from slowing.

As Scar teetered on the edge of collapse, Burn finally slowed and stopped, turning to face their oncoming foe. Scar's exhaustion lingered, muting the world like a drifting fog, but it gradually faded, leaving a sliver of recognition in its wake. This spot was familiar – and dangerous. Scar's memory flashed back to Burn and Ignis, to herself in someone else's form, to a man falling from the sky.

This was where he'd dropped. This was where they'd killed him. What a fitting spot to make their final stand.

Scar's distant thoughts blinked out in an instant as the blaster came sailing toward her. She barely had time to reach out before it hit her, and she fumbled to grab hold. Her hands gained purchase on the barrel and she looked up, relieved, only to find Burn staring at her in exasperation.

"Go!" she commanded. "Hide. And fix the damn thing before we're all torn to shreds."

Scar blinked as her brain caught up, then she hurriedly dashed down the street, throwing herself behind a low copse of faux bushes. Her hands got to work before she knew what she was doing. Parts pulled off, screwed off, disconnected, until a mess of components lay splayed in her lap.

The sound of gunfire pierced her concentration, and she glanced up just in time to see their villain come into view. It was Una Hyde, resplendent and utterly feral, holding a torn piece of steel like a shield before her. As she stalked forward, unhurried, she armed herself with pieces of the tier before sending them flying. Paving stones became projectiles as she ripped them from the ground, and sections of fence became her spears. She was cool, poised, and downright deadly, intent on destroying the world.

Ducking back, Scar redoubled her efforts, her fingers dancing between parts as she hooked up her tab to the blaster. The handful of seconds it took to think, to take stock of the damage, felt too timid, too slow to match the battle's frantic tempo. Scar jumped as an explosion of concrete and rock shook the ground beneath her, causing the parts to scatter.

The tab beeped as it completed its inspection, and Scar cursed at its results. The power cell verged on useless, all power drained from its clutches. Only weak sparks remained, like a ghost of its former function. She couldn't charge it, couldn't bring it back from the brink – but Fia could.

With hurried hands, Scar put the puzzle of pieces back together, slotting each in with the next until it was whole. Then she bobbed her head from behind her hedge, straining to see the action.

Even though the battle was now four against one, success remained elusive. Kaz lay on the ground, moaning, and Burn seemed too tired to do much more than bat away the rubble that Una flung her way. Beside them, Fia's bolts bounced weakly off Una's shield, sparking hopelessly to the ground. With every strike, her power was waning, sputtering feebly as her charge faltered.

Not knowing what else to do, Scar picked up a piece of shattered pavement and threw. It clattered to the ground unnoticed, nowhere near the action. Grunting in frustration, Scar tried again. And again. And again. Finally, one of her missiles managed to strike near enough to catch someone's attention. Kaz looked up from his place on the ground, confused. Spotting Scar, he furrowed his brows as she motioned in a crazed and frantic fashion toward Fia.

It took him far too long to rise – and even longer still to grab Fia's gaze and guide it toward Scar. When he eventually managed it, he slumped back down, his energy exhausted. But he had done his job. As covertly as possible, Fia withdrew from the battle. The others continued fighting, drawing Una's focus as Fia hurried across the space and threw herself behind the bushes.

"What's up?" she asked, her breathing ragged.

"I need you to charge the battery," Scar instructed, holding out the blaster. "Do you have enough power left to fill it?"

Fia looked uncertain, but she nodded. "I might have enough for one shot, but I'm almost empty. Will that work?"

Scar did the calculations, then smiled grimly. "It will have to. The blaster won't hold the charge for long, though, so I'll need to be quick. Can you make sure she's distracted?" Fia gave another nod.

"Good," Scar spat, "then let's get to work."

Fia closed her eyes, summoning up a spark. Placing both hands on the cell, she exhaled, releasing her power. Beneath her fingers, the weapon whirred to life, flickering then glowing with her energy. The moment Fia opened her eyes, Scar grabbed the blaster and ran.

Fia darted in the opposite direction, powerless but brave. Scar couldn't see what she did, but she heard it, making out the sounds of clattering rocks and violent shots and a scream. She couldn't look back, couldn't turn around, couldn't tear her eyes from the dome.

Skittering to a stop, she braced herself against the railing, her hands aimed toward the sky. Without another thought, she fired.

A flood of force cascaded from her hands, tearing at the layers of their cage. The sound of it echoed like an explosion through her ears as the glass above her fractured and fell. Looking up, Scar marveled at her handiwork – a giant hole wrenched from the side of the dome. It was the most beautiful thing she had ever seen.

In that moment, everything was peaceful, serene. Scar gazed at the night sky, enchanted. She could just feel the breeze as it tickled her face and see the stars as they twinkled before her.

The sound of her own name being screamed in fear brought her crashing back to reality. She turned to locate Burn, to find the source of her sister's terror, but before she could, something heavy hit her in the stomach and threw her back, flinging her up and over the side of the world.

The air whipped around her as she slipped softly through the sky, falling like an angel from the heavens.

Chapter 29

For one glimmering second, Burn felt like she was flying. The blaster had worked, the hole had appeared, and the air had swirled in around them, tempting them with salvation. Then, in an instant, everything collapsed. Her flying turned to falling as she watched Una heave a lump of stone from the ground and toss it with terrible precision toward Scar.

Burn stared in horror as her sister toppled over the banister and into the empty air beyond. She tried to go to her, to save her, but by the time she arrived there was no trace of her. Scar had simply vanished, disappearing into the smoke and wreckage of the city.

Burn fell to her knees on the spot, crying out in a sound composed of pure pain. She felt herself tumbling, plummeting to the ground beside Scar as if they were one and the same, two souls connected by a single fate.

She barely noticed as the world grew louder around her. It didn't register, didn't make it past the fog that had descended in her mind, cushioning her thoughts. Scar hadn't died. She couldn't die. She couldn't leave Burn alone.

The denial was easy. If she closed her eyes, she could wish the world away, rewriting the present into shards of possibilities. Alternative scenes danced before her, tempting her to give up, give in. They called to her with a siren song, a lure of lives capped with happy endings.

What came next was harder. Even as she struggled to hold on, the happy scenes dissolved, and Burn watched as Scar fell again and again, the past trapped in an endless loop before her. Her numbness burned away in a shower of ash as her blood began to boil. She howled again, dispensing with the hollowness of loss in favor of pure, untainted rage. It sparked through every atom in her body, visceral and raw, igniting her from within.

Burn wanted to fight, to drown her sorrow with blood. She wanted to make someone pay.

She rose, turning to face Una as a calmness descended across her mind. For the first time since Burn had known her, the woman looked scared, as if she finally understood her place in this drama. She was the villain, destined to die, and Burn was her executioner.

"What do we do now?"

The question rippled across the ether. Kaz hadn't said it out loud, hadn't asked the question on his mind, yet Burn had heard it, which could only mean one thing. Their plan had worked. Crete's serum had worked. The air from the wildlands was doing its job, making the mutants strong, giving them an edge. It was helping them win. But it could never bring back Scar.

"Now?" Burn said, turning to her friends with a cool, detached smile. "Now we finish this."

"Burn…" Nara started, tears sparkling in her eyes, but Burn cut her off, not needing to hear the end. She already knew what Nara was going to say.

"No," she said firmly. "I'm staying. But you should go. Take Fia and get somewhere safe. She needs your help more than I do."

"And him?" Nara asked, gesturing to Kaz on the ground. "I'm not sure I can carry them both."

Burn was about to reply when Kaz did it for her. "I'm fine," he said with a grimace before amending his words. "I'll be fine. Just go. We won't be far behind."

Nara opened her mouth as if to protest, but the words wouldn't come. Burn saw the thoughts swirling, the emotions crashing, the words eluding her, and she understood.

"I know," Burn said with a nod. "I'll make sure she pays."

The look Nara gave her said more than words ever could. Turning to go, she gathered Fia in her arms and set off into the city.

Una had, of course, run off while they were speaking. She'd sensed the change in the air, the turning of the tides, and hadn't stayed to see where it would lead. It didn't matter. Burn could hear her now. She could feel the woman inside her head, and she could track her.

"Auburn," Kaz said in warning, sensing her plan, "you can't take her on alone. Even with the air, she's stronger. Far stronger."

Burn met his gaze and held it. "I know," she said, "but it doesn't matter." With one last sideways look at her friend, she took off in pursuit.

Her injuries protested the jarring movements, but she didn't slow. The piercing blades of pain were muted to a dull throb by the surety of her mission and the grief coursing through her. Even the reports trickling in from around the city – of enhanced powers, of enemies dropping, of small and scattered victories – couldn't penetrate the shell.

Everything was changing. Everything *had* changed. The city had teetered and tipped and fallen. Eventually it would slide into the Lunaria's hands, finally freed from its bonds and shackles. Yet Burn couldn't celebrate, couldn't imagine a world beyond that day – a world without Scar.

"It would crush me!" Her own words to Scar came back to her with ringing clarity, suffusing her mind. "What is the point of creating a better world if you're not around to live in it with me?"

And she wouldn't be around. Scar would never be able to see the assembly fall, to watch as life under the dome evolved, to ring in the future by Burn's side. She had always thought they would explore the unknown together, that despite the odds they would always have each other. Without that hope, the future flaked away, peeling to reveal an existence just as desolate as before.

At some point, Burn armed herself. She picked up a gun, replenished her knives, and ran, caught in the clutches of déjà vu. This dance seemed familiar somehow, as if she'd done it all before, and she realized with a jolt that she had.

Scar had died, shot through the heart. Burn had mourned. Then she'd gotten angry. She'd chased the attacker, gun in hand, winding through the streets. She'd cornered him and killed him.

Only that time, it was Illex Cross in her crosshairs. Same war, different battle. Same villain, different face.

But in that instance, Scar had survived. She'd lived. What if she was alive now? Burn couldn't stop the wild hope from swelling inside her, from lifting her up and letting her soar. Yet soon enough she was grounded by reality.

No one could survive that fall. Ignis had been proof. His body, twisted and torn, rose in her memory as evidence. All his money, all his power hadn't saved him, and even Scar's cleverness couldn't compete with death. This time, she was really gone.

Burn heard Una long before she saw her. The woman had stopped running to take a stand, to fight, to finish this. She wanted Burn helpless and alone, ripped from her friends, separated from any source of support. She wanted Burn weak.

Una underestimated her. Then again, most people did.

Despite the change in the air, Una was still going strong. Her mind had not yet succumbed to hysterics and her body showed no signs of shutting down. It was only a matter of time, though. Only, Burn didn't want her to faint. She didn't want a feeble enemy. She wanted Una to fight.

The moment Burn came within view, a brick tore through the air toward her, aimed at her head. Burn dodged it with ease, unconcerned by its proximity. A second brick grazed her shoulder, nicking her skin, but she didn't feel it, too numbed by adrenaline and heartache to process the pain.

When Una finally gave up on projectiles in favor of her gun, however, Burn figured it was time to move. She trained her sights on a small marble inlet, a decorative bastion inlaid within a building's side, and dove for it, dodging a spray of bullets as she claimed refuge behind its foot of solid stone.

Her clear sightline across the space showed Una to her right, farther from the dome, shielded by a set of ornate columns attached to a soaring steel arc. The scene reminded Burn of some old-fashioned gunfight, some ancient shootout pitting bad against good. The only problem was that she was almost out of ammo – and so was Una.

The second Una's well ran dry, Burn heard it. Drawing out her spear, she pressed the familiar button along its side, savoring the sound as the steel shaft lengthened. Then she threw herself toward her prey, her mouth primed with the taste of blood, ready for more.

Una wasn't one to back down. Despite her earlier escape from Burn's clutches, she seemed more than happy to face her now. At Burn's approach, she sauntered around the pillar, her eyes alight and her breathing heavy as the air took its first steps toward a toll.

"Done running?" Burn asked tauntingly, her mind devoid of any trace of self-preservation.

Una just smiled. "Who said I was running? Didn't you ever think I might be leading you here?"

Her thoughts didn't match her words. Underneath the surface, her pure deviance melted away, replaced by an anxious sort of fear. She didn't know what was happening, and she didn't like losing control. She needed things within her power, people within her grasp. Yet, just like her sanity, her grasp was slipping.

Burn lunged, quick and efficient, aiming at Una's heart.

She was done playing games, done beating around the bush. She wanted to finish this.

It was no longer a battle between great forces, a duel pitting assembly against Lunaria. In that moment, it was only them – Burn and Una – two women fighting for their home. And soon, there would only be one left standing.

Unfortunately, it wouldn't be soon enough for Burn. Una sidestepped her attack, just managing to clear the area as Burn's spear descended. Instead of flesh, it struck stone, grazing the surface of a pillar as Burn threw her weight forward.

Una seized on Burn's imbalance, ripping an iron fence post from the ground to strike at Burn's back. The force of it sent her sprawling, and she landed with limbs splayed on the pavement. Una reared back, eager to deal a final blow, but Burn rolled across the cluttered ground, clutching her weapon as she spun.

She managed to get her feet beneath her in a crouch, swinging her spear toward Una as she rose. The blade bit through the fabric of her pants and into her skin, drawing an angry red line along her shin. Una grunted but refused to shout, too proud to show pain.

Beads of sweat began to dot Una's face as the chemicals from the wildlands leeched into her system. Burn could hear her thoughts slow and her body weaken beneath the force, but the woman fought it, struggling to keep hold.

The fog made Una's thoughts thick, heavy, like syrup dripping from a spoon. It also made them more difficult to follow, since they derailed from any linear path into the realm of the erratic. One thought didn't lead cleanly to the next, meaning each movement was disconnected from the last.

Una brought her weapon down on Burn in a wild arc, but she caught it, blocking with her own. They stood there for an excruciating moment, locked in a battle of brawn, with Una winning. Out of nowhere the woman withdrew, then placed a furious kick to Burn's abdomen, sending her flying.

Burn sailed through the air, weightless for a long second before skidding to an agonizing stop. Her back came to rest along the railing, its steel beams protecting her from the drop. By the time she rose, Una was there.

She brought her spear down once more on Burn's head, iron meeting steel in a furious clash, and this time she didn't let go. Burn's arms began to ache from the strain, and the metal of the fence dug deep into her back as she braced herself against its beams. Yet Una was still stronger.

The metal of Burn's spear grazed her chin as it sank to hover over her neck, threatening to choke her. Una's face lurked mere inches from her own, her eyes crazed and her smile wild. The sharp tip of her improvised spear scraped Burn's cheek, slicing a line along her jaw, and Una began to laugh in a frenzied cackle. The sound bounced off the dome, ricocheting back to Burn in sharp shards of echo.

"There's no one to save you now," Una said in between manic chuckles. "No one can help you. You will die here, alone, and mine will be the last face you see before you go."

Burn closed her eyes, letting a single tear roll down her cheek. Then she dropped her spear and bit back a cry as Una's weapon sank into her shoulder, slicing through skin and muscle and lodging itself in bone.

Una's face was resplendent with victory, her eyes shining in fevered delight and her mouth cracked in a euphoric grin. Yet in an instant, everything changed. As Burn's knife pierced her stomach, thrust upward into her gut, the light faded, her smile dimmed, and she released her crushing hold. Stumbling backward, Una pushed herself off the hilt and into the empty air beyond.

Her breathing was rapid and ragged, coming in shallow gasps. She tried to turn, to run, but she only managed to stagger, one arm wrapped around her wound as if that would save her.

Burn twisted the shaft of Una's makeshift spear, separating its sections until only its tip remained lodged within her shoulder. Reclaiming her weapon, she advanced, her vision tunneling until all she could see was Una.

Her steps were slow, measured, deliberate. Before long she arrived at the woman's side, dealing an angry kick that slammed her to the ground. She kicked again and again as Una groaned, grasping the pillar beside her for support.

A cracking sound was the only sign that something was amiss. Not even Una's thoughts betrayed her plan. Despite her injury, she still had her strength, and as Burn watched she began to pull the pillar from its place. Her face was a mask of agony as she tore apart stone and steel, grappling for a weapon. Above them, the arch swayed precariously, its balance disrupted by Una's fervor.

Burn tried to stop her, to drag Una away from her endeavor, but she was too late. Suddenly nervous, Burn backed away, retreating toward the dome with uncertain steps. In a moment, Una turned and rose, an enormous portion of pillar clutched in her bloody grasp. Then she charged.

It looked like Una planned to ram her, to subdue her

with blunt force, but at the last second she halted. With a bellow that was part pain, part war cry, part insanity, she hurled the stone into the air, drawing on all the fire she possessed. Burn ducked, rolling out of the way, and the post sailed past her and over the railing beyond. With a sudden shuddering crash, it collided with glass.

Loud cracks sounded as fissures appeared around them, splintering the dome into shards. Burn watched with horror as the jagged lines grew, branching out in wrathful forks and dividing the sky into a network of faults.

For one glorious, weightless moment, the damage ceased to spread, and it looked like cracks was all there would ever be. Then, in an instant, the sky began to fall.

It was beautiful in its destruction, their prison falling away to reveal a clear night sky. Burn looked up at the stars and the waning moon, marveling at their clarity. The world was falling to pieces around her, and for some reason all she could do was stare.

It took a ping of glass striking the ground beside her to rip her from her reverie. Glancing up, she watched as a massive section of the dome broke free and began to fall, heading straight for her position.

Spotting the inlet she'd used only minutes before, she made a break for it, but it was too far and the glass was falling too fast. Behind her, she heard Una drop to the ground with a scream. Burn glanced back, then up, following the woman's gaze as the fragment made its final push toward them.

Then, without warning, it splintered into a million shards of light, fractured by the arch which Una had so nearly destroyed. Glass rained down on Burn in piercing slivers.

She shielded her head with her arms, flinching as the pieces sliced her hands, her wrists, her back.

The tinkling of glass slowed and faded, but another sound rose to take its place, a low, rhythmic creaking. Against her better judgment, Burn searched for the sound – and found it. The archway was rocking, teetering on the breeze, threatening to fall. Then it was falling, rushing toward her in a whoosh of stone and steel, anxious to crush her.

Burn ran, glancing over her shoulder as her feet consumed the pavement. She heard the base of the pillars crumble, giving way. She heard the arch sail through the air, whistling as it fell. She heard Una's last, frantic thoughts before it landed, crushing her beneath its bulk.

The structure slammed to the ground behind Burn, narrowly missing her body. Yet she couldn't avoid the force of its fall – the push of air, the quake of earth, the sudden pressure. It flung her against a wall with a crack, and she landed in a pile of dust and debris, which covered her and cushioned her in equal measure.

Burn lay there for some time as the world continued to fall. Eventually, there would be no dome left – and no heavens, either. The weight of their cell would crush their jailers, turning their homes to dust. And Burn would be dust alongside them.

There was nothing left inside her, no anger or anguish or fear. It was only peace, calm and quiet. They had done it. They had won. Una was dead, the Peace Force vanquished, the assembly toppled. She had done her part, finished the game, wrenched victory from the jaws of defeat. She was done.

Someone else could pick up the pieces. Someone else

could put them together again. She was tired.

Burn closed her eyes, enjoying the warmth and the sounds and the feel of the breeze against her skin. She couldn't move beneath the pile of rubble, but she didn't need to. All she had to do was wait, and the world would take care of the rest.

"Auburn? AUBURN?!"

The sound of her name pulled her from her peaceful musings, dragging her back to the chaos.

"Leave me alone," she mumbled to no one. "I don't need to be saved."

"No," said a voice beside her, and Burn looked up to find Kaz staring down at her. "You told me to leave once, and I did," he said, his jaw set in a stubborn line. "I'm not making that mistake again."

With nimble fingers, he began to dig her out of her stone coffin, bringing her back to the surface. After a beat, Burn began to help him.

It wasn't what he'd said – although that didn't hurt. It was what he hadn't said, what he couldn't say. It was his desperation to find her, his fear that she had perished. It was his utter elation at seeing her alive. And it was the fact that he was still there, still fighting to save her even as the city crashed down around them.

She meant something to him, to all of them, and they meant something to her. Dying would be easy. Surviving took courage.

Together, they freed Burn from the rocks and rubble, hoisting her to her feet. She was dirty and bruised, bloody and still bleeding, but she could walk. Or, at least, hobble.

Kaz and Burn put their arms around each other, both lending strength to the other as they fled. The dome was weakening with every moment, threatening to collapse completely and bury them in the wreckage. They needed to find a way down, a way out – and they needed to find it fast.

With the aid of the air from the wildlands, Burn could feel the city pulsing around her, its shuddering heartbeat entwined with her own. After months of watching her power dwindle, everything sounded so loud, so urgent, as if the whole world were screaming for her to flee. Each shatter of glass, each groaning beam, each toppling structure sang to her, promising to crumble and threatening to take her with it.

Burn raked her ravaged mind across the remnants of the tier, searching for signs of life, yet precious few remained. As soon as the dome had begun to fall, most had escaped, dragging the wounded and carrying the weak. Those that lingered were as good as gone, already drifting through the shadows of this world and into the next. Burn recognized none of the voices she heard, none of the thoughts floating lazily across the toppling plain. That fact gave her strength, somehow, willing her onward toward the safety of the stairs.

The downpour was constant now. Glass and stone littered the street beneath their feet like a graveyard of glamorous lives, making every step a struggle. Here and there, limbs peeked out from beneath jagged mounds and bodies lay splayed across the pavement, still gripping their weapons in a frozen pantomime of war. Without Burn's gift, she and Kaz would have been the same, just two more bodies buried beneath the sky. Instead, every time a shard started to fall or a building began to crumble, she heard it, and they raced against its descent, vying for life in a field of death.

Eventually, they spotted the stairs and darted toward them, but a wall of hissing flames rose between them and their escape, blocking their path. Burn looked and listened, reaching past the crackling blaze to the safety of the street beyond, searching for a way through, but Kaz found it first. Taking her hand, he led her to a narrow gap in the inferno, to a place scarcely wide enough for a person to pass.

Kaz went through first, ushering for Burn to follow, but she couldn't. Something at the base of the fire caught her attention and held it, bringing with it a desolate calm. It was a body. Not just any body, but one she knew, one she had fought beside, one she had known for years. It was Ansel.

The flames licked at him with gentle tongues, welcoming him into their fold. As she watched, the fire – *his* fire – consumed him, using him as fuel to further the blaze. Burn had thought that fire couldn't touch him, couldn't hurt him, but she'd been wrong. It was a part of him, and after burning within him for so long, it was finally free to claim him.

Burn couldn't breathe. Smoke and sorrow filled her lungs in equal measure, straining to choke her. She coughed, and pain pierced through her broken chest, shocking her with its rage. Her mind felt hazy, and she watched as the streets gradually began to bleed into the sky.

Suddenly, Kaz was by her side. This time, instead of waiting for her to cross, he lifted her into his arms, carrying her through the fire and down the rickety set of stairs. It was almost heroic. If he hadn't dropped her a few feet later, panting from the effort, she might even have called him gallant.

"Ansel..." she said once they were clear of the steps, trailing off without knowing how to finish.

"I know," Kaz said in between heavy breaths. "I know."

And he did. She could see in his mind that he understood, that she was not alone in her despair. Yet she could also see the words he was going to speak next, and she sighed.

"We won't be safe here," Kaz said. "When the last of the dome comes down, that tier is coming with it. If we stay, it'll crush us. The lower we get, the better our chances of survival."

Burn didn't protest. Instead, she hobbled forward, waving for Kaz to follow.

They made it down two more tiers before Burn heard it. Whereas everything before had sounded soft and tinkling, like the breaking of fragile china, this was something else, something different. It was deep and resonant, the final sigh before the end.

Burn grabbed Kaz's arm and pulled him along as she dashed to the edge of the tier, straining for a glimpse as the city fell. She didn't know if they were safe – if any of them were safe – but it was too late to do more than stand by and watch.

The dome was a patchwork of sky and glass, held up by mere threads. Burn didn't know what was keeping it aloft, but she knew that it was failing. The remnants of their cage rattled ominously in the breeze, preparing for release. Finally, with an epic crash, the dome gave way.

Burn watched with awe as the sky exploded above her, raining down on the city in brilliant splinters. For a few seconds, it was achingly beautiful. The glass caught the light of the moon and the stars and the fire below and reflected it back, showering the city in silver and gold. The shards seemed to fall in slow motion, dancing through the air to their own quiet song.

Eventually, though, everything must land – and the glass did so in spectacular fashion. It collided with the heavens in the loudest cacophony Burn had ever heard, a combination of crumbling buildings, shattering glass, and groaning steel.

The weight of the impact shook the city, but it was nothing compared to what came next. Burn could hear the supports weaken, hear the crunch of steel as beams buckled and girders bent.

Reaching out, Burn grabbed Kaz's hand and held on as the city came tumbling down.

Chapter 30

The taste of burning city was not pleasant. It clung to her tongue and coated her lips, vaguely reminding her of the disastrous times she had actually attempted to cook.

The smell was also abhorrent, and the breeze didn't help. Although it tickled her skin with hints of sand and whispers of cool night air, its base notes were metallic and harsh, burnt and bloody.

At least the screams had died, the horrors blanketed by a layer of calm. Everything was oddly tranquil and serene. Even the ash and dust floated lazily through the air, idly searching for a place to settle. Some of it drifted down to her, softly coating her skin in the final remnants of the old world.

The war was over. It had to be. Even the Peace Force would not persist in the face of such destruction.

The heavens were gone. The realm of the rich and powerful had been reduced to piles of smoldering steel and crushed concrete. From where she lay, she could see that two of the tiers had collapsed completely, along with a significant portion of the third. The age of the assembly ruling untouchable from on high had come to a shuddering end, ushering in a brand-new day.

This was it. This was what they had worked for, fought for, what many had given their lives for. This was freedom. It felt...strange.

Maybe it was the grief churning inside her. Maybe it was the pain still coursing through her body. Or maybe it was the fact that dreams look starkly different in the light of day than they do when they're conceived on street corners and discussed in dingy back rooms.

When you've toiled toward something for so long and given so much, can reality ever measure up to the picture in your head? She didn't think so. There would always be some disconnect, some places where the pieces didn't match, where the edges would never align. That didn't mean it wasn't worth it.

Still, after all that struggle, it was deliciously tempting to stay put, to lie there forever in the serenity of the night, staring up at the stars. She couldn't see much of the sky, with her vision obscured by mounds of burning rubble, but what she could see was magnificent. A billion stars and a million worlds, and all of them seemed close enough to touch. She could have stayed there, staring blissfully at the cosmos, until the ashes of the world welcomed her fully into their fold.

Yet she knew she couldn't, no matter how easy it would be. She had to get up, had to keep going, had to *live*.

With a deep sigh and one last look at the sky, Scar rose from the rubble and limped away.

Burn was in rough shape. She had been kicked and punched and stabbed, and her shoulder was still bleeding steadily, oozing dark red blood from Una's final blow. In fact, the weapon's head remained lodged inside her collarbone, cutting off feeling to most of her arm. It was a miracle she could walk, let alone climb down stairs, but she did it, shuffling sluggishly through Kasis with Kaz at her side.

They'd been lucky. When the dome had collapsed – and the city with it – they had been certain it would crush them. The tiers had come down one after the other above them, shaking the ground with such ferocious tremors that they'd been knocked from their feet, thrown against the road, and rendered helpless.

When the tier above them finally fell, Burn had closed her eyes and waited, ready for the worst. The metal had groaned and swayed, threatening to give way with every breath. Each creaking beam, each cascade of debris had been torture, promising punishment that had never come.

Eventually, they'd picked themselves up and dusted themselves off, their movements achingly slow. They'd been terrified of disturbing the balance, of upsetting the tentative equilibrium of the tier. Yet with each step they'd grown bolder, braver, faster.

Now, several tiers down, they were able to breathe with ease, the terror of the last few hours gradually fading to a memory behind them. Its absence left them weak and exhausted, mere shells of themselves without substance, but they trekked on nonetheless, searching for survivors.

Burn and Kaz didn't speak. They didn't need to. Somehow, just being there, side by side in the aftermath, was enough. They'd shared something so powerful, so visceral that she knew there would always be a bond. Now they shared each other's silence, both comfortable in its warmth.

As they descended into the Peace Sector, they found the Lunaria hard at work. Each familiar face was a balm, a salve to Burn's aching heart, a shining droplet in a pool of darkness. The mere sight of them made tears prick at her eyes, yet she held them at bay, knowing that if she started she might never stop.

Just like they'd planned, the Peace Officers had succumbed to the air from the wildlands, and their unconscious forms dotted the space, blending with the bodies of the dead. Those that hadn't fallen were rendered harmless, and they wandered aimlessly through the streets with blank eyes and stupid grins.

The Lunaria were busy rounding up these survivors, corralling them into what remained of the Peace Station. What had once been their bastion would now become their prison, at least until the Lunaria determined what to do next. For the time being, though, they would learn what it was like to be captives instead of captors, to live their lives at others' mercy.

When Burn spotted Hale amidst the crowd and their eyes met, she nearly cried out in relief. She tried to run but rapidly realized it was a mistake and instead shuffled awkwardly between the throngs of people. Within moments, they stood before each other, each gazing into the eyes of the other. Then, tentatively, Burn reached out, needing to touch, to feel, to convince herself that he was real.

Soon, his lips were on hers, and she welcomed them, savoring the warmth. Eventually, the kiss ended, but he didn't let go, his hands twined around her in a gentle embrace.

"I didn't know if you'd made it out," Hale said, his voice gruff with emotion. "I couldn't find you. I didn't know if…" he trailed off, unable to speak his fears aloud.

"I'm here," Burn whispered into his shoulder. "I'm here."

"After I finished with the assembly's *guard dog*," he spat, referring to man with impenetrable skin, "I tried to fight my way to the edge to help you, but there were too many of them. The Lunaria needed me." He sounded repentant, like he had somehow let her down.

"You did the right thing," Burn told him. "Remember, I don't need you to save me."

Hale chuckled quietly, and the deep rumble made Burn's heart stutter. Of course, she had needed saving, but he didn't need to be her savior. Her thoughts turned to those who had helped her, to Kaz and Nara, Fia and Ava. And to Scar. Yet they quickly skimmed back to the present, unable to linger. She couldn't dwell – not here, not yet. It was too fresh, and it hurt too much.

Hale continued his story, and she refocused on him, craving the distraction. "When you broke through the dome, everything changed. I could feel my strength coursing back. It was amazing. All of a sudden, the assembly started dropping and we started winning. It was exactly like we'd planned."

Well, not exactly, Burn thought, recalling the moment with vivid clarity. The dome breaking, the elation, Scar falling. She closed her eyes, cutting off the memories.

Hale paused, waiting for her side of the story, but it didn't come. Somehow, she was certain that even if she tried, she wouldn't be able to say it. Instead, she remained silent, content to listen.

"When the dome began to crack," he continued after a beat, "my first thought was of you." His grip on her tightened ever so slightly as he relived his fears. "I didn't know where you were. I couldn't help you. But I could help the others, and I did. I grabbed as many of the injured as I could, and I carried them down. I tried to come back for you, but it was already too late."

Burn watched as the events replayed behind his eyes, and her heart swelled at his concern.

"I'm here," she said again, bringing him back to the present. "It's over. It's all over." And, standing there with Hale's arms wrapped around her, she finally realized that it was. It was over at last.

Something inside of her gave way, and she began to cry. Hale held her until the tears stopped, until the racking sobs subsided. When she finally looked up, she saw tears in his eyes, as well.

Burn could hear his sorrow, his grief. In fact, she felt it pressing down on her from all sides, from Lunaria members and Peace Officers alike. They had all lost someone. They had all seen their city fall. They were all mourning for something. In a strange way, it united them.

Breaking away from Hale, Burn felt a tap on her shoulder and turned, finding Nara standing solemnly behind her. Her beautiful eyes were red and her dark hair lightened by a layer of ash. She looked angry and heartbroken and desolate.

"Fia?" Burn asked, not ready to broach the subject lingering on both their minds.

"She's fine," Nara said, her voice and her body rigid. "A couple broken bones and a concussion, but she'll be alright – which is more than I can say for some." Looking down into Burn's eyes, she dealt a blow that landed hard with one word, one name. "Meera."

Burn closed her eyes as the grief took hold and she mourned this new loss. Then she, too, gave a name, lending it to the list of the dead. "Ansel," she said with sorrow.

"Innoxia," Hale continued, giving one more.

Over the next few minutes Ava, Kornak, and Lux joined the list, as did Ecco and Coal and so many others. Each name brought with it grief, but also closure, and the process seemed to help – at least until Nara said the one name Burn had been dreading.

"Scar."

It was so quiet that it might have been a whisper – or even just the wisp of a thought – but Burn's world spun and her vision blurred.

"I need to find her," Burn said as soon as she was able. What she meant was that she needed to find Scar's body, but she couldn't say it. The words wouldn't form on her tongue or even coalesce in her mind. All she knew was that she needed to see her sister, to bring her home.

"I'll go with you," Nara volunteered, but Burn couldn't stomach it. Her grief on its own was too much to bear; she couldn't handle Nara's too.

"No," Burn said quietly. "I have to do this alone."

Hale remained silent in his usual fashion, but she could

tell that he wanted to help, wanted to do something to make things better. Only, he couldn't. No one could.

Burn closed her eyes, rubbing at her temples. She didn't know where to start or even how to search for Scar in a city so filled with ruin. Her gift wouldn't help her. She couldn't track the dead, couldn't hear inside their silent heads. Instead, she would have to scour the tiers, wading through death and combing through dunes of smoldering rubble.

"Auburn?"

The voice sounded at her back and Burn jumped, so surprised that her feet nearly cleared the ground. Kaz was all but silent now, his movements cloaked by his bolstered gift. Even his thoughts were fading, retreating behind the shield that protected him. He was Burn's antithesis, she realized, his gift the perfect opposite to hers.

Burn spun, focusing her gaze on him. "What?" she barked, half out of surprise and half frustration. She wanted to leave, to be alone, to search for Scar in peace. Yet fate wouldn't give her the chance.

"I've found something," he said cryptically, with a strange, confused look in his stormy green eyes.

Without warning, a shape stepped out from his shadow, entering the hazy pool of artificial light. The shape was tall with a mess of red curls and wide swaths of silver skin.

"No," Burn stated, shocking everyone with her vehemence. Even Scar looked at her as if she'd gone mad, but Burn didn't care. "You died," she clarified, her brain struggling to move from one thought to the next.

"No." It was Scar's turn to shake her head and draw the attention of the group.

"You fell," Burn said, stating it rather than asking. She knew the events that had transpired. She'd seen them with her own eyes.

"Yes," Scar replied, confirming that she had, indeed, dropped from the sky. Burn was right on that account, at least. Yet Scar didn't volunteer more details, compounding Burn's vexation.

"How?" she whispered, sounding – and feeling – so incredibly small. After years of being the caretaker, provider, guardian, she suddenly felt every inch the little sister, gazing up at Scar for answers.

"It's because of you. Well, technically you and Ignis," she said, smiling slightly. "But you gave me the idea. Remember? Right before the Peace Force Ball."

Burn stared at her blankly, disbelief coursing through her veins. It was easier than processing Scar's sudden reappearance, the fact that she was alive, the fact that she was *here*.

"You can't be serious," she balked. "You made a ring that allows you to fly? That's impossible!"

"I said you gave me the idea, not that I followed it to the letter," Scar scoffed, her usual superiority on full display. She held out her wrists to show the cuffs that rested there, gleaming and intricate. "It's not actually flying," she admitted with a shrug. "It's more like controlled falling. They're just a prototype, but they seemed to work well enough. I only slightly crashed – but the building was already broken before I hit it. I swear."

Burn couldn't take it any longer. One moment she was standing still, and the next she had her arms wrapped around

Scar in a crushing embrace. "*You* are impossible!" she cried, her face buried in her sister's red curls.

"Improbable, maybe, but hardly impossible," Scar countered, accepting Burn's hug and returning it.

For the first time since Scar had reappeared, Burn let herself believe that she was real, that all of this was real. She hurt in a million different ways and grief still lingered bleakly in the shadows of her mind, but her heart sang in triumph. Sadness bumped into fury, which clattered against joy, surging through her in a cluster of messy emotions, yet she finally felt alive.

After hours of being half present, half herself, half trapped between this world and the next, she was finally whole. She could breathe. Burn looked around at the faces of those she loved and smiled. She couldn't help it. Hale, Kaz, Nara, Scar. This was her tribe, her family. This was her heart. For the first time since the dome had collapsed, it truly felt like they had won.

Scar was the first to let go. Switching her gaze to Nara, she walked tentatively toward the woman, her footsteps slow and even. Nara didn't speak, but her dark eyes took in every inch of Scar as she approached. Then Nara gently placed her head against Scar's, their foreheads touching ever so slightly. She brought her hand up to Scar's face, lightly brushing back her hair in a gesture that radiated pure affection.

The sight was so tender, so intimate, that Burn was forced to look away. She found herself considering Hale, who regarded her in return, his gaze filled with the same raw tenderness as Nara's. She smiled coyly at the large man, feeling her mind go fuzzy.

She took one step toward him, then another, but darkness began to prickle at the edges of her vision. The last thing she felt was Hale's strong arms catching her as she fell, holding her tightly as she welcomed oblivion.

Burn sat atop the ruins of Kasis, watching as the suns began to rise on a new day. The bottom edges of the dome still remained, jutting along the horizon in jagged fragments. Soon, they would break through even that, demolishing the last of the glass that encased them and venturing into the world beyond. But for now, it endured, a reminder of their past and of all they'd overcome.

Burn's injuries had been treated and stitched, splinted and bandaged. She'd lost a good deal of blood, and she still felt woozy, but she couldn't tell how much was from her wounds and how much was from the pure elation of victory. Or the back-alley booze they'd drank in celebration.

Spirits were running high across Kasis. The liquor helped, as did the carefree current that flowed through the air, wafted in by the wildlands. It would take some time for everyone to adjust, to grow accustomed to the air and their burgeoning powers, but for now Burn enjoyed the jubilation.

That didn't mean she didn't yearn for her bed. In fact, it called to her, promising the sweet release of sleep. After weeks of bunking with an ever-growing horde, she craved the solitude of her house and the comfort of her things. It had likely been ransacked by the force, stripped to the floorboards and beyond, but it didn't matter. As long as it was still standing, it was home.

But she couldn't leave quite yet. For one thing, she didn't think she could make the journey on her own. She'd only ascended to her current peak with Hale's help, and he had forbidden her from moving. For another, she knew she was watching history in the making, and she didn't want to miss a single second.

Burn heard Scar before she appeared, but she didn't move. Turning her head required far too much effort. Instead, she waited patiently while Scar scaled the heap of rubble and settled herself on the beam beside Burn.

It was quiet for a long time as they gazed out at the city beneath them and the wide expanse of world stretching out before them.

Like always, Burn was the first to speak. "You're not allowed to fight in any more battles, you know," she said, only half joking. "You've outwitted fate too many times already. Next time, you won't be so lucky."

"Lucky?" Scar asked with laughter in her voice. "It's not luck. It's intellect. Pure, unadulterated cleverness."

"And modesty, of course," Burn said sarcastically.

"One doesn't need to be modest when they're so much smarter than everyone else," Scar pointed out. "Plus, with the air from the wildlands, I can already feel my mind growing sharper."

"That's a scary thought," Burn exclaimed, shaking her head – and regretting it. Pain bit through her bandaged shoulder, making her wince.

"I have to keep up with you somehow," Scar said, shrugging. "I mean telepathy? You're going to be a nightmare to live with."

"Ouch," Burn said in jest, feigning offense. "You know I can turn it off when I want to. Plus, it's not like your thoughts are incredibly deep or fascinating. I have little interest in the mechanics of your mind," she said, enjoying their return to sisterly banter. "But if you're worried, there's plenty of space to spread out." She gestured to the world around them, to the desert and its dunes.

Scar seemed to consider her words, staring out at the glowing horizon. One of the suns had already crested, with the second rising in its wake, and they cast a soft orangish light across the world.

"I think I want to go," Scar said after a pause, the laughter gone from her tone. "I think I want to explore."

"Really?" Burn couldn't keep the surprise from her voice. Scar had never been the adventurous sort, never one to stretch beyond her comfort zone. She'd always preferred the safe to the unknown, the reliable to the risky. Then again, she'd changed so much within the past few months, growing and blossoming into someone else entirely.

"You've had your adventure," Scar said, gesturing to the world beyond the dome. "Maybe it's time I have mine. I mean, imagine what I can learn, the things I can see, the people I can meet." Her voice rose in anticipation, and her eyes lit up with delight.

"We don't even know everything that's out there," Burn cautioned, recalling her own trials in the wildlands.

"I know," Scar said. "Isn't that exciting?"

And Burn realized that it was. Their world continued on past Callidus, past Videre, into the desert beyond. There was no telling what was out there, what creatures or structures or towns. It was truly a world of possibilities, with the door flung open before them.

"Maybe I'll come with you," Burn said, smiling softly to herself. "Maybe I'd like to see the world, too." Scar laughed, and Burn turned to consider her. "What?" she demanded, glaring. "What's so funny about that?"

"Nothing," Scar said, shaking her head but still smiling. "Nothing. But look at everything you've done," she told her, pointing out at Kasis. "You raised an army and brought a city to its knees. You can't leave now – and I don't think you want to."

"I thought I was the mind reader," Burn said, glaring at her. "Or did you develop that gift, too?"

"No," Scar said. "You're just easy to read." Burn narrowed her eyes, and Scar continued, "You gave up happiness, a life in the wildlands to come back here. I know you think it was for me, but it wasn't, not completely. It was for this," she gestured around her. "It was for them. You are a leader, and they are in desperate need of someone to lead them. I know you. You could never walk away from that."

"I'm not a leader," Burn began, but Scar just scoffed.

"And I'm not an inventor," she said with derision. "Come on. You understand people – what they want, what they need. You can legitimately hear inside their minds. And you can inspire them. In the end, that's all anyone wants: someone to listen, someone to care."

Burn felt the truth of Scar's statement in her bones, yet her heart still tugged at the thought of Scar leaving without her.

"I'll miss you," she told her sister, placing her hand on top of Scar's and feeling the familiar metal beneath her fingers.

Scar was silent for a second before responding. "I'll miss you too, little sis. But I won't be gone forever. We have our whole lives ahead of us. I'll be back to bug you in no time. Trust me: This is only the beginning."

And it was. This wasn't the end, but rather a new chapter full of blank pages just waiting to be written. Burn didn't know what came next for them, what twists their futures held, but for the first time they were in charge of their own story, the authors of their own destiny.

Burn squeezed Scar's hand and focused on the horizon, watching as the suns burned their way across the sky and lit the world with brilliant color. She closed her eyes, soaking in the radiant warmth, and realized that for the first time in their lives, they were well and truly free.

AUTHOR'S NOTE
& Acknowledgments

I can't believe that it's over! This world and these characters have been my life for so long. They've been my friends and my enemies. They've brought me joy, sorrow, heartache. They've lifted me up when I was down. And I hope, in some small way, that they've done the same for you.

Maybe someday their adventures will continue – whether in a sequel or a prequel or a set of short stories – but *my* adventure is just beginning. I can't wait to explore other worlds, other characters, other stories. I yearn to travel the universe through the lens of fiction, and I hope that you'll come with me.

Thank you for taking a chance on this book and this series. My gratitude goes out to all the readers that have embraced these novels and found themselves swept away by the stories. This series started as a dream and now, three books later, it's honestly a dream come true.

Of course, this series never would have come to be

without the continued support and encouragement of my family and friends. Thank you to my husband, Robert, for providing his honest opinions, a primer on the basics of hacking, and generalized IT support whenever my computer decided to crash.

Thank you to my beta readers, Kayla Suhm, Kinnon Schreiber, and Greg Poppy, for helping me polish my rough draft into a fitting conclusion for the series. And thank you to everyone who has shared their opinions online, lent the book to friends, or recommended it to others. Your reviews and endorsements have helped spread the word and introduce countless new readers to the world of Kasis.

If I have managed to entertain you, distract you, make you smile or laugh or cry, or helped you see the world in a different way, then I have done my job well. I am and always will be a storyteller at heart, and publishing these books has allowed me to spread my stories across the world. I have enjoyed being part of people's lives, even if it's only for the span of a few hundred pages.

If this book or this series has resonated with you, please consider leaving a review on Amazon. If you want to do more, you can follow Glass Fish Publishing on Instagram, like us on Facebook, or join our email list at *glassfishpublishing.com*.

Thank you for being part of this wonderful adventure. Stay tuned for more adventures to come!

ABOUT THE AUTHOR

Brenda Poppy has spent more than a decade writing and editing for publications across the country, as well as lending her writing and graphic design talents to companies to help them craft their brands. With a degree in journalism and sociology from Marquette University, she loves to seek out unique stories and capture them for others to enjoy. When not writing, the Milwaukee native can be found acting in local theater, spending time with her adorable corgi, Darcy, or traveling around the world with her husband in search of craft cocktails, good food, and inspiration for her next novel.

Connect with Glass Fish Publishing on Facebook and Instagram, or join our mailing list at *glassfishpublishing.com*!